CHRIS RUSSELL

Songs About Us

Hodder Children's Books

HODDER CHILDREN'S BOOKS

First published in Great Britain in 2017 by Hodder and Stoughton

1 3 5 7 9 10 8 6 4 2

Text copyright © Chris Russell, 2017

The moral rights of the author have been asserted.

A CIP catalogue record for this book
is available from the British Library.

ISBN 978 1 444 92917 1

Typeset in ITC Berkeley Oldstyle by Hewer Text UK Ltd, Edinburgh
Printed and bound in Great Britain by Clays Ltd, St Ives plc

The paper and board used in this book
are made from wood from responsible sources.

Hodder Children's Books
An imprint of
Hachette Children's Group
Part of Hodder and Stoughton
Carmelite House
50 Victoria Embankment
London EC4Y 0DZ
An Hachette UK Company
www.hachette.co.uk

www.hachettechildrens.co.uk

To Mum and Dad, for raising me
in a house full of music

I stared into Gabriel's eyes, heart pounding in my throat. Memories were rushing back to me in broken fragments – the smell of his skin, lines from his songs. My feet were rooted to the ground.

'You know this toothpaste is on two-for-one, don't you?' said the check-out lady, waving for my attention. I tugged my gaze from Gabriel's face on the magazine rack.

'Sorry?'

She was pointing a tube of Colgate at me.

'Two-for-one,' she repeated.

'Oh. Right.'

I moved a block of cheese on to the conveyor belt, fighting a blush. Meanwhile, the check-out lady clicked her fingers at a lank-haired boy stacking baskets at the end of the aisle. He looked up, like a startled bird.

'Mav'll get it for you.'

The boy nodded, then shuffled off towards the toiletries. The woman went back to scanning my shopping.

'Sexy, isn't he?' she said. I watched the lank-haired boy scratching his bum as he wandered past the meat counter.

'Who, Mav?'

She snorted, and dropped a box of tampons.

'No, not Mav.' She nodded at the magazine rack. 'That Gabriel West.'

My eyes returned to the row of magazines. Ten Gabriels, standing side by side, gazing back at me from underneath the headline: 'GABRIEL WEST TOPS OUR SPRING HOTTIES LIST!! GET IN LINE, GIRLS!!'

'Um, yeah, I suppose.' I unfolded one of my tote bags. 'If you like that sort of thing.'

The check-out lady made a funny sound, a sort of 'mmm' mixed with a 'yeeeah', and stared off into the distance. Then she picked up a cucumber, and started waving it around.

'Mind you, that other one, Olly Samson, he's got a pretty face and all. He's from round here, you know.'

My phone beeped loudly in my pocket. The woman nodded at my hip. 'Who's that, your boyfriend?' she asked nosily. My mouth dropped open as I read the name on the screen.

'It's . . . Olly Samson.'

The woman froze, a bag of satsumas dangling from her hand. I realised I'd said the words out loud, and a quiet panic gathered inside me. I hadn't been recognised as 'that random groupie' for months – the world had,

2

thankfully, forgotten about me entirely – but even so, it was a stupid mistake to make.

She was staring at me, her forehead crinkled. Eventually, her features broke into a smile.

'Aaah, that's a good one, that is! "I got a text from Olly Samson".' She shook her head, and passed the satsumas through the scanner. 'And I suppose you've got Gabriel West on speed-dial, right?'

Relieved, I began filling my bag with shopping.

'Something like that, yeah.'

'I'd take any one of them, myself,' she said, with a musical sigh. 'But let's face it . . . popstars don't exactly fall for people like us, do they?'

On the way out through the car park, shopping bags in one hand, phone in the other, I read Olly's message.

Hey, Charlie!! It's been a while. How are you? :) x

I tapped back a reply.

I'm good. Great to hear from you. How's the tour? x

Exhausting, but SO much fun

I hadn't heard from Olly since December. After that night at the Rochester, he had sent me a single Facebook message

– If you ever need to talk, I'm here – but I hadn't replied. I'm not sure he expected me to. And then the band went away on tour, and he didn't make contact again. If I knew Olly, he'd simply been waiting patiently, while I drifted back to normal life.

Hearing from him again like this, out of the blue, was giving me an unexpected rush.

So where are you now? I replied.

Hotel in Tokyo. People keep bringing us sushi! You?

Been to the shops. We ran out of dishwasher salt. I waited a moment, then added: Sometimes I can't take the glamour.

:) :) :)

I searched around for Dad's car, and spotted it by the trolley rank. Another message hit my screen.

So . . . do you have any plans on Friday?

I picked up speed, typing as I walked. Why would he be asking that?

Don't think so. Why?

Thirty seconds passed. I reached the car and dropped the bags into the boot. He still hadn't replied.

Olly?

Sorry, Sian's just arrived – I have to go. TV interview!!

I walked round to the passenger door, clicked it open and dropped inside. Dad was still on the phone to a client.

So what's happening on Friday? I wrote.

I'll tell you later – but keep it free if you can. I promise it'll be worth it :) x

By the time I'd shut the door behind me, Olly had already gone offline.

2

Behind The Band, Part One
'Auditions'

The lights dim to a single spotlight, and the audience falls silent. A figure walks out on to the empty stage.

'What's your name?' asks a hard, gravelly voice, off-camera. As the figure comes to a stop centre-stage, white light falls across his face. He's around sixteen years old, handsome, but visibly nervous. He nudges a dark lock of hair from his eyes.

'I'm Gabriel.'

Girls whoop in the crowd. Barry King, the owner of the gravelly voice, raises a hand to quiet them. He leans forward on his elbows.

'And what are you singing for us today, Gabriel?'

Gabriel sniffs.

'"Cat's in the Cradle".'

Scattered cheering clatters around the auditorium. Barry sticks out his bottom lip.

6

'Unusual choice,' he says flatly. Gabriel doesn't reply. He just shifts on his feet, and swallows.

'OK, then, Gabriel,' says Barry, turning to the judge on his left. He whispers something in her ear, inhales deeply, and turns back to the stage.

'Show us what you've got.'

www.poptube.com *all the pop, all the time*

I wasn't supposed to be watching this video. I wasn't supposed to be watching anything.

I was supposed to be studying.

'Charlie . . . ?'

My father's voice drifted up from the hallway, and I heard the front door close behind him. Jabbing the space bar on my laptop, I paused Gabriel with his mouth open, just as he was about to sing the opening line to 'Cat's in the Cradle', and slid off the bed. I could claim that I didn't know what happened next in the video. That I didn't know how good Gabriel's voice sounded as he let loose that first line. That my spine didn't tingle when the mouths of the judges fell open, one by one.

But that would be a lie.

'Charlie?'

I crossed my bedroom, weaving between piles of textbooks, and nudged open the door.

'Yep?'

'Food's up!'

'Coming,' I called back, walking out on to the landing as the smell of battered cod wafted up the stairs. Fish 'n' Chips 'n' Movies Night was a new ritual for me and Dad, part of our joint effort to spend more time together, and I liked it. Tonight it would have the added bonus of taking my mind off the fact that, in less than twenty-four hours, I'd be getting my mock exam results.

If I'd screwed them up, my dad would never forgive me.

'Tony was on top form at the chippy,' Dad was saying, from the kitchen, when I reached the bottom of the stairs. I spotted my phone on the living room table and crossed the hallway to fetch it. 'He reckons the Reading football team swear by his kebabs.'

'He's crazy,' I replied, picking up my phone. There was a message on the lock screen. 'He told Melissa that Katy Perry came in once and ordered twenty-five chicken nuggets, which is . . .'

I trailed off as I read the message.

A text? From Olly Samson?? WHAT IS THE MEANING OF THIS???

Melissa Morris: my best friend, neighbour and just a tiny bit of a drama queen. I perched on the arm of the sofa, and tapped back a reply.

I'm not really sure

I DEMAND ANSWERS

¯_(ツ)_/¯ I guess we'll find out on Friday

I craned my neck towards the doorway. In the kitchen, I could hear my dad clinking around in the cutlery drawer, and the fuzzy murmur of the radio. Glancing again at my phone, I blew out my cheeks. I'd been a bit careless, leaving it lying around. I really didn't need my father reading my messages, especially not the ones about – or worse, *from* – a famous popstar.

Maaaaybeeee he's finally realised U Are The One and he's going to buy u a private island and a white elephant with a saddle on it and ur going to spend ur days riding around on the elephant eating mangoes and laughing.

I squinted at the message.

That sounds terrifying. Have you drunk too much hot chocolate?

A pause.

Possibly

Anyway, like I told you before, we're just friends. End of story.

'Charlie?' Dad was calling me. 'Can I have a hand bringing the dinner through?'

'One sec . . .'

In front of me, on the coffee table, was a giant bowl of buttered popcorn, a bottle of Diet Coke and an unopened packet of marshmallows. The television was paused on the menu screen of *Sleepless In Seattle*, a movie which, in the last two months, had become one of our favourites. I think my dad identified with Tom Hanks's character or something. I just liked the music.

Hmmm, came Melissa's reply. Not sure it's possible to be just 'friends' with Olly Samson. Just look at his face. HIS FACE. Oh, the humanity.

I laughed to myself, and Melissa's speech bubble pulsated as she typed.

Still, at least he's not being super-weird with you like SOMEONE I could mention

The 'SOMEONE' in Melissa's message was Gabriel. And she was right: he *was* being super-weird. Back in December, after finding him in a hotel room with a movie star, I'd told him I never wanted to see him again. But I'd got it wrong. He and Tammie Austin weren't together after all; the story had been whipped up by gossip sites. Problem was, we'd never got a chance to talk about it, to resolve it. And then he'd sent me the photograph. The photograph which proved that, somehow, we'd known each other when we were kids.

His letter suggested we meet up, that he'd 'meet me anywhere', but it had never happened. Fire&Lights were crazy busy with the album launch and getting ready for their tour, and I was trying my best not to ruin the peace I'd made with Dad. And then, after the band left the country, on the rare occasion that I heard from Gabriel, the photograph was all he talked about. I *wanted* to talk about it, of course I did – not knowing what it meant was driving me crazy – but weeks and weeks later, I still had no idea where we stood with each other. All I knew was that Gabriel didn't want to discuss anything but his dad's band, Little Boy Blue, and the fact that my mother had been among their biggest fans. If I tried to steer the conversation towards us, he would shut it down. He would suddenly realise he had a soundcheck to get to, or a plane to catch, and he would disappear, go offline, usually for days at a time.

As the months passed, my memories of us bleached out and lost their colour. It was as if whatever we'd been to each other had faded away overnight, like the December snow.

'Kiddo, it'll go cold.'

I looked up and found Dad standing in the doorway, a dishcloth draped over his arm. He tilted his head. 'You all right?'

I covered my phone with my sleeve.

'Yes, yep.' I shook it off. 'Can't get standard deviation out of my head, that's all. Let's eat.'

As I followed Dad into the kitchen, listening to his quiet humming, I tried to force Gabriel from my mind. If he was completely over it, then I would just have to be over it too. Everyone had moved on, and that was probably a good thing. It was healthy.

Besides, Gabriel or no Gabriel, I had an ordinary life to lead.

3

'Ohmyholygosh. I just heard the craziest gossip OF ALL TIME.'

Melissa was trailing her fingers through a hedge on the way to school, plucking out leaves and the occasional twig. Early morning traffic grumbled by on the road.

'Go on, then,' I said. 'Hit me with it.'

She slowed her walk and turned towards me. Her face was deadly serious.

'*Pop Gossip* . . . have just run a story . . . about Aiden . . . and *Kaitlyn Jones*.'

I pulled my mum's beanie hat down over my ears. It was still just about cold enough to wear it, but it wouldn't be for much longer.

'What about them?' I said.

'That they're *dating*.'

I made a doubtful expression. Aiden Roberts, the sweet, soft-spoken Irish boy out of Fire&Lights – the quiet one, and Melissa's favourite – dating Kaitlyn Jones, the limelight-hogging American pop starlet? Yuki used to joke sometimes about Aiden fancying her, but . . . the two of them together? It seemed unlikely.

'Well?'

Melissa was waiting for me to respond.

'Well . . . what?'

'Charlie, this is serious. We're talking about Aiden here. MY AIDEN. If he really is taken, I basically may as well move to the mountains and live as a nun for the rest of my tiny, tragic life.'

I linked my arm through hers and tugged her onwards, towards school.

'He'll come back to you one day, Mel.'

'I *told* you I should've let him touch my boob at that after-party,' she murmured, kicking a stone along the path. 'And to find out today of all days . . .'

'What do you mean?' I asked innocently. Melissa stopped again, and grabbed both my shoulders.

'You do know what happens today, don't you?'

I wrinkled my nose.

'Erm . . . if I've failed my mock exams, which I probably have, my dad skins me alive and posts me to China?'

'Well, that, obviously,' Melissa agreed, 'but more importantly, *Fire&Lights finish their winter tour.* They'll be back in Britain by lunchtime! Boy, has this been a long ten weeks . . .'

Passing through the school gates, we briefly separated

as we fought our way to the front entrance, dodging through the bustling crowds. All around, students were shuffling along in groups, chatting over each other and jabbing at their phones. Teachers strode across the tarmac, rifling through papers.

'Hey, Charlie. Have you seen this?'

We found each other again by the school noticeboard. Melissa was pointing at an A4 poster, tacked between the sports announcements and PTA notices, and bearing a familiar photograph. The photograph was familiar because I had taken it myself, the summer before, at a hot, humid gig in the school hall, and it featured sixth former Jody Baxter, lead singer of Caversham High rock band Diamond Storm. The poster read: 'DIAMOND STORM, LIVE AT CAVERSHAM HIGH, THURS 20TH MARCH, 7.30 p.m. £2 entry.'

'Shall we go?' mused Melissa, tugging at one of her plaits.

'I don't know,' I replied, unconvinced. 'I'm not really into them.'

Melissa pushed air out through her lips.

'Me neither, but what else are we gonna do on a random Thursday night?'

'Well,' I said, with a sniff, 'if it's anything like last Thursday, we'll be lying upside-down on your bed, naming the ants in your ant farm.'

Melissa beamed at me.

'Oh my gosh, you are so right. Marmaduke's had an *excellent* week . . .'

My gaze veered away from the Diamond Storm poster and landed on the stark-looking announcement pinned next to it.

Year 11 – please report to tutor groups immediately after lunch to receive your mock exam results.

I fought off a shudder.

'Ugh. How depressing is that?'

'Armageddon is upon us, people,' said Melissa, hitching her rucksack up her back. 'Let the battle commence.'

I checked the time on my phone, and felt my stomach crinkle like shrink wrap. Four and a half hours to go.

The worst thing about it was the waiting.

Slowly, laboriously, one-fifteen crawled around. We all filed into the classroom, barely talking, the rubber squeaks of our shoes reverberating around the empty corridor. Normally Mr Crouch had to work quite hard to keep us quiet during tutorial sessions, but this afternoon, we were muted.

Everyone knew what was coming.

'Seats, everyone, please. Lots to get on with today.'

I slid into my chair, a hollow feeling in my stomach.

Mr Crouch perched on the edge of his desk, waiting, until the scraping of chair legs and unzipping of bags eventually subsided.

He leaned forward.

'No doubt you're all keen to see your results, and sure enough, I have them right here.' He opened a drawer, pulled out a wad of paper and dropped it on the desk with a thud. 'But my first question to you all is: how do *you* think you did?'

There was a cascade of sniggers from the back of the classroom. A few of my classmates exchanged looks. I kept my head down.

'Bossed it, sir.'

That sounded like Jamie Wheeler.

'Pardon?' replied Mr Crouch, nudging his glasses up his nose.

'I reckon I bossed it.'

'Well, I'm not entirely sure what that means, Jamie, but from the smirk on your face I assume you're labouring under the assumption that you've done well.' More sniggers from the back. 'You have not.'

My phone vibrated in my pocket. That was almost certainly Melissa, keen to find out how I'd done. She was headed for straight As, but then she'd been headed for straight As since she was about three years old.

'On the whole, Year Eleven, you've let yourselves down,' said Mr Crouch, picking up the papers and

17

straightening them out with a quick tap against the table. 'Which is disappointing, because despite appearances I happen to think you're a rather smart lot . . .'

Mr Crouch began to pace the rows, handing out results as he walked. I slid my phone from my pocket and stole a look. A sudden warmth buzzed through me. The message wasn't from Melissa. It was from Olly.

'Charlie?'

I whipped my head up. Mr Crouch was staring down at me over the top of his spectacles.

'No phones in class, Charlie, you know that.'

I quickly stowed it away.

'Yes, of course. Sorry, sir.'

'Here you go,' he said, with a tight-lipped smile, extending a sheet of paper towards me. I placed it on the desk and, with my pulse racing, scanned the figures. As in English, French and Spanish. In history and physics, Bs. Several more Bs dotted further down the list, one more A, and the odd C. Thankfully, most of it was pretty much what I expected.

But then, at the bottom, was the news I'd been dreading.

I'd been given a D in photography.

'As you're perusing these results, Year Eleven, ask yourself this question: did I perform to the best of my ability? And if not . . . why not?'

This wasn't what I'd been predicted. I'd been predicted an A*. But in the months leading up to the mocks, I'd thrown my heart and soul into photographing Fire&Lights, and that was the one set of pictures I couldn't submit. All our coursework was shown to parents at the Christmas exhibition, and in my backstage photos for Fire&Lights, every lie I'd told my father would have been laid bare. I'd eventually admitted to him that I'd been photographing a 'school band', of course, but it would have been obvious from the photographs – even to my father – that Fire&Lights were no school band. And so I'd pulled a project together at the last minute, an album of uninspiring shots taken in Reading town centre, and now the one subject that really mattered to me was the only one I was flunking.

'OK, everyone should have read their results now, so let's have a little calm, shall we?' Mr Crouch stuck his hands on his hips, and looked around the room. 'Hopefully not too many surprises in there, Year Eleven. We reap what we sow, after all. But the question is . . . what now? How do you turn those Es into Cs, those Bs into A*s?' He plucked the lid off a marker pen, and turned to the board. 'It starts with learning from your mistakes . . .'

An uneasy feeling prickled my skin. What if my poor grade actually had nothing to do with Fire&Lights, and I just wasn't cut out to be a photographer? Sure, some of my backstage shots had been picked for the F&L fan book last year, but what if that had been a fluke?

'. . . I would recommend drawing up a five-point plan for yourselves,' continued Mr Crouch, unaware that half the class weren't listening to him. 'Set yourselves five actionable steps, working towards an achievable goal, and you'll be far more likely to improve your grade come the final exams . . .'

My phone buzzed again – a reminder that I hadn't read Olly's message – and I suddenly craved the distraction. With Mr Crouch still facing the whiteboard, I snuck a look.

Thought you'd appreciate this pic :) Proof that Fire&Lights are #supercool *ahem*

On my screen was a band selfie, the boys bunched together in front of a beautiful Japanese temple, wearing matching caps that read 'WE LOVE TOKYO'. Yuki's cap was pitched at a jaunty angle, and his tongue was sticking out the corner of his mouth. I drank in every detail of the picture, grinning, fingers curled across it to shield it from view.

But as I took in each of their faces, something was nagging at my chest. Something that could mean everything, or it could mean nothing. Something that, despite myself, I knew I'd be obsessing about for days.

Gabriel wasn't in the picture.

'Twelve A*s, Mel. *Twelve*. I'm so proud of you. You are all kinds of clever.'

We were walking along the Oxford Road, a scruffy, bustling main road on the edge of town lined with second-hand stores, Polish supermarkets and carpet shops. It was a blustery day, and the sky was a dirty white, the colour of used paint-water.

'Thanks,' said Melissa, the corners of her mouth curling into a smile. 'And you are all kinds of awesome.'

I let out a sigh.

'I think my D in photography would beg to differ.'

'You'll figure something out, Charlie. You always do.'

We came to a busy bus stop and parted ways, threading through the waiting crowd. On the other side, we joined up again.

'Oh, and speaking of photography . . . that selfie Olly sent you is *amaaazing*. Did you ask him about Friday yet?'

Friday: Olly's surprise. The evening I had to 'keep free' for an as-yet-undisclosed reason.

'Not yet. I figure he'll just . . . tell me when he's ready.'

'Ah, man. Here you are getting secret texts from a popstar, *again*, and I still can't even get a *normal* boyfriend. What am I doing wrong?'

I grabbed Melissa's hand, and squeezed it.

'You're doing nothing wrong, you understand me?' She nodded reluctantly. 'You're the smartest person I know.'

'If today was anything to go by, though, smart is not hot. Boys are not interested in smart.'

'The right boy will be,' I said, but it seemed to pass her by.

'After we got our results,' she said, her face scrunching up, 'Mr Swift made this big deal of me being top of the year group, and Danny Dreyfuss said "one A* for every cat you're going to own", and everyone laughed. Which I can understand, because for Danny Dreyfuss that was actually kind of witty . . . but still.'

Her lips puckered into an exaggerated pout. I looked ahead, then checked the map on my phone. We were less than a minute away.

'Danny Dreyfuss? You can ignore him. They used to send him home from nursery because he kept trying to eat soil.'

Melissa snorted with laughter, and her gloom lifted.

'That explains a lot.' She peered at my phone. 'So . . . remind me where we're headed today?'

'Music Madness, on . . .' I consulted my map. 'Argyle Street. We're nearly there.'

'And this is the last one on the list?'

'Yep,' I confirmed, scratching my head, through my hat. 'After this, we are officially out of options.'

Melissa buried her hands in her coat pockets.

'Well, we may not have found a single Little Boy Blue album on our travels,' she reflected, 'but if they ever need someone to write the West Berkshire Guide to Independent Record Stores, we'd be the perfect candidates.'

Melissa was right. We'd been to pretty much every music shop we could get to on foot, and pickings had been non-existent. Since neither Gabe nor I had been able to find any trace of Little Boy Blue on the internet, I'd decided to go old school, straight to the source. To the people who really *knew* about music. But we'd visited record store after record store, and nobody stocked the band. No one had even heard of them. We were heading for a dead end, and its name was Music Madness.

Arriving at the shop's grimy front window, we peered inside. Vinyl records were perched on plastic stands on a threadbare purple carpet, their edges frayed, cardboard sleeves yellowed by the sun. Mysterious names stared back at us from the covers: Captain Beefheart, Atomic Rooster, Uncle Funkenstein. Melissa ran a single finger down the glass, leaving a greasy mark.

'Wowser. Is this a music shop . . . or a *museum*?'

'Come on,' I said, squinting into the dark. 'Let's do this.'

A little bell rang when the door opened, and we stepped inside, clutching our rucksacks. As the door groaned shut behind us, we looked around, intrigued. The walls were blanketed with brightly coloured throws, pink and orange and violet, hanging like the sails of a pirate ship between dog-eared concert posters. *Jefferson Airplane at The Matrix. Blood, Sweat & Tears at the Grande Ballroom.* The cramped space was deadly quiet, shut off from the grumble of traffic outside, and filled to bursting with old records. They lined the shelves, covered the counter and sat in tall, wonky piles in every corner. I had the strangest sense that if you tugged at just one of them, the whole shop would collapse in on itself like a house of cards and disappear.

Behind the counter sat a middle-aged man with short, grey-flecked hair and tortoise-shell glasses. His face was a little droopy, like it had grown tired of holding on, and he was surrounded by a collection of small tools and a scattering of electronics. He watched us for a few seconds. He had kind eyes, but his face was shadowed by an air of suspicious confusion. No doubt he was wondering, as the other shop owners all had, what two teenage girls were doing in his second-hand record store.

'Can I help you, ladies?' he said, setting down his miniature screwdriver.

'I hope so,' I replied, heading straight for the L-M shelf. 'We're looking for some music by a band from the nineties . . . but they're kind of obscure.'

He perked up at this. Something I'd learned in the last few weeks was that middle-aged men who ran record shops *really* got a kick out of obscure music.

'Oh, right. What were they called?'

'Little Boy Blue.'

He leaned back in his chair, one eye closed. The legs creaked underneath him.

'It's not ringing any bells. Where were they from?'

'London,' I said, flicking through records. Little Feat, Little Richard, Little River Band . . .

'Were they well-known?'

'I'm not sure,' I said, running out of artists and feeling my shoulders drop. 'I don't think so.'

He puffed his cheeks.

'I can't say I've heard of them, I'm afraid. And I've heard of most people.'

The man's attention wandered from me to Melissa, who was rifling through vinyls on the other side of the shop, singing quietly to herself.

'You know that's the collectibles section, don't you, love?' he asked, watching her lift up a tattered vinyl sleeve with a pink, multi-limbed Hindu goddess on the cover. Her brow furrowed as she read the band name out loud.

'. . . And You Will Know Us By The Trail Of Dead.' She scrunched up her nose. 'Jeez, talk about depressing.'

The man cleared his throat, very deliberately.

'Actually, Trail Of Dead are one of the most important bands in the history of prog rock.'

'Frog rock?' said Melissa.

'Pr— never mind.'

I swallowed a laugh, and the man caught me doing it. His cheeks went a little red.

'What's your interest in the band, anyway?' he said, picking up his screwdriver again.

'Oh, I . . .'

I hesitated. Even after several of these encounters, I wasn't quite sure how to answer that question. Sometimes I would make up a story about having a big brother with an unusual taste in music; other times I would say it was for a school project. But before I could reply, from the other side of the room, Melissa said: 'She's got a thing for old bands who no one's ever heard of.' She slotted the Hindu goddess vinyl back on to the shelf, and lifted out another one. It dangled from her hand. 'What's a Pink Floyd?'

'Maybe if I played you one of their songs,' I interrupted hastily, turning to the shopkeeper, 'it might jog your memory?'

The man shrugged, and pumped air through his nostrils.

'Stranger things have happened. Do you have something with you?'

I opened my bag and pulled out Gabriel's Little Boy Blue album. He still hadn't asked for it back, and since

December, I had become extremely attached to it. Both to the record, and the photograph he had sent with it – the one of us playing together as children – which I kept hidden inside the album sleeve. I plucked out the CD, and passed it over the counter.

'A CD,' said the man, lifting his eyebrows. 'I didn't think girls your age knew what a compact disc was.'

His chair let out another creak as he reached over to an ancient-looking CD player beside the till. It was dusty and scratched, and buried beneath a stack of vinyls.

Melissa appeared at my side.

'Did you know,' she said, to no one in particular, 'in the olden days, if you heard a song you liked on the radio, you couldn't just stream it on the internet . . . you had to go to an *actual* shop and buy an *actual* single.'

The man regarded her with astonishment, the CD glinting between his splayed fingers.

'That wasn't the olden days, that was 1998.'

'Yeah, *exactly*,' insisted Melissa, her eyes wide. 'The olden days.'

With a click and a whir, the CD spun into motion and the opening track began to play. Driving, echoey piano, laced with a distant electric guitar, flooded the shop, and in my mind's eye I could almost see the pianist's hands, fingers blurred, as he pounded out the chords.

The shopkeeper nodded his head in time with the beat, his eyes narrowing as if he were searching his interior database for a match. Melissa hummed along happily with the track, twirling a plait between her fingers.

Then, over the piano chords, Harry West began to sing. After months of listening to the album, I knew every feature of his voice, every note and detail, every crack and imperfection. Deep and rich, with a catching, jagged edge, it was unnervingly similar to Gabriel's.

I met a girl in winter . . .

'Sorry, nope,' interrupted the man, sitting up suddenly and turning down the volume. 'Don't recognise it.'

I touched my fingers to the edge of the counter.

'Are you sure?'

'I'd know straightaway if I'd heard it before, love. Got an audiographic memory.'

'Right.' I scratched my temple. 'But maybe you could turn it back up, anyway? Just in case?'

He sniffed loudly, and reached for the volume dial.

'It's funny, isn't it, nineties music?' said Melissa thoughtfully, over Harry's stirring vocals. 'Kind of scruffy, you know? Untidy.'

'That because they weren't using computers, love,' said the shopkeeper, squinting at a small screw as he rolled it between finger and thumb. The item he was fixing was one of those old-fashioned music players: a small, black plastic box with 'SONY WALKMAN' written on the side. 'Real music, this is, not like the robot-generated rubbish they churn out of reality TV nowadays.'

Melissa turned down the corners of her mouth, and wobbled her head, but the man didn't notice. He was too interested in his tiny screw.

The track played on around us, the lyrics swooping and diving through the air, a guitar solo yawning out of the noise. Then, as the song dipped into its calmer, quieter middle section, I waited for those all-too familiar lyrics . . .

She lives her life in pictures
She keeps secrets in her heart
The whole world could burn around her

'Colin? Colin!'

A woman's voice, coming from somewhere above us. A steady thump troubled the ceiling as she descended the stairs to the ground floor.

'Colin!'

The shopkeeper, who I was beginning to suspect might be slightly deaf, seemed to be blissfully unaware that he was being shouted at. I pointed towards the beaded string curtain over his left shoulder.

'I think someone's calling you.'

With a start, he spun on his chair, knocking a shower of screws off the counter.

'Colin?'

With a burst of beaded strings, a woman with long reddish hair and a big, happy, ruddy face appeared at the back of the shop. She was wearing a floaty tie-dye skirt and a tour T-shirt for a band called Steeleye Span. Behind her, the beads slowly clacked to a halt.

She clocked me and Melissa, then wagged a finger at the man.

'This is Little Boy Blue,' she said, with a smile.

4

I stared back at her, my heart cantering. Finally, we had a lead.

'What can we do for you?' the woman said, brightly. 'I'm not sure we've had young people in the shop since about 1989!'

'You know this band?' I asked.

She rocked her hand from side to side. 'Well, not exactly. I haven't thought about them for nearly twenty years. But I heard the song from upstairs and thought to myself, blimey, Jenny . . . that's Little Boy Blue, that is.'

'We're trying to find out more about them,' I said, showing her the album case. 'For a school project.'

She walked forward, wiping her hands on her T-shirt. When she reached the counter, I passed her the album.

'This is all we have at the moment.'

She flipped the CD case over a couple of times.

'They were from London, weren't they?' she asked, scanning the cover with her bottom lip sticking out.

'Uh-huh.'

'I saw them live once, you know. At the Alleycat.'

My chest tightened. Maybe Jenny had been in the same room as my mum. Maybe they'd even stood next to each other in the crowd, their shoulders brushing in the dark . . .

'That's so cool. Did you meet any of their fans?'

She shook her head.

'Not really. There were lots of them, though. And I'll tell you this' – she combed her fingers through the length of her hair, and flicked it over her shoulder – 'their fans were *devoted*. Girls, mostly. And it was pretty obvious why.'

I glanced at Melissa, then back at Jenny.

'What do you mean?'

She leaned over the counter, a twinkle in her eye.

'They had this lead singer . . . and, *oh my lord*. Most beautiful man I have ever laid eyes on.' She nudged her husband's arm with her elbow. 'Apart from Colin here, of course.'

Colin glanced up from his electronics, and frowned.

'His name was Harry,' I said, and Jenny clapped her hands together.

'Yes . . . yes, of course. Harry. My god. Made you weak at the knees, just looking at him.'

'Imagine if he'd had a *son*,' said Melissa, her hands on her hips. 'That guy would be one serious hottie.'

I gave her a sly kick beneath the counter.

'I remember,' continued Jenny wistfully, 'he caught my eye during one of the songs, just for a split-second. He didn't know me, and there were plenty better-looking girls in the crowd that night . . . but he had this way about him. I'll never forget it. You felt like the floor was giving way under your feet. When he looked at you, it was like you were the only person alive on the planet.'

With a shiver, I remembered thinking the exact same thought, about Gabriel, on the empty stage in Brighton. Like father, like son.

'Mind you,' continued Jenny, brushing some dust off the counter, 'that's all just a rockstar trick, isn't it? They make you think they're singing to you, that they're singing *about* you, but really, you're just one more face in the crowd.'

I folded my arms. Was that what Gabriel had been doing to *me*, all that time? Playing rockstar tricks?

'Well,' said Colin, without looking up from his work, 'his band didn't last very long, did they, so he can't have been much of a rockstar.'

Jenny patted his shoulder, and winked at me.

'Neither did yours, darling, so I'd button it if I were you.'

'Folk Octopus were ahead of our time,' protested Colin, waving his tiny screwdriver around. 'The world wasn't ready.'

'Whatever you say, my love.' She turned back to us. 'Where were we, ladies?'

'Rockstar tricks,' I said, and Jenny's eyes gleamed.

'Oh, yes. That's right.' She sighed, her gaze drifting up to the ceiling. 'It was a great night, that. The Alleycat was a fabulous venue. Shut down now, of course.'

'Did you see them play again after that?'

'No, that was the only time. They split up not long after. Lead singer killed himself. Tragic, really.'

I became aware, once again, of Harry's voice over the speakers. The CD had moved on to track two, the one with the lyrics that, years later, Gabriel would re-work for his own song, 'Dance With You'.

Take me home
I've been dreaming of a girl I know
The sweetest thing, you know she makes me wanna sing
I still remember everything

The first time I read those words, I was seven years old and they were written in my mother's scrapbook. At the time, I'd assumed she was writing about me, but, in fact, she was just copying out lyrics from her favourite rock band.

'So do you think they might have a website somewhere?' I asked Jenny, shaking off the memory. 'Or an old fan page, or something?'

She scratched the top of her head.

'Couldn't say, I'm afraid. But this was in the days before people really used the internet, so I doubt it. Back then, when you were gone, you were gone.'

Melissa, who had been unusually quiet during our conversation, suddenly burst into life.

'Come on,' she said, gesturing around the shop. 'You must have *one* of their records in this place. You've got *all the bands* in here. Well, except Fire&Lights.'

Colin frowned.

'Fire and what?'

'Problem is,' said Jenny, perching on the edge of the counter and disturbing a pile of screws, 'I just don't think they released much music before they split up. So, in a way, you're chasing a ghost.'

I felt myself tense. Something about that phrase, *chasing a ghost*, made me very uncomfortable.

'Unless . . .' Jenny was staring into a far corner of the room, fingers resting on her chin. 'I wonder . . .' She slid off the counter, lifted a hatch and stepped out into the shop, motioning for me to join her. I followed her towards a collection of boxes by the door and watched as she dug into one of them. Over her shoulder I could see CDs stacked in rows, most of them inside cheap cardboard jackets or slim, cracked cases.

'Now, let me see . . . 1999 . . . 1998 . . . ah, here!' She lifted up one of the discs. '1995. *Unsigned & Acoustic.*

They used to put these out to help new bands get exposure. Stick 'em on the front of music magazines and such. And if I remember correctly . . .' Running a finger down the back of the case, she read the names to herself, her lips moving silently, until eventually her eyes went wide. 'Yes! I knew it. Little Boy Blue. Here you go.'

She passed me the CD case, which was thin and made of card. On the front was a wooden guitar with the words '*Unsigned & Acoustic*: Covers Edition' wrapped around it, and on the back, a track-listing, which I quickly scanned, searching for that familiar band name.

When I found it, a thousand memories stirred inside me.

Little Boy Blue: Cat's in the Cradle.

Of course, I thought. *Of course it's that song.* The song that always made me think of childhood, the song that Dad told me last year was Mum's absolute favourite. The song Gabriel chose for his *Make Or Break* audition, and the one he was singing when I first stumbled in on him beside the empty stage in Brighton. The song Little Boy Blue took their name from in the first place.

A chill swept over me as I imagined what the track might sound like, and whether, in fact, I had heard it before as a child. Underneath the credit, the short description read: *Piano-led indie-rock quartet, fronted by the enigmatic Harry West. This band are making serious waves on the London circuit . . . you heard it here first.*

'This is amazing,' I said, without taking my eyes off the case. 'Thank you.'

'We should listen to it,' suggested Melissa, from across the room.

'Yes, can we?' I echoed.

Jenny pointed at her husband. 'Do the honours, Colin.'

Colin tapped the eject button on the stereo with the tip of his screwdriver, and the plastic CD tray slid noisily from the machine. Walking back to the counter, I passed Colin the *Unsigned & Acoustic* album and he handed back Gabriel's Little Boy Blue CD, which I returned to its case.

We all waited patiently for the music to kick in, but when the track began, it didn't sound quite the way I'd expected. Little Boy Blue had put the song's trademark introduction on piano, rather than guitar, which gave it a stark, ghostly feel, almost church-like. Then, when Harry began to sing and his voice filled the tiny shop, it felt like it was seeping into the very cracks in the walls. With every listen, it was becoming harder to deny: he sounded so much like his son. That jagged edge, those deep, aching notes, the shape of the words as they fell from his mouth. It was like hearing the same voice, twenty years apart.

As the four of us stood there in the shop, listening, the story of the song unfolded around us. The father who never had time for his son. Who pushed him away, day

37

after day, year after year, until one day, when his son was grown up with a family of his own, he found himself rejected by his only child. Because he had *taught* him to be that way. His son was repeating his mistakes, and there was nothing he could do to stop it.

Heat gathered in my face as I remembered Gabriel's wild eyes, that night on the roof at the London Complex, as he slowly broke down in front of me. I could feel tears edging my eyes.

I'm turning into him, Charlie. I can feel it . . . He's in my blood.

'You OK, love?'

I looked up. Jenny was watching me, her forehead creased with concern. Secretly, Melissa linked her little finger around mine.

'Uh, yeah. Sure,' I said, wiping the corner of my eye. 'It's just . . . I've always loved this song.'

'Beautiful, isn't it?' agreed Jenny, a sigh in her throat. 'And that man's voice, it's something else. Goes right through you.'

We all waited as the track slowed to a finish, and the piano faded away. Jenny ejected the disc, and slipped it back into its case.

'You can keep this, if you like. On us.'

'That's so kind,' I said, accepting it from her and holding it close to my chest. 'Thank you. Thank you so much.'

Her face relaxed into a warm smile, while beside me, Melissa extended her arm and shook Colin's hand. His face was a perfect picture of bewilderment.

'Cheers to you, Mr Colin, sir. We will be sure to tell our chums to come here for all their musical needs,' she said.

Jenny laughed. 'That's sweet, my dear, but we don't really stock much modern music.' She held a flat palm at a right-angle to her mouth, and whispered: 'Colin doesn't like it. The last album he bought was *No Jacket Required* in 1985.'

Colin narrowed his eyes, but when his wife reached down and squeezed his forearm, the tiniest hint of a smile tickled his lips.

'You've no idea how much this means to me,' I said, buttoning my coat. 'I can't wait to listen to it again.'

'Enjoy, ladies. And come back any time you want . . .'

'Old people are cool,' Melissa was saying, moments later, as we stepped out on to the street. The musty calm of the shop was replaced by the grey, fuzzy sound of traffic, and the sharp March breeze on our cheeks. 'They have so many wicked stories . . .'

We turned the corner on to the Oxford Road, and I smiled.

I was still gripping the CD tightly in my hand.

Melissa and I said goodbye at her gate and I wandered down my garden path, my mind full of music, my mother and Little Boy Blue. I was so wrapped up in my thoughts that it wasn't until I stepped into the hallway and saw my father in the kitchen that I remembered what was about to happen.

'Hey there, kiddo,' he said, turning round, steaming cup of tea in hand. 'How did results day go? Didn't you get my text?'

I felt my face tighten.

'Oh, I did,' I said, turning away from him and hanging my coat on the rack. 'Busy day, that's all.'

'So . . . can I see?'

Dad had drifted into the hallway. We both looked at my rucksack, slumped on the floor.

'Of course, yeah. One sec.'

Slowly, I knelt down and unfastened my bag, aware of every click, every rasp of the zips. I pulled out my sheet of results, passed it to my father, then pretended to have something important to do on my phone.

Every few seconds, my gaze flickered upwards, waiting for Dad to reach my photography grade. A big, fat D for 'Disappointment'.

'Oh . . . Charlie.' He lowered his mug on to the phone table and adjusted his glasses. 'Your photography. How did that happen?'

My words faltered. I suddenly didn't know what to do with my hands.

'I-I don't know,' I said, shifting my weight from one foot to the other. 'I just . . . I guess I was busy with other things.'

Dad let out a long, thoughtful breath.

'Maybe this is partly my fault.'

'It isn't, Dad.'

'I don't know, Charlie, I can be so busy with work. And photography's not like chemistry, or history; it's not just learning facts. It takes time.'

I tugged my sleeves down over my wrists, listening to the clock ticking in Dad's study. He wagged a finger in the air, as if a thought was coming to him.

'Actually, I saw something on the way home today . . . an advert for an exhibition, in town?'

I knew immediately what he was talking about. Reading didn't run that many photography exhibitions, and I'd been looking forward to this one for ages. Carrie Shakes, the American rock photographer, was exhibiting a whole new set of concert photos at the Slash Gallery, starting next week. She was only about ten years older than me, but she was already one of the hottest music photographers in the world. She was one of my idols.

'Carrie Shakes,' I said, slipping my shoes off.

'Yes, that's it! Why don't I take you, one day this month?'

I smiled.

'Thanks, Dad. That would be nice.'

He picked up his tea again, curving his palm around the mug.

41

'Hey, come on. You have a passion, and that's a rare thing.' He swallowed. 'You have to hold on to that, you know.'

He broke his gaze, and I thought of the newspaper clippings I had found in his study, months earlier. 'Gifted PhD student begins ground-breaking research programme'. 'Ralph Bloom published in leading academic journal'. And the letter that revealed he'd given it all up, to take care of me.

'I will,' I said, with a nod. 'I promise.'

We fell silent. The steam from Dad's tea snaked upwards, towards the low ceiling. I bent to slide my shoes into the rack, next to his.

'Dad.' I looked up. 'Can I ask you something about Mum?'

Dad stopped with his cup of tea halfway to his mouth, his features suddenly taut, anxious. I could feel my heart beating in my throat. It stung, knowing he knew so much about Mum that he wasn't telling me. I was pretty sure he was trying to protect me from something, but I didn't want protecting. I wanted the truth.

'Did she have something she was . . . passionate about?'

It was a question I already knew the answer to, of course. Mum was passionate about music. She was passionate about Harry West's band, Little Boy Blue, passionate enough that she wore a T-shirt with their name on it and listened over and over to 'Cat's in the Cradle' and spent her days copying Harry's lyrics into an old notebook.

Say something, I willed my father silently. *Tell me about her.*

Dad's mouth flattened into a straight line.

'Of course she did,' he said finally. 'She had you. She was passionate about you.'

Beneath my skin, frustration writhed like a wild animal. *She was passionate about you.* In a way, that should have made me feel better. It was a nice thing to say, after all.

But it wasn't enough. It never would be. Because I knew, for a fact, that he was hiding something.

5

Tuesday afternoon, double history. Melissa and I were sitting side by side, reading about Renaissance surgery, while behind us, Sam Croft and Jamie Wheeler were talking in hushed voices about how one footballer had owned another footballer on Twitter.

'Uh, who's talking at the back there?' said Mr Crouch, looking up from his marking.

'I think it was Charlie Bloom,' said Sam, to sniggers from his friends. I kept my head down.

'Mr Croft, has it occurred to you, at any point this year, that you are taking your GCSE exams in six weeks' time?'

'I don't understand how this helps my life, though, sir,' retorted Sam, over the scrape of chair legs. 'It says here that: "Doctor Amb . . . Am . . . something-in-French discovered that wounds healed better when treated with a . . . soothing digestive".'

'That's a biscuit, innit?' said Jamie, and pockets of laughter erupted across the room. At his desk, Mr Crouch removed his spectacles, and rubbed the bridge of his nose.

'What exactly are you getting at, Sam?'

A pause.

'Well . . . how does that help me get a job on Sky Sports, sir?'

'It doesn't, Sam, but if you'd actually listened to wh—'

Mr Crouch was interrupted by a knock on the classroom door. Chatter bubbled all around us.

'Uh – reading in silence, please,' said Mr Crouch, standing up from his desk and crossing to the door. He opened it, but only halfway. I could just about see one of the office staff standing in the corridor.

The two of them conducted a whispered conversation; Mr Crouch glanced at his watch, then back over his shoulder at us. Finally, he nodded at her, and they parted ways.

'OK, Year Eleven,' said Mr Crouch, gesturing to the whole class, 'I'd like you to leave all your bits and pieces where they are, and follow me quietly to the assembly hall.'

At first, nobody moved. This was a fairly unusual development.

'Come on, no dawdling.'

Bemused, we all began setting down our pens and shuffling out of our seats. I threw Melissa a questioning look, but she just shrugged.

'What's going on, sir?' asked Jamie, casually flicking someone's pencil off their desk as he passed. Mr Crouch ran a hand across his balding head.

'Just . . . be patient.'

'Is it a bouncy castle?' said Jamie.

'I'm choosing to ignore that,' replied Mr Crouch, wearily. 'Just leave your seats without talking, everyone, and follow me to the hall.'

Five minutes later, we were sitting in our established rows at the back of the assembly hall, watching as the final Year Sevens filed in at the front. I scanned the line of teachers alongside us, trying to read their strangely blank expressions. We did have assemblies every other Tuesday, but they were usually in the mornings. It seemed a bit strange to pull us out of class without warning.

Mr Bennett, our headteacher, addressed us from the stage.

'I'm sure you're all wondering what you're doing here,' he said, prompting a sudden burst of conversation from every corner of the room. He waved a silencing palm at us. 'Quiet, please. Thank you.'

He looked very serious.

'But if you'll quiet down, I'll explain . . .'

He peered across the hall. Someone gave him the nod. 'OK. I believe we're ready to start.'

Onstage, Mr Bennett gestured towards the main entrance, and every head in the room turned in unison.

The door opened, and in walked Olly Samson from Fire&Lights.

6

Pandemonium.

The hall exploded into a cacophony of screaming and yelling, voices battling for attention, tearing the air, people shouting and laughing and shrieking and crying. The noise was so piercing, so overwhelming, that as I watched Olly walk up the steps to the stage, I felt light-headed. Like I was dreaming.

Was he really . . . here?

'Uhh, thank you, Caversham! Let's have a little quiet, please!' Mr Bennett was saying – well, shouting – from the stage. Melissa's hand was clamped against my leg, a fistful of skirt between her fingers.

'Is this real? Charlie? Is that . . . oh my GOSH. I am DYING . . .'

The noise rattled and thrummed as Olly reached the top of the steps, shook Mr Bennett's hand and turned to face the crowd. Cameras that I hadn't realised were in the room flashed and clacked, excited feet stamped and scuffled, and teachers *shush*ed uselessly, all around. Gripping the edge of my seat, skin stretched across my knuckles, I held my breath as I took in the familiar sight of Olly Samson, popstar. His short, brown hair, the toned curve of his shoulders beneath a clean white T-shirt, those bright, sparkling blue eyes.

The last time I'd seen Olly in real life, he'd been asleep on a hotel sofa, dawn breaking behind the curtains. A shaft of sunlight falling across his chest. And Gabriel's words had floated, uninvited, through my mind.

I'm the fire . . . he's the light.

'Hey there, Caversham High. I'm Olly Samson.'

The screaming began again, louder this time, if that was possible, and Mr Bennett descended the steps, waving both hands like he was frantically directing traffic.

'Quiet, everyone!' he repeated, throwing an apologetic look at Olly, who smiled and gave an easy, carefree shrug. Mr Bennett's face was turning slightly pink, but eventually, as people realised Olly was about to continue, a fragile calm settled. Rubber soles squeaked against the parquet floor; vending machines hummed behind our heads. The occasional feverish whisper tickled the silence.

There was so much pent-up energy in the building, you could almost hear the air fizz.

'You're probably wondering why I'm here,' said Olly, rubbing the back of his neck, 'and, you know . . . interrupting double maths.' (Laughter.) 'Well, you might have heard of my band, Fire&Lights' (more screaming, but Olly kept going) 'and some of you may know that I used to go to this school, before I joined the group . . .'

Busy chatter spilled out along our row, and I became aware of Gemma Hockley, sitting on the end with Sam and Jamie, pointing at me and smirking. I'd been secretly hoping my classmates had forgotten about my association with the band, but unlike the outside world, Caversham High was a small place with a long memory. Cheeks burning, I diverted my attention to the small group of photographers and local reporters in the corner of the room. They were holding digital recorders in the air, focusing camera lenses and scribbling on notepads.

'Anyway,' continued Olly, from the stage, 'we just got home from the latest leg of our world tour, and we all decided we wanted to get back to our roots. Seeing the world with Fire&Lights is awesome, but I never want to forget where I came from. So . . . here I am.'

More clapping and cheering. Underneath the racket, I could hear what sounded like sobbing coming from some of the Year Sevens.

'We don't have that long, but while I'm here, I wanted to talk to you a bit about my life before Fire&Lights. Because, not that long ago, I was sitting exactly where you are right now.'

Whooping and whistling echoed around the hall, peppered with shouts of 'We love you, Olly!' and

'Fire&Lights rule!' There were a few jeers too, from the older boys, but they were fighting a losing battle.

'There are people here who knew me when I was at Caversham High, and you might remember that I was into singing and stuff, but I wasn't really *that* great at it. I had to work at that part. I know I'm kinda famous now' – Melissa turned to me and repeated: '*kinda* famous?' – 'but I'm no different to any of you. I was looking up at this stage, less than two years ago, hoping that one day I might be a singer in a band. So I guess what I'm saying is, if you have a dream, if you have a talent, you should go for it. There are tons of you in this room with talent, amazing talent, and you shouldn't hide it. It's part of who you are.'

As those last words fell from his mouth, he paused, and his gaze seemed to lock on to mine. He was staring right at me. My heartbeat stumbled.

'I've been really lucky,' he said, looking away, 'but you can do all this without luck. You can make it happen for yourselves.' I stared at my hands, clasped together in my lap. I hadn't imagined that, had I? 'Don't let anyone tell you your ambitions don't mean anything, because they do. Trust me. And whatever it is that fires you up, maybe it's music, maybe it's football or baking or, I don't know, knitting underwear for cats,' (a big laugh from the crowd) 'whatever it is your heart's telling you to chase, go after it. Because that's what life is for.'

An awed silence. The whole room was transfixed.

'Now . . . there's one more thing I wanted to do before I go.'

Mr Burnham was walking up the steps to the stage, holding an acoustic guitar. Whispers rippled through the hall.

'Most of you won't know this,' said Olly, receiving the guitar from Mr Burnham and strapping it over his shoulder, 'but I've started writing my own songs. I'm not much of a guitarist, and this wasn't really part of the plan today, but I figure, hey . . . I'm here in the town I grew up in, so would you mind if I played you a song?'

A roar erupted from the floor, and Olly responded with a slow, happy nod. Smiling, he gave the strings a thoughtful strum, and cleared his throat.

'OK, here goes. This is a song called "She Is The Fire".'

My pulse quickened: Olly's song from the beach. The one he'd played to me first, before anyone else, on that cold, crisp November day on the Devon coast. And now, as he carefully plucked the chords and began to sing, a steady warmth washed over me. The melodies, the words, though I'd only heard them that one time, felt so familiar to me, like fragments from a recurring dream.

Then, when he reached the chorus, my heart began to shake.

She is the fire in my fingertips
The warm rain that tells me where the thunder is
And I know that somebody has found her heart
But that won't keep us apart

There were hundreds of people sitting in between us, but they may as well not have been there at all. Olly and I could just as easily have been back there on that chilly, windswept beach, birds circling above our heads, freezing ocean lapping at the shore, the two of us, alone, on the sand dunes. Our eyes locked again, across the sea of heads, and as Olly sang, he was singing directly to me.

And nobody knew but us.

She keeps a piece of herself inside
But she speaks, and every single star collides
And I know that somebody has found her heart
But that won't keep us apart

My classmates, the teachers, the walls, the floor and the ceiling melted away, and it was just us, just me and Olly, and his music. It may have been in my head, this whole thing, it may have been another case of 'rockstar tricks', but I didn't care. It felt amazing. He sounded . . . *amazing.*

Olly strummed the final chord of the song, and for a few seconds, it hung, delicate and ghostly, in the air.

Then the spell lifted, and everyone applauded, screeched and hollered, and I just sat there, unblinking, my chair shaking as everyone around me clapped and stamped their feet.

Across the hall, the cameras started up again, and I found myself drawn back to the huddle of journalists in the far corner. They were all busy clacking away and writing notes, some of them laughing and chatting to each other, genuine joy on their faces. But there was one reporter standing apart from the group. A man I hadn't noticed the first time around. A man with no camera, no notepad and no sound recorder. A man with small, dark eyes like black stones, and a grizzled, stubble-flecked face.

Paul Morgan, from *The Record*.

And he was looking right at me.

'Well, well . . . Olly Samson.' Mr Bennett's voice. I tugged my gaze away from Paul. 'Incredible stuff. Incredible . . .'

As the hall shuddered with applause, panic clenched my stomach. What was Paul doing at Caversham High? He wasn't a local journalist; *The Record* was a national tabloid. He didn't even look like he was reporting on Olly's visit. He'd been watching me, and not for the first time. He'd secretly followed me and Gabriel around last winter, on more than one occasion, and when he'd finally caught up with us, he'd made it very clear that he knew

Gabriel was hiding something. Not only that, but one day, he'd told us, he was planning to tell the world.

I dared myself to look up again, but he was gone. A few metres away, the main door swung to and fro, three times, before finally slowing to a stop.

'. . . What a treat for a Tuesday afternoon . . .' Pushing Paul Morgan from my mind, I returned my gaze to the stage, where Mr Bennett had reappeared by Olly's side. He was out of breath, and seemed weirdly starstruck. 'Another big hand, please, for Olly Samson!'

Olly gave us a small, humble smile, waved, then started to make his way down the steps. Mr Bennett watched him go, clapping enthusiastically, his hair uncharacteristically unkempt, fringe flopping over his forehead.

'Such a pleasure to see homegrown talent doing so well, isn't it?' he said, flicking his hair from his eyes. 'And, actually, on the subject of homegrown talent – uh, quiet down, please, Caversham – don't forget that our next generation of Olly Samsons, the sixth-form rock band, Diamond Storm, are performing a live concert in this hall next Thursday at 7.30 p.m. So be sure not to miss that!'

When Olly reached the bottom of the short staircase, he was greeted by two teenagers I didn't recognise, both wearing Fire&Lights T-shirts. The first was a small, strikingly pretty girl, seventeen or eighteen years old, sporting one of those achingly cool, half-shaved-head haircuts. A sweep of bright red hair arched across the top of her head and down into her face, just touching the corner of her left eye. Standing next to her was a boy of around the same age and similar height, with an open, trusting face and carefully combed brown hair that made him look a bit like a Lego man. Olly high-fived both of them as he stepped on to the floor.

'Charlie, my mind has been blown. Olly Samson in our ACTUAL school. It's just too much.' Melissa was still staring at the empty stage, shaking her head. 'Stick me in a jar, and call me a pickle.'

Meanwhile, the assembly hall had descended into chaos. Students were beginning to rush about, pushing past each other and climbing over chairs in search of Olly. He had, however, been spirited away by security.

'We'll do this one year group at a time,' Mr Bennett was saying, as he weaved between excitable students. Along with a handful of teachers, he was trying, and failing, to calm things down. 'Starting with the Year Sevens . . .'

He clicked his fingers in our direction.

'And, uhhh, Year Eleven history, Mr Crouch and I have some PTA matters to attend to, so if you could make your way to the library for the remainder of the period . . . quiet revision, please. There are only forty minutes to go before the bell, so . . . wait . . . Year Seven, in a line, please!'

Out in the corridor, on our way to the library, Melissa and I stopped at the lockers to pick up some revision textbooks. I was about to open my door when I spotted a piece of rectangular card protruding from the hinge.

I plucked it out.

Carrie Shakes: *Friends Of Mine*
Slash Gallery, 14th March

I frowned at the ticket. Was this from my dad? If it was, it seemed a very weird way for him to have delivered it to me. And anyway, the fourteenth was in three days' time, and the exhibition didn't open until the following week. The date had to be wrong. Unless . . .

I turned it over, and a strip of gold writing gleamed in the light.

< PRIVATE VIEWING >
Hope you're still free. Olly xx

'Whatcha got there, buddy?'

Melissa was standing behind me, her chin resting on my shoulder. I passed her the ticket without saying a word, and she stepped around me, eyes narrowing as she read the information. Then her jaw dropped, and she pointed down the corridor.

'You. Me. Library. Now.'

*

The Caversham High library was a shabby, neglected room in a forgotten corner of the school. It was home to an elderly and mostly deaf librarian called Mrs Horton-Parker, and its main function was to house random classes who had nowhere else to go. Currently, Mr Crouch's Year Eleven history students were scattered around the graffitied tables, chatting about Olly Samson, snacking on sweets and tapping away at phones.

'Right,' said Melissa, tearing open a packet of jelly babies. 'Talk to me.'

I picked at the corner of my French textbook.

'What do you want me to say?'

She waved the ticket in my face.

'*This is a date.*'

I snorted.

'It so is not.'

'Um, yu-*huh*, it's a date.' She rapped her fist against my forehead as if knocking on a very small door. 'Helloooo! Charlie Bloom! This is your sanity calling. *Olly Samson has a thing for you.*'

I threw a worried glance around the library. Ironically, people were too busy gossiping about Olly's visit to overhear our conversation.

'He's just doing a nice thing,' I said. Melissa set the ticket on the table and leaned in towards me.

'He told you himself, last year, that he "really, really likes you". And he told you that on a beach, which makes it a hundred times truer.'

'Mel, you're blowing this out of pr—'

'ON A BEACH.'

Without taking her eyes off me, Melissa reached into the sweet packet and plucked out a jelly baby. Then she pulled off its head, and offered it to me.

'For you.'

I took it, and a half-smile curled on to my face.

'Thanks. But, come on . . . that was last year. It was a different time.'

Melissa tapped her finger against the ticket.

'This is Carrie Shakes, dinkus! She's, like, your absolute favourite. Only someone who really cares about you would know that.'

She did have a point. I'd never talked to Olly about Carrie, so how did he know? It wasn't as if I wandered round in a Carrie Shakes T-shirt.

'Even so,' I said, chewing on the sweet, 'after everything that happened with Gabriel, it would be too weird. Too complicated. Just . . . no.'

'Uh, girls?'

Miss Horton-Parker stood up shakily from her desk, and pointed a finger somewhere in our general direction (she was a little blind as well). A wave of sniggers passed around the library.

'Quiet in the library, please.'

'Sorry!' chirped Melissa, opening her maths book to a random page. Then she lowered her voice a little, and glanced around the room.

'But, seriously, you're telling me that if Olly walked in here right now and asked you to be his girlfriend, you'd turn him down?'

I raised one shoulder in a slow half-shrug.

'It's not about turning him down, Mel. I just . . . I don't think I'm cut out to date Olly Samson.'

'Charlie?'

A male voice, just above our heads. Melissa and I twisted in our chairs to find Jody Baxter, lead singer of Diamond Storm, standing by our table. I pulled my textbook towards me, hoping he hadn't overhead our conversation.

'Oh . . . hi, Jody.'

He nudged a long, flat strand of straw-coloured hair from his face, and frowned. I'd always thought he looked like a skinny, slightly nervous, Kurt Cobain.

'I know this is kind of random,' he said, 'but the guys and I have a question for you.'

By 'the guys', I assumed he meant the rest of Diamond Storm. I didn't know Jody that well, but I wasn't sure I'd ever heard him talk about anything else.

'Oh?'

'Yeah.' He sniffed, scratching a thumbnail on the

tabletop. 'See, thing is, we're doing this gig next week, in the school hall? Mr Bennett mentioned it in assembly?'

'We're coming!' said Melissa, even though we hadn't discussed it yet.

'Ah, cool!' said Jody, his face brightening. 'I know it's lame, playing at school and stuff, but . . .'

No one said anything. Jody coughed, and rubbed the side of his head.

'Anyway, thing is, we love the photos you took of us last summer, and we've tried some other people since then, but' – he scrunched up his face – 'no one's anywhere near as good as you, so . . .'

He trailed off again. I kept quiet. Melissa sang a little tune to herself.

'I know you've done Fire&Lights now, so you're probably not interested, but if you *were* coming, maybe you could bring your camera, and . . .'

Jody left his non-question hanging in the air, and I turned it over in my head. Even though Aimee Watts's dad had, finally, agreed to replace the camera his daughter had destroyed, I hadn't taken that many pictures since I stopped working with Fire&Lights. Photography was beginning to feel like something I used to do. And since I had a grade to bump up, I could definitely use the practice.

'I'll think about it,' I said cagily.

Jody stuffed his hands in his pockets. 'Great. Thanks.' He wiggled his fingers inside his trousers. 'Hey, that was *intense*, wasn't it? Olly Samson just turning up at school?'

'Uh-huh,' I replied.

'I almost weed my pants,' said Melissa.

'Are you still friends with him?' asked Jody. I tried to avoid his gaze.

'We don't ... I mean, I haven't seen him since December.'

'Right. Yeah.' Jody gave a slight flick of his hair. 'Anyway, maybe see you around? At the concert?'

'Sure,' I replied, and he ambled off, nodding hello at some friends on a nearby table as he went. Melissa drummed her fingers against her maths book.

'So are we going, then?' she asked hopefully.

I threw my hands up.

'Why not? Maybe it'll be fun.'

'Yessssss.' Melissa glanced over her shoulder, watching Jody slope through the exit. 'Also, exciting to find out you're officially an in-demand photographer.'

I laughed.

'I think you need more than one person asking for you to be in-dema—'

I was cut off by the shrill ringing of the school bell, which sent the whole room into a frenzy of book-shutting, chair-scraping and bag-zipping. Melissa glanced at her phone.

'Dammit, I have to get to my violin lesson. And we still have so much Olly-gossiping to do.' She slipped her books into her bag. 'Tell you what, why don't you go straight to mine, chill with Mum for a bit, and I'll be back in an hour? She could do with the company. She's been working on this big piece about North Korea and it is *seriously* bumming her out.'

'Sounds like a plan,' I said.

'And remember' – Melissa plucked Olly's ticket from the table and dangled it in front of me – '*this is a date. Plain and simple*.'

She dropped it into my hand and gave me a parting salute.

'Later, potater,' she said, with a wonky grin.

7

'I think I have chocolate sauce on my nose.'

Melissa's mum swivelled round from her position at the kitchen sink, and her mouth lifted into a smile.

'Oh, yes,' she said, stepping forward. 'You do.'

She plucked a sheet of paper towel off the stand, crossed to the table and wiped the dab of sauce off my nose. I stared down at my hands in the bowl. They were a big, sticky mess.

'Mucky business, this,' she said, screwing up the paper towel and dropping it in the recycling box. '*Jeez Louise*. This is why Brian normally does the baking round here. "You do the political exposés, Rosie, and I make the flapjacks". Too right.'

I peered out through the kitchen doorway and into the office, where Rosie's laptop was open on her desk, papers scattered all around it.

'Oh ... yeah,' I said, licking the chocolate off my fingers. 'I'm sorry I interrupted your work.'

Rosie's mouth fell open.

'Oh, gosh, no, Charlie. I should be thanking you! I needed a break from North Korea.'

Rosie grabbed a handful of her red ringlets, spun them together and fastened them at the back with a hair tie. Then she slid the chocolate sponge, which was sitting on a cooling rack, off the counter.

'So, how's the photography going?' she said, setting the sponge in front of me. I glanced at my feet.

'Well . . . turns out I kind of mucked up my coursework last year. They just gave me a D in the mocks.'

'Ah. What did your dad say? That icing ready?'

I examined the contents of the mixing bowl, poking at the gooey mixture with a wooden spoon.

'I think so.' Rosie tipped the bowl in her direction, and nodded in agreement. 'I did all right in everything else,' I continued, 'so he didn't flip out or anything. But I could tell he was disappointed.'

She reached towards the sink and pulled a palette knife from the drawer.

'Were *you* disappointed?' she asked, handing it to me.

'Yeah. I was pretty gutted, actually.' I was gripping the knife like a microphone, sticking straight up in the air. 'So I just . . . slap it on?'

Rosie laughed softly.

'Yep. Just slap it on.'

For a while, I busied myself scooping up the thick,

brown icing and layering it on to the cake. Soon, I had covered almost the entire sponge.

Rosie watched me silently.

'I'm hoping to fix it, though,' I said, sweeping the knife across the top of the cake, to smooth it. 'This school band, Diamond Storm, want me to start taking photos for them again, so that could be my new project, I guess.'

'That's the spirit,' replied Rosie, rescuing a globule of icing that had dripped off the edge of the sponge. 'You'll run it by your dad this time, though, won't you? He got awfully worried last year.'

'Sure,' I agreed, with a nod. I sat down at the table. 'I don't want him to get mad at me again.'

'You know he only got upset because he loves you, don't you?'

Rosie caught my eye, and I slid the palette knife back into the bowl.

'I know. But sometimes it's hard to know what Dad's thinking. Like, with Mum, and stuff . . .'

Rosie sat next to me, and Melissa's cat, Megabyte, hopped on to her lap. She stroked her from nose to tail, and Megabyte arched her back, purring.

'He's a private man, your dad, but that doesn't mean he doesn't care. He's just been through some difficult times, and he finds it hard to open up. When he's ready, he'll talk.' She tickled Megabyte under her chin. 'In fact, the last time we spoke, I got the impression that Ralph was – I don't know – finally ready to move on.'

I felt my chest tighten. Move on?

'Really?'

Rosie shrugged.

'Who knows, maybe. I think it would be good for him. He gets a little lonely sometimes, and you won't be at home forever.'

I sat back in my chair, my gaze wandering to a photograph on the fridge door. Melissa was standing with her parents and her older brother, Tom, in front of the Colosseum in Rome. I thought about my own family photograph, of Mum and Dad in the park, with me as a tiny baby, wriggling on a picnic blanket. What did Rosie mean by Dad being ready to 'move on'? How *could* he move on from Mum? Why would he even want to . . . ?

With a bang, the front door swung open.

'Dudes, I swear, if I have to listen to another MINUTE of Snotty Barwick trying to play Sailor's Hornpipe on the viola, I am going to suck my own brain out with a hoover. *Jeez Louise.*'

Melissa clattered down the hallway, emerged into the kitchen and dropped her bag by the table. Her eyes lit up as she spotted the bowl of icing.

'I am not a dude,' remarked Rosie wryly, as she dried her hands on a dishcloth. 'I am your mother.'

'You so are a dude,' replied Melissa. She slipped past me and dipped her finger in the icing. 'Right, Charlie?'

'It's true,' I said matter-of-factly. 'You are a dude.'

Rosie fought off a smile.

'Well, in that case, this dude would like *these dudes'* – she pointed at us both – 'to get some homework done.' She patted Melissa on the bum, shooing her away. 'Upstairs, chop chop. Dinner at six-thirty.'

Melissa walked backwards, sucking the icing off her fingertip.

'How many words have *you* written today, Ma?'

Rosie made a guilty face.

'Not enough, to be honest. Still so much research to do. North Korea is a complicated place.'

'If it were up to me,' said Melissa, picking up her rucksack again, 'I'd get in a plane, and I'd fly over to Yongpang—'

'Pyongyang,' corrected Rosie.

'Pyongyang, and I'd fly right up to Kim Jong-un's house, knock on his door and give him a serious piece of my mind.'

Rosie smiled, and hung the dishcloth over a chair.

'That's my girl.'

I loved spending time with Rosie and Melissa. It was my happy place. But sometimes, somewhere behind my chest, it made me ache.

*

Upstairs, under the guise of history homework, Melissa and I were sitting cross-legged on her bed, mugs of steaming hot chocolate on her desk, planning my acceptance to Olly's invite. Melissa was holding my phone in her hand, index finger poised above it.

'Erm . . . right,' she said, staring into the ceiling. 'How about this? You could say: "'Sup, O, got the tkt, looks sick, c u there".'

'I could,' I said, retrieving my phone from her. 'Except I'm not a Detroit gangster.'

Melissa giggled.

'I'm just going to say something simple,' I added, starting to type. 'Like: "Thanks for the ticket, sounds perfect, meet you at the gallery".'

Melissa fiddled with the corner of her duvet.

'I liked my idea better . . .'

I nudged her knee with mine, and she nudged back.

'Well,' she said, shifting on the bed, 'while you write your boring message, I'm going to stare at pictures of Olly on the F&L website and imagine what it'll be like when he literally *sweeps you off your feet* on Friday . . .'

Melissa opened her laptop and started tapping away at the keys. Meanwhile, I re-read my reply several times, wondering if she was right. Was I being boring? Did that even matter?

I took a deep breath, added two kisses to the message and hit *Send*. Next to me, Melissa suddenly straightened up.

'Hey, have you seen this?'

She was gesturing at the screen.

'What?'

'Look, right here . . . on the fan site. Check it out.'

She spun the laptop so the screen was facing me and pointed to the bottom corner, underneath the photograph. A thread of comments immediately caught my eye.

Does anyone know whether Charlie Bloom is coming back to take photos for F&L?? Her photos were sweeeeeeeeet.

Dunno but her pix were the best :)

Definitely!! #bringbackcharlie <3 <3

My brow creased as I read the words. I'd assumed the fans had forgotten all about me. Or, at least, about my photography.

'That is so cool,' Melissa said, a smile spreading across her face.

'Yeah,' I replied, still not quite believing it. 'I suppose it is.'

'Look at that hashtag! I told you you're in demand. On both the music scene *and* the dating scene . . .'

'It is not a date!' I blurted out. 'How many times?'

Melissa pulled her laptop out of the way and wiggled round to face me, her lips pressed together, eyebrows raised. She started counting on her fingers.

'Let's go over the evidence, shall we? Number one: you and Olly have history. You come from the same place, you went to the same school, yadda yadda yadda. Two: he bought you your dream camera, out of the blue, and it wasn't even your birthday. Three: he sat next to you on a friggin' beach and played you a song which OH MY GOD IS SO OBVIOUSLY ABOUT YOU and then he said, and I quote, "I really, really like you" . . . and four: back when we thought Gabriel was a bit evil, Olly knocked him out for you, gave up his bed like the gentleman he is and didn't even try and touch your hair while you were sleeping.' She stuck her hands on her hips. 'Ipso facto, this is a date.'

She paused, and pressed a finger to her lips.

'Actually, we can't be sure about the hair touching. But, come on . . . this is Olly Samson.' She grabbed my hand. 'So you can downplay it all you like, Charlotte Katherine Bloom, but I see the truth, and I ain't afraid to say it.'

Melissa was right: I *had* been downplaying it. I had insisted that Olly and I were nothing more than friends, and he was just doing a nice thing for me. But secretly, my skin tingled at the thought of seeing him.

I felt a little rush every time I pictured it. And as for Olly, did he feel the same way? Those things he'd said to me on the beach, back in November . . . were they still true?

I guess I would find out on Friday.

8

I didn't normally get nervous walking down Reading high street, but tonight was a little different.

It was early evening, and Friday festivities were in full swing: revellers were pouring from the train station, girls in tight skirts spilled out of taxis, dance music blasted from crowded bars. Meanwhile, I was off to a secretive not-date with a popstar in an after-hours art gallery. And I wasn't really sure what to expect.

Chain Street was dead when I turned off the high street towards the Slash Gallery. This was hardly surprising, since its handful of shops and boutiques were, by now, closed for the evening. The only person in the narrow street apart from me was a tall, broad man wearing dark clothes and standing in front of the gallery with his hands clasped across his belt. I'd spent enough time around the Fire&Lights security staff to know he was one of them.

I approached him cautiously, and gave a little wave.

'Umm . . . hi?'

He turned his head, ever-so-slightly, towards me. His stony expression didn't change.

'I . . . don't know if you're expecting me?' I added. It wasn't really a question *or* a statement, and he didn't reply. My palms started to itch.

'I'm Ch—'

'Charlie Bloom,' the man interrupted, the hint of a smile breaking on to his face. I tugged at the rim of my hat.

'Uh, yeah. That's right. Charlie.'

He leaned back a little.

'Former schoolmate of Olly's, studying for her GCSEs, backstage photographer to the stars. Fan of Carrie Shakes. Weakness for Dr Pepper.'

The hint of a smile reached his eyes.

'How do you know all that?' I said. The man nodded backwards, into the gallery.

'Olly told me,' he said, with a wink. Then he opened the door. 'On you go, love. He's inside.'

I walked through the doorway and the guard closed it quietly behind me. The gallery was low-lit; dark in the centre but with spotlights dotted around the edges, each one illuminating a large Carrie Shakes original. Olly was standing on the far side of the room with his back to me, hands in his pockets, head cocked, studying one of the photographs. He clearly hadn't heard me come in.

I took a few steps forward, and when I spoke, my voice sounded crisp and clear in the dusky silence.

'Hey.'

Olly turned around. When he saw me, his face opened into a smile.

'Hey, yourself.'

We stood, just looking at each other, for a few moments, and then he took his hands from his pockets and walked towards me.

'Drink?' he said, motioning to a high table a few metres away from us. Two glass bottles of Dr Pepper were standing together on a silver tray, each with a stripy red-and-white straw sticking out of the top. I laughed, and nodded.

'Sure.'

'There's no bar in here,' said Olly, picking up the drinks, 'so I had to improvise.'

He passed one to me, and it felt cool against my fingers. We both took little sips.

'It's good to see you,' he said, looking right at me. I bit the inside of my cheek, trying to keep my smile under control.

'You too.'

He jabbed his straw against the bottom of his bottle.

'Sorry about dropping in unannounced the other day . . .'

'That's cool,' I said, taking another gulp of Dr Pepper. 'I mean, I'd been hoping the secret guest speaker would turn out to be someone a bit more exciting, like the guy last year who repaired machinery at Reading waste disposal, but hey. You can't have everything.'

We shared smiles again, and Olly rubbed the back of his neck.

'I thought it might be fun for us all to visit our old schools, you know? Remind ourselves where we came from.'

'So all four of you did it?' I asked. Olly picked at the label of his bottle.

'Well . . . except Gabe. He said his old school wouldn't want him back.' Olly sucked in a lungful of air, and I glanced at the floor, suddenly aware that I knew so much more about Gabriel's past than Olly did.

'How was the tour?' I asked, deliberately changing the subject. Olly's face lit up.

'It was totally unreal. Japan, Thailand, Brazil, Mexico City . . . I just can't believe I get to see all these places, all these incredible countries, and do what I love at the same time. And the fans are awesome out there. At the concerts, you could barely hear yourself think . . . it was electric.'

Olly glanced around the room at the spot-lit gallery of rockstars. In the silence, I could hear the soft rhythm of his breathing.

Then, once again, his eyes met mine.

'We missed you, though.'

I frowned.

'Shut up, you didn't.'

Olly held my gaze. In the distance, I could hear a

group of friends singing and laughing as they wandered towards the high street.

'Anyway,' said Olly, breaking away and gesturing around the space. 'What d'you say we take a wander round?'

I nodded and, still holding our Dr Peppers, we drifted over to a nearby print of Bruce Springsteen. The classic all-American rockstar, he was normally photographed in heroic poses, guitar raised high or fists pumping the air, but this picture was different. It had been taken at a live show, but he was glancing at the floor, as if deep in thought, a private smile on his face.

'How cool is this shot?' said Olly, entranced. I stood beside him, taking in every detail, my gaze finally settling on the caption card. It read, simply: 'Copenhagen, May 14th'. Strangely, the subject's name wasn't listed.

'I love it,' I replied, studying Bruce's mysterious smile and wondering what it meant. One of Carrie's trademarks was her ability to capture tiny, vanishing moments in the midst of these huge, sweeping occasions, and this shot was a perfect example. There had probably been fifty thousand pairs of eyes on Bruce Springsteen when that picture was taken, but Carrie had made it feel like it was just the two of them in the room.

'Can I ask you something?' I said, still looking at Bruce.

'Of course,' replied Olly.

'How did you know I was into Carrie Shakes?'

Olly wrinkled his nose, as if slightly embarrassed.

'I remembered it from your presentation.'

My eyebrows leapt upwards. The presentation he was talking about – the one the teachers had pretty much twisted my arm to give, in front of the whole school – had been nearly two years ago.

'What . . . really?'

'I know. Crazy, right?' Olly's cheeks went slightly pink. 'It just stuck with me. You said if you could pick any career, you'd want one like Carrie's. And when you said that, I realised . . . a dream isn't just a dream. It's something you can actually make happen, in the real world.' He fiddled with his straw. 'Anyway, then we had that chat in the corridor afterwards, and you suggested I go on *Make Or Break*, and so I did. And then . . . '

I peered at him, sideways.

'What are you trying to say?'

Olly laughed, and shook his head.

'Hey, I'm not trying to say anything,' he said, holding up his hands. 'But it *was* your idea that I audition for the show. And that's how I ended up in Fire&Lights.'

A shocked laugh burst out of me.

'You're not actually suggesting . . . ? Come on.'

Olly stuck out his bottom lip, and shrugged.

'Well, either way,' I said, burying a smile, 'I refuse to take credit for your pop idol status.'

'Whatever you say, Charlie Bloom,' replied Olly, with a grin. 'Whatever you say.'

We moved on to the next piece, a three-part series depicting a band called the Dresden Dolls onstage in Auckland, and then on to an intimate photo of Beyoncé in her dressing room, staring into the mirror while having her hair done. Next, The Cure in Rio, Ed Sheeran strumming his guitar by an open fire, and an old man with wavy grey hair – who Olly told me was Jerry Lee Lewis – sitting at home by his grand piano. Finally, five or six pictures in, we stopped at an image of two very familiar faces.

Olly Samson . . . and Gabriel West.

I gazed, startled, at the tall, imposing, black-and-white photograph. It was one of the most arresting images I'd ever seen.

'I had no idea she'd been working with you,' I said to Olly.

He pushed a hand through his hair. 'We met her at the end of last year, in São Paulo.'

In the picture, Olly and Gabriel were standing opposite each other onstage, microphones down by their sides. They were in an open-air arena, a crescent moon throbbing in the far distance, stage lights burning fiercely all around, and they appeared to be in between lines, as neither was singing or moving. They were simply staring at one another. Staring in a way only two bandmates could: a look that was bristling with emotion, and heat, and bad blood. A dark strand of hair had fallen down over Gabriel's face, and his skin glistened with sweat. Olly's jaw was clenched. Behind them, high above their heads, the image was repeated on the arena's big screen, so it was as if you were seeing two separate pictures at once. In front, the reality, and beyond, the mirror. The version the fans saw.

I realised, with a shudder, that the way they were standing reminded me of the moment they had faced off on the rooftop at the Rochester hotel, the rain pounding their shoulders, sirens wailing below.

'Don't screw me about, Olly. You never wanted me in Fire&Lights. And now you don't want me with Charlie.'

'She deserves better . . . Why can't you just let her go?'

'It's an incredible photo,' I said, mesmerised. I heard Olly swallow.

'It is.' He took in a slow breath. 'Though I find it a bit difficult to look at, to be honest.'

As I studied Olly's face in the picture, it was obvious why. Carrie had really got under their skin. She'd seen who they were. She'd seen every detail of their relationship: the cracks and the camaraderie, the arguments, the late nights, the rivalry. It was all right there, in their eyes. They knew so much about each other, they were tied by the closest of bonds, by months on the road together, but there was something invisible,

79

something unknowable, keeping them apart. It was eerie.

Touching the back of my neck, I realised that every hair on my skin was standing up.

'So . . . you know Carrie, then?' I said, turning to face Olly. His cheeks looked flushed.

'That's how I arranged tonight,' he said, setting his empty bottle down on the floor. 'I remembered you were really into her stuff, and I just figured . . . I don't know, I hadn't seen you in ages, and after months flying around the world I thought it would be nice to do something normal again. If that makes sense.'

I considered pointing out that being invited to a private viewing of a Carrie Shakes exhibition before it had even opened wasn't exactly normal for me, but I knew what he meant.

'Absolutely.'

'After Carrie had taken our pictures in Brazil, I told her our backstage photographer was a big fan, and asked if I could get an advance viewing. And here we are.'

I flicked at the neck of my Dr Pepper bottle.

'I'm not your backstage photographer, though. Not any more, I mean.'

Olly opened his mouth, and almost spoke. Then he stopped himself, and turned back to the picture.

'Anyway, it's kind of an intense photo, but I have to

admit . . . it's one of the best pictures I've seen of the two of us.'

I glanced at the caption. It read: 'The boys, Madison Square Gardens, June 12th.'

'I like how she doesn't write the artists' names next to the photos,' I said. 'It's like she's just showing us pictures of her friends.'

'That's what's so amazing about Carrie,' agreed Olly. 'She isn't interested in celebrity, she's interested in who you are *underneath* the fame. She gets to know you, and it sounds kind of corny, but you're right: she becomes a friend. Then, when she takes your photograph, she's not just recording a moment in time. She's capturing who you are.' His blue eyes settled on mine again. 'You remind me of her, you know.'

I arched an eyebrow.

'Now you're just telling me what I want to hear.'

'It's not just me,' protested Olly. 'Yuki said the same thing, and Aid too. Whatever Carrie has . . . you have it too.'

My breath caught in my throat. I was almost too stunned to speak.

'I told her all about you,' said Olly.

'You . . . what?'

'I told her how you were really into her work, and how great your shots are. She said you should drop her a line sometime.'

I stepped backwards.

'I should . . . wh— . . . Carrie?'

Olly reached into his back pocket.

'Here.' He pulled something out and handed it to me. It was Carrie Shakes's business card. On the back, her personal email address was scrawled in pen, underneath a short message:

Hey, Charlie. Holler any time! Carrie x

I glared at the message in disbelief.

'Oh my god . . . Olly. I can't believe you've done this. Thank you. Thank you so much.'

'It's nothing,' he said, with a half-shrug. 'I mean, nothing you don't deserve.'

I held the card in my hand, still not quite believing it was real. Carrie Shakes, my idol, wanted to hear from *me*.

'So, listen.' Olly shifted his weight from one foot to the other. 'I did sort of have an ulterior motive for inviting you here.'

I looked up from the business card, remembering what Melissa had said when she'd found out about tonight. *This is a date, Charlie.* Was she right? Was this the moment where—

'We want you back,' said Olly, locking his gaze on to mine. My mouth fell open. What did he mean? 'We've talked about it, the whole band, and the work you did with us last year was just so great . . .'

I closed my mouth, rubbing my forehead with my fingertips.

'Olly, the thing is—'

'And the fans want you back as well. They're all talking about you on the fan site, and it's obvious why. You see us differently, Charlie. You've got this . . . unique touch. Like Carrie.' He slid his hands into his back pockets. 'We've got a radio interview at City Sounds next Saturday, and the Pop4Progress concert the week after. Be great to have you along . . . ?'

I sighed, and lowered my empty bottle to the ground.

'I don't know. Things are . . . complicated for me right now.'

Olly's forehead creased.

'Is this about Gabe?'

I drew in a breath. I could understand why Olly would think that, but seeing Gabriel again might actually give me some closure. At least if we were in the same room, he wouldn't be able to avoid me.

'Believe it or not, no . . . it's about my dad.' I fiddled with my sleeves. 'For the first time in years, we're actually friends. We're kind of happy. And with my exams coming up, there's no way he'd let me hang out with a band every weekend. Not after last year, and all the lies.' I tugged at the back of my hat. 'I wish there was some way round it, but right now . . . it's impossible.'

Silence fell. Olly nodded slowly, though he couldn't hide the disappointment in his eyes. Outside on the street, the security guard coughed into the night.

'I'm sorry,' I said, after a while.

'No, come on . . . I get it. In fact, I feel the same way. Family's everything.'

Hearing Olly say those words, I felt my lungs expanding, goosebumps rushing my skin. Because he was right. Family *was* everything.

He slid out his phone and checked the time.

'Hey, have you eaten?'

I shook my head.

'We could order takeaway, if you like?'

'To here?' I said, pointing to the floor. 'Won't we get in trouble?'

Olly scratched his jaw.

'You can eat takeaway in an art gallery, can't you?'

We looked at each other and frowned. Laughter bubbled out of us.

'I guess you can,' I replied, rocking back and forth on my feet. Olly unlocked his phone.

'Now, as luck would have it,' he said, 'I grew up around here.' He began searching his contacts for a phone number. 'And I just happen to know a really, *really* great pizza place . . .'

*

Two hours later, I was sitting on the back seat of a bus, hat pulled over my ears, a smile lingering on my face. It was nearly ten o'clock, and Reading rang with the clatter and chaos of bars, and the distant throbbing of nightclubs.

Melissa and I were texting furiously.

And then we just sat on the floor eating pizza and chatting for ages

My heart, Charlie!!! That is super romantic. I'M MELTING.

I beamed at my phone.

It was pretty magical

Melissa's speech bubble flickered as she typed.

Sooooo. What else . . . ?? #tellmemore

He said the band want me back to take photos

AAAAAAAARRRRRRRGGGGGGGGGHHHHHHHHHHHHH!

A pause.

Wait. U said yes . . . right??

CHARLOTTE

The bus slowed to a stop, doors opening with a mechanical hiss. An old man boarded, then we set off again.

You know I didn't. There's no way I could do this. Too many complications.

This is a disaster!!! From now on u take me on all future dates. Capiche?

I smiled.

Well, since I go on about one a year, that's fine by me

HA HA very much HA. But srsly. I won't let u throw this chance away again. I'll think of something, u mark my words.

I sent Melissa her three favourite emojis – the turtle, the fried egg and the trumpet, in that order – then leaned my head against the window, still smiling, still warm inside from the hot, delicious pizza, the random chats and the laughter.

I wasn't sure when I'd see Olly again, but there was one thing I did know. That had been a really lovely night.

Olly had asked me to text him when I got home, so after saying hi to Dad ('How was the movie, kiddo?' . . . 'Uh, kind of average') and making myself a cup of tea, I padded upstairs to my room, dropped on to the bed and pulled out my phone.

I'm home. Thank you for a super-fun evening :)

It was the best. So good to see you again.

You too

And if you change your mind about the photos . . . just shout ;)

I will. Night xx

Night xx

If I change my mind about the photos. I wanted to say yes, more than anything, but it was too risky. Even if I *could* come up with a believable cover story for Dad, our exams were less than two months away and anything non-school-related was pretty much off-limits. Besides, thanks to Olly,

I had a possible 'in' with Carrie Shakes. A chance to find out what a top photographer thought of my work.

All I needed now was the courage to send the email.

Carrie,

I'm Charlie Bloom, a friend of Olly's from Fire&Lights. I hope you don't mind me emailing you out of the blue, but Olly passed on your business card so I thought I'd say hi.

I really, really love your pictures. I'm still at school but I've started doing music photography in my spare time and you are one of my biggest inspirations. I wondered if you wouldn't mind checking out some of the photos I took for Fire&Lights, and maybe letting me know what you think? Only if you have time. I've posted a link below.

Thanks,

Charlie

Was that any good? I had no idea. Still, I couldn't just sit there all night obsessing over it, so after several deep breaths and few quiet words to myself, I posted the link and hit *Send*.

Almost instantly, my laptop pinged with a new email. A delivery failure, maybe? Had she given me a false address so I wouldn't pester her? People like Carrie probably had to do that sort of thing all the time.

But no. It wasn't from Carrie, or Melissa, or one of the various newsletters I kept meaning to unsubscribe from.

It was from him.

From: Gabriel West
To: Charlie Bloom
[no subject]
Today at 23:17
I know we thought there was no trace of Little Boy Blue online, but we were wrong. I found something. Something you should see.
http://www.real-music-chat.com/music-memories/27778-little-boy-blue.html
G

No greeting. No small talk . . . nothing. By now I had got used to the idea that Gabriel was entirely over me, but did he really have to make it so obvious?

Still, despite the cold tone of the message, my pulse was racing. I needed to see what he had found.

Sucking in a shaky breath, I slid the cursor downwards, and clicked on the link.

9

The page loaded and I was presented with a clunky-looking chat forum, all garish colours and spiky fonts. The posts were out-of-date – getting on for a decade old – and the site looked like it had been inactive for years.

There can only have been a handful of people in the world who would be interested in the post Gabriel had linked to. But I was definitely one of them.

> 20:01, June 10th 2005
david_loves_rock78: Hey guys, how's it going? I just joined this forum & I'm looking for people who remember a band I used to follow in London called Little Boy Blue.

Those three little words seemed to glow on the page: *Little Boy Blue*. Underneath was a string of replies.

> 16:34, Nov 21st 2005
REALmusicfan: Ummm, yeah, think I do. Lead singer's name was Harry something???

> 17:46, Nov 21st 2005

david_loves_rock78: Yeah, that's it!!! Ah, man, such great days going to their gigs.

> 12:08, Nov 28th 2005

sabbathrules: Decent band. Shame it all went so wrong.

> 12:17, Nov 28th 2005

david_loves_rock78: What do you mean. Do u know what happened????

> 09:25, Nov 30th 2005

gemstar001: I loved LBB!!!!!! We followed them everywhere, got this cool pic of me & my mates with the band outside the Troubadour Club.

I was drawn, at first, to the tantalising reply from SabbathRules: 'shame it all went so wrong'. But the user had left no other posts, and the trail seemed to have gone cold. Scrolling down to Gemstar's reply, I noticed that her photograph hadn't loaded, so I clicked on the question mark and watched as a picture matching her description filled the box.

Four men in their mid-twenties were standing on a London street outside a venue called the Troubadour. Two were holding guitars, one had his drumsticks in the air and the fourth was balancing a keyboard on its end. My eyes flitted across the picture, settling on the guitarist on the far right, and the strings around my heart tightened as I recognised his face.

It was like staring at a forgotten ghost of Gabriel.

This was Harry West, band leader and songwriter. The man who had abandoned Gabe at the age of five, sending him to a foster home, before committing suicide some months later. His hair was much lighter than his son's – Gabriel's black, wavy locks almost certainly came from his Brazilian mother, who had died of an overdose earlier in the year – but the way Harry's gaze hit the camera, simultaneously intense and detached, was disturbingly familiar. Almost unsettling. In front of the band, and gathered on both sides, was a group of excited-looking fans, most of them wearing Little Boy Blue T-shirts and grinning at the camera.

But that wasn't all. Because kneeling in front of the keyboard player, her face lit up with the widest, happiest smile, was a woman with big brown eyes, pale skin and messy, milk-chocolate hair spilling out from underneath her blue knitted beanie.

It was Mum.

My stomach seized and I sat back against the pillow, heart hammering in my chest. Across the room, that very same hat was perched on the corner of my chair, a few blue threads hanging loose. Suddenly, it seemed like a relic from the past that had travelled through time and fallen out of the photograph into real life.

I returned my gaze to the picture on the screen, my heart still thudding with nervous excitement. I was so used to seeing the handful of pictures I had of my mother that it was strange and disorienting to see her in a different place, with different people. Here, she looked about twenty-five, so this must have been only a couple of years before the accident. I zoomed in on her face, soaking up every detail – her chestnut-brown eyes, a stray lock of hair curling around her neck – and a slow calm settled over me. She looked happy and carefree, and like she was among friends.

But someone very obvious was missing from the picture.

My father wasn't there.

I pushed the thought to the back of my mind and moved my hands towards the computer keys. I had a lead now . . . Gemstar001. There was a direct message function on the site, and though I knew it was an insanely long shot, I had to give it a go. I had to contact her. It was nearly ten years since whoever Gemstar was had made that post, and the chances of her still being active were slim to none. But if she'd known my mother, even if only in passing, I had to try and talk to her.

Hurriedly, I signed up for an account and wrote her a short message, leaving my email address at the bottom.

After I fired it off, the confirmation screen was taking ages to load, so while I was waiting, I replied to Gabriel.

I made my words as blunt and cold as his original message.

I think that forum is probably dead . . . but I guess it's a lead? I've sent Gemstar001 a message. She might know something. Maybe you could try SabbathRules?
Charlie

The swooshing sound effect of my reply disappearing into the ether was followed by a *ping* from my internet browser. A chirpy auto-response had popped up on the screen.

YOUR MESSAGE HAS BEEN SENT!! LET'S HOPE GEMSTAR001 GETS BACK TO YOU SOON!! ☺ ☺ ☺ ☺ ☺ ☺ ☺ ☺ ☺

I closed my eyes, and let out a deep sigh. Something told me I could be waiting a very long time indeed.

As I peered through the lens of my camera, my ears were ringing with the clash of guitars. I could feel the urgent thump of the bass drum in the soles of my feet, and the heat from the crowd on my skin. Coloured lights bathed the boys' faces in atmospheric blues and angry reds.

Adjusting the focus, I zoomed in on Jody's head and shoulders. His hair was plastered to his forehead with sweat, the collar of his T-shirt tangled beneath the weight of his guitar. For a brief moment, he looked down at the floor, and smiled to himself. *Snap*.

It was good to be at a gig again.

'So how's everyone doing?' called Jody, from the stage, his arm extended towards the crowd. Everyone whooped and yelled, and the drummer – who went by the nickname Thumper – unleashed a volley of smashes and crashes from the kit. 'We've got a pretty awesome announcement to make tonight,' continued Jody, 'and it's coming up just as soon as we finish our next song. So stick around! This one's called "Robot Romance" . . .'

I lowered my camera and surveyed the room. It wasn't a bad turnout – well over a hundred people – and Diamond Storm were clearly enjoying themselves. They'd really improved since last summer too. They were starting to sound like a proper band.

As the boys thundered into their next song, I crept along the front of the stage, taking close-up snaps of the floor: feet pressing guitar pedals, leads coiling over one another. A chilled bottle of water, condensation clinging to the plastic. Then I caught the guitarist as he swept into an over-the-top, but admittedly quite impressive, guitar solo. I followed his fingers up and down the neck of the instrument, capturing the veins tensing in his arms and the taut white peaks of his knuckles.

The song clattered to an end, and Jody wiped his face with a grubby-looking towel.

'Cheers, guys, thanks!' he said, chucking the towel behind an amp, and I suddenly became aware of a group of girls edging towards the stage, a few metres away from me. They were immaculately made up, flashing shoulders and cleavages, and several of them even had the band logo – a diamond over a lightning bolt – scrawled on their arms in black marker. They hollered and whistled at Jody, who gave them a slightly embarrassed wave.

'So here's the thing,' he said, fiddling with the tuning pegs on his guitar. 'We've been talking to some venues around Reading and London, and we've booked our first-ever tour . . .' The girls in the front row screamed. 'Ha, thanks! We're seriously pumped for this, and we really hope you guys can come down and see us. We'll stick the dates on Facebook, so check 'em out if you can . . .'

There was a pause while Jody finished tuning his instrument. The bass player hit a couple of random notes, and Thumper spun a drumstick in one hand, tugging at his sweat-drenched vest with the other. I took the opportunity to buff my camera lens, while close by, the Jody Baxter Fan Club argued over his best features.

'I don't normally fancy him, but . . . *seriously*.'

'I think it's the guitar.'

'Look at his arms.'

'*So* hot.'

'His hair is, like, pure sex right now.'

Snap. Without thinking about it, I took a picture of them, their open faces craned up at the stage like wide-eyed worshippers in church. The girl nearest to me turned at the sound of the shutter, and her eyes flashed at me in the dark. Just as I was about to slink away, she signalled to her friends, and they all turned around in unison, posing for the camera. Pouting lips, big eyes.

I took a second photograph, and made a mental note to delete it later.

'Thanks, Charlie,' they chorused. Then the first girl added: 'Say hi to Gabriel from us!'

'Yeah, like he still hangs out with *her* . . .'

The band started up again, and the girls forgot about me almost instantly. The mention of Gabriel had stirred a forgotten sickness in the pit of my stomach, but I figured I should be grateful. If this was all I had to deal with at school these days, things had definitely improved.

'Charlie, Charlie. Charlie.'

I spun round. Melissa was standing behind me, holding a fizzy drink and jiggling up and down. She started yelling at me over the noise, but I couldn't make out a word.

'WHAT?' I yelled back.

'HUH?'

'WHAT ARE YOU SAYING?'

'I CAN'T HEAR YOU,' bellowed Melissa.

'WHAT?'

'WE'RE GOING OUTSIDE.'

I was in the middle of shouting back, 'BUT I HAVE WORK TO DO' when Melissa seized my hand and led me across the hall towards one of the side doors. Soon, we were standing in the starkly lit, eerily empty school hallway, the sound of the band a muffled thump through the walls of the building.

'What's going on?' I said, lifting my camera off my neck. 'I am sort of supposed to be taking photographs in there.'

'Like I was saying, I have had the BEST idea.'

I began scrolling through the exposure settings on my camera. Without looking up, I said: 'It's not that thing about replacing teachers with robots again, is it?'

'No, no. Although that would totally work.' She waved a hand in front of her face. 'But no, it's about *you*. And it's a good one.'

'Okaaay . . .' I said doubtfully. Melissa took a sip from her drink.

'I've been thinking,' she said.

'Always dangerous.'

'About you, and your family, and this crazy connection to Gabriel. You see, when you break it down, it *must* have something to do with Fire&Lights.'

I squinted at her.

'In what way?

'Think about it. Yes, it's a weird coincidence that you and Gabriel knew each other when you were kids, but it's not the *only* coincidence. You also happened to grow up round the corner from his future bandmate.'

'And your point is . . . ?'

'Whatever's connecting you and Gabe must involve Olly in some way. Or, at least, it must involve Fire&Lights. Otherwise it's the world's most ridiculous coincidence. And since I'm a mathematician *and* a rationalist, I don't believe in coincidences.'

Melissa stuck her hands on her hips and waited for me to reply. Over her shoulder, through the swing-door windows, I could just about make out Diamond Storm's lead guitarist playing his instrument behind his head.

'Well . . . I guess you're right. But why are you telling me this now?'

She sighed dramatically.

'Even if you're not prepared to admit that Olly is crushing on you something *hectic*—'

'Come o—'

'Still talking!' she said, holding up a single finger. 'Even if you're not prepared to admit that, you shouldn't be passing up his invitation to spend time with the band again. I mean, obviously it would be the funnest thing ever – EVER – but it's also the only way you're ever going to figure out what happened with your mum. Well, aside from asking your dad and coming clean about everything and then being grounded until, I don't know, the year 2078, by which point you'll be' – she went quiet, but for only a split-second – 'eighty-one years old, which is older than my grandma, and boy is she *old*. Like, her toilet seat has a furry cover.' She blinked at me. 'A FURRY COVER.'

I waited for a few seconds, but she seemed to have finished.

'That was a lot of talking, Mel. Even for you.'

She beamed at me.

'And . . . I guess . . . everything you've said is true,' I continued gingerly, 'but we've been over this. It's too risky. Dad'll suspect something, and I've got tons of revision to do, and—'

'Wait!' interrupted Melissa, raising her palm up in front of me, like a police officer. 'There's more.' She cleared her throat grandly. 'Did you, or did you not, screw up your photography mock because you spent most of last term taking pictures you couldn't submit?'

I let out a hollow laugh.

'Way to make me feel better, Mel, but . . . yep.'

'And wouldn't a final project made up of amazing photographs of Fire&Lights be, like, the ULTIMATE way to nail that A* you so obviously deserve?'

'Well, yes, but—'

'*So* . . . you simply tell your dad that, to bump up your photography grade, you're going to follow this band from school, Diamond Storm, on their upcoming tour, and take their pictures. Sure, that means you might be away some evenings, but *it's all in the name of schoolwork.* You see?' Melissa was frantically nodding at her own genius. 'The minute your dad hears that, he'll be all: "Hell, yeah, sister, I am *so* down with this."'

'Wow. It's like actually having my dad in the room.'

'Shut up,' said Melissa, with a smile. 'But here's the thing. When you say you're at Diamond Storm gigs, you'll *really* be at Fire&Lights gigs . . . and good old Pop-Pops will never know the difference.'

I considered this for a moment, gazing into space. At the far end of the corridor, two girls were stumbling towards the main doors, laughing, their arms draped around each other.

'Still sounds risky to me.'

'Hey. Charlie. HEY.' Melissa clicked her fingers at me. 'What do we always say? Huh? Risk it for a bourbon biscuit.'

'I don't think we do say that.'

Melissa drained her drink, and wiped her mouth with her hand.

'Look,' I said. 'Even if I agreed that this was a good idea . . .'

'Which it is.'

'Even if I agreed with that, how exactly will this *actually* help my photography grade?'

'Oh, Charlotte. How greatly you underestimate me.'

She crushed the empty can between her fingers. 'I've thought of that too. Your final batch of coursework won't be shown in any exhibitions, right?'

'Uh-huh.'

'So your dad will never see it.'

'Riiight . . .'

'*So* . . . you could submit your Fire&Lights photos for your final grade, and no one would be any the wiser.'

My face fell into a frown.

'Apart from my teacher, that is.'

'Mrs Robertson is fifty million years old! She wouldn't know Gabriel West if he came up and kissed her in the darkroom.' Her eyes glazed over. 'I would so kiss Gabriel West in a dark room.'

I raised both my eyebrows.

'Sorry,' said Melissa, with a hiccup. She tossed her can into a nearby bin. 'I know he's, like, your ex- . . . whatever. But still. Hubba hubba.'

Back in the hall, Diamond Storm piled into a cover of a Bruno Mars track, and I found myself staring at the school noticeboard on the opposite wall, turning the idea over in my head. To her credit, Melissa had thought of pretty much everything.

'Whaddya reckon, CB?' she said, with a tilt of her head.

I chewed on my lip, and stared back at her. I wasn't exactly ready to admit it, but there was a chance her plan might actually work.

10

'Hi there!' said the woman at the door. 'Welcome to the Slash Gallery. Have you been to a Carrie Shakes exhibition before?'

I shoved my hands deep into my jean pockets, and looked at the floor. Dad started undoing the buttons of his coat.

'No, we haven't!' he said cheerfully. 'Charlie's a big fan, though, aren't you?'

I nodded, feeling the colour rush to my cheeks.

'Well, you're in for a treat,' replied the woman. 'No one does rock photography like Carrie. Enjoy!'

Dad and I wandered into the familiar, low-lit space, the heels of Dad's work shoes clipping on the wooden floor. A few other people were scattered around the gallery, talking in low voices and nodding to each other. Dad leaned sideways, towards me.

'I'm glad we're getting the chance to do this together. I know how excited you were to see it.'

'Me too.'

I gnawed on a fingernail. I'd been in this precise room,

exactly a week earlier, hanging out with a popstar, when Dad thought I was at the movies. I was basically returning to the scene of the crime.

'Thanks for leaving work early for me,' I said, and I meant it. He hardly ever did that.

He ran both hands through his tousled hair.

'Believe me, it was a pleasure . . .' He glanced around the room. 'Anyway, what do we do here? I've never been to a photography exhibition.'

I laughed.

'You don't really *do* anything, Dad. You just look at the photos.'

He scratched his neck.

'Well, I know that. It's just . . . oh, I don't know. It's your thing. Why don't you lead the way?'

This will be fine, I told myself, as I led my father towards the picture of Bruce Springsteen onstage in Copenhagen. The picture that I had already examined in intimate detail. *Just act normal. You've never seen this before. This is totally new to you.*

'Ah, The Boss,' said Dad, pointing at Bruce's face. 'Born in the USA.'

I smiled to myself. It was actually kind of sweet, how hard he was trying.

'Got it in one,' I said. 'But do you see the way she's captured him?'

Dad's brow crumpled.

'What do you mean?'

I gestured at the photograph.

'Springsteen is the quintessential American rockstar, right? So most photographers would pick a shot of him with both hands in the air, or jumping from the drum riser . . . but Carrie doesn't do that. She knows it's been done before, all that clichéd rock stuff, so she tries to get *underneath* it. She tries to bring out things the fans don't normally see.' I pointed to Bruce's curious smile. 'Like here, the expression on his face. It's this fleeting thing, this private moment, and in real life it probably lasted less than a second . . . but Carrie managed to capture it. And that's what I want to do with my pictures.'

We went quiet for a while, standing side by side, peering into the photograph. After nearly a minute, Dad jingled the change in his pockets, and cleared his throat.

'You're so smart, Charlie,' he said, turning his head towards mine. I looked back at him, and he swallowed hard. 'Just like she was.'

We held eye contact for a moment, and a warm feeling fluttered inside me, like a tiny flock of birds. Little by little, Mum was creeping back into our lives. Since we had started making an effort to spend time together, it had become natural for Dad to mention her, now and again, without it seeming forced or awkward. We were beginning to feel like a small, broken, almost real family.

105

And maybe, sometime in the future, just like Rosie said, Dad would be ready to talk. To tell me everything about her.

But until then, I would have to take matters into my own hands.

'Dad, can I ask you something?'

He scratched his jaw pensively.

'Sure.'

'It's about my photography grade.'

'Oh, yes.' He made a clicking sound in his throat. 'That needs fixing, eh?'

'Uh-huh.' We meandered onwards, heading for the second photo in the series. I concentrated on my hands.

'So I've had this idea,' I said. 'I just . . . I need to make sure you're OK with it.'

Dad stuck out his bottom lip, intrigued. We stopped as we arrived at the triptych of the Dresden Dolls.

'Ooh, crikey,' said Dad, gawping at the pictures with raised eyebrows. 'Who are these two? They look a bit scary.'

I pointed to the banner at the back of the stage.

'They're called the Dresden Dolls.'

'What happened to the rest of her clothes?'

'Um, Dad? My idea?'

'Sorry, yes. Go on.'

I adjusted my hat, and took a deep breath.

'It involves . . . I mean, there's this band.'

My father straightened up. I thought I saw his face tighten, but it was probably my imagination.

'The band I told you about, last year? Diamond Storm.'

'OK . . .'

'They're at Caversham High, in the sixth form. I started taking shots for them last summer.'

Dad nodded to himself, very slowly.

'And then . . . well, then I went away to Devon without telling you, which was really bad, but it won't happen again.'

Dad's eyes darkened as he recalled the moment. *A band? What band?* he had said, his voice curdling with anger. *They asked me to go on tour with them and take photos*, I had replied, carefully spinning a truth from my web of lies. *It's no big deal . . .*

'They've just booked a tour around Reading and London,' I continued, 'and they need a photographer. They've asked me.'

Dad stepped away from the photograph and sucked in a long, drawn-out breath. I tucked a stray lock of hair inside my hat.

'I'm good at this, Dad. I just need the chance to prove it.'

He glanced at his feet, then back up again.

'You're right, Charlie. Of course you are. You *are* good at this. And who knows' – he waved a hand across the room – 'maybe one day it'll be your pictures in this gallery.' His shoulders relaxed. 'Plus, I'll admit, this does seem like a good way to sort out that grade. I do have one condition, though.'

I moved us on again, towards Beyoncé.

'Oh?'

'I'd like to see you in action.'

We slowed for the photo, and my toes curled in panic.

'What?'

'I'd like to come to a gig. Not all of them, obviously, just one or two.' He gave me a goofy smile. 'I won't embarrass you. I'll stand at the back, pretend I'm the drummer's dad, or something.'

I frantically sifted through the idea in my head, straining to keep my face blank. What could I say? If I turned him down, he would know something was awry. And as things stood, I had about three seconds before he started to wonder what—

'Charlie?'

Dad was waiting for my response. I blinked at him.

'What do you think?' he said. 'I promise I won't try and dance, or anything awful like that.'

He laughed at himself, and a realisation came over me. Diamond Storm were playing the Black Hat in Reading in two weeks' time. What if I actually *did* take Dad along? All he needed to see was evidence of me working with them, and I'd be in the clear. I could keep a low profile, take a few snaps, maybe even bring Melissa along for solidarity.

My alibi would be set in stone.

'Um ... yep, yeah. Sure,' I said, concentrating on Beyoncé's face. Her flawless skin, keen eyes. 'You should come to a show.'

'When are you planning to see them next?'

'Tomorrow,' I replied, without thinking. Then I quickly covered my tracks. 'It's not a gig, though, it's a radio session. But they're headlining the Black Hat on the second, if you fancy it?'

'Whatever you like,' said Dad. 'You're in charge. You just tell me where to go, and when, and I'll be there.'

We continued plotting a course around the gallery, wandering idly past The Cure, onstage in Brazil, Ed Sheeran by his log fire, and Jerry Lee Lewis. A surge of nerves coursed through me as I realised I'd actually done it. I was going to see Fire&Lights again. When I got home, I'd message Olly and tell him I'd changed my mind, and within twenty-four hours, I'd be hanging out with the boys. I'd get to see inside a proper radio station, watch a live session and document it all in pictures along the way. With all the stress and deception, I'd almost forgotten how exciting the whole thing was.

'I might be a little out of place around all the young people,' Dad said, as we stopped again. 'But I do think it'll be good for me to see Diamond Storm in action.' He lowered his voice. 'You see, boys in bands ... they can be ...'

Dad trailed off. I was waiting for him to finish his sentence, but he was utterly transfixed by the photograph we'd just arrived at. I turned to see which one it was, and my spine turned to ice. It was Fire&Lights.

And Dad was staring directly at Gabriel.

'How . . . strange . . .'

Hectic thoughts began to pile up inside my brain, throbbing against my skull. Harry West, in that photograph outside the Troubadour . . . he had looked so much like Gabriel. And whatever it was that happened with Mum and Little Boy Blue back in the nineties, Dad must have known Harry by sight. So how could I have let this happen? I *knew* there was a photo of Gabriel in the exhibition, but I'd been so caught up in everything else that it hadn't even occurred to me to avoid it. If Dad made the connection with Fire&Lights, and started looking into it, pretty soon he'd figure out—

'Who is this band?'

My heart was slamming against my ribcage, and I could feel beads of sweat building at my hairline. I pulled my hat off, panicking. Dad was reading the caption, searching for clues, but as he leaned closer, I remembered that it was one of Carrie's trademarks not to include artists' names beside her photos. That simple fact was about to save my skin.

'I dunno,' I said vacantly. My blood was singing with fear.

'Really? I thought you knew everyone.'

I studied the photograph nonchalantly.

'They look like a boy band, Dad. You know I'm into indie, right?'

Dad lingered on Gabriel's face, his fingers twitching in his pocket. It was taking everything I had not to yank him away and drag him out of the gallery all together.

'It's just, it's somehow . . . there's something . . . familiar . . .'

Dad's eyes went a little foggy, and I breathed a secret sigh of relief. He hadn't made the Harry West connection. But if we hung around too long, there was every chance that he might.

I had to get him away from that picture.

'Come on, Dad, let's push on. There's a band over here I really want to see . . .'

As I dragged Dad in the direction of a random photograph on the other side of the gallery, the cogs in my brain were spinning ten-to-the-dozen. *Dad had recognised Gabriel*. And if he'd had longer to look at the picture, maybe he would have worked out why. He'd have joined the dots, realising it was Harry West he'd been reminded of, recalling that Harry had a son who by now would be in his late teens, with music in his blood. And from there, all it would take would be for him to search 'Gabriel West' on the web and he'd be led straight to Fire&Lights, from Fire&Lights to Olly Samson, from

Olly Samson to Caversham High, and from Caversham High to me. And then the whole house of cards would come tumbling down around me.

'Kiddo?'

I was wrenched from my hurricane of thoughts by Dad touching my arm.

'You OK? You were miles away.'

I stared back at him, clutching my hat.

'Yep, fine,' I said flatly. 'Just thinking about photography . . .' I was playing a dangerous game here, but there was no way around it. While I didn't like deceiving Dad, as long as he was intent on keeping things from me, I didn't have much choice. And as we drifted towards another of Carrie's pictures, I thought how strange it was that he had no idea how close I was to the truth about Mum. And that, come to think of it, neither did I.

For now, this was how it was going to be.

My father would keep his secrets, and I would carry on keeping mine.

)

It was early Saturday afternoon in West London, and I was standing on the front steps of one of the biggest record labels in the country. Busy-looking people streamed in and out of the revolving doors, brandishing coffees and talking into mobile phones, barely noticing me as they passed. Glancing upwards, I shielded my eyes against the brassy March sunshine as it glinted off the imposing entrance sign.

WELCOME TO KINGDOM RECORDS.

These were the London headquarters of Barry King, music industry giant, foul-tempered TV personality and the man behind the Saturday night talent show, *Make Or Break*. Barry's acts dominated the charts on a weekly basis, but his most successful creation by far was the world-conquering boy-band sensation, Fire&Lights.

I was about ten minutes away from seeing the band again, and it was making my fingers tingle.

'Oh my god . . . it's *actually* Charlie Bloom.'

A hand touched my shoulder and I spun on my heel to find two teenagers, a boy and a girl, standing on the steps behind me, beaming. They looked strangely familiar.

'Oh . . . h-hello,' I said, adjusting my hat. 'Do I . . . have we met?'

'No, sorry,' said the boy, with a flustered laugh. 'I'm getting totally ahead of myself. I'm Campbell.'

He extended a hand, eyes gleaming. I shook it, taking in his very neatly combed, Lego-man hair – and suddenly remembered where I'd seen them before. They'd been at the school with Olly, that day last month when he'd played in assembly. Olly had high-fived them after his performance, and it had made me wonder who they were.

The girl stepped forward.

'Duffy,' she said brightly, shaking my hand. She was small and incredibly pretty, with a dramatic sweep of pillar-box red hair that cascaded across her head in a striking wave. The opposite side of her head was shaved, and she had these dark, bewitching eyes that were hard to turn away from. They looked like they'd been designed by Walt Disney.

'Nice to meet you,' I said, gripping the strap of my camera bag.

'Excuse me.'

A woman in a sharp suit passed between us, forcing us all to step out of the way. When she'd gone, Campbell leaned towards me.

'It's so exciting to finally talk to you.'

I felt my eyebrows sliding together.

'Really?' I said, with a laugh. 'How do you even know who I am?'

'You're Charlie Bloom,' he replied, cocking his head, as if I'd asked a crazy question. 'If you *really* know Fire&Lights, then you know Charlie Bloom.'

I turned to Duffy, and she nodded in agreement. I scratched my head through my hat.

'So you guys are . . . fans, then?'

'*Super*-fans,' corrected Campbell, with a dimpled smile. Duffy showed me a small metallic badge that was pinned to her T-shirt.

'We run the new VIP fan club: the FireLighters.'

'We organise secret competitions, meet-and-greets, that sort of thing,' explained Campbell. 'Which means we get to hang out with the band *loads*. Plus it counts towards our media studies, so *ker-ching* . . . tons of time off college.'

I let out a sigh of understanding.

'So *that's* why you were at my school, with Olly?'

Duffy clicked her fingers, and pointed at me.

'Exactly.'

'Sorry we couldn't say hi on the day,' said Campbell. 'There just wasn't time. Your school was nice, though!'

'Yeah,' I said doubtfully, thinking about the decomposing fox behind the canteen bins. 'It's a regular . . . Hogwarts round there.'

115

Campbell chuckled infectiously, and I started to laugh too.

'Come on,' said Duffy, jerking her head in the direction of the main doors. 'We'll help you sign in. We've been here before, so we know the ropes.'

'And *then*,' said Campbell, as we ascended the steps together, 'we get to see something *really* exciting. Did management tell you?'

We stepped inside the revolving doors, and through the tinted glass I could see a big plasma screen fixed to the far wall, playing a Fire&Lights music video.

'Tell me what?' I asked. Campbell clenched his fists in excitement.

'Just you wait. This. Is. Going to be. *Awesome.*'

The Kingdom Records lift glided upwards through the building, smooth and silent, its glass back wall offering an impressive aerial view of the open-plan offices. Young assistants scurried back and forth between meetings, executives reclined on leather chairs in long boardrooms, steam rose from endless coffee cups.

On one side of me stood Campbell, bouncing slightly on his toes, and on the other, Duffy, running a hand over her glowing sweep of red hair. I tugged my camera case up my shoulder.

'So where are we actually going?'

The two of them exchanged looks, their eyes alight.

'Have you ever been in a recording studio before?' asked Campbell.

'Nope.' He looked slightly surprised. 'Barry King doesn't seem to think I have chart potential,' I added. He grinned at me.

'Ah, this is so exciting! So basically, the boys are upstairs, finishing off a recording session. And if we're not too late' – he checked the time on his phone – 'no, we should be fine. We'll get to watch them laying down vocals on one of the new tracks.'

New tracks? Olly hadn't mentioned anything about that at the gallery.

'The band have new material?' I asked, wondering why Olly had chosen to play 'She Is The Fire' during the school visit, rather than one of the band's new songs.

'They're releasing an EP in May.' Duffy leaned back against the wall. 'They've been working on it during the tour. We've heard some early versions, and they sound epic.' She glanced over my shoulder. 'Gabriel's lyrics are just . . . *the best*.'

I turned round, following Duffy's gaze, to find a framed photograph of Gabriel fixed to the wall behind me. It was a recent GQ magazine cover shoot, and Gabriel was dressed in a sharp, designer tuxedo, the collar of his shirt open, black strands of hair cascading down over his eyes. The headline read: 'Gabriel West: there's more to this teen idol than meets the eye . . .'

117

I wasn't sure if it was the weightlessness of the lift, or my nerves unravelling, but as we slowed to a halt I began to feel a little queasy.

'This is it, fifth floor,' said Duffy, leading the way into the corridor. Plush, thick carpet stretched out in front of us, and the walls were decorated with signed posters, framed press clippings and expensive-looking modern art. At the far end of the corridor, gleaming brass letters on a large blue door read 'Studio Six'.

As we drew closer to the studio, the reality of the situation sank into my bones. What would I actually *say* to Gabriel when I saw him? The only thing we'd talked about in months was Little Boy Blue, and even that was in short, broken messages, often going weeks without a reply.

When we reached the studio door, Duffy pressed her ear against it, then knocked three times. While we waited, I rehearsed some opening lines in my head.

Hey, you.

What's new?

Fun tour?

No, no and no.

'Oh, hey, guys!'

Standing in the open doorway was Tara, a tall, middle-eastern-looking twenty-something with corkscrew curls, who I remembered as one of the band's personal assistants. She had a headset on, as she almost always did, and was eating a sandwich.

'Did we make it in time?' asked Campbell, as Tara ushered us in.

'Just about,' she said, closing the door behind us. 'Gabe's still got one or two takes to lay down, so you *should* get to see some action. I'll be back with you in two secs . . .'

Tara slipped away into a corner, talking into her headset in a low voice, while the three of us glanced around the room. The recording studio was a wide, dusky, peaceful space, softly-lit and luxurious. Everything was velvety blues and deep purples, so it felt a bit like being underwater in some mysterious, secret cavern. There were comfy sofas for lounging on, guitars and keyboards in every corner, and stretching the entire length of one wall was a huge, sloping mixing desk, its citadel of knobs and faders winking green in the darkness.

A woman with short, spiky blond hair sat at the desk, her back to us, adjusting some settings. Above her head was a large glass panel acting as a window into a second, adjacent room, complete with polished wooden floors and a grand piano. There were booths for singing in, towering guitar amps and a small metal fridge stacked with mineral water. On top of it, purple blobs swam lazily inside a lava lamp.

This was clearly the live room, where the musicians recorded their tracks. Which meant that, in all probability, somewhere inside it was a musician.

And that's when I saw him. Gabriel. He'd been concealed by one of the vocal booths, but had slipped out to adjust his headphones and was passing a hand through his tousled hair, singing to himself. He hadn't noticed us arrive, which suggested that, like us, he couldn't hear anything through the glass panel. Finally happy, he slipped the headphones back on and slowly raised his head. I felt my throat tighten.

Any second now, our eyes would meet.

'Charlie B!!!'

Gasping, I swivelled round to find Yuki Harrison moving towards me at pace.

'Yu—!'

Before I could finish his name, Yuki had picked me up clean off the ground. He hugged me hard, squeezing me until I burst out laughing.

'Where have you *been* all my life, homie?!' he said, dropping me again, his voice giddy with excitement. His chaotic hair, spiky at the back and messy at the front, was even crazier than I remembered, and he was wearing ripped jeans, a faded leather jacket with the collar popped and custom-made, hi-top sneakers. He looked every inch the rockstar.

'I've been at school, like a normal human being,' I said, adjusting my hat. I gave him a playful push. 'You're the one performing to sell-out crowds in Bangkok.'

'They *make* me do that, man!' said Yuki, clamping his

hands on top of his head. He reeled for a moment, like he was about to fall over, then leaned towards me and spoke in an exaggerated whisper. 'Seriously, dude, they lock me in the luggage rack on the tour bus and only bring me out for gigs and interviews, and they beat me in my sleep and feed me baked beans from a shoe.'

'You, surviving on baked beans?' scoffed Olly, appearing behind his bandmate. He laid a hand on Yuki's shoulder, and turned to the rest of us. 'I have seen this man eat seven McDonald's cheeseburgers in less than ten minutes.'

Yuki's gaze bounced around the assembled group.

'What?' he said, incredulous. 'What? They're *really* small . . .'

'How are you guys doing?' said Olly, turning to Campbell and Duffy. Campbell immediately blushed, and Duffy, almost subconsciously, flicked her hair from her eyes.

'We're cool,' she said nonchalantly.

'*So* exciting to be in the studio,' added Campbell. 'Do you think we'll get to hear Gabriel sing?'

Olly's smile faltered, for a split-second.

'Maybe,' he said, running a hand around the back of his neck.

'Hi, Charlie.'

This new voice was Irish, softly-spoken, and belonged, of course, to Aiden Roberts. He had stepped quietly into the group, sipping from a bottle of water, a row of coloured wristbands striping his arm. There was something different about him, which at first I couldn't put my finger on, but then it came to me: his hair, previously a shaggy blond mop that fell in front of his eyes, had been lifted up, quiffed, making him look taller and several years older. He looked less like a little boy, now, and more like the heart-throb the world had always wanted him to be.

'Hi, Aid,' I said, feeling my chest swell. It was so good to see them all again.

'We missed you,' said Aiden, his eyes wide. 'Loads.'

'You soppy idiot,' said Yuki, dangling his arm around Aiden's neck. Then he cupped one hand next to his mouth, and whispered at me: 'I MISSED YOU MORE.'

'OK, folks. Everyone good?' Tara had returned, clipping the plastic lid on to a fresh, steaming coffee. She glanced at me, and blew a stray curl out of her face. 'They're not bugging you, are they, Charlie?'

'Nah,' I said breezily. She gave me a wink.

'Good to have you back.'

I smiled at her, surprised. In a way, I was shocked that she even remembered me. When we'd first met, back in November, Tara had assumed, perhaps understandably, that I was some kind of hanger-on. A hapless groupie.

This time around, maybe things would be different.

'Anyone need anything before we head off?' she added, lifting her drink as a prompt. 'Tea, coffee, water?'

122

'Ooh, ooh . . . Tara.' Yuki tapped a finger against his lips. 'Do you have any cheeseburgers?'

'Cheeseburgers?' She screwed her face up. 'You ate lunch fifteen minutes ago.'

Yuki shrugged.

'I know, but Olly said "cheeseburger", and now I want a cheeseburger.'

'You are such a child,' said Tara, shaking her head, a smile teasing the corners of her mouth. 'So, we need to leave for City Sounds in about, uh' – she checked her watch – 'fifteen minutes, so don't wander too far. Oh, and the FireLighters have some merch for you to sign before we head off, don't you, guys?'

Campbell and Duffy nodded in unison.

'Grand.' Tara clicked her fingers at Yuki and Aiden. 'Yuki, Aid, let's do that now. We'll set up in the corner.'

Tara led the way, with Aiden and the FireLighters in tow. Yuki wagged a finger at me as he followed them.

'Charlie, you see anyone with, like, a bacon burger, or one of those, y'know, chicken towers, with the bread, and the . . . all the *chicken*, you call me immediately, OK?' he said, making a phone gesture with his hand, while Aiden dragged him off by the sleeve. I smiled from ear to ear.

'You bet,' I said, watching him swagger off.

'So . . . what's new with you?'

Olly was standing beside me, hands in his pockets. I shrugged.

'Oh, you know, just hanging out in the studio with my popstar buddies. Gonna "lay down some tracks".' I buffed my fingernails against my top. 'It's no biggie.'

Olly's face softened into that world-famous smile.

'Tara's right, you know,' he said.

'What?'

'It's good having you back.'

I returned his gaze.

'It's good to be back.'

We held eye contact for a moment, and I felt a sudden pang for our evening in the art gallery. It had been such an amazing night, such a strange and lovely time, wandering around in that spot-lit room, talking about photography and music, and then nothing much at all. It felt timeless and surreal, almost like it hadn't happened.

Awkwardly, I broke away, remembering that Gabriel was standing in the next room. Olly stepped backwards and stared at his feet.

'So this place is pretty impressive,' I said, attempting small talk.

'Not bad, eh?'

Over Olly's shoulder, I could see a shiny silver disc hanging on the wall, framed in gold. The inscription underneath read:

Fire&Lights
'SONGS ABOUT A GIRL'
Kingdom Records
1million+ copies sold

'A million . . .' I said, struggling to get my head around the number. 'That's insane.'

Olly followed my eyeline.

'Yeah, I guess it is.'

'Did you record the album in here?'

'Yep. This is where they do all the Kingdom albums.'

'Oh.' I thought about the number six I'd seen on the studio door. 'What do they use the other five studios for, then?'

Olly's eyes narrowed.

'What other five studios?'

'This is the only one?' He nodded. 'Why number six, then?'

'Barry's lucky number. He's the youngest of six brothers. It's a superstition thing.'

I laughed and frowned at the same time.

'Barry King is superstitious?'

'Surprised me too,' said Olly. 'But that's just the way he is. Like, apparently he opened his first office on the Old Brompton Road, even though there are no other labels there, because he has some sentimental attachment to that part of town. Weird.'

Coincidentally, at that precise moment, a door at the back of the live room opened and Barry King stepped through. He was talking on the phone, and looked slightly red-faced. I was suddenly reminded that I had a job to do.

'I should really take some pictures,' I said, unzipping my case and lifting out the camera. Olly watched me switch it on.

'The fans'll be pleased,' he said, as I began scrolling through settings. 'They're still talking about you online, you know.'

'Pressure,' I said, with a nervous smile. 'I hope I haven't lost my touch.'

Slipping the camera strap around my neck, I decided to begin with a few shots of Yuki and Aiden on the far side of the studio, autographing T-shirts and albums. Yuki was singing as he worked, in a quivering, falsetto voice, and making the FireLighters laugh. Aiden signed every item at a slow, methodical pace, thinking carefully each time about what he was going to write. I managed to capture a nice shot of him sitting there, pen in mouth, his green eyes bright with contemplation.

Then, as I was zooming in on Aiden's hand, pen poised between his fingers, a familiar sound snatched my attention. It was Gabriel's voice, coming through the intercom system.

'Can I have more track, Suze?' A pause. 'Thanks.'

I swung back towards the mixing desk, where the producer was adjusting dials and pulling faders.

'Actually . . . drop the kit, just a bit,' continued Gabriel. 'Perfect.'

I raised the camera and trained the viewfinder directly on him, watching as he took a swig of water and moved closer to the microphone. *Snap.* He cleared his throat, gave Suze a thumbs-up and she began to play the track. *Snap.* At the back of the live room, leaning against the wall, Barry watched on proudly, toying with a gold ring on his little finger.

Snap.

As Gabriel leaned into the mic, he closed his eyes and lightly touched his fingers to his left headphone. I fired off a long round of shots, trying to ignore the uneasy, guilty feeling in my gut. We still hadn't spoken, or even looked at each other since I'd arrived, and something about that fact was making me feel like one of the paparazzi. Like I was taking his picture against his will.

Finally, with the track building to a crescendo underneath him, Gabriel began to sing.

Hearing his voice in real life, up close, never lost its power. He wasn't singing lyrics, just a long, soaring note, but it didn't matter. It gripped you. It sank into your skin like pounding rain, swam around your bones like a fever. Lifting my finger off the shutter release, I lowered my camera, the breath stalling in my chest. Around the studio, everyone had stopped what they were doing, just to listen, and we were all transfixed. I found myself thinking about what Jenny from Music Madness had said about Gabriel's father's voice, as we'd listened to him singing 'Cat's in the Cradle' . . .

That man's voice, it's something else. Goes right through you.

Pushing the memory to the back of my mind, I pointed the lens at Gabriel again, and carried on shooting. Soon, his long note faded and he stepped away from the mic very slightly, taking a deep breath to ready himself for the next line. As he did so, his gaze lifted and he looked straight into my camera lens. His expression shifted. His eyes darkened. I kept shooting, because I couldn't stop myself, but it felt wrong, somehow. Like he was trying to communicate with me, and there was a machine in the way. What did the look on his face mean? Was he angry with me? Did he want me to stop? Or did he just want to talk?

'Stop. Suze! Stop the track. I can't do this now.'

There was a minor commotion in the studio as Suze turned the music off and, in the far corner, Yuki and Aiden stood up, whispering to each other and trying to catch a glimpse of Gabe in the live room. Barry had walked over to him and they were deep in conversation, but the intercom had been turned off and we couldn't hear what they were saying. All I knew was that Gabriel was shaking his head, his face tight, and glancing occasionally in our direction. But was he looking at me . . . or Olly?

'Is Gabe all right?' I said cautiously, my camera now hanging at my side.

Olly pushed out a weary sigh. 'Who knows? You're probably asking the wrong person.'

I gritted my teeth. This was exactly what I'd been afraid of. The signs were small – Olly's reluctance to look at their photograph in the Slash Gallery; the way he had reacted, just a few minutes ago, to Campbell's question about Gabe – but they were undeniably there.

'Is everything OK, Olly? With you and Gabe, I mean?' Olly pressed his thumbs into his eyes.

'I don't know. It's been . . . difficult, on tour.'

'Oh?'

Olly thought for a moment, throwing guarded looks at each of his bandmates. Then he laid a hand on my shoulder and guided me to the outskirts of the room, stopping by an upright piano. He kept his voice low.

'Ever since . . . *that night*, at the Rochester, there's been something different about him. He won't talk to me about it, which isn't that surprising . . . I mean, I hit him, right?'

I winced. At the time, I'd thought Gabriel deserved that punch. But the driving force behind it, his apparent one-night stand with Tammie, turned out not to have happened. So where exactly did that leave us? And would it really be that surprising if he was holding it against Olly?

'Anyway,' continued Olly, 'I don't know what's up with him, and neither do the others. But there's something on his mind. Something big.'

Of course there was something on his mind, I thought to myself. *We just found out we knew each other as kids, and we don't know why.* But nobody could know about that. I had to keep it from Olly, from everyone, no matter how tempting it was to tell them.

Olly ran a thoughtful finger along the lid of the piano.

'It's not even all about Gabe, to be honest. It's Barry too.' When he said Barry's name, he tossed a glance into the live room and lowered his voice even further. 'You remember I played my song the other week, at Caversham? Well . . . I wasn't supposed to. I got in a lot of trouble.'

'With Barry?'

'He said it wasn't "on-brand". He said I was putting myself ahead of the band.' He dropped his head back against the wall. 'But that's not true, you know? I love this band. They're like family to me. It's just . . . I can do more than sing, and smile at the fans. But when I ask Barry to listen to my stuff, he brushes me off. It's like he thinks only Gabriel can write songs, and I'm just some wannabe. Second best.'

Through the glass panel, Barry was giving Gabriel a pep talk, a hand on each shoulder. Like a sports coach.

'There's something between him and Gabriel,' continued Olly, 'and I don't know what it is. He's so protective over him, and I can't get past it, no matter what I do.'

Olly was right; I'd noticed it myself. The way Barry seemed to favour Gabriel, pushing him harder than the rest of the band. It was almost like a father-son relationship.

'I'm not asking Barry for any guarantees,' said Olly, his eyes still on his manager and his bandmate. 'We have to use the best songs, of course we do.' He threaded both hands through his hair. 'But why won't he give me a chance?'

Olly hung his head, and I wished I had something to say that would make him feel better. I hated seeing him this way.

'I don't want to make it all about me,' he added, 'but sometimes . . . I feel like I'm being pushed out of the ba—'

'Charlie's back.'

We both looked up guiltily at the gruff sound of Barry King's voice. He folded his arms across his broad frame.

'How you doing, Bloom?'

I nodded, tight-lipped. Even though I suspected his TV persona was largely an act, it was hard not to be a little bit scared of Barry King.

'I'm all right, thanks.'

'Yeah,' he said thoughtfully, running a big hand around his stubbled jaw. 'That you are.'

Awkwardly, I lifted my camera off my shoulders and dropped it into its case. I stole another quick glance into the live room, but it was empty. Gabriel had disappeared, without even saying hello.

Barry made a sweeping motion with both arms, ushering us from the room.

'Come on, then, you two. Get your arses downstairs. Your carriage awaits.'

Olly pushed away from the wall.

'You're travelling with us, right?'

I zipped my camera case up and tugged it over my shoulder.

'Uh . . . I don't know.'

He blinked a few times and forced a smile, as if trying to shake off his dark mood.

'I think you should. We're not going far, but it'll be worth it.' He nodded towards the door. 'I guarantee.'

12

As it turned out, spending time in a recording studio wasn't going to be my only first that day.

Minutes later, we were cruising through central London in the most extraordinary car I had ever seen. It was a stretched silver Bentley, big enough to carry at least ten people, with winged doors that opened upwards and an interior like a high-end nightclub. Music pumped from in-built speakers, coloured lights spun in the ceiling and miniature fridges stacked with fresh fruit and alcohol hummed quietly in the corners. In the centre, doubling as a table, was a fully functioning aquarium, home to four beautifully spotted tropical fish, and there was even a hot tub at the far end, illuminated from above by a halo of twinkling fairy lights.

It was, to be honest, totally ridiculous.

'Wait,' Olly was saying, leaning forward on one of the curvy leather sofas. 'You're actually telling me . . . that you think Bert and Ernie would beat Mr Potato Head in a fist-fight?'

Yuki, who was sitting opposite him drinking a can of Coke, threw his free hand up in the air.

'It's a tag-team situation, bro. Two against one.'

'Bert and Ernie are muppets, Yuk. They're carpets with eyes.'

Yuki shook his head despairingly.

'Oliver, Oliver. Mr Potato Head is made of detachable parts. He's not built for hand-to-hand combat. Plus . . .' He set down his drink on top of the fish tank, and pressed a finger to each of his temples. 'Dude's a freaking *potato*. Ernie would mash that right up.'

Peeking out from behind my camera, I threw a secret smile at Aiden. He returned it.

'This isn't over,' said Olly, shaking his head and trying to keep a straight face. Yuki eyeballed him, and soon enough, Olly burst out laughing. I pressed the shutter release, and caught it on camera.

'Who's your money on, Gabe?' asked Aiden. Gabe glanced up, briefly, from his phone.

'Bert's an animal, man,' he said slowly. His voice sounded husky and tired. 'Forget about Ernie, Bert could take Potato Head on his own.'

It was the most I'd heard him say for the whole journey. We still hadn't spoken, or even really acknowledged each other, since I'd arrived. I could barely bring myself to photograph him after the way he'd looked at me in the studio.

'Hey, do you know what two things would improve this

little trip?' said Yuki, tugging me from my thoughts. He was poised on the edge of his seat, waiting for an answer, but no one replied. He began a count on his fingers.

'OK, number one. Rub-a-dub-dub, let's get in the tub.'

Yuki picked up his drink from the table, drained it and wandered over to the hot tub. He crouched down and started poking at the controls.

'I don't think that's a good idea,' said Olly, watching his bandmate. 'In fact, I believe Barry's exact words were: "If any of you idiots get in the hot tub, I'll pull your arms off".'

'Ah, come on!' protested Yuki, trying out the buttons, one by one. 'They put the thing *in* here, bros, that means we're *obliged* to use it . . . a-HA!'

The tub burst suddenly into life, water bubbling and frothing, its interior lamps pulsing through different colours. They cast a fetching rainbow glow across the surface.

'Now *this* is what I call a party,' said Yuki, rubbing his hands together. 'All we need now is a pick-me-up.'

'We're out of Haribo,' revealed Aiden, waving an empty sweet packet.

'Not that kind of pick-me-up,' said Yuki, reaching into the nearby mini-fridge and pulling out a chilled bottle. '*This* kind.'

I zoomed in on Yuki's hand, and as it sharpened into focus, I lowered the camera. He was holding a bottle of Jägermeister.

The air in the car seemed to tighten.

135

'Yuki, seriously.'

Aiden, who was closest, reached over to take the bottle, but Yuki dodged him.

'Just a little one.'

I held my breath, wondering whether I should carry on taking pictures. Aiden and Olly exchanged a meaningful look.

'Yuks, come on,' said Olly patiently. 'We're on the radio in ten minutes.'

'This is Jäger!' protested Yuki, lining up two shot glasses. 'It's barely even booze.'

Yuki filled each glass to the brim and, after a shifty look through the glass divider in the direction of the driver, extended them towards us.

'Who's joining me? Charlie?'

'Ah, no, thanks,' I said, trying to keep the mood light. 'I had three vodka martinis with lunch, so . . .'

For a moment, nobody spoke. Then Gabriel reached forward.

'Go on, then,' he said, taking the glass from Yuki. Olly squirmed in his seat.

'This'll liven up the live session,' said Yuki, slipping on a pair of shades and clinking glasses with Gabriel. They knocked back the shots, and I felt Olly and Aiden tense. Yuki swallowed.

'That is *fine liquor*,' he said, gazing into his empty glass. 'Round two?'

'Nah, man,' said Gabriel, waving a hand and wincing. 'I'm good.'

'Suit yourself.'

Yuki poured himself another glass, lifted it to his mouth and, as he drank, tripped backwards over the lip of the hot tub and plunged into the water. He landed with a loud slap, causing a hot, frothy wave to break over the lip of the tub. It soaked down the edges and on to the floor.

There he was, sitting in the tub, shades on, legs hanging out over the edge with a bottle of Jäger in his hand, laughing. I couldn't resist taking a picture.

'Jesus, Yuki.'

Olly walked over to help him out, but Yuki waved him away.

'I'm good, I'm good. This is actually kinda refreshing.'

Olly jabbed at the controls until the bubbles stopped.

'Tara is going to crucify you.'

I peered out of the window. We were pulling in through a large set of security gates, and any minute now, management would appear to escort us inside. If we were lucky, they wouldn't smell the alcohol on the boys' breath, but there was no hiding the fact that the hot tub had enjoyed a spot of unauthorised usage.

Still, whether or not he got away with it this time, one thing was very clear.

There was something going on with Yuki.

13

'Come on, we're running late! Go, go, go!'

We were bundled out of the Bentley in a flash of arms and legs, ushered through a waiting tunnel of security guards and into the studio buildings, Tara striding up front with her clipboard. We passed endless doorways into dressing rooms, radio booths and equipment stores, and studio employees rushed by, talking into radio packs and tapping at their phones.

I was taking photos as we went, while up ahead, Tara walked backwards, calling out instructions.

'Everything's been set up for us in the live lounge, and the band are all ready to go, so we'll just— Yuki, what the hell happened to you?'

Yuki gave a non-committal shrug, and passed a hand through his wet hair.

'I got hot-tubbed.'

Tara's eyebrows climbed her face.

'For god's sake . . . you know they *film* the live lounge sessions, don't you?'

Yuki turned around and gave us all a guilty look. *Snap.* With his hair all over the place and his clothes dripping wet, it made for a fantastic photo.

Tara touched a finger to her ear.

'Sian, can we get some fresh clothes for Yuki and, uh . . . a towel and a hairdryer in the studio, please? Immediately. Thanks.'

She lingered on Yuki, shaking her head, then went back to addressing the rest of us.

'So . . . it's into the live lounge, sing three songs, then five or ten minutes of chat in the main studio. Olly, don't forget your announcement. And the three tracks are "Dance With You", "2am" then "Meet Me At Midnight". OK?'

I peeked out from behind my camera lens. 'Meet Me At Midnight'? I'd never heard of that song. Was it from the new EP?

'Gotcha,' said Olly, who was leading the pack, with Aiden and Yuki flanking him and Gabriel trailing at the back. While he was facing away from me, I snuck a few shots of Gabe's head and shoulders, his tumbling locks of black hair, his tanned face in profile.

'This is it, boys!'

Tara had stopped at the end of the corridor and was holding a door open. One by one, the band members slipped into the room, and soon I was standing in the doorway myself, unsure whether or not to follow them in. I hesitated, but Tara smiled.

'After you,' she said, and I swept into the room.

'Lads, that was *epic*!'

Shakia Lloyd, City Sounds' most popular presenter, was sitting at a round table, opposite the boys, talking into a large microphone. She was tiny but athletic, with short, cropped hair and a long tattoo – a rose tangled in barbed wire – snaking all the way along her left arm. She was also, for such a small person, startlingly loud.

'BOOM! What a cracking session,' she said, whacking the table with the flat of her hand. Aiden jumped, and I squeezed the shutter, capturing the moment.

'Thanks for having us,' said Olly, with a smile.

'Don't mention it, Ols. You were absolutely storming. In fact, I'd eat every single one of you for breakfast, and I'm not even into boys.'

She laughed her loud, scattershot laugh, which sounded like someone letting off firecrackers in a bin.

'Oh, and "Meet Me At Midnight"?' she continued. 'Stellar choice.'

Turns out there was a reason I hadn't heard of 'Meet Me At Midnight'. It wasn't a Fire&Lights song.

'We're all partial to a bit of Kaitlyn Jones, here, but I gotta ask you: covering one of her bonus tracks? That's kind of a fanboy thing to do, isn't it?'

'Sure it is,' replied Gabriel. 'We're big Kaitlyn fans.'

'All of you, or . . . one of you in particular?'

The studio went quiet. Aiden happened to be sitting closest to Shakia, and she dug an elbow into his ribs.

'*You* know what I'm on about, yeah?' She squeezed his cheek, and I took a picture. 'Miiiister Roberts?!'

Aiden laughed, but I could tell it was forced.

'Kaitlyn's cool,' he said softly. 'We really dig the new album—'

'And what else d'you dig about her? Right? Come aaaaahn.'

Shakia's grin was threatening to split her face in half. Aiden searched for the right words.

'Well, her music is—'

'Seriously, buster, let's get down and dirty here. Everyone's seen the pics of you two hanging out in Shanghai, in that noodle house. You're together, right?' She reached over once more, mussing up Aiden's hair. 'Come aaaaahn,' she said again.

Aiden blushed, and carefully rearranged his new quiff.

'Well . . . yeah. Yeah, I guess we are.'

I actually grimaced behind my camera. Melissa would be devastated.

'I knew it!! Gimme all the goss.'

'Actually, Shak,' interrupted Olly, leaning forward on his elbows, 'there's something very special we wanted to tell you about first.'

141

Shakia lolled her head from side to side.

'Hmmm, I dunno, I kind of wanna hear more about Aiden and Kaitlyn.' She drummed her fingers on the desk. 'Hashtag . . . Kaidlyn? That is CLASSIC.'

Olly held up his hands, palms open.

'Trust me, you want to hear this. It's a genuine exclusive.'

Shakia perked up at the word 'exclusive', and spun a little on her swivel chair.

'Very interesting. Let's hear it.'

Secretly, with the smallest of nods, Aiden thanked Olly for shifting the spotlight. *Snap*, I caught it on camera.

'So,' continued Olly brightly, 'no one else knows about this yet, 'cos it's been top secret until now, but . . . we're releasing a new EP.'

Shakia *oooh*-ed right into her microphone.

'No way! That is a City Sounds *exclusive*, people. Brand-spanking-new material from Fire&Lights, and you heard it here first.' A look of confusion flashed across her face. 'But, hang on. I thought your second album wasn't due until the winter?'

'It isn't,' said Olly. 'But some unexpected material kind of . . . fell into our laps.'

'We wrote it on the last tour,' added Gabriel, prompting a fleeting, sharpened look from Olly. Shakia sat back in her chair.

'And does this EP have a name?'

142

'*Songs About Us*,' replied all four boys, in unison. There was a pregnant pause, then everyone laughed, and Shakia's mouth curled into a grin.

'Did you rehearse that?' she said.

'For hours,' said Yuki, sipping his coffee. He'd drunk at least two cups since we'd arrived at the radio station.

'*Songs About Us*,' said Shakia, bobbing her head. 'Great title, sounds smashing. What's the music like?'

'Better,' said Gabriel.

'Than what?' replied Shakia, eyeballing him. He eyeballed her right back.

'Than our old songs.'

'I like your old songs,' protested Shakia.

'I like our old songs,' agreed Yuki. 'Well, except that cover of "Flying Without Wings" Barry made us release during *Make Or Break*.'

Aiden kicked him under the table.

'Come on!' said Yuki, his hands in the air. 'In some countries, that song is technically a violation of human rights.'

'So when do we get to hear this new EP?' said Shakia, smirking at Yuki.

'Friday the twenty-fifth of April,' replied Olly. 'Stick it in your diaries.'

'Whaaat? That's ages away.'

'Genius takes time,' offered Yuki, pressing his hands together, as if in prayer. Shakia rolled her eyes at him.

'Whatever you say, dude. But come on, you have to give me something. Like, the title, *Songs About Us*. Kinda begs the question . . . who exactly are these songs about?'

Silence. Shakia spun on her chair to face Gabriel.

'I'm looking at you, Mr Broody. You write the lyrics, right?'

Gabriel rubbed a thumb into his palm, his brow knitted. He looked a little uncomfortable.

'Uh-huh.'

'So who, pray tell, is the "us" in *Songs About Us*?'

'Some secrets aren't meant to be told, Shak,' he said, managing to fake a rakish smile. It was actually quite impressive how easily he turned it on.

Shakia laughed, shaking her head, and wagged a finger at him.

'Ohhhh no, no no no. You don't get out of it that easily.' The tone of her voice became suddenly conspiratorial. 'Because here's the thing. I've had an anonymous tip-off about you and Clara Fitzcharles, hanging out in Singapore, getting a little bit cosy over a chicken satay. What do you say to that? Is Clara your new squeeze?'

Gabriel squirmed in his chair. My stomach began to churn.

'Come on, West. Beans. Spill.'

'Rumours don't mean anything, Shak. You know that.'

'Is *this* one just a rumour, though?'

Gabriel sucked in a breath, as if he was about to reply. But no reply came.

'He's not denying it, listeners!' exclaimed Shakia, delighted. 'Gabriel West is *not denying it*, which I think makes it official. Gabe and Clara, sitting in a tree.' She let out a whistle. 'I'm impressed, she's a stone-cold hottie. Are you still together?'

Gabriel shook his head, the ghost of a smile playing on his lips.

'You don't give up, do you?'

'Nuh-uh.'

'OK . . . yes, we hung out in Singapore, and yes, sometimes, we hang out here. That enough for you?'

Shakia pressed a series of buttons on her mixing desk, and eyed him sideways.

'You little vixen, Gabriella. You little vixen.'

She pushed and pulled at various faders, and a track began to play. I lowered my camera, heart stuttering, a prickly heat on the back of my neck.

'Right, I'm afraid we're out of time with the Fire&Lights crew, but, boys, it's been a pleasure. And, you kids at home, keep your eyes peeled for the new EP, *Songs About Us*, chronicling Gabe's whirlwind romance with society beauty Clara Fitzcharles. For now, taken from the band's million-selling debut, this is the chart-topping "Have You Seen My Girl".'

As the track took over, Shakia walked round the table, shaking the boys' hands and patting their shoulders, and I tried with all my might to keep my eyes off Gabe. I'd never asked to be his best friend, or to know every tiny detail about his love life.

I just wished he'd had the decency to tell me himself.

14

Behind The Band, Part Four
'Boot Camp'

A spiky-haired, half-Japanese boy is sitting in a busy waiting room, the camera trained on his face. His name flashes up on the screen: 'YUKI HARRISON, sixteen years old'.

'So, Yuki,' begins the interviewer, off-screen, 'how do you feel it's going? You're through to boot camp, you're a favourite with the fans at home and the crowd here absolutely love you.'

Yuki blows air out through his lips.

'I don't know, bro. I just came here for the free sandwiches.'

The interviewer laughs, and Yuki sips from a can of Fanta.

'You'll be back in front of a live audience this weekend,' continues the interviewer. 'Think you'll make it through?'

'Who knows? I'm just gonna get up there and try not to fall over. Other than that . . . we'll see.'

There's a burst of music, and the video cuts to the famous Make Or Break *stage. Yuki appears from the wings and, on*

147

his way towards the spotlight, spins on his heel and moonwalks into the centre. The audience screams with delight.

Once calm has settled, Barry addresses him from the judges' table.

'Why do you want to be a popstar, Yuki?'

Yuki thinks about this, scratching the side of his head. In the crowd, someone shouts, 'Marry me Yuki!'

'You know those tiny bottles of shampoo you get in hotels?'

Barry's brow folds.

'I love those,' says Yuki, wide-eyed. 'They're amazing. And popstars get AS MANY AS THEY WANT.'

The audience collapse into laughter, but Barry is unmoved. He rests his chin on his hand.

'Seriously, though. Why?'

'I am serious!' insists Yuki, his hands in the air. 'Tiny shampoos, bro! That's the dream.'

Barry sighs, ever so slightly, and sets his pen down. Next to him, eighties popstar, Kaz Allbright, is beaming at the stage.

'I like you, Yuki,' she says, her immaculate teeth glinting in the light. 'I think you might be trouble.'

Yuki folds his arms, and arches an eyebrow. The camera cuts back to Kaz as she leans forward on the desk.

'Are you?'

Yuki cocks his head and a curious smile colours his face.

'That depends what you mean by trouble.'

‹ www.poptube.com *all the pop, all the time* **›**

'I think there's something up with Yuki,' I said to Melissa, as we weaved past a crowded bus stop on the way home from school. 'He seems . . . different, somehow. Since the tour.'

Melissa was fiddling with a loose thread on her coat.

'In what way, different?'

'I don't know.' I thought back to the incident in the limousine, with the Jägermeister. 'He's still the same awesome Yuki, he's just . . . wilder. He was drinking all these shots on the way to the radio station.'

Melissa went quiet for a bit, deep in thought. Then she slid out her phone.

'I don't know if this has anything to do with it,' she said, scrolling the screen with her thumb, 'but when they were in Japan, he was tweeting *loads* of selfies with this random punk band. Look.'

She showed me her screen, which was open on Yuki's Instagram feed. There was a series of shots of Yuki, wearing shades and looking bedraggled, pictured with three intense-looking punk rockers with piercings, tattoos and day-glo hair. They were all drinking spirits.

'They look kind of . . . hardcore,' I said, staring at the shortest one, who had a pink mohican and a tattoo of a naked woman on his neck.

'Well, maybe,' replied Melissa, pocketing her phone, 'but Yuki can look after himself. It's Aiden I'm worried about. I mean, Kaitlyn Jones? She is so not his type.'

'How do you know Aiden's type?'

Melissa pouted.

'Well, I don't, it's just . . . I know it's not her. She's way too glitzy.' She shoved her hands into her pockets. 'I don't know, though. I'm sixteen in two months . . . maybe I should stop obsessing about being some popstar's girlfriend.'

I buried my chin in my scarf, my cheeks burning bright. Melissa winced at herself.

'Sorry, I-I didn't mean . . .'

I smiled, and my eyes flickered in her direction.

'I know you didn't.'

'We can talk about it, if you want?'

'Talk about what?'

She lifted her eyebrows pointedly.

'Come on, Charlie. About Clara Fitzcharles.' She pulled a sour face. 'Or, as I like to call her, Blahra Fitzblahblah.'

I laughed, despite myself, and Melissa waved a hand in the air.

'To be perfectly honest, CB, I think it's for the best. It totally clears the runway for you and Olly.'

I closed my eyes, and sighed.

'Olly . . . god.'

'*A* god, more like it.'

'He's the best. He really is. He makes me feel . . . safe. And *so* happy. But just thinking about him and Gabriel, it

150

frightens me. There's something really weird going on between them.'

'I don't want to sound harsh,' said Melissa, 'but Gabriel's moved on. You should be allowed to move on too.'

'With one of his friends?'

'*Are* they friends, though? Aren't they just . . . bandmates?'

I stared into the middle distance, and shook my head.

'To be honest, I really don't know the difference any more.'

'Well, all I can say is this: the heart wants what the heart wants.' We passed the local corner shop, and Melissa stopped outside it, patting her belly. 'More importantly, the stomach wants what the stomach wants, and right now that's TWELVE JAMMY DODGERS.' She took a step inside. 'Fancy anything?'

'No, you go on.'

Melissa wandered into the store and I waited for her in the doorway, watching a messy train of Caversham High students snake along the pavement on the other side of the road. Jody was there with the rest of Diamond Storm, flicking the hair out of his eyes, laughing at one of Thumper's jokes. In just over a week's time, I would be taking my dad to their concert at the Black Hat club, and pretending to be their official tour photographer. *That'll be fun*, I thought, *and in no way awkward*.

'You OK there, miss?'

The shopkeeper was watching Melissa with suspicious eyes. She was rifling through the biscuits, her face taut with concentration.

'Just … looking for … where are your Jammy Dodgers?'

'Next to the digestives. Careful, you'll have the shelf down!'

I knew it wasn't a good idea, but I found my eyes drifting away from Melissa, towards the front of the shop, and settling on the magazine rack.

Fire&Lights heart-throb reveals sensational new romance!

Gabe & Clara – how adorable is that?!

Gabriel West & Clara Fitzcharles
IS THIS THE HOTTEST NEW COUPLE IN BRITAIN?

'Found 'em!'

Melissa was walking towards me again, pocketing her purse. Guiltily, I pulled my gaze away from the magazines, faking a smile, and watched her tear open the biscuits.

'They try and hide them, but I smoke 'em out every time.' She paused, reading my expression. 'You all right?'

I flicked at my thumbnail.

'I kind of . . . accidentally read some headlines about Gabriel and Clara.'

Melissa looked at me, at my hunched shoulders and red face, and looped her arm through mine. I laid my head on her shoulder.

'Come on,' she said, as we ambled home. 'Forget about them. Talk to me about Kingdom Records. Was it cool? I bet it was SUPER-cool. Did you get to meet Barry's monkey butler?'

I stood up straight, and blinked at her.

'Say what?'

'I read this blog once,' she continued earnestly, 'about Kingdom Records, and how instead of normal, like, servants or whatever, Barry King has a monkey butler.'

'Mel, there are so many things wrong with that sentence, I don't know where to start.'

Melissa bit into a Jammy Dodger and a small shower of crumbs escaped into the folds of her scarf.

'So are you saying he *does* have a monkey butler, or he doesn't?

I stopped in the street.

'You're asking me whether Barry King, the manager of Fire&Lights, dresses a monkey in a little suit and tie and employs him at his record label?'

Melissa swallowed the last of her Jammy Dodger.

'That is exactly what I'm asking.'

'Then, no, Mel. He does not.'

She produced a second biscuit from her pocket, and slipped it, whole, into her mouth.

'Ah, man,' she said, chewing. 'That means I owe Becky four pounds fifty.'

We continued on our way and, as I watched Melissa munching on her biscuit, not a care in the world, I started laughing. The image of Barry's monkey butler, standing there in his little suit scratching his head, wouldn't leave my mind, and soon I was cry-laughing. I couldn't stop. I was choking, and happy tears were brimming in the corners of my eyes.

Melissa frowned at me, swallowing her biscuit.

'Dude, are you broken?'

'You, Melissa Clementine Morris,' I said, catching my breath, 'are the strangest person I have ever met.' I smiled at her. 'Just as well you're also the loveliest, isn't it?'

I grabbed her hand and, with Melissa still shaking her head and me drying my eyes, we turned the corner into our road.

'Is that a dead frog in my shoe? In my *shoe*?!'

From Melissa's bedroom, we could hear her dad talking to himself downstairs. Her bed was littered with open school books, but we'd hardly given them a single look.

'That sounds pleasant,' I said, flicking through Instagram on my phone.

'Yeah.' Melissa made a face like she was sniffing a bin bag. 'Megabyte's developed a . . . *thing*. For frogs. She kills them, then kind of eats them a bit, then leaves them around the house. It's rancid, but I love her.'

'That cat could get away with anything.'

'Well, we all have our flaws, don't we?' replied Melissa, scrolling on her laptop. 'Becky's got a weasel that won't stop farting, and she lets it sleep on her pillow. Mind you, Becky is out of her tree.' She spotted something on the screen, and sat up straight. 'Oh my gosh! Check this out.'

'What?' I said, looking up from my phone. She was pointing at her computer.

'This is *awesome*.'

She spun her laptop round and presented me with a familiar webpage: Fan HQ on the official Fire&Lights site. My photos were already online.

'Your pic of Yuki in the hot tub is blowing UP!' she said, scanning the comments. 'I'm stealing that for my wallpaper, stat.'

If I did say so myself, Melissa was right: it was a really cool picture. The startled expression on Yuki's face – and the way I'd managed to catch him blowing a drop of water off the end of his nose – was priceless. But as I looked at the photo again, I felt my insides twist. Maybe all this reckless behaviour was just Yuki being Yuki, but something told me there was more to it than that.

'And have you seen what the fans are saying?' said Melissa. 'So much love for you on here, dude.'

I dragged the computer towards me, and studied the most recent comments.

This is soooooo adorable!! Yuki forever :) :) xoxoxoxo

Yuki is my favourite!!!!!!!! This photo is THE BEST.

I'm crying right now . . . I WANT TO MARRY FIRE&LIGHTS

'What's going on in here, then?'

Instinctively, at the sound of an adult's voice, I shut the laptop. Melissa's dad was standing in the doorway.

'Nothing,' said Melissa, in a way that suggested we were definitely up to something. Brian smiled.

'Don't worry, I'm not checking up on you. Is Megabyte in here?'

We all glanced around. No sign.

'Hmm,' said Brian, stroking his jaw. 'She's probably hiding, the little rascal. I found a dead frog in my shoe.'

Melissa gave a one-shouldered shrug.

'She's expressing herself, Dad. In cat years, she's a teenager now, so you should probably cut her some slack.'

'Oh, should I?' said Brian knowingly.

'Yep,' confirmed Melissa. 'Teenagers are complex creatures, and when they misbehave it's usually just their primitive way of expressing love.'

'Can you back that up with science?' replied Brian, giving her a sceptical glance. She crossed her arms.

'I can back *anything* up with science.'

Brian smiled at her, his face colouring with pride. Suddenly, from nowhere, I found myself thinking of the unmailed letter I'd found in my dad's study, late last year. The words that I longed to hear from him in person, just once. *You'd be so proud of her . . . I know I am.*

Emotion stirred in the pit of my stomach.

'You staying for dinner, Charlie?' said Brian, checking his watch. I smiled the feeling away.

'That would be great, thanks. Dad's working late, so . . .'

'Excellent.' Brian rubbed his hands together. 'I've made a fresh pizza, deep pan, since Rosie's away.'

Melissa leaned closer to me.

'Mum thinks deep pan pizzas are an American abomination. Which is kind of true, but they are also SWEET CHEESY HEAVEN.'

'Dinner's in forty, so I'll leave you guys to it,' said Brian, stepping out of the room, one hand still on the doorknob. He narrowed his eyes. 'And if you see that cat, tell her to be afraid. Very afraid.'

He gave us a big grin, closed the door and padded

away down the stairs. Melissa grabbed her laptop and lifted the screen.

'Where were we? Ah, yes. Checkin' out the Charlie-Bloom love.'

Next to the photograph of Yuki in the hot tub was one of the pictures I'd taken of Gabriel, in the studio, headphones on, between vocal takes. He was looking straight into the lens, his keen, amber eyes locked on the camera like a wild animal staring down the barrel of a gun. It felt like he was gazing right at me, through time, through the camera, through the screen. My throat clenched.

Melissa was pointing at the comments underneath.

'This is so cool! Have you read this . . . ?'

Anyone else think these pix might be Charlie Bloom's?? They're totally her style.

Charlie was lit, hope F&L are bringing her back 4 good

Did she actually have a thing with Gabe? if so ....
LUCKYYYYYYY <3

Shut up, who cares. I heart her photos big time.
#bringbackcharlie

'D'you know who else has a recognisable style?' said Melissa, idly undoing one of her plaits. 'Carrie Shakes.'

I rolled my eyes.

'Yeah, whatever.'

'Seriously, I'm not kidding. You're following in her footsteps. Did she get back to you yet?'

'Nope,' I said, with a quick shake of my head. 'And come on, I doubt she will.'

'Either way, Charlie, you can't deny it.' Melissa set about re-doing her plait, purple hair tie wrapped around her wrist. 'The people have most definitely spoken.'

Even I had to admit, this was a thrill I'd missed. Seeing strangers praise my work online was an incredible feeling, and I knew I shouldn't take it for granted. But I knew better than anyone that there was a darker side to fandom, and after last November, it wasn't the praise I was worried about.

It was the inevitable backlash.

15

For most sixteen year olds, bringing your dad to a gig is up there on the embarrassment scale with having to wear a gross PE kit from lost property, or accidentally calling a teacher 'Mum'. Fortunately for me, I wasn't too concerned about looking cool, or being embarrassed in front of my classmates, and that – in combination with the elaborate lie I'd recently talked myself into – was how I ended up at an all-ages rock concert with my forty-one-year-old father.

'Are you pumped for the show, Mr Bloom?'

The three of us – Melissa, me, my dad – were standing in the queue for the Black Hat, a grubby live music venue in the centre of town. Several members of the Jody Baxter Fan Club were huddled in front of us, discussing in staggering depth the various merits of volumising versus lash-defining mascara. When, at one point, one turned round to wave to a friend, they looked my dad up and down and threw me a passing, but loaded, glance.

'Yes, I think so,' said Dad, nodding at Melissa. 'A little . . . strange to be seeing a live band again, but I'm excited to see Charlie in action.'

My camera was hanging off my shoulder. In my own way, I was excited that Dad was seeing me in action too. Even if the whole thing was basically a charade.

'How old are these two?' said the bouncer, addressing my father. After being closed down the year before, the Black Hat had a zero tolerance policy on underage drinking. Dad was about to answer when Melissa interrupted him.

'Fifteen years and ten months,' she said proudly. The bouncer flared his nostrils and, locking eyes with my dad again, nodded in my direction.

'And Charlie's sixteen,' said Dad. The bouncer pressed the 'underage' stamp into both our wrists, and we passed into the club.

'Hey, Mr Bloom,' said Melissa, as we stepped into the darkened main room. A thudding dance track assaulted our ears. 'When did you last go to a gig?'

'You know you don't have to call me Mr Bloom, Melissa,' said my dad, raising his voice above the booming bassline. 'But, erm . . . I'm not sure. 1999, perhaps?'

'No. Freaking. Way,' said Melissa. 'That's in, like, the last *century*.'

'I was never that into gigs,' continued Dad. 'I used to go with Charlie's mum sometimes in London, though. Place called the Troubadour. No idea if it's still there . . .'

He tailed off, and pinpricks swarmed my skin. *Dad knew the Troubadour.* So while he hadn't been in the photograph, he'd almost certainly been to Little Boy Blue concerts with Mum. For all I knew, he'd *taken* the photograph.

'You OK, Charlie?'

I looked at my father, the blood rushing to my face. Could I ask him about it? Could I bring up the Troubadour, without giving away that I knew about Little Boy Blue?

'Charlie?'

'Oh, y-yep . . . yeah, I'm fine,' I stammered, tucking a lock of hair behind my ear. 'Shall we . . . find somewhere to sit? Would you be happier sitting?'

Dad gave me a confused smile.

'I'm not a hundred years old, kiddo.'

'Right. Yeah.'

I glanced around the room. This was really awkward.

'Look, it's like I said earlier,' continued Dad, taking a step towards me. 'You two go off and do your thing, and I'll amuse myself. I know it's not especially trendy to be seen in public with your dad.'

'Sure. OK.' I didn't move. 'Sure.'

'Ooh, a jukebox!' said Melissa, spotting one in the corner. She set off to investigate it, leaving me alone with Dad. He swallowed, and rubbed the side of his neck.

'I think it's great what you're doing here, Charlie. Following your passion. I was only hard on you last year because you went behind my back.' The reminder stung

162

us both, but Dad waved it away. 'I want to support you, in any way I can. And I promise not to cramp your style.'

'Thanks, Dad,' I said, though it was lost in the deafening climax of the music. It felt almost like the track was inside my head, my brain pulsing with the relentless thump of the bass drum. There could be no question now that my father had known Harry West, in some way or other. And Melissa was right: somewhere, there was an explanation for how Gabriel, Olly and I were connected, and my dad almost certainly knew what it was. But he was the last person in the world I could ask.

'Word up, homies.'

Melissa had reappeared beside us. Dad slipped his wallet from his pocket.

'I'll get you both a drink, then I'll leave you to it. What do you fancy?'

Melissa placed a hand on Dad's shoulder.

'Mine's a lychee martini, Ralph, old boy. Shaken, not stirred.'

Dad recoiled.

'Do you even know what one of those is?'

'Totally,' insisted Melissa. 'Take a lychee, whack it in a martini. Job done.'

'I'll get you both Cokes,' said Dad, with a wry smile. 'See you in a mo.'

Dad made his way to the bar, carving a course through the lively crowd of Caversham High students, and joined the drinks queue. I watched him tapping his foot slightly out of time with the music.

'I feel weird.'

'It's fine!' exclaimed Melissa, re-applying her lip gloss in a pocket mirror. 'We just need to get through tonight, avoid any fudge-ups, convince your dad that you're genuinely hanging out with Diamond Storm and you'll be off the hook for the rest of the term. Until our exams, anyway.'

'I don't like lying to him,' I said, switching on my camera.

'Lying is bad,' agreed Melissa. 'But then Fire&Lights are *sooo* good, they effectively cancel each other out.'

'What?'

'Ancient Chinese proverb,' she said, nodding sagely. 'Now let's go and join the mosh pit.'

Diamond Storm played a really strong set, to a very excited crowd. Although 'mosh pit' had been a touch optimistic, Melissa enjoyed being up the front, half-singing along to any words she could remember, while I hung back at the sides, darting from one space to another to capture the band from a variety of angles. Every so often I would catch Dad's eye, as he sat in a booth in a distant corner, nursing a bottle of beer. He would give me a little smile and a nod, and I wouldn't know whether to feel happy or ashamed.

At the end of the show, I crossed over to the bar to

fetch a drink of water. While the barman tipped ice into a tall glass, I leaned against the counter, scanning through my pictures. It had been great to see the band playing in a proper venue, rather than the school hall, and there were actually some pretty nice shots in my gallery. I was lingering on one of Jody pointing into the crowd, his face glowing under red lights, when I heard Melissa's voice beside me.

'Um, Charlie?'

She was chewing gum and gazing at the stage.

'What?' I said, concentrating on the picture.

'What's your dad doing over there?'

I looked up, and the second I saw what Melissa was pointing at, my entire body tensed. My father was talking to Jody.

16

Moving as fast as I could without actually running, I dragged Melissa across the room towards the stage.

'Dad, what are you doing?'

Dad swivelled round, surprised, and gestured at Jody.

'Oh, hi, Charlie. I was just talking to the lead singer here, um . . .'

'Jody,' said Jody, pushing his sodden hair back from his face.

'Jody, that's right. Fabulous band you've got. Really fabulous.'

This was the last thing I needed: my father getting chummy with Diamond Storm.

'I think it's probably time w—'

'I have to say, Jody,' continued my dad, undeterred, 'I'm delighted that Charlie's joining the tour. Where are you headed next?'

'Oh, hello there!' said a new voice from behind me. Grateful for the interruption, I turned round to find a woman, about the same age as my dad, standing underneath the flickering lights. I threw a panicked glance at Melissa. How had this suddenly turned into Parents' Evening?

'Oh, hello,' said Dad perkily. 'I thought I was the only old fogey here.'

The woman reached over to shake Dad's hand. Bangles rattled on her wrist.

'Christine,' she said. 'I'm Jody's mum.'

'Ah, I see. Ralph. I'm here with Charlie, the photographer. Though keep that to yourself: I don't think I'm doing her street cred any good!'

'Me neither,' agreed Christine, placing a hand on her chest. 'Still, someone's got to drive all the gear home.'

I tugged at Dad's wrist.

'We should . . . go?' I said. Slightly deflated, Dad glanced at Jody, then back at me.

'Y-yes, of course. School in the morning.' He nodded at Jody's mum. 'Lovely meeting you, Christine.'

'You too, Ralph, and thanks for coming. I know the boys appreciate it. And, Charlie, good luck with the photos. I'm sure they'll turn out great.'

I mumbled some unconvincing thanks and began herding my father and best friend away from the Baxters. As we neared the exit, Dad and Melissa chatting happily to each other, I looked over my shoulder and cast a final glance towards the stage. Jody caught my eye, and gave me an off-putting smile. A smile that suggested he was starting to put two and two together.

*

Dad and I walked through the front door into our darkened hallway, and he clicked on the lamp by the phone. He pulled off his coat and dropped it on to the hook.

'Well done tonight,' he said, nodding at me. 'You looked like you were doing a grand job.'

'Ah, I didn't do much, really.'

Dad scratched his head.

'I know this all started because of your grades, but I see now that it's more than that. It's about . . . who you are. And you're a pretty amazing young woman, Charlie.'

As our eyes met in the low light, I thought about how strange it was that I was working with this world-famous band, chasing my dream and following in the footsteps of my idol, and yet I couldn't tell my father. Instead, I had to pretend I was doing some watered-down version of it, taking photos for an unknown school band in local nightclubs. And for the first time since I'd started this whole thing, I suddenly felt sad that I couldn't talk to him about it.

'Thanks, Dad.'

'Any time, kiddo. Goodnight.'

'Night.'

Upstairs, after getting ready for bed and turning off the light, I lay back against my pillow for a while, snug beneath the duvet, texting Melissa.

So that was kinda stressful.

Naaaaah, it was fine. We were on it the whole time.

!!! Dad was about two seconds away from blowing my cover

I paused for a moment, listening to my father in the bathroom, brushing his teeth and humming to himself.

I've been thinking, I added, maybe it would be easier if I just told him the truth?

WOOOOOAH THERE, cowboy

Melissa sent me four horse emojis.

U tell your dad the truth and it's all over, she wrote. No more F&L, no more concerts, no more Olly, no nothing.

I took a deep breath, and slipped down further beneath the covers.

You're right, I replied. I know you are. Just tell me it's worth it, would you?

My phone went quiet for a while. Across the hall, I heard the toilet flushing, the sound of Dad's bare feet padding along the wooden floor and then his bedroom door gently closing.

My phone buzzed again.

Put it this way. In 2 days u get to hang out with Olly again. Backstage at a massive concert. DON'T U PRETEND THAT'S NO BIG DEAL, SISTER. <3 <3 Night, Charlie Cheese xxxxxx

Sleep well, you maniac xxxxxxxx

Melissa had made me smile, again, just like she always did. And she was right. Friday would be awesome: a chance to do the thing I loved most in the world, at an incredible venue, hanging out with some of my favourite people. Locking my phone and sliding it on to my bedside table, I sank my head into the pillow and stared up at the ceiling.

I couldn't wait to see Olly again.

17

I was unzipping my case and reaching inside for my camera when I heard a commotion, looked up, and through a gap in the curtains saw Elton John.

Sir. Elton. John.

'This is blowing my mind,' said Campbell, transfixed. 'We are *actually looking at Elton John.*'

He looked weirdly familiar, Elton John, like a distant uncle you'd met once before, but were too young to really remember. He was in a different room to us, in the VIP area, but a narrow gap in the curtains was giving us an illicit view of the action. What's more, he wasn't the first celebrity we'd spied that evening. The Pop4Progress concert was the very definition of star-studded.

'I can't believe it's really him,' continued Campbell dreamily. 'I love *The Lion King . . .*'

Backstage at the London Complex, the building was buzzing with activity. Stage technicians zig-zagged through the wide, industrial-looking space, caterers handed out sandwiches, management types conducted urgent-sounding phone calls in quiet corners. Through the walls, you could hear thousands of people streaming into the auditorium, and the sound of the warm-up presenter making cheesy jokes over the speaker system.

Duffy was frowning at Campbell.

'You know Elton John has made, like, tons of seminal albums, don't you?'

'Yeah, but, Duff, come on. *The Lion Ki*— WHOA. Get out.' Campbell was pointing through the curtain. 'It's Kaitlyn Jones.'

Pulling out my camera, I shifted sideways to get a better view and managed to catch a glimpse of Kaitlyn as she touched a hand to Elton's shoulder, laughing sweetly. Duffy was doing her best not to look interested, but even she couldn't resist a glance.

'Shall we see if they'll let us in?' said Campbell, toying with the laminate pass around his neck. 'We might get to meet her.'

'Seriously, Kaitlyn Jones?' Duffy threw a weary glance at me. 'Sometimes, Cam, I wonder whether you only became a FireLighter to meet celebs.'

Campbell's cheeks turned pink. I hit the switch on my camera, and waited for it to power up.

'Don't take this the wrong way, Duffy,' I said, 'but isn't that why you joined?'

Her face opened with surprise.

'No way, I'm not some fangirl. I want to be a journalist. This is a stepping stone for me.'

172

Campbell and I shared a guilty look, and he smiled at me, brushing his immaculate Lego hair off his forehead.

'Sorry, Duffy. I didn't mean—'

'To be honest,' she said, 'I want what you've got.'

I glanced up, confused.

'What do you mean?'

'You know what you want, and you're making it happen. That's pretty cool, if you ask me. And if I'm going to be a reporter, I need to do the same thing. My dad keeps saying I'm being impatient, and he wants me to go to university first, but what's the point of that? I can start my career now, I just need a break. I just need to meet the right people.'

I paused, finger poised over my camera's touch-screen. I could see Duffy's point. I was only really here because I knew Olly.

'Actually, Duff,' said Campbell, tapping her on the shoulder, 'that thing we were talking about . . . Charlie might know someone.'

A look of realisation flashed over Duffy's face.

'Know someone for what?' I said, with a frown.

'We need a—'

'Elts! Elts, my boy, how the devil are you?'

We were torn from our conversation by the sound of Yuki's voice, spilling from the gap between the curtains. We all peered through to the VIP area and found him standing next to Elton John, teaching him to fist-bump.

Behind them, Kaitlyn greeted Aiden with a quick kiss, and took his hand. His eyes dropped instantly to the floor.

'God, I love Yuki,' said Campbell, with a sigh.

'Everyone loves Yuki,' agreed Duffy, turning back to me. 'You should see some of the fan-mail he gets. People have sent in actual locks of their hair and been, like, "Can you give these to Yuki for me?". Freaky.' She waved it off. 'Anyway . . . sorry, I was saying. Cam and I have been talking, and we've basically decided . . . we need a third FireLighter.'

I took a quick look through my camera's viewfinder, then lowered it again, pulling a cloth from my pocket.

'What do you need a third person for?' I asked, polishing the lens.

'I want to do more vlogging for the fan site,' said Duffy. 'Making videos, writing up the events and stuff. That's what I'm good at. But if I'm doing that, Cam'll need someone around at the concerts to help him look after the competition winners. Someone who's *super* into the band, but isn't a total headcase. We thought you might know someone . . . ?'

A laugh burst involuntarily out of me. Duffy searched my face.

'What?'

'Sorry, it's just . . . I think I know the perfect person. I mean, she is a *bit* of a headcase, but only in a good way.'

'Amazing! Do you think she'd be up for it?'

'Oh, yes,' I said, nodding deeply. 'Melissa would literally chew her own arms off for this job.'

Duffy and Campbell both beamed.

'That is so exciting!' said Campbell, clapping his hands.

'We'd need to do a FaceTime interview or something,' said Duffy, 'but if she's cool with you, I'm pretty sure she'll be cool with us.'

'Sure,' I agreed, imagining Melissa's face when I told her. It was very likely her head would explode.

'Dudes!'

We all twisted round to find Yuki and Aiden approaching us, Aiden with his hands in his pockets, Yuki grinning from ear to ear. He had sunglasses pushed up into his hair, and was carrying a pair of beers in each hand.

'Hi, guys!' said Campbell, as they drew closer. He dropped his voice. 'We just saw you chilling with Elton John. That is the coolest. What did you talk about?'

Yuki jerked his head, and his shades dropped down in front of his eyes.

'Mostly, he wanted to know who on earth I was. Beer?'

Yuki stretched out his arms, proffering the drinks. We all shook our heads.

'Dammit,' he said. 'Now I'm going to have to drink all four.'

My gaze met Aiden's. He smiled, but it didn't quite reach his eyes.

'Cam, we have to dash,' said Duffy, checking her

phone. 'The comp winners are getting here in five minutes.' She flicked her hair at Yuki and Aiden. 'Nice to see you guys.'

'Have a great show!' said Campbell, as the two of them drifted away. 'I know you're going to kill it.'

'Thanks,' said Aiden, with a small wave. Yuki tipped his beer at them, then turned to me.

'Just us then, Charlie B?'

I lifted up my camera. 'Wanna shoot some photos?'

Yuki smiled, and slung an arm around Aiden's shoulder.

'I thought you'd never ask.'

Yuki and Aiden were sitting opposite each other in the Fire&Lights dressing room, knees nearly touching. They each had three multi-coloured balls in their lap.

'You really think this'll work?' I said, from behind my camera. Yuki took off his shades.

'Charlie.' He pointed one of the balls at me. 'As the saying goes: you can't teach an old dog new tricks, but you can teach an Irishman how to juggle.'

'In under five minutes?'

'Hell, yeah.' He turned back to Aiden. 'Now, Aid. I want you to imagine that you are Neo and I am Morpheus, and I am about to upload all the juggling knowledge that exists in the universe directly into your brain.'

Aiden looked at me, and sighed.

'He thinks he's in *The Matrix*. He's always going on about *The Matrix*.'

'Oi, pipe down,' said Yuki, clicking his fingers in Aiden's face. He took a swig of beer, then picked up all three balls. 'This is the bit where you have to follow me *very closely*.' He leaned closer to Aiden, eyeballing him, and Aiden started to laugh.

Snap.

'OK, OK,' conceded Aiden, pushing Yuki away. 'I'm watching. I promise.'

Yuki distributed the balls so there were two in his left hand and one in his right hand. He nodded at Aiden, who did the same.

'Now . . . you're going to throw *one* of these balls from your left hand into your right hand.'

As he described the action, Yuki carried it out, with Aiden watching. *Snap*. Concentrating hard, his tongue sticking out the corner of his mouth, Aiden tried it himself, but failed to catch the vaulting ball and it fell to the floor, rolling under a chair.

'Crash and burn,' remarked Yuki, laughing. Aiden dropped down to retrieve the ball.

'Man, this is tricky,' he said, returning to his chair with all three balls cradled clumsily in his hands. 'You make it look easy.'

I smiled at the concentration on Aiden's face. He was trying so hard.

'Try it one more time,' said Yuki, repeating step one. 'Throw one ball from your left hand to your right hand, niiiice and easy.'

Aiden tried it again, but this time, not only did he fail to catch the flying ball, but in lurching for it managed to propel it across the room into Yuki's collection of beer bottles, sending them tumbling like skittles. *Snap*.

'Dude, precious beer!'

Fizzy, frothy beer gulped from two of the bottles, cascading in a pair of sad, brown waterfalls to the carpet. Yuki grabbed both and returned them to a standing position, but not before they'd been nearly entirely drained.

Aiden grimaced. *Snap*.

'Sorry, Yuk,' he said, his arms loose by his sides. 'This is way harder than it looks.'

Yuki stood up and walked backwards, his palms in the air.

'I give up, Charlie B, I was wrong. This is like trying to teach a hedgehog to speak Italian.'

'Hey!' said Aiden, mock-offended.

'Don't worry, Aid. Luckily for you, Kaitlyn's not interested in your circus skills. Just your boyish good looks.'

Yuki winked at his bandmate and, though I might have imagined it, Aiden suddenly seemed a little uncomfortable. I took his picture, but he turned away, and as I stared at his back through the camera lens, I realised that I could hear 'Meet Me At Midnight' through the walls. Across the building, in the auditorium, Kaitlyn was opening the show.

'Right,' said Yuki, throwing his juggling balls, one by one, over his head, and catching them all in the same hand. He discarded them on the table, next to his almost-empty beer bottles. 'I'm off for a walk, locate some more booze.'

'Maybe you should just chill?' said Aiden, looking up at him from beneath raised eyebrows.

'I *am* chill,' said Yuki distractedly, draining one beer, then the other. 'I . . . am . . . *super* chill . . .' He grasped the doorknob. 'When's our first set again?'

Aiden pursed his lips.

'Eight-thirty.'

'Roger that. See you then.'

Yuki pulled open the door, saluted us both and sauntered out into the hallway. I lowered my camera and glanced at Aiden, who was looking a little red-faced.

'You OK?'

Peering down at his lap, he nodded slowly.

'Yeah. Yeah.' He made eye contact with me. 'Sort of.'

I studied his expression, wondering if it was Yuki's drinking that was clouding his thoughts. I wanted to talk to him about it, but it didn't feel like my place to ask.

'Can I ask you something?' he said, scratching his jaw. 'It's sort of . . . private.'

I set my camera on a nearby chair.

'Of course.'

Aiden reached over to the open door and gave it a nudge. It closed with a soft click. He took a breath.

'It's about Kaitlyn.'

'Oh.' I hadn't been expecting that. I decided to keep the mood light. 'You've broken my best friend's heart with that one, you know,' I said. Aiden laughed reluctantly.

'Melissa? Say hi from me, would you?'

I nodded, sliding backwards on to the counter so that my legs were hanging off the edge.

'So what's going on with you two?' I asked casually. Aiden started to answer, then hesitated. He turned to face me.

'Did you ever get together with someone, and then . . . like, the idea of that person, and the reality, turn out to be two different things?'

I almost laughed at how familiar this was. There was the idea of Gabriel West, The Popstar, and then there was the 'real' person underneath. Sometimes, they may as well have been two separate people.

'Definitely,' I replied. 'But you're totally into Kaitlyn, right? Everyone's talking about you guys.'

'That's exactly it,' said Aiden, glancing at the wall. With the door closed, no one would be able to hear us, but he lowered his voice anyway. 'Everyone's talking about us. And, like, I thought I was into her, I honestly did. She's cool and fun, and super-talented. We had a nice time hanging out in Shanghai, and people at the label kept saying to me, "Oh, Aid, you guys would make a great couple", and I sort of went along with it. But now that we're actually *together* . . . something doesn't feel right.'

My fingers gripped the edge of the counter. I felt like I was on the verge of learning a big secret, and I was carrying around enough of those as it was.

'Don't get me wrong,' continued Aiden, 'I like Kaitlyn, but . . . I think . . . I like her as a friend. Does that make sense?'

'Of course it does,' I said. 'So just tell her. She's a grown-up, she'll understand.'

Aiden covered his face with his hands.

'It's not that simple, though, because apparently it's "great for record sales", and there's a whole hashtag and everything. I can't just break it off.'

Frustrated, I tipped my head back, and stared at the ceiling.

'You can, Aiden. It's your life. If she's not the girl you want to be with, then tell her.'

'But that's just it. I don't know if I want to be with *any* girl right now.'

I opened my mouth, but couldn't think of a response. In fact, I wasn't entirely sure what he meant.

'Look, I'm not an idiot,' he said, picking at the label of an empty water bottle. 'I know that some people think I'm . . . you know . . . into boys, and stuff. They look at me, and they're, like, he's in a boy band, he's the quiet one, he must be gay. But I'm not. At least . . . god, I don't know what I am.' He blushed. 'This is making me sound crazy.'

'It isn't,' I said, trying to catch his eye. 'Honestly.'

He looked up at me.

'Teenagers are supposed to fall in love, or in lust, all the time, right? But I don't know if I ever have.' He stopped, biting back emotion. 'Or if I ever will.'

We both fell silent. Distant strains of Kaitlyn's breakthrough hit, 'If U Wanna Be My Boyfriend', seeped through the walls.

'I read somewhere,' continued Aiden, trying to ignore the music, 'that some people, they're not into boys . . . *or* girls. They just have these intense friendships, but nothing more.' He tore a long strip of label off the bottle. 'That probably doesn't make any sense.'

I nodded.

'No . . . it does.'

'Anyway, I don't know if that's what I am or not. I feel like I might never know.'

Aiden ripped off the last scrap of label, and set the bottle down next to him. I tried to imagine what it would be like to feel the way he did, and be the person he was, and a lump rose up in my throat. This sort of thing was hard enough for any teenager, but Aiden was going through it with the whole world watching.

'You shouldn't put so much pressure on yourself,' I said.

'What do you mean?'

'You are who you are. Maybe that'll change, maybe it won't. As long as you're happy, none of it matters.'

Aiden slid both hands into his hair.

'I'm famous, though. People expect things of me. My managers, my label, the fans.'

I could feel the heat rising to my cheeks. This was unfair, and it was making me angry.

'You might be in the public eye, but you shouldn't . . . I mean, you don't owe anyone anything.'

I glanced at Aiden's juggling balls, lined up neatly on the counter, and then at Yuki's, scattered among the discarded beer bottles.

'Have you talked to Yuki about this?'

Aiden shook his head sadly.

'I can't, Charlie. He's changed. Something's happened, and he won't talk to me about it. He spends all his time with this punk band he met on tour, Scorched Earth, and he's drinking, and . . . I don't know, I just feel like he doesn't want to hear about my problems.'

'Of course he does,' I protested. 'You're his best friend. Best friends tell each other everything.'

Aiden frowned, deep in thought.

'This will sound a bit strange,' he said, 'but . . . I miss him. You know?'

Aiden gritted his teeth, his face flushed. I nodded.

'I know. But whatever's going on with him, it doesn't change your friendship. He's a good person, Aid. He cares about you.'

Aiden looked over at me and, ever so slightly, his face brightened.

'You must think I'm pretty weird.'

I smiled.

'Sometimes, when I'm hanging out with Fire&Lights, I think you're the only sane person in the whole building.'

The door swung open, and noise from the corridor rushed into the room. We both turned to find Yuki standing in the doorway, holding a cold beer in each hand.

'Kids, this is happening right now!' He pointed a bottle at Aiden. 'One for the road?'

Aiden inhaled patiently.

'Yuks, give it a rest. We're onstage in five minutes.'

'Playing, like, three songs. The after-party starts here, dude.'

Aiden swallowed his concern, and peered out through the open doorway.

'I can hear Tara,' he said, subtly taking the beers from Yuki and secreting them behind the sofa. 'Let's go.'

Aiden pushed Yuki out of the door and, just before they disappeared from sight, he turned and glanced back into the room. He caught my gaze, and the look in his eyes said, 'Thank you'.

'Ladies and gentlemen . . . are you ready . . . for the biggest boy band . . . on the face of the earth?!'

As I waited at the side of the stage, I was haunted by a mess of conversations, twisted and tangled inside my head. Olly, frustrated at being pushed aside by Barry. Aiden, trapped in a relationship invented for the media. Yuki, acting out and getting drunk before shows. And Gabriel . . . Gabriel, doing whatever it was he was doing right now, withdrawn, distant. Dating some society It Girl.

From where I stood, cracks were appearing in The Biggest Boy Band On The Face Of The Earth. But of course, for the next ten minutes, none of that would matter. Because when those four boys hit the stage, they lit a fire inside your soul.

'It's the incredible . . . Fire . . . AND . . . LIGHTS!'

All around the auditorium, bright white spotlights flickered and spun, settling on four trapdoors on the upper level of the stage. There was a momentary silence, a sound like a shotgun being cocked, and then Gabriel, Olly, Yuki and Aiden were launched through the trapdoors from some secret chamber beneath the floor, a cavalcade of strobe lights capturing their vaulting path through the air. As the lights framed their soaring silhouettes, it was no exaggeration to say that they looked like they were flying.

Seconds later, they landed simultaneously on solid ground, triggering a volley of fireworks from both sides of the stage, and wild, rapturous cheers from the crowd. The musicians were pounding out the introduction to 'Hollywood Movie Star' and the boys were streaming towards the audience, their hands above their heads, inspiring a mass clap-along from all corners of the arena. I smiled helplessly, caught in the moment, high on the band's infectious energy. Backstage, through the lens of my camera, they had been vulnerable, they'd been flawed. Ordinary teenage boys, with ordinary teenage problems. But out here, in the smoke and the noise and the lights and the music, it was absolutely undeniable.

They were superstars.

Part of me wanted Yuki to be useless. I wanted the drinking to wreck his performance and teach him a lesson, but it didn't. He was as brilliant, as energetic, as irresistible as ever. He ran along the front of the stage, his hand passing across the fingers of the lucky fans on the front row, and many of them wept and screamed as he passed, clutching their hands to their chests. I had looked down on those people once, but not any more. Tonight, I felt every atom of their passion in my blood, and as the boys began to sing, I realised I was welling up. Not because I was sad about the things that had changed, but because hearing them sing, watching the way they lifted the spirits of every single person in that room, made me happier than almost anything else in the world.

They thundered through 'Hollywood Movie Star' and straight into 'Have You Seen My Girl', and thousands were on their feet, singing, laughing, fists pumping the air. Confetti canons exploded from the ceiling during the choruses, and giant, glittery balloons bounced across the heads of the audience, hands reaching up high to send them careering off in every direction.

Then, in the break before their final number, Olly wandered on to the large, semi-circular platform that jutted out into the auditorium, and addressed the crowd.

'How's everyone doing?' he said, his wide, bright smile illuminating the big screens. Below, girls reached for him, waving their banners and calling out his name. 'We've got something a bit different planned for our final song,' he added, as behind him, a stage tech appeared inside a spotlight, carrying a stool. She set it down, then retreated back into the darkness. Olly moved to the edge of the stage, knelt and addressed a girl in the front row.

'Would you like us to sing to you?'

Watching the action unfold on the screens, the crowd lost it, and the girl clamped both hands to her mouth.

'Is that a yes?' said Olly, with a laugh. The girl, still covering her mouth, nodded hard, and Olly held out a hand. Everyone cheered and roared as he wrapped his fingers around hers and, with the help of the bouncers, lifted her on to the stage. He guided her over to the stool, and she sat. Music began to build from the back of the stage.

'This one's called "Dance With You"', said Olly, and the building shook with the screams. Guitars rang out, keyboards soared, and Olly turned to the girl and began to sing.

Take me home
'Cos I've been dreaming of a girl I know . . .

It had been a while since I'd heard those words.

Words I'd first read as a seven-year-old, in my mother's scrapbook. Words that I'd fantasised were about me, about how any day now she was going to come home. What I didn't know at the time was that, one day, I'd hear them again in the songs of a world-famous boy band, and I'd start learning things about my mother that I might otherwise never have known. That Katherine Bloom loved music, just like I did, and was obsessed with a band called Little Boy Blue. If she'd been with me beside that stage at that very moment, I was certain she'd have felt the same way I did. Overwhelmed. Alive. Our hearts turning like the wheels on a freight train, unstoppable, rushing; heat on our skin, fire in our bones.

I looked back at the stage. Sitting on her stool, the girl was trying to stay calm, but her shoulders were shaking. The four boys were taking turns singing to her, and on the big screen, you could see the tears streaming down her face.

After a while, the guitars, keyboards and bass dropped out, but the drums played on – an anthemic *boom-cha, bmm-cha* – and Yuki, Aiden and Gabriel swept to the front of the stage. Soon, they were leading the crowd in an almighty singalong, twenty thousand voices belting out the words as vast, swooping spotlights danced over their heads. Meanwhile, Olly invited the girl off the stool, held out his arms and danced with her, ballroom style, in small, gentle circles. Tears were still tumbling down her cheeks, and she brushed them away with the back of her hand. Then Olly leaned forward slowly, and whispered in her ear.

Something tightened inside me.

Was this making me . . . jealous? Surely not. It was just an act, another rockstar trick; I knew Olly wasn't actually *into* her. Or was he? I folded my arms, willing the thought away, but I couldn't ignore the burning sensation in my chest, or the craving in the pit of my stomach. Because, whether or not I was prepared to admit it, I didn't want Olly to be hers.

I wanted him to be mine.

I wanna dance with you, girl, till the sun goes down
I wanna feel every rush that you feel
I wanna hear every sound when your heart cries out
So sing it with me tonight

Shaking my head, I turned away from the action and fell against the wall, pushing my fingertips into my eyes. *Pull yourself together, Charlie. It's just a performance. It doesn't mean anything.*

'Yep, I'm bringing her through, meet us at door seven.'

I was jolted back to reality by an approaching stage tech, talking into a receiver on his shoulder. He was leading the girl off the stage, straight past me, her cheeks red and shiny. 'I love Olly so much,' she was saying, to no one particular, 'I just love him so much . . .'

The MC was thanking Fire&Lights, stoking the hysteria in the auditorium, and after waving to the adoring crowd, the boys filed through an exit on the opposite side of the venue. Tara had suggested I hang out with the band between their sets, so with a final glance across the stage, I slung my camera over my shoulder, tugged my hat over my ears and headed for the dressing room.

Arriving outside the closed door, I reached for the handle and paused, momentarily, at the sound of music coming from inside. A guitar, softly picked, and a single voice.

Olly's.

She is the fire in my fingertips
The warm rain that tells me where the thunder is
And I know that somebody has found her heart—

Click. I opened the door as quietly as I could, but he heard me straightaway, and stopped.

'Sorry, Olly. I-I . . .'

He twisted round on his chair, and his face lit up.

'Oh . . . hey!'

I stepped into the room, and looked around.

'Where are the others?'

'Doing press photos.'

I tilted my head.

'And, what, the press aren't interested in Olly Samson all of a sudden?'

He smiled.

'I finished mine earlier. Thought I'd come back here for some peace and quiet before round two.'

I closed the door behind me.

'Actually, since you're here, mind if I take some pics myself?' I said, unzipping my camera case. 'I've got tons of Aiden and Yuki from tonight, but . . . I mean, I don't want to interrupt.'

Olly beamed at me.

'Not at all. I'll keep playing, if that's OK?'

I glanced at his left hand, his strong fingers curled around the neck of the guitar.

'Go for it.'

Olly picked up where he'd left off and, switching on my camera, I began to roam around the room. I took a whole series of shots, some from behind, capturing the slope of his shoulders, and some from the side, framing the angle of his jaw as he sang. The whole time, at the back of my mind, was the image of him dancing with that girl, the shape of their silhouettes, and the roar from the crowd. The entire spectacle being caught on the big screens.

And I know that somebody has found her heart
But that won't keep us apart

Skirting the space, I rolled off a batch of photos and then sat opposite Olly, on the arm of the sofa, so we were less than a metre apart. I took a few more snaps, stopped and then lowered my camera, just watching him, weighing up the best angle.

She keeps a piece of herself inside
But she speaks, and every single star collides
And I know . . .

Olly stopped playing. He was looking right at me.

'You OK?' he said, his fingers poised on the strings.

'Yep, fine. Why did you stop?'

'You were just . . . looking at me funny,' he said, with a curious expression on his face.

'Oh, no. That's just how I look when I'm figuring out a shot,' I said. There was a short silence, then we both laughed at the same time. Olly cleared his throat.

'Charlie?'

'Uh-huh?'

He turned his plectrum over in his fingers.

'We're cool, aren't we?'

'You and me?' I concentrated on my camera screen, flustered. ''Course.'

With heat blossoming on my cheeks, I opened up the image gallery on my camera. In the last picture I'd taken, Olly was staring straight into the lens, but somehow beyond it, right at me. His eyes were spellbinding.

'That was really sweet, you know,' I said, after a while. 'What you just did onstage.'

'I think she enjoyed herself. I hope so, anyway.'

'Are you kidding?' I replied. 'She looked like she was going to evaporate into thin air.'

Olly laughed.

'I guess it would blow anyone's mind, being up there in front of so many people.'

'I saw you whispering in her ear,' I said, trying to sound casual. 'What did you say?'

Olly placed his plectrum on a nearby table and leaned forward, arm resting on top of his guitar.

'I asked her if she wanted to dance, and she said she was scared. And I said I was scared the first time I got onstage, too; in fact, I still am, every time. But I told her that all she had to do was trust me, and she'd be OK.'

We looked at each other, and his eyes seemed to repeat the words to me. *All you have to do is trust me, and you'll be OK.*

'She was totally mesmerised,' I said, my heart beating faster, my skin prickling. 'It really felt like you were singing right to her.'

Olly's blue eyes sparkled in the light. All I could hear in my head was the girl's voice, repeating over and over: *I love Olly so much . . . I just love him so much.*

Before I knew it, the guitar had slipped from Olly's arms, and he was moving towards me.

And his lips were on mine.

'Yo, Samson, have you seen Charl—'

We broke apart instantly at the sound of the door opening and a voice carrying across the room. Yuki had paused in the doorway, next to Aiden, their faces frozen in surprise. Disoriented, I slid away from Olly, and as I did so, I noticed a third person standing behind them.

It was Gabriel.

18

Time seemed to slow down.

My heart was thudding in my ears, and I felt like I was underwater. The only sound I was aware of was the metallic ringing of the guitar that Olly had dropped on the floor, and nobody said anything, or moved, for several seconds. I wanted to catch Gabriel's eye, but I was afraid. Afraid to find out what he thought of me.

Then, in a split second, the world seemed to rush back in, and Olly was running his hands down his face, breathing hard, and Aiden was pressing his fist to his mouth, and Yuki was staring at me, unblinking. Footsteps echoed in the corridor outside.

As for Gabriel, he was just standing there, looking at Olly. His expression was flat, emotionless. The only tell was his jaw shifting, very slightly, from side to side.

'So, erm . . .' Suddenly, Yuki was talking. 'Hey, what does everyone think about that cow in Japan that can play the trombone?' Silence. 'Anyone? No? Oooookay.'

I stood up, not really knowing why, camera still

hanging round my neck. My head was swimming, and I felt sick. Dizzy, and sick.

'I should go,' I said, half to myself. Gabriel stepped forward.

'Charlie, don't.'

I froze. They were the first words he'd said to me in months.

He pushed a hand through his hair.

'Can I talk to you in private?'

I glanced instinctively at Olly, who was looking red in the face, his shoulders rising and falling. After a pause, he nodded, jaw clenched, and stood up. He walked over to Yuki and Aiden, leaving his guitar on the floor.

'We're on again in fifteen minutes,' he said, in a clipped, business-like voice.

'Uh-huh,' said Gabe, with his back to the rest of the band. Olly looked at me, his brow knitted, then stepped into the doorway.

'See you onstage,' he said to Gabe's back, and with that, the three boys filed silently from the room, closing the door behind them. I waited for their footsteps to fade away down the corridor.

'So,' I began. 'About . . . that.'

Gabriel sighed heavily, and a dark strand of hair broke free in front of his eyes.

'I don't know what it is yet,' I continued.

'Charlie, just listen.'

196

'And to be honest, it's not really anyone else's business.'

'This isn't about him.'

'Of course it is—'

'*Charlie*.'

Gabriel snapped at me, his voice unusually hard. I held my breath, confused, fists clenched at my side.

'Would you just . . .' He took a deep breath. 'Would you just *listen* to me for a second? This isn't about Olly.'

I looked around.

'What?'

He blinked: a long, slow blink.

'I need to talk to you about Little Boy Blue.'

At that moment, the door opened, and Tara poked her head through.

'Gabe.'

'*What?*' he said impatiently, barely turning round.

'We need you backstage in five, OK?'

Gabe was staring right at me, amber eyes burning.

'I'll be there.'

Tara threw me a quick smile, then closed the door. Slowly, I lifted my camera off my neck and lowered it on to a nearby chair, my heart still juddering. I didn't know how to feel. Gabe wasn't laying into me about Olly, and I should have been happy about that. I should have been relieved. But I wasn't.

Why didn't it bother him?

'That photo we found online,' he said, sliding his hands into his back pockets, 'on the music forum . . .'

I rubbed my eyes, trying to push Olly from my mind. For some reason, Gabe was talking about Gemstar's picture. The one taken outside the Troubadour club. The band were all lined up with their instruments, and a clutch of fans – one of them, my mother – were standing and kneeling around them, smiling and laughing.

'Wh . . . what about it?' I asked, my voice barely there.

'The other three guys in Dad's band,' said Gabriel, 'Owen, Kit, Jermaine . . . you remember I said last year that I'd never met them? Well, I was looking at that picture again, and something didn't add up, and . . .' He stopped for a moment. On the other side of the wall, there was a clattering of footsteps, and the sound of someone barking instructions. 'God, how do I put this?' He fixed his gaze on mine. 'OK. Owen, Jermaine, I've no idea who they were. But think about it. What's Kit short for?'

I frowned, and scratched the back of my neck.

'I don't know. Christopher, isn't it?'

Gabriel nodded.

'Sure. But what else?'

I sighed. My brain hurt, and my heart hurt, and I didn't really fancy playing Gabriel's games right now.

'Look, Gabe, I've got no idea what you're getti—'

'*Katherine*,' said Gabriel, stepping backwards, both

hands in his hair. I swallowed hard, feeling my throat close. 'It's short for Katherine.'

As the name, my mother's name, sank into my skin, my entire body bristled. Gabe was still looking at me, his eyes unblinking.

'Our parents, Charlie ... they were in the band *together*.'

19

Behind The Band, Part Seven
'The Seychelles'

The camera sweeps across a remote island setting, an atmospheric club soundtrack pulsing in the background. Blue-green ocean twinkles beside lush forest terrain, while in the middle distance, a luxury mansion overlooks a horseshoe of white-golden sands.

A female voiceover narrates the action.

'It's week nine of Make Or Break, *and we're here in the Seychelles at a top secret studio location with our incredible finalists, where there's been a dramatic turn of events for hotly-tipped four-piece boy band JOYA. This is what members Olly Samson and Jake Woodrow had to say to us yesterday when we asked how things were going . . .'*

'We're so excited,' says Olly, his smile stretching wide across his clean, tanned face. He is sitting next to Jake on a rocky outcrop, overlooking the water. 'It's a dream come true.

To be out here with all these amazing artists, and the judges . . . I just can't get over it.'

He turns to his bandmate, and they grin at each other. Jake is a skinny, handsome sixteen-year-old with trusting eyes and an open, boyish face. His hair is plaited into corn-rows, and he wears a silver pendant around his neck.

'And you two didn't know each other before your audition?' asks the interviewer.

'You wouldn't believe it,' says Jake, his palms upturned. His voice has an unexpectedly soft, high tone to it. 'We've known each other less than two months, but we're tight now. Real tight. It's the music, you know? It changes everything.'

Gradually, the soundtrack shifts and darkens, and the camera cuts to a low-lit room in a plush-looking house. An infinity pool twinkles in the distance, and large white candles flicker in every corner.

The female voiceover returns.

'. . . But the boys had a shock in store for them that evening, when Barry King gathered them together to discuss the future of the band . . .'

'I've brought you here, lads, because I have some news.'

Barry is sitting in a large leather chair, legs crossed, his tanned skin orange in the fluttering candlelight. The four members of JOYA sit opposite him, arms around each other's shoulders.

'I'm afraid it's not good.' He inclines his head to the side. 'At least, not for Jake.'

201

Jake sits up in his chair.

'What?'

'I'm sorry, Jake,' says Barry. 'The band dynamic, it's not working. I'm going to have to let you go.'

Jake looks at Olly, confused and blinking.

'But you can't do that,' says Olly, turning to Barry. 'We're a band.'

'I know it's tough, Olly,' says Barry, pressing the air with his open palm, 'but this is a tough industry. I've been watching you guys, and you're not short of talent, any of you, but the band's missing something. It's missing star quality.'

'We'll try harder,' insists Olly, and Jake nods in agreement, his eyes wide. Next to him, Yuki sinks back into the sofa, and blows out his cheeks. Aiden seems to have frozen in his seat.

'It's out of your hands now,' says Barry, as a woman with a headset appears onscreen, and places a hand on Jake's shoulder. 'Sorry, Jake. You've got tons of potential, but this just isn't your time.'

The woman starts to lead Jake away, towards the exit. Olly clamps his hands on top of his head, his face disbelieving. The voiceover returns.

'Barry had one more surprise in store for the boys that evening, one that would change the course of their lives forever. After a day adjusting to life without Jake, the three remaining members of the band – Olly Samson, Yuki Harrison and Aiden Roberts – were gathered together, just before midnight, to receive some unexpected news . . .'

'Look, I know this has been a hard day for you, lads, but that's about to change.'

Barry is standing with Olly, Yuki and Aiden beside a perfectly still swimming pool. The boys look tired and disheartened, their eyes hooded, shoulders slumped. Barry gestures to a nearby set of double-doors.

'Say hello to your new fourth member.'

The doors swing open, and out walks Gabriel West.

He stops a few metres away from the rest of the band.

'Hi,' he says, with a slight nod. His hands are hidden in his back pockets.

'Gabriel West,' says Yuki, impressed. 'Welcome to the jungle.'

Yuki offers his hand up for a high-five, and with a half-smile, Gabriel obliges. Behind them, Aiden and Olly look shocked.

'We've never done this before,' says Barry, 'but as you know, Gabriel's been making waves in the solo category, and I was re-watching his tapes last night, and it just came to me. He's your answer. He's the fourth member of this band.'

Gabriel's eyes meet Olly's. They both force a smile, then Gabriel looks away.

'I'll leave you guys to get acquainted,' says Barry, 'but before that . . . there's one other thing.' All four of the boys look at him. 'Your name. It's no good. JOYA? Sounds like a charity shop. So Gabriel and I have been talking, and we've come up with something new.' Barry nods at the band's newest recruit. 'Gabe, care to do the honours?'

Gabriel scratches the back of his head, and shrugs.
'What do you guys think of Fire&Lights?'

'So, wait. You're telling me that your mum wasn't a *fan* of Little Boy Blue . . . she was actually *in the band*?'

I nodded solemnly. Melissa blinked back at me.

'Holy hashtags, Charlie. That is AWESOME.' She shook her head, staring out of the window. 'Katherine Bloom was a rockstar.'

I smiled flatly. Melissa was right – it *was* amazing – but inside, something was gnawing at me. Dad must have kept this from me for a reason, and I was beginning to understand what that reason might be.

'I wonder if she had one of those keyboards you wear over your shoulder, like a guitar? They are SO COOL . . .'

Last November, I'd found an unmailed envelope in Dad's study. Inside was a letter he'd written to my mother in America, where I now realised she must have been touring with Little Boy Blue. Dad's words had puzzled me at the time, but since I'd discovered that Mum was in the band, the things he'd written were beginning to sink in. And they wouldn't leave me alone. *We can't go on like this any more . . . I've hardly heard from you in weeks . . . Charlie needs a mother . . . Please come home . . .*

I was proud of Mum for doing what she believed in. I really was. But she'd left me when I was a tiny baby, and my dad had to give up his PhD, and his own ambitions, to look after me.

In a way, she'd abandoned us. Hadn't she?

'This whole thing is bad-ass,' continued Melissa, sipping at her hot chocolate. 'Your mum must have been one epic lady.' She waved a hand in my direction. 'She made you, for a start.'

I picked at a fingernail. The thought was still sitting in my stomach like a ball of barbed wire.

'Yeah . . . I guess.'

'Come to think of it, you should probably feel a bit guilty for assuming she was a groupie.' Melissa pointed at me. 'The sisterhood judges you.' She plucked a mini-marshmallow from her drink, and popped it in her mouth. 'So how did Gabriel figure all this out from one random photograph?'

Pushing my doubts aside, I coaxed my laptop from sleep mode, clicked through to the Real Music Chat forum and brought up Gemstar's photograph.

'See these four guys at the back?'

I indicated, in turn, the four men standing at the back of the picture. On the far right was Harry West, the two in the middle were Owen and Jermaine, and we'd assumed the fourth one, holding the upturned keyboard, was Kit. We'd been wrong.

'What have three of them got in common?' I asked. Melissa peered at the photo, and shrugged.

'Terrible nineties outfits?'

'Well, yes. But look at their wrists.'

I pointed to the screen. Melissa squinted.

'Three of them are wearing red wristbands,' I explained. 'If you zoom in, you can just about read what they say: "Artist Access".'

Melissa looked confused at first, then slowly her face opened.

'But the piano player . . .'

I nodded, scrolling over towards the man holding the keyboard.

'The piano player,' I said, zooming in, 'isn't wearing a red wristband. He's wearing a black one, for crew. Because he isn't actually the piano player.'

Melissa sat back against the wall, her mouth open.

'Because the pianist is actually *your mum*, the ass-kicking rockstar Katherine Bloom. *Man*, that is the coolest.'

I navigated downwards until Mum's left hand came into view.

'There it is, the fourth red wristband.'

Melissa let out a long whistle.

'That is some epic detective work, Charlie. It's like being in an episode of *Scooby Doo*.'

I zoomed out again, pausing over Mum's face. Her big,

chestnut eyes, so much like mine, and her dark, mussed-up hair. Our blue beanie, pulled down over her ears.

'Gabriel is Shaggy,' continued Melissa excitedly. 'You're Velma, and I'm . . .' Her face fell. 'Ah, rats. I'm Scrappy Doo, aren't I?'

'You are,' I said, grabbing her hand. 'But then Scrappy Doo was always my favourite.'

She squeezed my fingers, and sighed.

'So . . . how does Gabriel feel about all this?'

My shoulders dropped.

'I have no idea. After he explained about the wristbands, he had to leave for their second set and I didn't see him again. He hasn't been in touch.' I picked up my phone, ran a finger across the screen, then dropped it again. 'God . . . it's all such a mess. The kiss with Olly, and everyone bursting in . . . I just don't know what'll happen next time I see them.'

The WorldPOP Awards were less than a week away, at the StarBright Arena. It was a huge event, and in theory we could keep our distance if we needed to, but I was their backstage photographer. It was my job to stick close to the band.

I guess, just recently, I'd been getting a little *too* close.

'This probably isn't appropriate right now,' said Melissa, looking up at me from beneath a lowered brow, 'but OH MY STARS, YOU KISSED OLLY SAMSON.'

Despite everything, my face opened into a smile. I crossed my arms.

'Actually, *he* kissed *me*.'

'Whatever.' She put a hand on each of my knees. '*What was it like?*'

A warm, intense feeling rushed over me as I recalled that moment, the moment our lips connected, however briefly, before the rest of the world crashed in.

'Mel, it was unreal. It was *everything*, but . . . argh, I just can't stop thinking about the door opening, and . . . I feel like I'm going to lose Gabriel now, completely. As a friend, or . . . as anything at all.'

'Come on,' said Melissa, pinching my sleeve. 'He said it himself: you guys are connected. That hasn't changed. And hey, at least now you know why there's a photo of you playing together as kids. Your families must have been friends.'

I nodded, lost in my memories of the dressing room. The dulled sound of music coming from the auditorium; Olly's kiss, soft but urgent against my lips; the expression on Gabriel's face when he found us. Steely and emotionless.

'Do you mind if we listen to the album?' I said. 'Little Boy Blue, I mean?'

Melissa smiled.

''Course not, CB. Play that funky music.'

I opened the music library on my laptop and clicked

Play on track four. Soon, a thoughtful, meandering piano riff began filtering through the tinny speakers, the notes twinkling and tumbling like freshwater flowing in a stream. I thought back to our time at Music Madness, when we'd listened to the driving chords that opened the album, and I'd imagined the pianist's hands pounding them out. Little did I know, back then, that the hands I should have been imagining were my mother's.

> *Take me home*
> *I've been dreaming of a girl I know*
> *The sweetest thing, you know she makes me wanna sing*
> *I still remember everything*

As it always did, Harry's voice infected me, right to my bones. He was Gabriel, but rougher round the edges, worn with age.

> *I call her name*
> *I keep her picture in a silver frame*
> *So she will know, just as soon as I come home*
> *That she will never be alone*

As she listened to the song, Melissa's brow was knitted, her eyes darting left to right.

'Maybe I'm being dense here,' she said, 'but . . .'

She tailed off. I nudged her knee with mine.

'What?'

'You told me that Harry wrote all the songs on this album, right?'

'That's what it says in the sleeve.'

Melissa chewed her lip.

'I don't know . . . that made sense when we thought your mum was just a fan, and she was copying out the words to her favourite songs. But now we know she was actually *in* the band?' I nodded. I knew exactly where she was heading. 'Charlie, these lyrics, they're so obviously about you. Just like you said from the beginning.'

The same thing had occurred to me, the night before, as I was falling asleep. It was a comforting thought – if she'd written those words, maybe she really had missed me, and cared about me, after all – but as I'd worked through it all in my head, I'd begun to feel uneasy. Had my mother written songs that Harry had passed off as his own?

'I think you're right,' I said. 'But I have no idea what to do about it.'

'We need the full story, that's what we need,' said Melissa, staring up at the ceiling.

I leaned back against the wall, and ran a hand down my face.

'I've been in touch with the woman who took the photo, but I doubt I'll ever hear from her. And I can't talk to my dad, obviously.'

Melissa went quiet, her eyes narrowed.

'What about your grandma?'

I looked right at her.

'Gran?'

Melissa twisted to face me. 'I know you hardly ever see her, and she sort of blames your dad for your mum's accident, but she's pretty much the only extended family you have. And who knows ... she might tell you things you can't get from your dad.'

I let out a long sigh, tugging my sleeves over my hands and trying to remember the last time I'd seen Gran. She and Grandad had never got over Mum's death, and when Grandad passed away the following year, everyone said it was the stress of losing Mum. So my relationship with Gran had always been a little distant and strained.

I closed my eyes, trying to picture her face, and realised it had been over two years since we were last at her house. 'Do you think she'd even want to see me?'

I opened my eyes again, and Melissa caught my gaze.

'It's got to be worth a try . . . hasn't it?'

20

The following afternoon, I was sitting under a tree on the school playing fields, waiting for Melissa to come out of a Year Eleven council meeting, when Olly texted.

Note to self: if you're in a boy band & you go out for milk in your PJs, someone WILL pap you :)

It was early April, the first properly warm day of the year. Mottled sunlight was dancing across my school skirt, breaking through the swaying branches above. I smiled at my phone.

I saw that. You looked cute.

Cute . . . or dorky?

Hmmm. Bit of both?? ;)

So how you doing? Since Friday, I mean?

My smile dissolved, and I let out a sigh.

> I still feel really weird about it, tbh

> The kiss?

> God, no, not the kiss . . . the kiss was perfect

> I thought so too xx

> But . . . you know

> I know

I plucked a few blades of grass from the ground.

> I just hope it doesn't ruin everything

'Hey, Charlie.'

I stowed my phone in my sleeve sharpish, and looked up to find Jody Baxter's tall, skinny frame standing in front of me, blocking out the sun.

'Oh. Hi, Jody.'

I stood up, leaning backwards into the tree trunk. There was a strange pause, then Jody's eyes suddenly went wide, as if he'd just remembered how to speak.

'So how are you?'

213

I picked at a loose flap of bark on the tree.

'I'm all right, thanks.'

'I, um . . . I wanted to say thanks for taking photos for us last week, at the Black Hat.'

I shrugged. 'That's OK.'

'I didn't know you were coming, actually?'

His voice was a little stiff, as if reciting lines from a play.

'Oh, right. We thought it'd be fun, and I figured I may as well bring my camera, so . . .'

Jody forced out a laugh.

'Can't believe you had to bring your dad.'

I glanced towards the main school buildings. Still no sign of Melissa.

'Yeah. Sorry about that.'

'My mum was, like, if I'm driving you there and picking you up, then I'm staying for the gig. So lame.' He kicked absently at an exposed tree root. 'Why *was* your dad there, by the way?'

The expression on Jody's face seemed painted on. It was like he was doing a bad impression of a confused person.

'He just . . . I mean, my dad thought . . .'

Jody's eyes were locked on mine. He was barely blinking.

I had to be honest with him.

'Look,' I said, keeping my voice low, 'the truth is, I

had to bring my dad with me. I'm . . . I've started taking photos for Fire&Lights again, but there's no way Dad would allow it, so I've told him I'm following you guys round on tour, taking *your* pictures. As a cover story.'

Jody nodded slowly, his mouth open.

'You *have* to keep this a secret,' I said. 'Please.'

'Oh, no, no, course. I won't tell anyone.' He ejected a short, breathy laugh. 'It's pretty cool, though.'

I folded my arms across my chest.

'I s'pose. But my dad can't find out. Seriously.'

'Sure, yeah. Whatever.' Jody went quiet, as if listening to his internal monologue. Then he pointed back over his shoulder. 'You knew Olly was coming to the school the other week, then?'

'No, I had no idea. It was all a big secret.'

'But you are friends with the band, right?'

I held my breath. In the circumstances, it seemed best to play this down.

'Not really. Not . . . *friends*. They're too busy being popstars to worry much about m—'

My phone pinged, and we both heard it. I slid it out from my sleeve, and felt my cheeks burn up.

Olly Samson
If you need to talk, I'm here. Call me any time x

'That's Melissa,' I lied, stepping away from the tree. 'I have to go meet her.'

Jody tugged his jumper down at the sides, and with a twitch of his head, flicked the hair from his eyes.

'Right, cool. That's cool.' He didn't move, so I began to walk past him. 'See you around?'

'Sure,' I said, hurrying away across the sun-speckled grass. I didn't look back, but I could tell, as I walked, that he was watching me.

My encounter with Jody was on my mind hours later, as Melissa and I made our way home from school. The sun was still shining and we had our jumpers tied around our waists. Melissa was eating a green liquorice lace.

'The thing is, Mel, Jody knows I have a secret now. And he was being really weird about it at lunchtime.'

'He *is* a boy, though,' said Melissa, chewing thoughtfully. 'And let's face it, all boys are a bit weird.'

I smiled, but it quickly faded.

'There's just something about him, and I can't put my finger on it. Something off-putting . . .'

A bus trundled by, brakes creaking as it slowed, and I ran through the facts in my mind. My dad knew who Jody was, and Jody knew I was lying to my dad. And from the way he was acting on the playing field, he wasn't planning to let it lie any time soon.

'I do know what you mean,' replied Melissa, as we

passed the corner shop. She glanced inside, but kept on walking. 'Maybe he's a Scientologist, or a fruitarian. Or, ooh . . . maybe he's in one of those weird cults where they dress up like Jedis and chop the heads off swans.'

I peered at her sideways.

'That's not a thing.'

'I'm pretty sure it is a thing.'

We pushed on, past the park and the library, Melissa humming happily to herself. My phone buzzed and I pulled it out, half-expecting a message from Olly.

Did you ask your friend about joining the FireLighters?
D

Duffy. I stopped in the middle of the pavement, one hand on my mouth.

'I completely forgot.'

'Forgot what?' asked Melissa, tugging at her liquorice lace with her teeth, like a puppy chewing on a slipper. I looked at her.

'So . . . you remember I mentioned the FireLighters?'

'The VIP fan club dudes, yep.'

'Well, I meant to tell you . . . they're looking for a third member.'

Melissa's face went blank, then her features began to shift, her mouth fell open and she pointed at her chest.

'Wh . . . wait, that's me! The third member!'

217

I laughed.

'Yeah, that's what I said.'

'You're not telling me . . . I could actually *be a FireLighter*?'

I started walking again, tapping out a reply to Duffy. Melissa followed me, hanging on my every word.

'Duffy's trying to break into journalism,' I explained, 'so she wants to focus on vlogging. Which means Campbell needs an extra pair of hands at events to look after competition winners and stuff.'

Melissa waved her liquorice lace at me.

'Charlie, I was born to do this job.'

I smiled.

'I know.'

She grabbed my shirt sleeve.

'No, I don't think you understand. *This is the reason I'm alive.*'

'That's what I said,' I replied, tugging my arm from her grip. 'Let me just text her back.'

Yep, she's definitely keen :)

'This is unbelievable,' said Melissa, as we approached the corner of our road. 'I'm going to be on Team Fire&Lights. This . . . is . . . EVERYTHING.'

Ping.

Awesome. Shall we do a FaceTime interview tonight? 7pm?

Sounds perfect. I'll ask her.

Then if she's free on Saturday she can maybe come to StarBright?

'They want to meet you tonight, over FaceTime. Seven o'clock.'

'Shut. Up.'

'Then, if it goes well, you can come to the WorldPOP Awards on Saturday.'

Melissa sucked in a sudden gasp of air and, for a moment, I thought she was going to cry. She held her breath for ages, then an avalanche of words tumbled out of her.

'Thank you, Charlie. Thank you thank you thank you—'

'Hey, I didn't really do anything. And they'll love you, I know it.' We stopped at Melissa's gate. 'There is just one thing, though.'

She leaned towards me, desperate for the answer.

'We have to keep this between us,' I said. 'You can't tell anyone, not at school, not your parents.'

Melissa shrugged it off.

'No sweat: I'll just tell the 'rents the same thing you

219

did. I'm "helping out Diamond Storm on tour". I could say I'm selling merch, or something.'

I stared up at Melissa's bedroom window, deep in thought. Having my best friend by my side would be amazing, but it wouldn't be without its risks. In fact, it would basically double my chances of getting found out. Of Dad discovering my lies, and my sneaking around, and my secret prying into Mum's past. And once that secret was out, it could break our little family apart.

'I just hope we don't get busted.'

'Nah,' said Melissa breezily. 'It's foolproof. Two lies are better than one, right? Or something.' Her voice dropped to an excited whisper. 'So . . . where shall we do the interview?'

With a deep, slow breath, and a flexing of my fingers, I pushed all my worries to the back of my mind. As long as we both stuck to our story, we'd be fine.

'I guess your place is safer. You're better at bluffing your parents.'

'I am pretty good at that,' agreed Melissa. She grabbed both my hands. 'This is so, so exciting. You're THE BEST. Come over at six-thirty, OK?'

'Got it.'

She was about to turn away when something over my shoulder caught her eye.

'Hey, whose car is that in your drive?'

I followed Melissa's pointing finger to a blue Volkswagen Polo sitting in our driveway. I'd never seen it before.

'That's . . . weird,' I said distantly.

'Anyway, see you in a few hours,' said Melissa, peeling off down her garden path. She threw her arms in the air. 'You are the light of my life, Charlie Bloom . . .'

Wandering down our driveway past the Polo, I stole a look inside. There were a few toy soldiers on the back seat, and an empty coffee cup in the holder, but nothing to identify the owner. It didn't make sense. Dad was hardly ever home from work early, and even if he was back and had some kind of visitor, where on earth was *his* car?

I slid my key into the lock, but before I could turn it, the door opened of its own accord. My father was standing in the doorway, a cryptic expression on his face. As my eyes adjusted to the light, I realised there was a woman standing behind him.

And that woman was Jody Baxter's mum.

21

Standing on the doorstep, I felt my heart tumble and trip inside me like a frantic hamster on a wheel. This was unbelievable. I *knew* Jody had been acting strange at lunchtime, but I'd never expected this. He had dobbed me in *already*.

And now I had about two-eighths of a second to come up with an excuse.

'Dad, I can explain, the thing is—'

'Let's not be rude, Charlie,' said my father, his face still unreadable.

'What? Sorry, I just mean that—'

'Calm down,' he said, putting on a Laid-back Dad voice that, to be honest, was creeping me out a little bit. 'Why don't you come on in? I'll put the kettle on.'

I walked slowly, as if on the moon, into the hallway. Come on in? Put the kettle on? I felt like my brain was short-circuiting.

'Hi, Charlie,' said Jody's mum, with a little nod.

'This is Christine,' said Dad. 'Christine Baxter. She's—'

'Jody's mum,' I said breathily. 'I . . . I remember.'

222

No one said anything for a while. The air felt itchy.

I decided to take matters into my own hands.

'I know this seems bad, Dad, but, really, it's not what it looks like.'

Dad frowned at me, and Christine struggled to maintain her smile. I was expecting one of them, either of them, to start lambasting me at any moment. But they did nothing.

I remembered the Volkswagen in the driveway.

'Where's your car, Dad?'

'Bit of a nightmare at work,' he said, fiddling with his shirt cuff. 'The office servers went down at lunchtime, so they sent us home for the afternoon. Five minutes later, I'm in the car park and the damn car won't start, and who turns up but Christine!'

Christine gave a little wave, in case I thought Dad was talking about one of the other Christines in the hallway.

'Anyway,' continued Dad, slightly giddy, 'she only works on the floor directly above me! She's been there for years.'

Christine laughed. Dad laughed. I attempted a smile, but it was paper-thin.

'We've used the same photocopier!'

They both laughed again, and I tried to cover a wince.

'I gave your father a lift home,' offered Christine.

'Yes, Christine gave me a lift home, and we had a cup of tea, or three, and . . . uh . . . well, there you go.'

Christine smiled modestly, and I struggled to process

223

the emotions piling up inside my brain. On the one hand, I was relieved. Christine wasn't here because Jody had told her my Fire&Lights secret, and that was definitely a good thing. But something about the way the two of them were acting was making me anxious. Why was she still in the house?

I caught Dad's eye, and motioned towards the kitchen with my head.

'Dad, can we talk in the kitchen for a minute?'

He blinked at me.

'What?'

'Kitchen?' I said, leading the way.

'Do excuse us,' I heard him say to Christine.

'Of course,' she replied.

Once we were in the kitchen, I carefully closed the door and spoke in a whisper.

'What's going on, Dad?'

'Going on?' His brow creased. 'Nothing, we just . . . we got chatting about work, and then you kids, and Christine's divorce and . . . well . . . we've decided to go out. Tonight.'

'What do you mean "out"?'

'You know,' he said, with a tilt of his head. '*Out* out.'

'What is "out out"?' I said, untying my jumper from around my waist. 'Unless . . . you don't mean on a *date*?'

Dad's mouth went small, and he suddenly looked like a little boy.

'I suppose it is a date, yes. Dinner at the Pear Tree.'

I dug my nails into my jumper, my ears burning. Jody's mum was dating my dad? *Jody's mum?* But of course. Because that would make my life so much easier, wouldn't it? It's not like I was keeping a massive secret from him that just happened to involve her son.

And also: she was *dating my dad*.

'But I don't understand, you don't . . .' I was going to say 'you don't date', but then I realised how that might sound. 'What does this mean?'

Dad sighed.

'It doesn't mean anything, Charlie. She's just a nice woman, and I don't often meet nice women, or *any* women, for that matter. We just got talking and . . .'

'The rest is history,' I said, half to myself.

'You don't mind, do you?'

I felt my cheeks redden. I did mind. I hated it. But I also knew that I had no right to feel that way. It had been thirteen years, after all. And from what Rosie had said to me the week before, this had been on the cards for a while.

'Of course not,' I said, trying to sound genuine. 'I . . . think it's a good thing.'

I didn't think he'd ever be over Mum. I'd got so used to him being closed off about her, it had never occurred to me he might open up to someone else.

'I know this must be strange for you, kiddo, but will you make an effort? For me?'

I nodded, resting my hands on the back of a chair,

fingers tightening around the wood. Dad blinked at me, patting his trouser pockets, then opened the kitchen door and walked back into the hallway. Christine gave him a funny little smile.

Turning away, I stared out through the kitchen window and across the garden, chewing on a fingernail. I had to talk to Jody, and I had to do it soon.

I bring good news and bad

It was early evening, and I was sitting in my bedroom, texting Melissa and waiting for Dad and Christine to leave the house. It was childish to be avoiding them on purpose, but the idea of sitting around making polite conversation made me feel a bit queasy.

Melissa's reply lit up my screen.

Bad news??! Have the FireLighters decided not to hire me? WHY GOD WHY?

I smiled, and shook my head.

Chill, you nutcase. The good news is: we can do the interview here cos I have a free house tonight.

Yessssssss!

The bad news is: my dad's going on a date

What??? Ew.

She's here right now

DOUBLE EW

I paused, and took a breath.

It's Jody Baxter's mum

No reply from Melissa. I sat up on my bed and looked out across the driveway into her bedroom, at the ant-farm on her window sill and the Fire&Lights posters on her walls. She was standing in the middle of the room, glaring at her phone, face bathed in bluish light.

Jeepers creepers, she wrote back.

What am I gonna do?

Melissa glanced around, grabbed a jumper from the floor and hit the light switch, plunging the room into darkness.

I'm coming over

A minute later, the doorbell rang.

'Hey, Mr Bloom!'

'Oh, hello. How are you, Melissa?'

'Ruddy bloody good, thanks. You?'

I could hear Dad jingling his keys. 'Actually, we're just on our way out. But Charlie's upstairs.'

Scritch-scratch. Melissa wiped her feet on the mat.

'Hi, Melissa, I'm—'

'Jody Baxter's mum. I know.'

An awkward silence.

'Anyway,' said Dad, clearing his throat. 'We must dash. Off out for, um, a bite to eat. See you later.'

There was some mumbling that I couldn't make out, then I heard Dad and Christine crunching up the driveway. Melissa called to them from the doorstep.

'Have her home by midnight, Mr Bloom, or she might turn into a pumpkin!' She closed the door. 'Oh, no . . . wait. It's the carriage that turns into a pumpkin, isn't it?' She was talking to herself now, walking down the hallway and up the stairs. 'So, hang on, what does Cinderella turn into? A . . . horse? A frog? No . . .'

My door opened.

'Hello,' I said.

'When the clock strikes twelve,' said Melissa, stepping into the room, 'Cinderella turns into . . . what? A mouse? A shoe?'

'Mel, I need help.'

I gestured at my laptop, which was open on Jody Baxter's Facebook page. Melissa sat next to me and examined the screen.

'What are you doing?'

'This is Jody's Facebook page. I'm going to message him and tell him what's going on.'

Melissa shook her head vigorously. She seized the laptop and dragged it across the duvet.

'No. Nooooo, no, no, no. Not Facebook.'

I frowned.

'Why not?'

She shrugged, typing away.

'Between you and me, I think Jody fancies you a bit.'

'Get out.'

'And if you hit him up on Facebook, he'll get all clingy and weird and start making collages of your holiday photos. But if you message him on Twitter, which you basically never use, you can pile in there, do the business and get out before things get icky.'

I rubbed at my temple.

Her argument did make sense.

'Is he even on Twitter, though?'

'I don't know,' said Melissa, holding one finger up in the air, 'but Diamond Storm definitely are. And I'll bet you a sackful of Aiden's hair that Jody does all the tweeting.'

She loaded Twitter, and I watched her type 'diamond storm' into the search box.

'Please tell me you don't have a bag of Aiden's old hair hidden under your bed,' I said. She looked at me.

'Would I be over here if I did? COME ON NOW.' She pointed two fingers at the screen. 'Ah-ha! Here they are.'

Melissa had found the Diamond Storm Twitter feed. They'd used two of my photos from the Black Hat gig for their banner and profile pic, and they actually looked pretty good. Most importantly, they'd tweeted only ten minutes earlier, so there was a decent chance they were still online.

Diamond Storm

@diamondstormband

Brand new indie rock band, straight outta Reading, UK!!!
Tweets by Jody (singer) & sometimes the drummer, when he can be arsed!!!! :-)

'Told ya,' said Melissa. 'Now we just DM the heck out of them, and wait.'

She started to type, and I grabbed her sleeve.

'What are you saying?'

'Just a straightforward opener,' she replied, waving me off. 'There. Done.'

Hurriedly, I read Melissa's message. Fortunately, it was harmless.

Hey, is that Jody, by any chance?? It's Charlie B.

'And now, we wait.'

Melissa sat back against the headboard, fiddling with one of her plaits. I realised she was watching me, and looked up.

'What?' I said.

'Talk to me about your dad dating. I mean, apart from the obvious . . . *grossness* of the whole thing.'

I sucked in a slow breath, one palm splayed across my stomach.

'I feel sick. And guilty. And sad.'

Melissa reached over and took my hand.

'He's not trying to replace her, you know.'

A sudden swell of emotion rushed through my body, almost spilling out as hot tears, but I swallowed it.

'I know.'

She rubbed my finger with her thumb.

'I know it must be horrible, but you want him to be happy, right?' I nodded. 'And no one's ever going to take the place of Katherine Bloom, real-life rockstar. I promise.'

Blip. A new Twitter message. We both turned to the laptop, and Melissa gave a mini-fist pump.

'Yessss. Jackpot.'

Jody had replied.

Charlie, hi!! How's it hangin?! J x :D :D

Already planning my response, I took to the keyboard and the words flew from my fingers.

Not bad, thanks. Although . . . this is a bit weird, not sure
if you know, but . . . our parents are dating

At first, no reply. I tapped impatiently at the edge of the
screen.

Yeah, I heard!! They're having dinner right now.
Weeeeeird!!!

I know I already said this, but we need to be REALLY
careful about this whole F&L thing. Could you just tell
your mum I'm taking photos for you guys? If Dad asks
and she doesn't know, it might look a bit odd

I hit *Send* and waited, my heart thumping. I needed him
to be with me on this.

Actually, I already did. Before she went out. You're safe
:D

Oh my god, thank you!

And she won't be at the gigs either coz Thumper's mate
in yr13 is gunna roadie 4 us:)

Thank you, Jody!! Seriously. I owe you one

He sent a few more smiley faces, and I fell back against the wall, relief washing over me. Melissa held up her hand for a high-five, and I obliged.

'Mission accomplished, CB.'

As I was about to sign off, though, another message arrived.

Actually, there IS something you could do for me ....
Lol.

I winced, and showed Melissa the message. She gawped at me.

'Oh my god, he's going to ask you out.'

I thought for a moment, then wrote back.

Sure, what were you thinking?

Umm, like, could you get us a support slot with
Fire&Lights?? That could totally launch our band!!!
Lmao.

I rubbed my eyes.

'What? He's asking me to get them a support slot with Fire&Lights,' I said, my brow knitted. Melissa sat up.

'What a fruitcake! I mean, they're quite good for a *school* band, but . . .'

'It's fine. I'll just fob him off.'

I'd love to help, I wrote back, but honestly, I have no
sway over anything like that.

Please. Just try. It would mean everything to us ;) !! Are
you seeing them soon?

In three days, to be precise. Problem was, I couldn't get
Diamond Storm a support slot with Fire&Lights any
more than I could get myself one. But he'd backed me
into a corner. I needed Jody, maybe even his entire band,
on my side.

OK, I'll try. But it's a long shot.

AWESOME!! The boys will be proper excited. Catch you
later :D :D

See you soon

I blew an errant lock of hair from my face.

'That's it, then,' I said, shutting the message thread.
'Though he seemed pretty excited about the support slot
thing, which is obviously never going to happen.'

Melissa was filing her nails. She waved the file at me.

'He's seventeen years old. He'll get over it.' She gave
her nails a once-over, then popped the file back into my
pencil cup and clapped her hands together three times.

'Is it time yet? It must be time.'

I checked my phone.

'Six fifty-seven. Let's do this.'

Closing my web browser, I opened FaceTime, found Duffy's number and hit video call. She answered almost straightaway.

'Hiiiiii!' exclaimed Campbell, waving at us. He and Duffy were sitting on adjacent coloured beanbags, in the light of a tall, curvy lamp, in what I assumed was Duffy's bedroom. There was a flat-screen TV bolted to the wall, flanked on either side by posters for cool-sounding movies like *Citizen Kane* and *Fear and Loathing in Las Vegas*. Two hot drinks sat on the table in front of them.

'Hey, guys,' I said.

'Helloooo!' sang Melissa, grinning widely. Duffy shifted on her beanbag, so she was sitting cross-legged, and picked up a notebook from the table.

'I'm Duffy, this is Cam.' Campbell waved again. 'So nice to meet you! Charlie's told us all about you. She said you might be up for joining the team?'

Melissa craned her neck forward.

'Ummm . . . *does a one-legged duck swim in circles?*'

Duffy and Campbell exchanged puzzled looks. I moved closer to the screen.

'She says yes.'

'Sorry, guys,' said Melissa, tugging at her collar. 'I'm just a bit over-excited.'

'Don't worry!' said Cam, picking up his tea and wrapping both hands around it. 'Excited is good.'

Duffy tapped a pen against her notebook.

'So, if it's not too dorky, we thought we'd maybe do a quick interview-thing with you? From what Charlie says, you'll be perfect for the job, but I don't know, it might be more fun this way.'

'Bring it on,' said Melissa, giving her a double thumbs-up. Duffy leaned towards Campbell and whispered in his ear. Campbell thought for a moment, his eyes slightly narrowed, then nodded.

'OK, here goes.' Duffy looked right into the camera, her big, bewitching Disney-eyes sparkling in the lamplight. 'What was Aiden's favourite subject at school?'

'He didn't have one,' Melissa replied, without hesitation. 'He liked English, Music and Drama the same.'

Campbell set down his tea and gave Melissa a miniature round of applause. Duffy smiled, impressed, and crossed the question off her list.

'Where did Gabriel get his tattoo, and what is it?'

'Flamin' Eight, in Camden.' Melissa pointed to her back, just above her hip. 'It's a small black cat, on his lower back.'

'Why a cat?'

Duffy lowered her brow, ever so slightly, as if she knew this would stump Melissa. Campbell shook his head.

'It's OK,' he said. 'Hardly *anyone* knows this one.'

'It's a song reference,' said Melissa calmly. 'But he's never said which song.'

The FireLighters looked at each other, eyebrows raised, apparently already sold on Melissa's credentials. Meanwhile, I felt my pulse begin to race. Melissa had told me about Gabriel's tattoo earlier in the year, and though she'd never reveal it to the FireLighters, we were pretty certain which song it was. It had to be 'Cat's in the Cradle'.

'OK, this is a *really* tricky one,' said Campbell, pressing his hands together. 'Where did Olly's mum go to university?'

Melissa barely flinched.

'Technically, it wasn't university. It was drama school. She trained as an actor in London, but it didn't work out. That's why they moved to Reading.'

Duffy put down her notebook and pen and sank back into her beanbag.

'I've got a feeling we could do this all night and never catch you out.'

Melissa beamed.

'In that case . . .' Campbell looked at Duffy, then back at us. 'Melissa . . . I'd say you're in, if you want it?'

Melissa's eyes widened.

'Well, butter my face and call me a crumpet.'

There was a short pause, and then we all burst out laughing.

'I take it that's a yes?' said Duffy, picking up her tea.

Melissa nodded, eagerly. 'A thousand times, yes.'

'Yay!' Campbell bounced a little on his beanbag. 'We are going to have so much fun this weekend.'

'Actually,' said Duffy, 'speaking of the weekend, we've got some pretty exciting news about Saturday. The boys thought it would be cool for the fans to get a better look at where they live, and for me to vlog about it, so before we leave for the awards ceremony . . . we're all going to meet them at the Fire&Lights house.'

Melissa dropped her head into her hands, breathed deeply, and then slowly rose up again as if emerging from prayer.

'Thank you for coming into my life.'

'The house is epic,' said Campbell. 'Have you seen any of their pics on Instagram?'

'Hell, yes,' replied Melissa, her arms outstretched. 'It's RIDIC. They live next door to Barry King, in Maida Vale.'

Duffy shook her hair from her eyes.

'Wow. You really do know everything.'

Melissa shrugged happily, and Campbell let out a contented sigh. He linked his arm around Duffy's.

'We are going to make an *amazing* team . . .'

22

Maida Vale was an extremely fancy part of London. Walking the wide, leafy streets, you could almost smell the money in the air: the roads were immaculate, the trees were lush and tidy and the people passing by all had glowing skin and stylish, expensive-looking clothes. The gigantic houses were mostly set back from the road, separated from the pavement by wrought-iron gates, their spacious driveways dotted with luxury cars.

As we arrived outside the Fire&Lights mansion, we caught the attention of a gaggle of die-hard fans, camped out across the street. They whispered and pointed, and starting snapping us on their phones. I quickly turned away.

'Looking forward to seeing inside?'

Tara, who had met us at the tube station and walked us over, pressed the buzzer on the gatepost and waited for a response. We all watched ourselves on the little video screen beneath it, throwing nervous, excitable glances at each other. Above our heads, security cameras recorded our every move.

'Best day ever,' said Campbell, jiggling on the spot.

'Totally,' agreed Duffy.

The gates opened in front of us and Tara led the way across the gravel drive to the big, black front door. We ascended the steps and, as we stood on the doorstep waiting to be let in, Melissa chatted away to herself.

'This is unbeLIEVable. Are we really going inside? I must be dreaming.' She turned to me. 'Charlie, punch me.'

I smiled at her.

'I think you mean "pinch me".'

'Normally, yeah, but this is a big one. You're going to have to punch me.'

The door opened, slowly and majestically, to reveal Yuki Harrison, standing in the magnificent entrance hall, dressed in a purple smoking jacket and holding a snooker cue. He grinned like the Cheshire Cat.

'Welcome to my humble abode.'

Tara stepped into the building and, gingerly, we all followed her in. The grand, gleaming hall was nearly the size of my entire house, and was decorated with curvy sculptures, a stack of vintage guitar amplifiers and a twinkling chandelier. The white walls bore a series of huge album cover prints – The Beatles, Fleetwood Mac, Kings Of Leon – and speakers in the ceiling filled the air with folky acoustic tunes.

We gathered in a cautious semi-circle around Yuki.

240

'FireLighters!' he exclaimed. 'You're looking well. And Melissa: tip-top to see you again.'

'I . . . bfah . . . dji . . .' Melissa shook her head, like a small dog. 'Sorry, I've forgotten how to speak.'

Yuki hooked his arm through hers.

'Don't worry, no one talks sense around here anyway.' He gestured towards the staircase. 'So what d'you fancy seeing first? Pool room? Swimming pool? Ball pool? It's mainly pools.'

'Wait,' said Melissa. 'You *actually* have a ball pool?'

'Hell, yeah.'

Tara rolled her eyes, and shook her head.

'Installed it last week,' continued Yuki, with a sniff. 'I asked Barry, and he said, "Are you five years old?" and I said, "Yes, Barry, as a matter of fact, I am. And I demand a ball pool." And because I am the boss of him, I got one. Milkshake?'

Melissa swallowed, and tried to catch her breath.

'Wh . . . a milkshake? You mean, right now?'

'Sure. We have a Milkshake Butler, so your wish is his command.' He leaned towards her, their arms still entwined. 'I mean, *technically* he's the head chef, but I call him the Milkshake Butler and no one's stopped me yet.'

'Yes, please,' said Melissa, shell-shocked. I'd forgotten how adorable she was around the Fire&Lights boys.

'I can recommend the Peanut Butter & Cookie Dough,'

said Yuki, making a little circle with his thumb and forefinger. 'It'll melt your freaking face off.'

'Right, I'm off next-door to see Barry.' Tara tapped a finger against her clipboard, and raised her eyebrows at Yuki. 'Yuks, you can look after the guys until we leave, right?'

'Roger that, skipper.'

'See you in twenty.'

Tara strode out of the door, disappearing down the front steps into the fading light. Yuki closed the door behind her, then spun round on his heel.

'Time for the tour! We'll do milkshakes in the interval.'

Campbell let out a little squeak, and beamed at Melissa. Duffy brushed her bright-red hair away from her face.

'Where are the others?' she asked. Yuki puffed out his cheeks.

'Aiden's in the salon, having his hair quiffed. Olly's in his bedroom, serenading himself, and Gabriel's . . . erm . . . who knows? Moping around somewhere.' He propped his snooker cue against the amplifier stack. 'Come on, kids. Let's start in the basement.'

Yuki led us all down the richly-carpeted staircase, and as we neared the basement, the temperature rose dramatically. Seconds later, we emerged into the long, luxurious pool room, and I let out a little gasp.

'Wowsers trousers,' said Melissa, her eyes running the

full-length of the tranquil, low-lit space. The walls were checkered white and grey, subtle uplighters were dotted every few metres and thick, red-brown wooden beams stretched across the ceiling. There was a jacuzzi at the far end of the pool, and beyond, glass doors led to a steam room on one side and a sauna on the other. In front of us, the water in the pool was perfectly undisturbed, like a sheet of blue glass.

Yuki stretched out his arms.

'Yep, this is where I do most of my lane work, and my meditation. Bikram Yoga on Mondays, Tai Chi on Fridays. Also, it's *superb* for bombing.'

'Hey, everyone.'

We all turned to find Olly standing behind us, dressed in black jeans and his sky-blue, V-neck T-shirt, the one that matched his eyes. He threw the briefest of looks at me, and I felt my heartbeat skip.

'Olly!' said Campbell, running a hand across his hair, flattening it. 'How's it going?'

'Not bad,' replied Olly, with a smile. 'I see Yuki's giving you the grand tour. Though don't let him trap you in the movie room, or he *will* make you watch *Sharknado*.'

'Hey!' said Yuki, pointing at his bandmate. '*Sharknado* is a modern classic.'

Olly nodded at me.

'Can I borrow Charlie for a sec?'

Something fluttered in my chest, and my face began to colour. Hastily, I looked at the floor, keen to disguise it. Campell and Duffy had no idea about me and Olly, and I wanted it to stay that way.

'Fine,' said Yuki, with a shrug. 'But I'm afraid she *will* miss the Space Invaders tournament.'

'Another time,' I said, smiling at him. I gave Melissa a little wave, and then Olly and I wandered back towards the staircase together. Yuki was still talking as we climbed the bottom step.

'Follow me, dudes. You're gonna lose it when you see the underwater bar . . .'

I followed Olly back to the entrance hall and up a second flight of stairs, heading for the upper floors. We stepped on to a long, spacious landing and I looked both ways, counting at least six rooms leading off it.

'This is me,' said Olly, opening the nearest door. Inside was a cosy-looking, blue-walled bedroom, and as I walked across the threshold, I caught Olly's scent in the air, sweet and spicy, like ginger and cinnamon. The room was tidy but welcoming, the bed neatly-made, an angle-poise lamp shedding a circle of light across the desk. Rows of books lined the walls.

The Fire&Lights house was truly extraordinary. It had to be worth tens of millions of pounds, and I'd never seen anything like it before. But looking around, Olly's bedroom was reassuringly ordinary. Clothes hanging on the back of his chair, photographs of family and friends pinned to a corkboard. A well-thumbed copy of *Paper Towns* on his bedside table.

'I can't believe it,' he said, swinging his arms.

'What?'

'Charlie Bloom's in my bedroom.'

We locked eyes for a moment, and both started to laugh.

'Smooth,' I said, lowering my camera case on to the soft carpet. I glanced back out of the open door. 'So, your place is all right, then. Bit pokey, obviously.'

Olly smiled.

'We like it. Although living with your bandmates can be . . . interesting.'

'I can imagine.'

He leaned against the chair.

'Sometimes we have slumber parties, though, and that's cool. We watch *Mean Girls* and have pillow fights and bitch about boys. The usual.'

I laughed, and my eyes fell into his. It was comforting to be there with Olly, in his own private space, but some distant emotion was stirring in my gut.

'Olly?'

'Uh-huh?'

I thought of Gabriel, sitting somewhere in the house, maybe above us, maybe below. The indecipherable look in his eyes when he'd walked in on us at the London Complex. The slight shifting of his jaw.

'I'm a bit worried about tonight.'

Olly frowned.

'Why?'

'After last Friday, I just . . .' I glanced nervously towards the open door. Olly nudged it closed. 'I mean, how do we act around each other? Are we . . . different now?'

He moved closer, and took my hand. His skin felt soft and warm against mine.

'We're exactly who we've always been. Olly and Charlie.'

'It's just . . . Gabriel—'

'You don't answer to Gabriel. He can look after himself.'

I stared at the floor. I knew Olly didn't like it when I brought up Gabe, but we had to deal with it some time. The situation wasn't going away.

'I know, but . . . god, I just don't want to be "the girl who came between Fire&Lights". I don't want to be that person.'

Olly smiled, shaking his head.

'What? What are you smiling at?' I said.

'You don't get it, do you?'

'Get what?'

He took my other hand and ran his thumb across the back of it, firing little shivers up my arm, like tiny silent fireworks.

'Charlie, you're the *opposite* of that. You're like a glue for this band. We need you.' He stared at the wall for a moment, then returned his gaze to me. 'People don't realise this, but it can be lonely being a celebrity. When everyone knows who you are, sometimes it can feel like no one really *knows* you at all. But since you and I have been . . . well, whatever we are now, I don't feel that any more. I feel grounded. I feel . . . safe.'

He bowed his head slowly, until our foreheads were touching, and in my ears, I could hear my heart beating. The roar of silence. Then he touched two fingers to my chin, gently lifting it, and pressed his lips against mine. One of his hands uncoupled from my own and moved around my waist, settling into the small of my back, and I fell into him, running a hand around the back of his head, my fingers in his hair. I was floating, drifting, my vision splintering into light, my body weightless. I was falling.

'Um, guys . . . ?'

With a jolt, we broke apart. It was Yuki's voice, coming from a room across the hall. I touched two fingers to my lips, my head still swimming.

'Guys? I think you should come and see this.'

Olly crossed to the door and opened it again, just a centimetre or two.

'See what?'

A pause.

'Just get in here. Right now.'

247

Olly looked back at me, laughed softly, and gestured into the hallway. As I walked past him, our hands brushed, and I felt my lungs fill with air.

'Third door on the right,' said Olly, from behind.

Walking into the room, I found myself in some kind of chill-out area, complete with beanbags, pinball machines, a jukebox and a plasma screen bolted to the wall. Everyone was standing beneath the television, necks craned upwards: Yuki, Melissa, Duffy, Campbell and Aiden too, who gave me a half-smile as we walked through the door. The only person missing was Gabriel.

'So, as we were saying just before the break: big, big news today about boy band superstar Gabriel West. And the news isn't good.'

Onscreen, a peroxide-blond woman and an off-puttingly orange man were sitting together at a desk, beneath a photograph of Gabriel in an airport terminal, wearing dark glasses. I recognised this straightaway as a *Pop Gossip* 'news' report, much like the one about Gabe and Tammie Austin that Melissa had played me back in December. It seemed *Pop Gossip* were particularly big fans of Gabriel. Or, at least, fans of the ratings he brought to their channel.

'Gabe? Gabe, get in here.'

Yuki was shouting across the hallway again. A door opened in the distance.

'What is it?' Gabe's voice.

'I don't know yet, but you need to see this.'

'A mysterious video has surfaced on YouTube,' continued the blond woman on the television, in a sugary American accent, 'that suggests the eighteen-year-old heart-throb may be hiding *quite* a few skeletons in his no-doubt-very-expensive closet . . .'

At that moment, Gabe wandered in, his feet bare, his hair dishevelled. He was in the middle of putting on a dinner jacket over a white shirt, but when he saw the screen, he froze, one arm still caught inside the sleeve.

'The video is called "Gabriel West: Popstar or Petty Criminal?",' added the orange-faced presenter. 'And it appears to have been shot actually *inside* a correction facility, by an inmate. Crazy stuff.'

The woman clasped her hands together.

'So, let's give it a look . . .'

We all watched silently as a video began to play. It was grainy and shaky and looked like it had been filmed on a phone, inside a prison cell, just as the reporter had suggested. A teenager, about Gabriel's age, was talking to camera.

'Check me out, I'm famous!'

The boy laughed at himself, lifting his fists like a boxer. Someone spoke up from behind the camera.

'Tell 'em, Desi. About the big man.'

Desi sniffed, bobbing his head.

249

'Oh, yeah. So, yeah, I knew Gabe West. He was with the Wembley lot, we chilled sometimes.'

In the room, an icy tension crackled. No one dared look at Gabriel.

'We'd knock about and smash up stuff, scare people and that. Rob a few shops. Gabe didn't talk much, so we didn't know where he came from or nothing. He was just some kid.'

At this point, he leaned towards the camera, and prodded the screen.

'Only difference between me and Gabe is: they caught me. Just 'cos he's a millionaire now, don't make him any different. He's still one of us. I mean, good luck to him, he made it out. Fair play. But he's crooked, yeah? Always will be.'

Desi glared into the lens, chewing his tongue, as if squaring up to Gabriel. Then he turned away, muttering something under his breath.

'Hey, Desi. Desi.' The voice behind the camera again. 'You got a message for Gabe?'

'Oh, right. Yeah. Gabe?' Desi lifted both arms and pointed towards the camera. 'Your songs are dodgy as, mate.'

Laughing, Desi tried to bat the phone away, and the video ended on a freeze-frame of his snarling face. The feed cut straight back to the *Pop Gossip* studio, but Yuki lifted the remote control and muted the sound. A thick silence settled over us, like a cloak.

'We should get going,' said Gabriel finally, turning away from the screen. Yuki walked over to him, and laid a hand on his shoulder.

'Dude, what about the video?'

'What about it?' said Gabe, shaking him off. Yuki swallowed.

'Well . . . is it true?'

For the first time since entering the room, Gabriel glanced around, taking in the seven pairs of eyes trained on him. A look flashed across his face; he was suddenly exposed, vulnerable. Stripped of his popstar armour. It was exactly the way he had looked when he'd told me about his father's suicide.

'We'll be late,' he said, tugging his cuffs from his sleeves.

And he walked out of the door.

23

'. . . Guys, you join me outside the StarBright Arena on a crisp April evening for one of *the* most star-studded nights in the British music calendar: the WorldPOP Awards! And the celebs are already swarming the red carpet . . .'

Melissa, Duffy, Campbell and I were being led alongside a chain-link fence by Tara and two security guards, heading for the arena's back entrance. On the other side, a noisy crowd of fans and journalists was gathered on the fringes of the red carpet, shouting for the attention of the passing guests. An enthusiastic reporter was clutching a big, square microphone and talking to camera.

'Predictably, tonight is looking peachy for gorgeous pop idols Fire&Lights, who are up for *three* separate awards: Best Band, Best Album and Best Music Video. Their nearest contender, Kaitlyn Jones, is vying for Best Solo Artist and Best Album . . . but could this, I wonder, cause any awkwardness between Kaitlyn and her *brand-new boyfriend*, Aiden Roberts? I guess we'll find out later . . .'

Melissa nudged me with her elbow, and pointed. A band called Nine Miles West was striding past the reporter, waving at the assembled crowd. The dashing, diving spotlights glinted off their sunglasses, and all around, paparazzi jostled and yelled for their attention.

'. . . And while we're talking Fire&Lights,' continued the reporter, 'how will Gabriel respond to the disturbing "prison video" leaked on the web this afternoon? He's always been cagey about his past, and maybe now we know why.' She adopted a serious face. 'In short, you have to wonder: what do we actually *know* about Britain's most talked-about popstar . . . ?'

The cameraman pointed over the reporter's shoulder, and she swivelled to find Fire&Lights stepping out of their limousine and on to the red carpet. Yuki first, then Olly, Aiden and, at the back, Gabriel, all four of them dressed in tuxedos. As the fans and journalists noticed their arrival, they surged towards them like iron filings towards a magnet, and the noise doubled in volume.

'Here they are,' said the reporter, raising her voice above the hubbub. 'Let's see if we can snatch a minute with Gabriel West.'

She weaved through the crowd, carving a path to the red carpet. Raising a hand, she called for Gabriel's attention. 'Gabe! Gabriel!' Her cries, though, were swallowed by competing voices.

'Gabe! Tell us about Clara.'

'Olly, over here!'

'Yeah, Gabe. Clara Fitzcharles. You guys've been together for two months now! What's the goss?'

'Aiden, where's Kaitlyn?'

'Yuki! Yuk!'

'Talk to us about the video, Gabe. The fans want to know . . .'

The reporter with the square microphone was still trying her luck with Gabriel, but he was too far away to notice. Changing tactics, she reached out a hand, clicking her fingers, and managed to hook Yuki as he was walking past.

Something about the looseness in Yuki's shoulders told me he'd had a drink on the journey over.

'What do *you* think about the leaked video, Yuki?' she said, thrusting the microphone towards him. He lifted his sunglasses.

'It was OK, but to be honest, I prefer Desi's earlier work.'

The reporter tilted her head.

'Come on. This is a *huge* revelation, and who knows what other secrets Gabe's hiding? Will it cause tensions in the band?'

'We're a happy family,' said Yuki, as Olly arrived behind him, touching a hand to his shoulder. 'Don't you worry about us, lady.'

I felt a broad palm on my back, and realised that the Fire&Lights security team was ushering us away, towards the doors. More guards were stationed on either side of the back entrance, and there was a brief pause while our names were checked off on a tablet. Then, walking in pairs, we passed into the cavernous building, the commotion from the red carpet soon replaced by the sound of our footsteps on the concrete floor. Melissa glanced at me, excited, her eyes glinting in the dark.

Flanked by security, we were funnelled down corridors, through back-rooms and across starkly-lit hallways. After a few minutes, we reached a bustling open space, wide and low-ceilinged, with catering tables lining the walls and staff pacing every which way. People wearing headsets shouted instructions, steam rose from tea and coffee urns and static hummed from walkie-talkies.

The band's security guards gave us a nod, then peeled away.

'OK,' said Duffy, turning to Campbell and Melissa. 'This is it. The VIP fans are arriving in ten minutes, so I need you guys to head in that direction' – she pointed towards a nearby door, signposted to the main entrance – 'and I'll meet you backstage in half an hour.' They both nodded. 'Mel, you ready for this?'

'Born ready,' she said, clenching her fists. 'Bowl of Ready Brek. Call me Ready Eddie. Sorry, I'm babbling.'

Duffy smiled.

'You'll be fine. Now, I've managed to wangle a meeting

with a journalist, so I need to head out for a bit, but I'll see you in thirty. Have fun, everyone!'

With that, she strode away in the direction of a nearby exit, eyes glued to her phone, texting. Melissa turned to me.

'I don't think I'll see much of you tonight, CB.'

'That's cool.' I smiled. 'You have a job to do.'

Campbell sucked in a deep breath.

'Right, partner,' he said to Melissa, smoothing his hair at the back. 'Let's do this. See you in a bit, Charlie.'

He gave me a little wave, then the two of them headed off together, chattering excitedly. Left alone, I unzipped my camera case and pulled out my Canon.

'. . . All I'm saying, Gabe, is give me a chance.'

I turned my head cautiously to find Olly and Gabriel standing at one of the catering tables. Gabriel was picking at the fruit bowl. Olly looked a little red in the face.

'Barry won't listen to me,' continued Olly, 'but he will listen to you.'

Gabe bit into a strawberry, chewed for a while, then swallowed.

'I don't make the decisions, you know.' He finished the strawberry and reached for a can of Coke. 'I just write lyrics, and sometimes they get used.'

'I'm not asking for much. I just want a chance to be part of it.'

Gabriel yanked the ring pull off his drink, and it

opened with a crunchy fizz. He took several long gulps, and wiped his mouth with the back of his hand.

'Talk to Barry, that's all I can say. I don't understand the guy any better than you do.'

'That's not true, and you know it.'

Gabriel's brow furrowed.

'What the hell are you talking about?'

Olly glanced into a far corner of the room, where Barry King was issuing instructions to Tara and Sian. Then he picked up a bottle of water from the table, and lowered his voice.

'Ever since *Make Or Break*, you two have been in this weird little club, and we don't get to be a part of it.'

Gabriel let out a short, breathy laugh.

'Mate, you're starting to sound paranoid.'

'I'm not paranoid.'

'You act like I'm trying to push you out of the band or something. Like it's my fault Barry doesn't want your songs.'

'Doesn't *want* my songs?' choked Olly. 'He's never even listened to them.'

'Hey, guys.'

While they were talking, I had walked over to the table, camera cradled in my hands. I'd decided it was time to confront Gabriel head on.

'Oh . . . hi, Charlie,' said Olly, rubbing his neck. Gabriel took another sip of his drink, avoiding my eyes.

So here we were, finally. The three of us. As Olly and I exchanged cagey glances, my fingers worried at the dial on my camera, and I thought about what he had told me earlier that day, in his bedroom in Maida Vale. *We're exactly who we've always been. Olly and Charlie.*

I felt like my skin was shrinking on my body.

'So . . . where's everyone going to be for the next hour or so?' I said, lifting my camera. 'I don't want to miss the backstage action.'

Olly's eyes flickered towards Gabriel, then to me.

'Um, Aiden's off somewhere with Kaitlyn, I think. And Yuki . . . I don't know. He's probably at the bar.'

Gabriel set his can on the table and, as he looked up, I caught his eye, for just a second, before he broke away.

'I need a proper drink,' he said, more to Olly than me. 'I'll see you onstage.'

A sudden surge of courage fired up through my body, from the soles of my feet, and I felt the words shooting out of my mouth.

'You don't have to leave because of me.'

Gabriel froze, surprised. He very nearly looked me in the eye.

'Yeah,' he said, his fingers twitching. 'I think I do.'

Before I could reply, he was walking away, hands buried in his pockets. Olly watched him go, sighing long and low.

'Man. It's going to be a long night.'

He lifted his water bottle to his lips, and I dropped my camera back into its case, zipping it up.

'I'm going after him,' I said. Olly lowered his bottle.

'You don't have to do that.'

'I do. I've had enough of this.' I watched Gabriel pass through a set of double-doors on the opposite side of the room. 'The way he was just talking to you . . . and he barely even looks me in the eye. We can't go on this way.'

Olly almost fought me, but I could tell, from the way his shoulders dropped, that he agreed with me.

'Yeah . . . I guess you're right.'

I scanned the space quickly, to make sure no one was looking, then gave him a peck on the cheek.

'What have I done to deserve that?' he asked, with a half-smile.

'Everything,' I said, with a shrug. 'See you in a bit.'

Walking behind Gabriel, I kept my distance, hoping to bide my time and catch him somewhere secluded. Somewhere we could talk. I followed him along corridors, up staircases and down narrow hallways until, eventually, we emerged into the main arena, and I stopped dead in my tracks.

The StarBright Arena looked incredible.

In the centre of the huge space was a massive circular stage, surrounded by thick, twinkling clusters of coloured lights, hanging down like vines off a tree. The rest of the space was filled with glittering tables, adorned with candles, miniature ice sculptures and golden champagne bottles. Important-looking people sat in the chairs, their elbows on the tables, knocking back drinks and laughing uproariously. Music blasted from speakers high above our heads.

For a moment, my concentration lapsed and I almost lost Gabriel, but I soon spotted him powering ahead of me, snaking through the jungle of tables and dodging between waiters carrying trays of champagne flutes. I pushed on, feeling like an intruder among all the beautifully-dressed guests, keeping my head down as I narrowed the gap between us.

Finally, I caught up with Gabriel, and in desperation, grabbed him by the arm and pulled him through a gap between two ice sculptures. There were six in total, arranged in a semi-circle, and they acted as an effective barrier between us and the rest of the arena.

'What the—?' He stepped backwards, one hand in his hair. 'Charlie?'

I caught my breath.

'We need to talk.'

Finally, with nowhere else left to look, his eyes settled on mine. They seemed to soften, almost, before he turned away again. His chest rose and fell with his breathing.

'Were you following me?' he said. I took a deep breath.

'We can't go on this way.'

Gabriel gestured into the arena.

'What, with you following me, you mean?'

'No, Gabe, with you treating me like I'm invisible. I know you've moved on, but I'm still here, I still exist.' I stepped towards him. 'What is with you lately?'

Gabriel's mouth was pinched, and he was breathing heavily, through his nose. He closed his eyes, summoning a reply, but just as he was about to speak, a familiar voice called out from beyond the sculptures. We turned to see a wiggly shape darting along behind the dripping blocks of ice, and moments later, Yuki emerged from between a swan and a harp-strumming cherub. His face opened up when he saw us.

'Charlie, Gabe! I knew it. My all-time favourite will-they-won't-they twosome.' He eyed us suspiciously. 'Westie, you look seriously gloomy, bud. What's going on in here?'

Gabriel pressed a thumb into his palm.

'Yuks, we're kinda busy—'

'Charlie B!' interrupted Yuki, pointing at me. 'What have you been saying to the poor guy? You've bummed him out.' He looked at me more closely. 'Did you tell him you don't like his hair? Because he's real sensitive about that.'

I crossed my arms, and cleared my throat.

'We were just ... you know. Taking a break from the madness.'

'Nonsense!' said Yuki, grabbing us both by the hand. 'Tonight is all *about* madness. It's a P-A-R-T-Y-U-K-I.' He arched a single eyebrow. 'OK, that made no sense. But what the heck, I'm buying you both a drink.' He dragged us out past the ice sculptures and into the path of an oncoming waiter. 'And when I say "buy you a drink", I mean "hand you a free one".' He swiped four glasses of champagne, passed one to each of us, and kept hold of two for himself. 'But it's the thought that counts, right? VIP bar?'

Before we could protest any further, Yuki was leading us through the arena, waving hello to random guests as we walked. All around, cameras flashed, glasses clinked and people talked in loud voices about record sales and the quality of the table wine. I quietly discarded my drink on an empty tray.

After a few minutes, we arrived at the VIP bar, and Yuki tipped his champagne flutes at the security guard, who unclipped a silver rope to let us in. The bar, which was pill-shaped and glowing with purple neon, had been built into the tiered seating high above the action, and provided a spectacular view of the arena. Discarding his empty glasses on the counter, Yuki held up a finger, and within seconds a tray of cold beers had been delivered to him. He took two in each hand, and offered them to us.

'Charlie, can I tempt you to – *oof!*'

Beer splattered our clothes as three punks crashed

simultaneously into Yuki, nearly toppling him over. Gabriel and I stepped out of the way, brushing the liquid from our arms and chests, and watched as Yuki emerged from the scrum, handing out beers.

'Sorry, dudes. These guys can get a bit . . . over-excited.'

The punks were dressed in ripped jeans, Doc Martens and one of them had a pink mohican. Another had a row of chunky eyebrow piercings. I would have put money on this being Scorched Earth, the band Yuki had met on tour.

'Bloody hell,' said the third, a wild-eyed skinhead with anaconda tattoos creeping up both arms. 'It's Gabriel West.'

'Hi,' said Gabriel, keeping his eyes low. Yuki spread his arms wide.

'These are my boys: Ratty, Grimes and BossEye.' He clocked the look on my face. 'I realise those may sound like made-up names, but that's because they are.'

The pink-haired one thumped him on the arm.

'So how come we didn't get to meet you in Japan, Gabriel West?' said the skinhead, swigging his drink. 'You too famous to hang out with us?'

Gabriel shook his head patiently.

'No, I'm not. I was just . . . I had a lot going on out there.'

'Like what? Signing little girls' pencil cases?'

His tone was teasing, but there was a trace of malice in his eyes. Gabriel held his gaze.

'Something like that, yeah.'

'And who's this little hottie?' said the one with the pink hair. I realised he was referring to me, and fixed him with a death-stare.

'I'm Charlie. I take photos for the band.'

'Well, Charlie Who Takes Photos For The Band, pleasure to meet you. I'm Ratty.'

Ratty had a tattoo of a naked woman on his neck. His jugular vein was pulsating beneath her belly, so it almost looked like she was breathing. My stomach turned.

'Why do they call you Ratty?' I said.

'Wouldn't you like to know?'

'That's why I asked,' I replied drily. Ratty rubbed at the back of his head.

'Well, yeah. It's because, uh, because I freak some people out, I guess.'

'Oh. Not because you carry the plague, then?'

Ratty's face fell, and his bandmates jeered at him. He sniffed, and rolled back his shoulders.

'So, uh, listen, Charlie Who Takes Photos. Do you drink . . . *absinthe*?'

The bandmate with the eyebrow piercings produced a bottle of bright green alcohol from behind his back, and passed it to Ratty. I'd never drunk absinthe before, but I'd heard how strong it was.

'No, I don't. But thanks.'

'You're missing out,' he said, turning to Gabriel. 'Gabriel West must drink absinthe. You're an *artiste*, right?'

Gabriel coughed into his fist.

'I'm good, thanks.'

'One shot, mate. Come on.' Ratty's features hardened. 'Surely your minders will let you have one itty-bitty shot.'

At first, I thought Gabriel was going to let this go. But then I saw his muscles tighten.

'I'm onstage in half an hour, so no.' He leaned towards Ratty. 'Mate.'

Ratty's eyes flashed in the dark.

'I get it. You're a teeny bopper. You can't take your drink.'

Gabriel's breathing quickened.

'What exactly is your problem?'

'I just want to have a drink with the all-powerful Gabriel,' said Ratty, holding the absinthe aloft. 'Just a quiet drink between two lads. But turns out . . .' He unscrewed the lid of the bottle. 'Turns out he's a pussy.'

There was a pause, then Gabriel went for him. In less than a second, he had Ratty up against the bar by the collar of his T-shirt, liquid sloshing from the bottle. People were beginning to stare.

I ran forward and pulled them apart.

'What the hell are you two doing?' I hissed. 'There's paparazzi everywhere.'

Ratty smoothed down his vest top.

'So? This'll be gold in the tabloids.'

'For you, maybe,' I said, glancing at Gabriel. He hadn't taken his eyes off Ratty, who was now flanked by the rest of his band, bristling like a pack of wolves.

If I knew one thing, it was that I had to get Gabriel out of there before somebody got hurt.

'What is Yuki doing hanging out with those morons?'

Gabriel was pacing the rich, red carpet of the Fire&Lights dressing room, flexing his hands. Behind him, four bottles of chilled champagne sat in glistening ice buckets, one for each band member. Through the walls, muffled merriment throbbed in the main arena.

'What are *you* doing starting a fight in a room full of journalists?' I said, dropping on to the arm of a sofa. 'What if someone took a picture?'

Gabriel wheeled round.

'What if they did? The world already thinks I'm a criminal.'

I buried my face in my hands, trying to gather my thoughts. I looked up again.

'This is what I'm talking about, Gabe.'

His brow knitted.

'What?'

'All . . . *this*.' I gestured to the door. 'Starting fights, acting weird around everyone. I know this prison video stuff must be stressful, but you can't take it out on the rest of us.' Standing up, I slid my camera case off my shoulder and lowered it to the floor. The strap coiled on the carpet. 'I just . . . I don't *get* you any more, Gabe. You ignore me for months, you won't talk to me about anything except our parents, then you walk in on me with . . .' I paused, and his eyes locked on to mine. I swallowed hard. 'You find me with Olly, and you don't even seem to care. Will you just tell me what's going on inside your hea—'

'It's killing me, Charlie. OK? Is that what you want to hear?' His open palms were outstretched, pleading. His breathing was ragged. 'It's killing me.'

I took a small step backwards, and the arm of the sofa dug into my thigh.

'Wh . . . what? But . . .'

He pressed his fingers to his temples.

'I can't sleep, I can't write. I can't do anything. I can't stop thinking about you.'

'What are you talking about?' I said, in disbelief. My voice sounded stretched and thin. 'What about Clara?'

His eyebrows climbed his forehead.

'Clara Fitzch— *Her*? I barely know her.'

'But she's your girlfriend.'

He tipped his head back, and closed his eyes.

267

'Barry planted that story to get airtime for the EP. It's all lies. And not for the first time.'

Blood rushed to my cheeks. He was talking about Tammie Austin. I had believed the gossip back then, and now I'd fallen for it again.

'They'll say anything to sell records, you know that.'

My fingers twitched, and my mouth felt dry. Something was bubbling up inside me. I couldn't tell whether it was confusion, or guilt, or pain, but it was making me angry.

'Well, maybe you *should* date her,' I said, folding my arms. 'Apparently she's a stone-cold hottie.'

Gabriel paced backwards, and then forward again, his hands buried in his hair. He almost smiled, but the smile died before it stuck.

'This is the thing about you, Charlie. The thing that drives me *crazy*. You believe the hype about all these girls, these movie stars and TV stars. You think they're better than you because they've got shiny hair and perfect skin and endorsement deals, but it's all meaningless. It means *nothing*. You . . .' He pushed the heels of his palms into his forehead, breathed in, then out, and stared right at me. 'Charlie, you are the best person I've ever met. OK? That's all I know. You are the best person I've ever met, and I'm in love with you, and I've been in love with you since that day on the cliffs.'

He stopped suddenly, and his words hung in the air between us like a fine mist. I pressed a palm to my chest, feeling it shudder with the thrumming against my ribs. I had been aching, for weeks, for him to look at me, and now that he was, it was so intense I could barely stand it.

'Still . . . I guess you probably don't want to hear that right now.'

I could hear my own breathing inside my head, thunderous, uneven. Something Olly had said to me in the recording studio at Kingdom Records was echoing through my memory.

There's something on his mind. Something big.

'It . . . that . . . doesn't make sense.' I couldn't move. I felt like my feet had been bolted to the ground. 'I don't believe you.'

He went quiet for a moment, his eyes glinting. For five seconds, then ten, he said nothing. Time slowed and stretched, like honey falling from a spoon, and we just stood there, watching each other, waiting for something to happen.

Finally, he broke the silence.

'I remember what you were wearing the first time we met, at Reading Arena. Dark green top, blue pattern. I remember your coat, with the hood and the big buttons. The middle button was missing. I remember passing you a can of Coke, which you didn't drink. I remember the sound of the door as you closed it on your way out, and I remember the next time I saw you, you wanted to know why I was singing "Cat's in the Cradle", and you said you were lost. We lay on the stage and I made up constellations in the lights and you told me you didn't have that many friends, and I . . .' A soft, short laugh burst out of him. He was staring into the floor, but beyond it, somehow, into the past. 'I just thought, how is this possible? How do other people not see what I see, this girl who has absolutely no idea how mesmerising she is, who's so perfect that sometimes it hurts just to look at her, and . . . and I didn't know how to act around you. I'd never met anyone like you. You saw me. No one ever sees me, not really, but you do. You see . . . *everything*.'

I began to feel light-headed, like we were standing on a mountain-top and the air was thinning around us. Pressure was building behind my eyes, and I could feel my fingers shaking, the back of my neck prickling. Gabriel swept a tanned hand through his thick, dark hair, and two strands broke loose at the front, dropping down in front of his eyes.

'And you think that seeing you . . . you and Olly . . . you think that didn't bother me? Charlie, *it keeps me awake at night*. But what am I supposed to do? You said it yourself.' He blinked at me. 'When you're around me, bad things happen.'

Words fell out of me in stilted, broken shards.

'So . . . w-what . . . you just decided *not to be around* any more?'

He shrugged. A sad, defeated sigh of the shoulders.

'But you can't . . .' I clenched my fists. 'You can't just

decide these things on your own. What about me? All this time, I thought you hated me.'

His face shifted, and his eyes glazed over.

'You told me you never wanted to see me again.'

His words sank in, one by one, and I could feel cracks spidering across my heart, like splintering glass just before it shatters. It didn't matter what I said, because he was right. I had told him that: *I never want to see you again*. And at the time, I'd really thought that I meant it.

There was a sharp, urgent knock at the door.

And again.

'Who is it?' said Gabriel, without taking his eyes off me.

'The awards are about to kick off, Gabe. We need you out there now.'

We were breathing in-sync now, our eyes still locked. He clenched his jaw.

'I have to go,' he said, reaching for the door handle. I wanted to do something, I wanted to stop him, but I didn't know how. I was paralysed. Everything I'd assumed about him since Christmas had been wrong. How had I got it so wrong?

All I could do was watch as Gabriel walked out into the corridor and shut the door behind him, leaving me standing there alone, listening to the pounding of drums in the distance.

24

I stood in the centre of that room, without moving, for minutes on end. I kept waiting for the things Gabe had said to sink in.

You are the best person I've ever met, and I'm in love with you.

But my mind was racing, and I couldn't think straight. The words refused to settle, like fresh snow falling on wet ground.

And then I thought about Olly.

I was with Olly now. Or, at least, Olly and I were . . . *something*. And whatever it was, there was no room for Gabriel. I didn't have feelings for him any more. I hadn't *allowed* myself to. It was all too messed up. It was impossible.

'Charlie?'

Startled, I looked up. Tara had popped her head inside the door.

'Everything OK?'

I tucked my hair behind my ears.

'Uh, sure.'

'Gabe said you were still in here.' She smiled at me: a curious, lopsided smile. 'You can join us in the VIP box, if you like? Best view in the house.'

I looked around the room. There was no point in me staying there; I had no one to photograph, and I was starting to feel a little claustrophobic.

'That would be great. Thanks, Tara.'

'You'll love it up there. It's *very* fancy.'

The Kingdom Records VIP box was on the upper level of the StarBright Arena. It had a silver drinks bar, leather sofas and a balcony overlooking the auditorium, and it was full of middle-aged men drinking whisky from thick-bottomed tumblers and laughing at each other's jokes. I'd been standing alone on the balcony since the awards had begun, my arms wrapped around my body, a stubborn chill on my neck. Down below were flashing, swooping lights, waiting staff dashing right and left and thousands of people, some still at tables, some gathered at the various bars, bellowing at each other and popping bottles of champagne. On one side of the stage, cordoned off from the tables, was a kind of sunken pen containing a rippling crowd of excited fans. Melissa was in there, somewhere, messaging on her phone.

Tonight has been SOOOOOO much fun, CB. I get to boss people around and everything.

#livingthedream, I wrote back.

Yep, although . . . these guys are mega MEGA fangirls.
I'm like, dudes, srsly, there's more to life than F&L. A
pause. That's a lie, obviously, but I'm tryna look cool.

I managed a weak smile, and wished Melissa was up on the balcony with me. She would make everything better, just by being there.

'Ladies and gentlemen of the twenty-fifth WorldPOP Awards!' A massive, slow cheer drifted up from below, and onstage, the lights began to change. 'This is the moment you've been waiting for . . .'

The presenter, standing onstage in a flowing gold ballgown, was Jane Delaney, a popstar from the nineties who now did the kind of TV shows where celebrities were forced to eat live beetles and shower in public. She held a hand in the air, and four spot-lit columns materialised behind her in the centre of the circular stage.

'Performing a brand-new song from their upcoming EP *Songs About Us*, you've just seen them walk away with Best Music Video *and* Best Album, this is the incredible . . . Fire&Lights!'

Jane swept off the stage, and I dropped my phone into my camera case. Darkness descended, and an excitable quiet fell over the arena as, very slowly, Gabriel, Olly,

Yuki and Aiden rose up through the stage into the spotlights. A lonesome, haunting piano part began over the speakers.

I leaned against the chrome balcony, curious about the unfolding song. I'd expected something upbeat from them, something high energy, but this sounded like a ballad.

Then, as another cheer swelled up from the crowd, three of the spotlights faded away, leaving only Aiden, and he sang the opening lines.

Turn off the TV
Shut off the phone
I know what the headlines are

A second spotlight returned, illuminating Yuki, and he took the next verse.

You were beside me
On a road to nowhere
But I can never go, I can never go back there

As Yuki sang, I thought back to the radio interview at City Sounds. Shakia had announced to the world that Gabriel had written the songs on the new EP about Clara, but just now, he'd told me he barely even knew her. The whole thing had been a lie.

Onstage, Gabriel reappeared in his spotlight, lifting his microphone, ready to take the lead. And as the chorus opened up, realisation swept over me like a fever.

When we were wild inside
I believed you and I could do anything
When we were wild inside

Back in December, a few days before the night on the hotel rooftop, I'd been sitting in the school canteen at lunchtime, messaging Gabriel. I'd told him I 'wasn't cut out for drama', that it 'doesn't suit me', and he'd disagreed. *'Course it does, Charlie Brown*, he had replied. *You're wild, inside.*

And what had I thought, in that moment? *That sounded like a song lyric. Perhaps, in a month's time, I'd hear it on the radio.*

I gripped the balcony railing, stunned, the tips of my knuckles turning bone-white. Gabriel's song wasn't about Clara Fitzcharles, or Tammie Austin, or any of the other women the world was so desperate for him to fall in love with.

It was about us.

When we were wild inside
You were mine, I'd have given you everything
Everything

I stepped backwards, reeling, and bumped into a man behind me. I turned to apologise, but he waved it off, giving me a smile. A small part of me wanted to run, to get out of there, but all the VIPs had moved towards the balcony to watch the performance, and my path would have been blocked. More importantly, I needed to hear the rest of this song. I needed to know what Gabriel thought about us.

I drifted back to the edge of the balcony, the music ringing in my ears, and watched Gabriel step forward, the spotlight moving with him, to sing the next verse. There was something familiar about the tone of the song – the pulsing of the piano, the bittersweet ring of the chords – and as I stood there, entranced, it came back to me. This was the song Gabriel had been trying to record when we'd arrived at Studio Six, at Kingdom Records. I'd been standing with Olly, watching Gabe sing, and he'd suddenly stopped. When he told the producer that he couldn't go on, I thought Olly might have been putting him off, or maybe he was just being difficult, or stubborn. But that wasn't it.

It was because he couldn't sing it while I was in the room.

The fire in your heartbeat
And the light of your skin
The memory of you is pulling me further in

Olly moved forward, next to Gabriel, and took his turn. His turn to sing Gabriel's words.

Maybe I'll see you
After my show
And maybe you will smile, or maybe you will never know

I held my breath as the chorus returned, led again by Gabriel. A thatch of lasers was firing across the stage, dry ice billowing around the boys, a tumbling drum beat propelling the song to a rousing climax.

When we were wild inside
I believed you and I could do anything
When we were wild inside

When we were wild inside
You were mine, I'd have given you everything
Everything

'This is a great song,' said the lady standing next to me, sipping at her cocktail. The woman to her right nodded, and finished her drink.

'New sound for them,' she said. 'They've gone a bit Coldplay.'

The first woman chased an olive round her glass with a cocktail stick, skewered it and popped it in her mouth. She chewed for a moment, listening to the lyrics.

I know we can't be together
I know you gave your heart to him
I only want to see you one last time

'Gabe wrote it, about Clara Fitzcharles, you know,' she said.

Her friend nodded.

'So I hear.' She shook her head. 'He must have seriously fallen for that girl. Another martini?'

Onstage, strobes fired and spotlights whirled, and the song came to an end. A huge roar erupted from the crowd and, as the boys left the stage, Jane passed them on her way up the staircase.

'Thank you, boys! Incredible stuff.'

She sashayed back in front of the audience, clapping a hand against her microphone.

'Fire&Lights, everyone, with their latest single, "Wild Inside". What a song. I tell you, if I was twenty years younger . . .' Laughter rippled through the auditorium, and Jane, smiling to herself, picked up a silver envelope from behind the podium. 'So here we go, people. The big one: WorldPOP's Best Band award.' A twinkling graphic appeared on the big screen. 'To read out the nominees – you saw her onstage earlier, and she's already walked away tonight with the gong for Best Solo Artist – it's the gorgeous, not to mention impossibly talented, Kaitlyn Jones!'

Kaitlyn, wearing a spectacular turquoise dress that

fanned out at the sides, appeared on the stage and swept across to join Jane, enthusiastic applause ringing out all around. They took their positions on either side of the podium.

'So, Kaitlyn, congrats again on your award.'

Kaitlyn smiled sweetly.

'Thanks, Jane.'

'Who's your money on for Best Band this year?'

'I couldn't possibly say,' she said, raising laughter from the audience. Jane planted her tongue in her cheek.

'Might that be because your boyfriend's in one of the nominated acts?'

'No comment,' said Kaitlyn, winning another bout of laughter.

'But, come on, you're gonna tell us a bit more about the two of you, right?' pressed Jane, tilting her head. 'Kaidlyn. Pop's golden couple?'

On the big screens, you could see every facial expression Jane and Kaitlyn made. It had to be tough up there, hiding your true emotions, and if Kaitlyn had any inkling of the way Aiden was feeling about their relationship, the next few seconds weren't going to be easy.

'That's hella sweet, Jane. But Aiden's pretty private. I don't think he'd want me shooting my mouth off in front of y'all.'

Kaitlyn maintained her dazzling, beauty-pageant smile. Jane rolled her eyes.

'You young'uns, you're so coy. But surely it'll make your next date a bit awkward that he beat you to Best Album, no?'

My phone buzzed. A text from Melissa.

Ooh, that was bitchy

'I don't think so,' replied Kaitlyn placidly. She wasn't rising to the bait.

'Well,' said Jane, 'if that's all we're getting, I guess it must be time for the nominations.' She aimed a shallow smile at Kaitlyn, and handed her the silver envelope. Kaitlyn moved behind the podium, which meant Jane had to step backwards, out of the light. She clenched her jaw as her face went dark.

'And the nominees for Best Band are . . .'

Slow-motion footage began to play on the big screens.

'. . . Nine Miles West!'

A wave of applause clattered and swelled over a video montage of Australian pop act Nine Miles West, and I found myself, for some reason, thinking of my mother. Was this what she had hoped for with her band, in those early days, as they toured around small venues, building their audience, one fan at a time? Had she daydreamed about being nominated for awards, attending glitzy ceremonies, being recognised the world over? Would she be proud of me, I wondered, for being up here, among the record executives, part of the Fire&Lights entourage?

'Jailbreak Anthem . . .'

Perhaps she'd hoped that, one day, Little Boy Blue would be nominated for Best Band, or Best Album. That they'd get a chance to walk up to that podium and make a speech, their faces lit up on the big screens, adoring fans cheering them on.

'Fire&Lights . . .'

Of course, Mum never got that opportunity. It was taken away from her suddenly, before she'd had a proper chance to make it happen.

'. . . And last but not least, You Me & The Universe!'

Still gripping the balcony rail, I willed Mum to the back of my mind and tried to focus on the screen, where Kaitlyn was pulling the winner's name from the silver envelope. The soundtrack grew to a crescendo, and she read the name to herself, then leaned into the microphone. There was a sudden silence.

'The winners are . . . Fire&Lights!'

Music and noise and cheering reverberated around the arena, and moments later, the boys began walking towards the stage in an uneven line. They mounted the steps and, as they gathered around the podium, a slow dread congealed in my stomach.

Looking at their faces, and the way they were standing, I could feel it in my bones. Something bad was about to happen.

25

They looked wrong somehow, standing up there. Too far apart. Yuki was wearing shades, his hair a complete mess, and carrying a half-empty bottle of champagne. Gabe and Olly were stony-faced, while Aiden hovered at the back, his expression unreadable.

When they'd performed, just minutes earlier, they'd been a band. The unstoppable force that the world so fiercely adored. Now, without the spotlights and the dry ice and the pounding music, they looked strangely exposed. Like four lost boys, waiting to be saved.

'How about that, ladies and gentlemen?' said Jane, returning to the podium, and displacing Kaitlyn in the process. Kaitlyn retreated to the back of the group, taking Aiden's hand. He didn't respond.

'Gabriel, Yuki, Aiden and Olly: the extraordinary Fire&Lights! How do you feel, boys?'

There was an awkward pause. Olly moved towards the microphone, but Gabriel blocked him, beating him to it. He picked up the award, and turned it over in his hands.

'Cheers, guys. We've pretty much thanked everyone already tonight, but—'

Gabriel stopped abruptly, as Olly took the award from him.

'What are you doing?' he said, glancing at the crowd.

'Chill, bud,' said Olly, faking a smile. 'So I guess it's the fans first—'

'What do you mean, chill?' interrupted Gabriel. 'I was talking.'

'And now I'm talking.'

'Dudes, dudes!'

Yuki stumbled between them, champagne bottle swinging from his hand, and leaned an elbow on the podium. I felt relieved, at first, that he'd interrupted the stand-off, but the relief didn't last long.

'What's this one for again?' he said, and a small chorus of boos volleyed towards the stage. Yuki pouted, and waved them away.

'Hey, whoa! Guys. GUYS. We've won a bunch of these tonight, and it gets hard to . . . y'know, *remember* . . .'

The booing got louder. Yuki stepped backwards, one hand in his hair, and bumped into Olly and Gabriel, who barely noticed. They were engaged in a private conversation, and it didn't look friendly. Jane's eyes began to panic, and she stammered into her microphone.

'Uh . . . so . . .'

The video feed went black for a second, before

powering up again with a shot of Aiden and Kaitlyn holding hands. The camera zoomed in, super-close, and at that exact moment, Aiden's hand fell away from hers.

Kaitlyn stared right ahead, her eyes round and shiny.

'Um . . . a-anyway,' stammered Jane, with a nervous laugh, 'thank you, guys, and congrats again. Three awards in one night, that's quite something. Ladies and gentlemen, Fire&Lights!'

Scattered applause, still peppered with booing and jeers, accompanied the boys back down the stairs and into the crowd. Over the speakers, Jane kept talking, but nobody was listening. Every last person in that room was wondering what the hell was wrong with Fire&Lights.

As quickly as I could, I made my way through the executives in the VIP box, out into the corridor and down the stairs, heading for the floor below. I wanted to catch the band before Barry did. I wasn't sure what I'd say when I found them, but I had to do something. I had to find out what was going on in their heads.

When I reached the door of the dressing room, I pressed my ear to the wood. Nothing. Maybe they weren't even heading this way. Maybe—

'Seriously, I'm telling you, Kylie Minogue is definitely less than four feet tall.' Yuki's voice, approaching from around a corner. 'I've seen her, she's *teeny tiny*. She's out there right n— Oh, hey! It's Charlie B.'

He stopped when he saw me, his big sunglasses docked in his hair. The rest of the band slowed to a halt behind him.

'Hey,' I said, tugging at the strap of my camera case.

'Hi,' said Olly, his voice cracking slightly. He had a bottle of water in his hand, and I watched his grip tighten around it.

'What just happened out there?'

No one spoke. Behind Olly, standing half in shadow, Gabriel shook his head, very slowly. Aiden ran a hand down his flushed face.

'I'm worried about you. What are people going to say? What are the fans going to say?' Still, there was silence. It was starting to feel like I was having a conversation with myself. 'You can't throw this away, you know. Some people would give *anything* for what you have.'

A shiver of sadness swept over me as I thought of Mum, sitting onstage at a piano. All her dreams, lost in an instant.

Olly pressed a palm into his forehead.

'Charlie, we . . . it's just . . .'

My phone buzzed, and I pulled it from my pocket. Melissa. I began to back away from them.

'Where are you going?' said Olly.

'I'm meeting Melissa at the bus stop. We have to head home.'

'Can I walk you there?' he asked, stepping forward. Over his shoulder, Gabriel's eyes flickered in the dark.

'No, you can't,' said a gruff male voice, behind me, and I spun round to find Barry King standing by the dressing room door. He twisted the handle and nudged it with his fingertips, letting it open into the room.

'Lads, in here, now.' He gestured inside with a flick of his head. He glanced at me. 'Sorry, Charlie.'

'It's . . . fine,' I said, pressing awkwardly against the wall to allow the boys past. Gabriel was the last to walk by me, and as he did, a sudden heat prickled up my arms.

Barry shut the door behind them, and I was alone.

A light drizzle was falling as I walked across the vast arena car park, a high chain-link fence on one side, endless rows of sleeping cars on the other. Most of the guests were still inside the building, enjoying the after-party, and when I arrived at the bus stop, it was deserted.

A message lit up my phone.

Aargh, sorry! Just finishing up with Duffy + Cam . . . out in 5 mins!! x P.S. WHAT is going on with F&L?????

The chaos and noise from the arena had been replaced by a chill darkness, and the occasional sweep of car headlights. Planes passed overhead, dragging their distant

287

roar through the night's sky, and orange lamps cast a mournful glow across the rows of parked vehicles. I sat down on the bus stop's cold metal bench, and began writing a reply.

'Oi, Charlie.'

I stopped typing. A man in a long, baggy coat was approaching through the cars, a furred hood casting a thick black shadow across his face. His features were lit only by the angry orange tip of a cigarette.

I pocketed my phone and pulled my camera case tight against my body.

'Charlie Bloom, as I live and breathe.'

I stood up, looking left and right for signs of life. There was no one else around.

'How do you know my name?'

The man stepped into the harsh yellow light of the bus stop and dropped his hood. He had suspicious little eyes, sallow skin and a jaw patched with stubble. It was Paul Morgan, the reporter from *The Record*. My toes curled.

'We're old friends. Cigarette?'

I shook my head, keeping my eyes low.

'Kids these days.' He flicked ash on to his boots. 'You're supposed to smoke when you're sixteen, Christ's sake.'

My pulse began to gallop. The fact that he knew my exact age was like a fingernail down my spine.

'You were at my school,' I said. 'Last month.'

He drew his head back, giving himself a double chin.

'I doubt it, sunshine.' He scratched his stubble, and a heavy gold watch dropped down his skinny wrist. 'But since I'm here now, I have something to run by you.'

He took a long, slow draw on his cigarette.

'I'm not interested.'

'Oh, you will be.' He fixed me with his small, black eyes. 'Your old flame, Master West, he hasn't been entirely honest about his family, has he? Turns out there's things in his past he doesn't want the rest of us to know about.'

I gritted my teeth. The prison video. Did this mean Paul was behind it?

'I don't know what you're talking about,' I said, and he laughed. It was a thick, smoker's laugh, and it soured into a cough.

'Sure you don't,' he said, wiping his mouth.

'I'm meeting my friend in a minute, so you should probably go—'

'Actually, I don't think I will.'

His face hardened, and he took a step towards me.

'You see, Gabriel's past ... I think it involves you.'

I tried not to flinch.

'I really think you should go now, before I call the police.'

He glanced over his shoulder, then pointed his cigarette at me.

'You're not going to call the police, love, and here's

why. Unlike Teen Angel in there, you're not a millionaire. And you could make some serious cash from this story, believe me. Give me an interview and I'll make it worth your while.'

'I don't want your money.'

'They all say that, but you wait until there's a cheque in your hand. We're talking thousands.'

I took a side-step away from him, holding his gaze. Then, as quickly as I could without running, I turned and made a break for it, heading towards the maze of cars. He called after me.

'This isn't a negotiation, sweetheart!'

I increased my pace, no clue where I was heading, and soon I could hear his footsteps behind me, boots slapping on the damp concrete. Seconds later, his fingers closed around my arm. I froze, my heart slamming against my ribs.

His hot breath felt wet on my neck.

'I could make things very uncomfortable for you, Charlie,' he said, in a low voice. 'Just you think about that for a mo—'

Paul's voice was suddenly muffled, and I could feel his fingers being yanked off my arm. I spun round to find him being hauled backwards, an arm wrapped around his neck, his cigarette falling to the ground, spilling hot sparks. He struggled against his assailant, jabbing with his elbows, until he managed to break free.

Gabriel was standing behind him, dark loops of hair falling across his face. Paul straightened his crumpled coat.

'Speak of the devil.'

'Didn't you listen the first time?' said Gabriel, sweeping his hair out of his eyes. 'We're not interested in your stories.'

'You don't really have a choice, Gabe.' Paul jabbed at his temple with a rigid finger, his gold watch clinking. 'I know things. I'm working things out. I see you.'

Gabriel sneered at him.

'You're bluffing.'

'Suicide,' said Paul, with a calm shrug. 'It's the coward's way out.' He tilted his head. 'Don't you think?'

Gabriel snapped and charged towards him, slamming him with an almighty crack against the plastic wall of the bus shelter. He grabbed his shirt collar and twisted it.

'You have *no idea* what you're talking about.'

'Oh, really?' choked Paul, still somehow managing to laugh. 'Turns out your old man was a bit of a bastard, eh? Abandoned you, am I right?'

For a sickening moment, my mother flashed up in my mind.

Abandoned you . . . am I right?

'Shut up,' spat Gabriel. 'You didn't know him.'

Paul smirked.

'Neither did you.'

'Charlie, what's happening?'

Melissa's voice. She had appeared behind Gabriel and Paul, clutching her handbag, eyes shining in the dark. I pointed towards the arena.

'Just go, Mel. Back inside. I'll come and find you.'

'No, I . . .' Her face was white with fear. 'What's going on?'

Gabriel still had Paul pinned to the bus shelter. Paul was short of breath, but that wasn't stopping him from talking.

'I mean, if I was you, I'd be thinking: damn, what if that's who I am? What if I'm turning into him?'

'Shut up. Just shut up.'

'We can't escape what's in our blood, can we?'

Gabriel had been holding fast, but now, he began to weaken. His body sagged, and Paul managed to free one arm. He hissed angrily into Gabriel's face.

'He never cared about you, did he, Gabriel? You were *nothing* to him.'

'You didn't know my dad, you don't know anything.'

'He had his band, he had his drugs. He didn't want some dumb kid messing up his life.'

'Stop it.'

'Christ, the man killed himself to *get away* from you.'

'Shut up, just . . . *shut up* . . .'

Gabriel's shoulders slumped as Paul overpowered him. Tears were pooling in his eyes.

'Stop it . . . please . . .'

Paul straightened and pressed his face into Gabriel's, so their eyes were only centimetres apart.

'Why don't you make me?'

Before he had time to think about it, Gabriel had thrown Paul to the ground and was launching blows into his face, neck and chest. His fists were clenched in anger, but when I looked at his eyes, they were shut tight, dripping tears. He barely knew what he was doing.

I was about to run over and drag Gabriel away when I heard a battery of clicks coming from behind my head. Wheeling round, I saw a camera flashing from the window of a car.

'Gabriel, stop!'

I snatched Gabriel's arm and tried to pull him away, but it was too late. Paul was already staggering to his feet, touching a hand to his bleeding mouth. Then he ran to the car, pulled the passenger door open and jumped inside, slamming it shut behind him. The driver reversed, with a screech of tyres, and drove at speed out of the car park.

We were enveloped by a cold, empty silence, and I looked at Gabriel, the freezing wind lapping at our faces.

Voices shouted to us across the tarmac.

26

<><><> www.popgossip.co.uk <><><>

BOY BAND SUPERSTAR IN VIOLENT ATTACK!!
*Gabriel West assaults stranger outside
glitzy awards ceremony*

We can hardly believe it here at PG-HQ, but the pictures speak for themselves: **Gabriel West was caught last night violently assaulting an unidentified man** in the car park of London's StarBright Arena. West's band, the almighty Fire&Lights, had just swept the board at the WorldPOP Awards, winning Best Album, Best Music Video and Best Band – but if you think the F&L boys are on top of their game right now, think again. Judging by last night's bizarre acceptance speech, **this is a band in crisis**. (Click here for the video!!!)

As for Gabriel, it seems he's had a lucky escape this time. The victim wasn't hospitalised and, as far as we know, isn't pressing charges. But after last week's revelation that Gabriel has been hiding a troubled past – including **shoplifting, vandalism and hanging around with street gangs** – the *evidence is clear. He's a messed-up guy, and there's no telling what he might do next.*

More news as soon as we have it!!

RELATED STORIES

> *Does this GIF prove that Kaitlyn and Aiden are an industry hoax?! #kaidlynhands*

> *Yuki Harrison splashes cash in West End nightclub with punk-rocker buddies*

<><><> www.popgossip.co.uk <><><>

'This is not good, Charlie.' Melissa was sitting cross-legged on my bed, computer on her lap. Her eyes were wide with worry. 'This is *nicht gut.*'

The story had broken in a matter of hours, and the photographs had spread like wildfire. There were articles, blogs and Tumblr pages, and thousands of memes were being shared across social media. The backlash against Gabriel was gaining momentum, and some of the fans had already turned on him.

I'd been worried, for a while, that Paul would run the photos in *The Record.* But he didn't. He hadn't even identified himself when he leaked them to the gossip sites. This didn't make much sense to me at first, but as I'd lain in bed that morning, glued to my phone screen, a dark realisation had crept over me. Paul was building up to a bigger story, just like he'd said. And he didn't want to blow his cover before his moment of glory.

'Poor Gabe,' said Melissa, grimacing at a meme on Tumblr. Above a grainy picture of Gabriel punching Paul in the chest, the text read: *Don't tell Gabriel West his music sucks.* Then, underneath: *YOU MIGHT GET A THUMPING.* 'Have you heard from him?'

It hurt my heart to hear what people were saying about Gabriel. That he was violent, aggressive. A loose cannon. He'd only been there at all because he was trying to protect me.

'Only once,' I replied, glancing at my phone, which was lying in the folds of my duvet. I'd messaged Gabe when I woke up that morning, to find out if he was OK, and all I'd got back was a single line.

I'm sorry I dragged you into this x

I opened my messages and passed the phone to Melissa. She read Gabe's reply, and sighed.

'God. I still can't believe he dropped the L-bomb last night.' She wrinkled her nose. 'How do you feel?'

I slumped against the wall.

'Mel, I'm dating Olly. I can't feel anything about Gabe.' She swallowed, looking at her fingers.

'Sure. 'Course.' She sniffed. 'But that song, "Wild

Inside" . . . I mean, it's *beautiful*. How could anyone actually believe it's about Blondey FitzDoodah?'

I rubbed the sleep from my eyes.

'They need to keep on believing that,' I said firmly. 'I don't want any attention for this. Not after last year.'

I plucked a grape from the open punnet sitting between us, and rolled it between my finger and thumb. Melissa tugged at one of her plaits.

'Hey, did Duffy tell you about the secret gig yet?'

'What secret gig?'

'Wh . . . hang on. I have insider band knowledge *before Charlie Bloom*? Check me out.'

I smiled despite myself, and threw the grape at her.

'Anyway,' continued Melissa, chasing the grape as it rolled off her leg, 'it's on the twenty-fifth, for the EP launch. VIP fans and press only. It's perfect for me, 'cos there'll be tons of competition winners to look after.'

'Where is it?'

'They don't know yet. But it'll be in London, Duffy said. Somewhere small and intimate.'

I pulled my knees up to my chest. The idea of being somewhere small and intimate with both Olly *and* Gabriel wasn't a comforting one. Did Olly have any idea how Gabriel felt about me? What would he do if he found out? And how did I even feel about the things Gabe had said . . . ?

297

I noticed Melissa watching me. She snapped my laptop shut.

'What?' I said, confused.

'Look, d'you fancy doing something normal this week?' she said, twisting round to face me. 'You know, cinema or something. Friday night? We could watch that new movie about the singing dogs.'

'Actually . . . I was hoping to go see my gran on Friday. You know, ask her about Mum.'

Melissa nodded, and smiled.

'Ah, yes. I still think that's a great idea, you know.'

I narrowed my eyes at her.

'It was *your* idea.'

'Really?' she said, pressing a hand to her chest. 'Was it? I guess I must be full of them, then.' Her smile softened. 'But seriously, CB, she's your gran. She should be in your life anyway, whatever happens with all this Little Boy Blue stuff.'

'Yeah. I guess you're right.'

She set my laptop aside.

'This mess will all work itself out, eventually. You'll see. And until it does, I'm here for you, twenty-four seven. Your trusty sidekick, Scrappy Doo.'

I lowered my head on to her shoulder, and sighed.

'Thanks, Mel. You're the best.'

'No,' she said, resting her head on mine. 'I think you'll find you are.'

That week, at school, I kept a low profile. From the minute the bell rang on Monday morning, the disintegration of Fire&Lights was on everyone's lips, and the corridors were crawling with rumours, alive with gossip. It felt like it was in the walls, seeping from the brickwork. So when I first saw Jody – the only person at Caversham High, apart from Melissa, who knew I was working with the band again – I planned to walk right past him with little more than a nod. But he wasn't alone.

'Hey, yo. Charlie.'

Jody had his bandmates with him, standing behind him in a crescent. Like bodyguards.

'Hey.'

His eyes were skittish, darting this way and that. I tucked my hair behind my ears.

'You good?' he said.

'I guess. You all right?'

'Yeah, sort of.'

I waited for a moment, but he seemed to have run out of words. I was about to move on when Thumper, the drummer, stepped out from behind him and into my path.

'What Jody's trying to say,' he explained, 'is that we need something. From you.'

I frowned. Thumper was very tall and broad, and

could probably have picked me up with one hand. I'd never liked him that much.

'Like what?' I said. 'More photos?'

Jody scratched his neck, avoiding my gaze.

'You remember you mentioned ... getting us a support slot with Fire&Lights?'

I closed my eyes, and exhaled.

'Actually, Jody, *you* mentioned that, not me. And I said I couldn't do it. That stuff's all organised by management.'

Thumper drew himself up to his full height, and slid a heavy arm around my shoulders.

'Charlie, come on. Everyone knows you dated Gabriel.'

I threw him off, pulling my rucksack up my back.

'Don't be a creep, Thumper. And that was months ago.'

Thumper shared a look with his bandmates, then turned to me again, rubbing his big palms together.

'Fine. We'll do it this way. We've heard about the secret gig they're doing next Friday.'

I glanced back and forth between Thumper and Jody.

'How do you guys know about that?'

'My kid sister,' said Thumper. 'She's a big fan of "F&L".' He made air-quotes with his fingers. 'She won two VIP tickets, 'cos she's, like, the world's biggest fan or something, and they sent her details last night. It's at some random venue called the Troubadour.'

My whole body tensed. The Troubadour? It couldn't be.

'Do you mean ... in London?'

Thumper sniffed.

'Yeah, that's the place.'

I turned towards my locker, my shirt collar feeling suddenly tight around my neck. *The Troubadour?* It could have been a coincidence, of course, but what were the chances of that? Like Melissa had told me, back in March, whatever was connecting me to Gabe *had* to involve Fire&Lights, and Olly, in some way, otherwise the odds were too astronomical to believe. And now, right in front of my eyes, here it was: a connecting factor. An obscure London venue that my mum and Harry used to play at, chosen for a secret Fire&Lights EP launch, twenty years later. What did it mean? Did it mean anything at all?

Or was I slowly losing my mind?

'So, anyway,' Thumper was saying, when I tuned back in, 'I checked the place out, and it's tiny. We could easily play there.'

I shook off thoughts of my mum and Harry and Little Boy Blue, and looked up at him.

'I've already told Jody, they don't pick support bands this way.'

'Yeah, except *we're* old schoolmates of Olly's, and I reckon he'd give us a break, since he's such a decent bloke. Unlike your ex, the violent criminal.'

Thumper sniggered at his joke, and the two as-yet-silent members of Diamond Storm joined in. Jody did not.

301

'Don't talk about Gabriel like that,' I snapped.

Thumper's eyebrows shot up his forehead.

'OK, whatever. I take it back. But seriously, just ask Olly. Tell him it's all about school spirit, or something.'

'Aren't you listening to me? I can't help you.'

'Tell her, Jody.'

Everyone turned to Jody. He stared at his feet.

'Well, you know . . . my mum is, like . . . sh-she's—'

'What my man here is trying to say,' interrupted Thumper, tossing some gum into his mouth, 'is that his mum is currently copping off with your dad, and you don't want Daddy accidentally finding out about your latest "arrangement" with Fire&Lights.' He made air-quotes again. 'Right?'

So Jody had let the rest of the band in on my secret, then. And now they were using it against me.

'What are you trying to say?' I replied, anger stirring inside me.

Thumper stared at me, chewing lazily.

'I think you know.'

I did know. I knew exactly what he was saying, and there wasn't a thing I could do about it.

'You're a jerk, you know that?'

'Yeah,' said Thumper, grinning at me. 'I do.'

'Jody?'

Appealing to Jody was the last card I had to play.

302

I knew he was a decent guy, underneath all the rockstar ambition.

'Sorry,' he said, still not looking at me. 'Just sort it out for us, OK?'

With that, Diamond Storm sloped off down the corridor, leaving me on my own. Just as they were being swallowed by a passing stream of students, Thumper swivelled round, raised his hands to his mouth and shouted: 'Remember . . . people talk, yeah?'

He slung an arm around Jody's neck, pulling him into a headlock, and they disappeared from view.

'Fish and chips are in the house!'

From the living room, where I was sitting with my feet up on the coffee table, I could hear Dad manoeuvring through the front door and throwing his keys in the dish. I lowered my phone.

'In here, Dad.'

He popped his head around the door. He was holding a blue plastic bag, stuffed with takeaway food. I could smell the batter from across the room.

'Still on that mobile, I see.' He narrowed his eyes, amused. 'I don't understand what you and Melissa *say* to each other all evening. You see her every day.'

'Oh, it's pretty boring,' I replied. My phone pinged.

Olly Samson

Fancy flying to Manchester to film a live TV show on
Saturday??

'You know, teenage girl stuff,' I added casually. Dad raised
the bag of food in the air, and pointed at it.

'I'll be back in two minutes, with the nosh. Stick the
movie in, if you like.'

I dragged my feet off the table, sat up and reached for
the DVD case. *The Shawshank Redemption* was a film from
the nineties about a prison break, which Dad had been
going on about for weeks, and now he'd chosen it for
Fish 'n' Chips 'n' Movies Night. I flipped the case over,
scanning the synopsis. In a way, two hours of escapism
was exactly what I needed. It might take my mind off
Paul Morgan, and Diamond Storm, and Gabriel's flaying
in the press.

Plucking out the DVD, I crossed over to the player
and dropped it in. I tapped a reply to Olly.

A TV show? Which one?

Blake Hadaway. Barry pulled in a favour. He thinks an
interview could turn the tables for us.

You guys can work your charms live on air

Exactly. We could grab lunch before we fly if you want, in the first class lounge??

Are you asking me on a date?

A pause.

I might be

Then, yes, I am totally there

I smiled, my heart lifting at the idea of finally going on an official date with Olly. Like we were normal people, in a normal relationship. And, of course, it would be the perfect chance to ask him about Diamond Storm. But as I imagined us there, eating lunch and chatting, anxiety crept over my shoulders. Things had changed since the StarBright Arena. I wasn't going to tell him about Gabriel, obviously, but by keeping Gabe's feelings a secret, who was I trying to protect? Fire&Lights . . . or myself?

'Right, then,' said Dad, walking into the living room, carrying two steaming plates of food. He set them down on the table, next to the popcorn. 'Ah, you've already sorted it.'

He nodded at the screen, where the DVD menu had loaded and a stirring, operatic aria was playing over a clip from the movie.

'You are going to love this film,' he said, positioning a knife and fork beside each plate. 'It's all about guilt and innocence, truth and lies.'

I bit one of my fingernails, thinking about the deception I'd agreed to only seconds earlier. To get on a plane and fly to the other end of the country, with the biggest band in the world, without my father having any clue where I was.

'I'm looking forward to this,' Dad continued, loosening his tie. 'It's been a hectic week at work.' He bent to untie his shoe laces. 'Still, Friday tomorrow. You up to much over the weekend?'

I held my breath, watching him loosen the knots with his fingers. My brain was working double-time.

'Erm, not really . . . Diamond Storm are rehearsing on Saturday, so I'll probably go and hang out with them.'

I'd learned from Twitter that Diamond Storm actually rehearsed *every* Saturday afternoon, in some grotty studio on the Milford Road, so with any luck, this alibi would be watertight.

'Oh.' Dad kicked off his shoes. 'Do they really need a photographer at a rehearsal?'

'I . . . don't know,' I replied, trying to sound disinterested. 'I think they want the fans to know what it's like behind the scenes, or something.'

Dad shrugged, then grabbed his beer from the table

306

and popped it open. I needed a change of subject, and quick.

'Dad, can I ask you something?'

'Sure, kiddo.' He took a hearty slug of his beer, and smacked his lips. 'Fire away.'

'Would it be OK if I went to see Gran?'

He froze, drink in hand. His eyes flickered towards the television, then back to me.

'Wh . . . your grandmother?'

I nodded. 'Uh-huh.'

'But . . . when?'

'Tomorrow.'

Slowly, he sank back into his seat, bottle paused halfway to his lips. I tugged at a loose thread on one of the cushions.

'I know you guys don't really talk any more, but I just think it's really sad. That I hardly ever see her, I mean.'

Dad nodded, his eyes glazed.

'Yes . . . I suppose you're right.'

'I could take the train there and back in one evening. I'm sure she wouldn't mind.'

Dad stared into the distance for a moment, then turned to me.

'No, I'm . . . sure she wouldn't.' He took a cautious sip of beer. 'Have you asked her, though? She might not be in.'

'She's seventy-five, Dad. She's hardly going to be out clubbing.'

Dad looked at me, a strange expression on his face. Then, unexpectedly, a little laugh burst out of him, and he touched a hand to his mouth, like a naughty schoolboy. I couldn't help myself, and laughed too. We smiled at each other for a moment, and then he cleared his throat and his face went serious again.

'You're right, though, Charlie. It's my fault that you barely see her. I should have done something about it a long time ago.'

'Don't, Dad. You always take responsibility. I know things weren't easy after Mum . . .' I rubbed one eye, a lump rising in my throat. 'After Mum was gone.'

He nodded at me, tight-lipped, and all of a sudden, I felt an intense urge rising inside my chest. The urge to just ask him *everything*. To find out the whole story about Mum, in one go, and get everything out in the open. I already knew so much more than he realised, and maybe . . . maybe he wouldn't be mad. Maybe he'd understand about all the lies, and the sneaking around.

But no. That would ruin everything, and I knew it. And as I sat there next to him, our knees lightly touching, I felt the urge sigh away, like a wave retreating on a beach.

'Actually,' said Dad, picking at the label on his beer bottle, 'since we're talking about your mum . . .'

We were suddenly both aware of the shrill, piercing tones of the opera singer on the television. Dad slid the remote control off the table.

'Let me just mute this . . . ah, damn.'

He'd pressed the wrong button, and the screen flicked to a random channel. I picked my plate up off the table and set it on my lap.

'Never mind,' said Dad, 'I'll switch it back in a sec.' He turned the sound off, and shifted round to face me. 'I wanted to say, Charlie, about this whole dating thing . . . I'm not trying to replace your mother. You know that, don't you?'

I nodded, heat flushing my cheeks. I prodded at my chips with a fork.

'It's just, it's been such a long time, and I feel like I ought to at least *try* to move on with my life. Does that seem fair?'

'Sure.'

'And Christine, she's a very sweet person. We actually have lots in comm—'

'Oh my god!'

I dropped my fork and sat up abruptly, scattering a handful of chips across the floor. On the television, on whatever random channel Dad had ended up on, was a picture that had been taken at the WorldPOP Awards.

And I was in it.

'Charlie, are you OK?'

I pushed my plate on to the table, and fumbled for the remote. Fortunately, Dad was rescuing chips from the floor and not looking at the TV, because if he had been,

309

he would have seen a photograph of Gabriel pressing a pink-haired punk-rocker against the VIP bar at the StarBright Arena, while behind them, I looked on in shock.

The headline read: 'THE BAD BOY OF POP STARTS YET ANOTHER FIGHT – GABRIEL WEST CAUGHT IN THE ACT'.

'Crikey, there's chips everywhere . . .'

Just as Dad rose up from the carpet, I managed to get purchase on the remote, and switched channels.

'What's going on?' he said, dropping on to the sofa. 'Have I upset you, talking about Christine?'

I tried to control my breathing. My heart was doing somersaults.

'No, sorry, Dad . . . I just . . . I thought I'd swallowed a fish bone. But I haven't. It's fine. Panic over.'

He looked at me, unconvinced.

'Sure you're OK?'

'Mm-hmm.'

'And you don't have anything you want to ask about Christine?'

'Nuh-uh.'

Dad pressed his lips together.

'Right. Right. And do you want these chips?'

He still had the dropped chips cupped in his hand. I wrinkled my nose.

'They've been on the floor.'

'Five-second rule,' he said, with a shrug. I narrowed my eyes at him.

'How do you know about the five-second rule?'

Dad laughed.

'My generation *invented* the five-second rule.'

Smiling at me sideways, Dad retrieved the remote from the table and clicked back to *The Shawshank Redemption*. My chest tightened as I gazed at the image on the screen: hundreds of blank-faced inmates, standing motionless in a prison yard.

It's all about guilt and innocence, truth and lies.

27

Gran lived in a medium-sized red-brick house just outside of Basingstoke town centre, and had done for most of her adult life. Mum had grown up there, and though I'd only visited a handful of times since she died, just standing on the driveway made me feel closer to her.

I walked to the front door and reached for the bell. As my finger hovered in front of it, questions rushed through my mind. What was I about to find out? Would this change things? What might Gran be prepared to tell me that my father wasn't . . . ?

I had called her, at lunchtime, to ask if I could come.

'Hello, three-double-four-two-seven-eight?'

I'd smiled to myself. I liked the way old people told you their phone number when they answered a call.

'Gran, it's Charlie.'

A pause.

'Oh. Oh, Charlotte.' Another pause, then the sound of Gran sitting down in a creaky chair. 'Hello, my dear. Well, this is a surprise . . .'

We'd talked a little, about this and that – school,

Melissa, my exams – and when I'd asked her if I could come and visit that evening, she'd said yes straightaway. Several hours later, I took a train to Basingstoke.

And now I was standing on the doorstep, pressing the bell.

After thirty seconds or so, the door opened.

'Charlotte. Charlotte. It's so lovely to see you.' Her mouth trembled into a smile. 'Come on in, I'll put the kettle on.'

Gran's house never changed. There were always the same ornaments on the window sills, and the same pictures on the walls: an inky watercolour next to the coat rack, all rolling fields and tumbledown barns, and a series of framed dressmaker's sketches leading towards the kitchen. There were photographs of Mum as a little girl too, with her big eyes and long, dark hair, and a picture of me, about the same age, at primary school, against a blue background. We looked so very similar.

'You take a seat in the front room,' said Gran, heading for the kitchen. 'I'll be through in a mo.'

'Don't you want some help?'

'You're my guest,' she said, with a wink. 'You just make yourself comfortable.'

I drifted into the living room and sat in one of the armchairs. From the kitchen, I could hear the bubbling of the kettle, the clinking of cutlery and the shuffle of Gran's slippers on the tiled floor.

Five minutes later, she appeared in the doorway with a tray full of drinks and biscuits.

'Wait, let me get that for you,' I said, standing up and crossing the room. She allowed me to take it, and I lowered it carefully on to the table. We sat down in opposite armchairs.

'I must say,' she began, reaching towards the tray, 'I was surprised to hear from you today. A lovely surprise, of course.'

I felt my cheeks turning red.

'I'm sorry I haven't seen you in so long.'

She shook her head.

'That's not your fault, sweetheart.'

Gran poured the tea into two delicate china cups, and I glanced around the room. A clock ticked on the wall, steady and sure.

'I wanted to ask you about Mum, Gran.'

Gran paused, the teapot still in her hands. Her face went a little pale, and she placed it back down again, blinking.

'She was in America when she died, wasn't she?'

'She was,' replied Gran, reaching for the milk jug. 'Milk and sugar?'

'Just milk, please.' I leaned forward in my chair. 'Why was she there?'

I was pretty sure of the answer, of course. She was almost certainly on tour with Little Boy Blue. But I needed to know if Gran would tell me herself.

She poured milk into both cups and stirred it, thoughtfully. The spoon clinked against the china.

'Well . . .'

There was a slightly pained expression on her face. She wanted to tell me, it was obvious, though I knew she wasn't going to. Like Dad, it was as if she was trying to protect me. But what were they protecting me from?

'Your father hasn't told you?' she said.

I shook my head. 'No.'

She slid the tea cosy back on to the kettle, very slowly.

'Well, I don't feel it's my place. You must ask him. But I'd say you're old enough to know everything now.'

To know *everything*? What was 'everything'?

I twisted a little in my seat, my gaze settling on the upright piano in the corner of the room. Before, it had always just been part of the furniture, but it was so much more than that now. It was almost certainly the piano that Mum had learned to play on; the place where she had sat, day after day, dreams breathing to life inside her head.

On the lid of the piano, there was another photograph of her, clutching a scroll at graduation. I felt a tingle in my fingertips.

'I miss her, Gran. Every day.'

Gran nodded, reaching for her drink. As she lifted it off the table, the cup trembled slightly on its saucer.

'So do I, my dear.' Her eyes went shiny. 'So do I.'

I picked up my cup and, for a few moments, we sat there in peaceful silence, drinking our tea. A lorry grumbled by on the road outside.

'Do you blame Dad for what happened?' I said, after a while. Gran touched a wrinkled hand to her chest.

'Of course not.'

'Because he thinks you do.'

She sucked in a long, shaky breath, and her forehead sank into a frown.

'Death can scar a family, I suppose. And sometimes those scars don't heal.' She shook her head, staring into the middle distance. 'I admit your grandfather did blame Ralph, at first. In a way. But he was just looking for somewhere to aim his hurt, his anger. He never really meant it.'

I set down my cup.

'You should make up with him, Gran. We should be a family again. Don't you think?'

She looked at me curiously, as if for the first time. A quiet smile lifted the corners of her mouth.

'Yes. Yes, I do.'

We held eye contact, and it occurred to me, in a way it never had before, that Mum had had her mother's eyes. Which meant that I did too. Maybe I shared more things with my grandmother than I realised.

Steam danced from our teacups and disappeared into the air. I stretched forward and picked up a shortbread biscuit from the neat little pile Gran had made on a doily. I took a bite.

'Do you have anything of hers?' I asked, rescuing a crumb from the corner of my mouth. 'That I could look at, I mean?'

Gran pointed towards the door.

'Plenty, upstairs. In her bedroom. In fact, if you look in the top desk drawer, there's a whole box of her childhood things. You could bring it down, if you like.'

Leaving the remains of my biscuit on my china saucer, I stood up, walked into the hallway and mounted the staircase. It was a long time since I'd been upstairs in Gran's house; it almost felt like a foreign country.

On reaching the first floor, I glanced across the landing and spotted a door with Mum's name on it, in chunky wooden letters. 'Katherine', it said, next to a carving of a piano keyboard and two musical notes. I remembered sneaking in there once, on an Easter visit, when I was about eight years old, but I wasn't sure how much it had meant to me at the time. I had almost no memory of what it looked like.

I padded across the carpet and nudged the door open. It creaked a little, and I kept pushing until it opened out to reveal what was, essentially, still a teenager's bedroom. There were music posters on the wall – Prince, Bon Jovi, Michael Jackson – and a little pot of pens on the desktop, next to a stapler and a hole punch. There was a single bookshelf above the bed, stuffed to bursting with books like *The Secret Diary Of Adrian Mole* and *To Kill A Mockingbird*, and an acoustic guitar, with only four strings, leaning against the wall in the corner. The room smelled dusty, and slightly fragrant. Sunlight streamed in through a bay window.

It was a bedroom frozen in time. After Mum had moved away from home, my grandparents clearly hadn't changed a thing.

Crossing to the desk, I opened the top drawer and found a shoebox inside with Mum's name written across the top. I lifted it out.

'Have you found it, dear?' I heard Gran call.

I brushed my fingers across the writing. *Katherine.*

'I have!'

Walking back towards the landing, I paused, breathing in the scent of the room. Then I took one more look around, and closed the door behind me.

'Yes, that's the one,' said Gran, as I sat down again in the front room. The box was sitting on my lap, unopened. 'Why don't you have a look through?'

I lifted off the lid, setting it aside, and found a little collection of toys and trinkets nestled inside. A plastic orange yo-yo bearing the Fanta logo, its tattered string tangled up around the spindle. An eraser in the shape of an ice-cream cone. A *My Little Pony* toy, with long, purple hair and shooting stars painted on its back.

318

'Hey, I used to play with these,' I said, stroking its mane.

'These fashions always come back round again,' said Gran, with a knowing bob of the head. 'Little Katherine and little Charlie, you'd have been two peas in a pod, really.'

Still clutching the pony, I peered into the box again and noticed a white envelope buried beneath a pile of beaded necklaces. I pulled it out and turned it over. The writing on the front read: 'For Charlie'.

My heart leapt.

'What's this?'

'Oh, gosh,' said Gran, lowering her teacup. 'Katherine's letter. I'd forgotten all about that.'

My brow creased.

'This isn't a childhood thing.'

'No,' said Gran distantly. 'I'm not really sure what it's doing in there, to be honest.'

I turned it over, and ran my finger along the seal.

'You haven't opened it.'

Gran smiled.

'It's addressed to you, dear. And I remember now: I'd always planned to give it to you, when you were old enough.' She nodded. 'I think you are now.'

I held up the envelope, my chest thumping. This was a little piece of her. This was exactly what I had yearned for my entire life, and never imagined I would have. A part of me was sad that I hadn't been given it years earlier, but, really, that didn't matter. Because here it was. Finally, I had something of hers that was meant only for me.

'You keep that,' said Gran, setting down her empty teacup. 'And as for the rest of it . . . you can come back and look at it any time. Any time you like.'

'Thanks, Gran,' I said, dropping the letter into my handbag. She smiled at me.

'So tell me more about your photography,' she said, pouring more tea. 'I want to hear it *all* . . .'

Two hours later, full of tea and biscuits, I stepped out of the house, Gran waving me off from the doorstep. As I hurried towards Basingstoke station, a nervous energy fizzed in my bones. I was excited to see Mum's letter – I'd been burning to read it ever since I'd lifted it from the box – but what if it made things worse? What if it just turned out to be a reminder of how she'd left us behind, when I was too young to understand where she was going? What if she'd never really cared for me at all, and this was how I finally found out?

As soon as I sat down on the train, I slipped the envelope from my bag, broke the seal and pulled out the letter. My heart was racing as I unfolded it, curled up against the window and began to read.

My darling Charlie,

It might seem strange to write you a letter while you're still just a toddler. But then, when you eventually read this, you won't be a toddler any more. You'll be all grown-up, and I'll probably have already told you this in person. I just wanted to write down my thoughts while they were fresh in my heart.

I'm going away, my love. With the band. We've got a tour booked in the USA, and it starts next month. The label says this could be our big break — American radio stations are going crazy for the album, and if we can get a buzz going in the States, it could launch us all over the world. It's everything I've dreamed of, ever since I first sat down at a piano. And if it works out, I'll be able to take care of you, and your dad, and when you're older, you can come on tour with me. You can ride on the tour bus and stand beside the stage at our concerts and sit next to me on the piano stool while I perform. You'll love it, I know you will. It's in your blood.

But all of this, Charlie, it means leaving you while you're still so very tiny. And it has to be now. If we wait until next year, the buzz will be gone and it'll all be over — that's how this industry works. I'll only be away for a few months, but knowing I won't see you during that time breaks my heart in two.

I love you, with all that I am. But I hope you can understand: this is my chance to make something of myself. To prove to you that you can be _anything_, Charlie. You can be anyone. You are the most important thing in my life, and I want the world for you.

She'll never tell you this herself, but my mother was an artist,

321

once. She designed dresses, the most beautiful dresses you could imagine, and before she married Dad, she was studying fashion in Paris. Her tutors told her she could have been a top designer, but it never happened. Back then, mums were expected to stay in the home, simple as that, and it broke her a little, every day. I could see it in her eyes. I still can.

So I'm telling you now, my baby, to find the thing that fires you up, and chase after it. Chase after it with everything you have. I just know you have crazy talent in that little beating heart of yours, and I don't want you to waste even one drop of it.

Your father is a wonderful man, and he will look after you while I'm gone. I have your picture in a silver frame, and I'll keep it with me wherever we go. I will write to you every week, and I'll be home soon. You will never be alone, my perfect, perfect girl.

I love you.

Mum

'Are you OK, love?'

I glanced up to find a bearded train inspector looking at me, his brow crumpled with concern. I sat up and touched a hand to my face. It was wet with tears.

'You seem upset,' he said, pointing at the letter. I shook my head.

'No, no, I'm fine . . . it's good,' I said, sniffing, smiling through the tears. 'It's a good letter.'

'I see,' he said, smiling back. He had very kind eyes. 'I'll let you get on with it, then.' He tapped the ticket machine hanging at his side. 'You look trustworthy. And don't you let go of that letter, now. It seems important.'

He ambled off happily, and I wiped my eyes with the back of my hand, returning to the letter. A thrill buzzed through my body. This letter contained the answers to so many of the questions in my head. Had Mum abandoned us to go on tour with Little Boy Blue? No, not really. She was doing it *for us*. For me. She was trying to break a cycle that had begun with my grandmother, by seizing the opportunities her mother never had. And those dressmaker's sketches in Gran's hallway? They were almost certainly her own. I glanced out of the window as Gran's hometown disappeared behind me, and felt a pang in my chest. Knowing you had that talent, but were never allowed to do anything with it, can't have been easy to live with all these years.

As the train thundered along the tracks, I re-read the letter for a second, then a third time. And as I reached the last paragraph, I began to see lyrics emerging, ghost-like, from between the handwritten lines. Fire&Lights lyrics, from 'Dance With You', that had begun their life as Little Boy Blue lyrics. *I keep her picture in a silver frame . . . just as soon as I come home . . . she will never be alone . . .*

I knew now, for certain, that the inscription 'All songs by Harry West' in the Little Boy Blue album had to be a lie. This was unsettling, but it wasn't the most pressing thought on my mind. Because something else Mum had

323

written in her letter was bothering me. *I will write to you every week*. The unmailed letter I had found in Dad's study, back in November, told a different story. The story of a man desperate to hear from his wife, unsure even of where she was in the country. And this left two options: either she'd betrayed the promise she'd made to us, which I knew in my heart wasn't true . . . or something had happened to those letters.

28

The waiter laid my plate down with a flourish, and offered a serene smile.

'Madam, for you: roasted tomato tart served with an aubergine caviar, drizzled with basil oil and dusted with tomato powder.' He turned to Olly. 'And for sir: pan-fried fillet of British plaice, seasoned with fennel pollen and served on dill-crushed new potatoes with buttered and sautéed samphire and tomato concasse.'

He gave a very slight bow.

'Enjoy.'

We thanked him, and he walked away across the extremely plush carpet, leaving us alone in our booth. I peered at my food. A little reddish tart sat in the centre of a large, white plate, surrounded by a slim trickle of oil.

'It's very small, isn't it?'

I looked up. Olly tried, and failed, to hold in a laugh.

'We can always nip into Burger King afterwards for some proper food, if you like.'

He picked up his cutlery, and peered at the immaculate pile of fish and vegetables sitting in front of him.

'Sorry, this is the world's weirdest date, isn't it?' he said, skewering a potato. 'I mean, who takes a girl out for lunch in an airport?'

I shrugged.

'Hey, at least it's original.'

Olly smiled, but it wasn't the gleaming smile I was used to. There was a cloud behind his eyes.

'Oh, and we're going to have to eat fast, I'm afraid.' He checked the departures screen on the wall. 'Not long until we fly.'

I lifted my tomato tart with my fork, peering underneath it for evidence of more food.

'Just as well it's so tiny, then, eh?' I said, dropping the tart and picking up my knife.

As I sliced into the warm, flaky pastry, I tried to ignore the persistent memory of Thumper Wilson's grinning face, as he backed away down the school corridor. I'd known for days that this would be the best opportunity to bring up Diamond Storm – I had no other choice – but I wasn't exactly looking forward to it. *Killer date conversation, Charlie.*

I took a sip of water.

'Can I ask you something?' I said. Olly glanced up.

'Always.'

I picked at the corner of the tablecloth.

'There's this band at Caversham High, Diamond Storm—'

'The band in your photos.'

I paused, surprised that he had remembered them. But, then, that was Olly. He always remembered everything, and everyone.

'Yeah, that's them. And, I don't know, this might sound crazy, but I was thinking about the EP launch, how it's in a really small venue, and I wondered whether . . .' I could already feel myself wincing. 'Whether it might be cool to have them as a support act?'

Olly's mouth turned down at the corners, and he looked away, staring at the wall. I shook my head, and my hands.

'It's a dumb idea. You hate it. I shouldn't even—'

'No, Charlie, relax.' He smiled. 'I think it's a great idea.'

I twisted my fork in my hands.

'Really?'

He nodded.

'Really. We normally have Barry's latest act off *Make Or Break*, but it'd be nice to share a stage with someone who isn't famous, for once.'

I thought about Barry King, and the ruthless way he ran his all-conquering business empire. Something told me he wouldn't be a massive fan of this idea.

'I'm not sure your management will see it that way.'

Olly shrugged.

'With Barry, you just need a strong PR angle. I'll tell

him it'll look like we're "supporting grassroots music", or something. The press'll love it.' He broke off a corner of his fish and coated it in the sauce. 'I mean, I can't promise anything, but I'll give it a go.'

'OK, cool.' I took a breath, dabbing my mouth on my napkin. 'Thanks.'

'That's . . . no problem,' he said, looking at me searchingly. He frowned momentarily, then returned to his food.

We ate for a while, gentle classical music playing through speakers in the ceiling, the waiter briefly returning to refill our water glasses. Planes took off periodically in the distance, roaring like thunder above our heads.

'Charlie, are we OK?' said Olly suddenly, lowering his cutlery. I was still chewing on a mouthful of tart. I swallowed.

'Us? Why do you ask?'

Why do you ask? That wasn't the right response. The right response would have been, 'Yes, of course'. Because we *were* OK. Weren't we?

'It's just . . . I don't know, you've felt a bit distant since Saturday night.' He held up a hand. 'And don't get me wrong, I know why. Things got really weird at the awards. We let everyone down, including you.'

'You didn't let me down,' I said hurriedly. 'To be honest, it's none of my business. And these things happen.'

328

Olly leaned his elbows on the table, and raked his fingers through his hair.

'I just ... I can't get over Gabriel. We did enough damage with that awful acceptance speech, and then he goes and lays into some random stranger, right in front of the paparazzi.' He looked up, his forehead creased. 'I mean, what was he even doing out there in the first place?'

He was looking out for me, I thought. But I couldn't tell him that. I couldn't explain who Paul really was, or why he was targeting us. Gabe had been very clear: he didn't want anyone apart from me and Barry to know the truth about his past, and even if I thought it might do him good, I couldn't betray that trust. Not even to Olly.

'I guess he just ... has a lot going on right now.'

'Maybe,' said Olly, nudging his almost-empty plate away. 'But that's no excuse. I know he has a difficult past and he doesn't want to talk about it, but we're a band. We can't get through this unless we work as a unit.' His eyes dropped to the table. 'I tell you, one of these days, that guy is going to push us all to breaking point.'

'What guy?' said a voice above us. I looked up, and the breath shot out of me.

'Gabe,' I said, my eyes unblinking. Olly twisted round to find Gabriel standing at his shoulder, and his face immediately coloured.

'Fancy lunch,' said Gabriel, nodding at my food. 'What's that green stuff?'

I poked at it.

'Aubergine caviar.'

A thorny silence fell. I squirmed in my seat.

'If you ask me,' I said to the tablecloth, 'aubergine caviar does *not* need to be a thing.'

For a few moments, we all listened to the clinking of cutlery from other tables, and the distant ringing of flight boarding calls. Gabriel scratched the top of his head.

'Charlie, can we talk?'

'What . . . now?' I glanced at Olly, who was chewing his bottom lip and concentrating on his plate.

Gabriel didn't reply. He just gave me a look: an intense, dark look that told me this was something private. Something Olly couldn't know about.

Awkwardly, I pulled the napkin off my lap and slid across the leather seating.

'Sorry, Olly . . . you don't mind, do you?'

Olly looked back at me, a little lost.

'No, sure,' he said, pushing his knife and fork together. 'I should probably . . . check my passport anyway.'

I looked at him one last time, managing a weak smile, before walking away with Gabriel, my skin too tight, my fingers fidgeting in my sleeves. As we left the restaurant, I glanced over my shoulder and saw Olly toss his napkin on to the table and drop back against the seat, his hands in his hair.

'Did we really have to do this now?' I said, crossing my arms. It was making my heart ache.

'Sorry,' said Gabe, running a hand down his face. 'I didn't realise you were with . . .' He trailed off, and I clenched my jaw, keeping my eyes low. He pulled his phone from his pocket. 'It's just . . . I think you're going to want to see this.'

'What?' I said, with a sigh.

He drew in a long, deep breath.

'I know how our parents died.'

We were sitting in a secluded corner of the bar, still in the first class lounge, nursing tall glasses of Coke. The room was empty apart from a smart-looking middle-aged couple at a nearby table, drinking red wine and not talking to each other. The woman noticed us at one point and looked at Gabriel as if she recognised him, then returned to caressing the stem of her wine glass.

Gabriel passed me his phone.

'That guy from the forum, SabbathRules. He got back to me.'

I took the phone, my eyes widening.

'Oh. Wow.'

When I'd suggested contacting SabbathRules last month, I'd assumed Gabriel had just ignored me. I guess the lesson of the last couple of weeks was: Stop Assuming Things About Gabriel West.

'I posed as some guy called Adam, told him I was researching old indie bands from the London area.' He took a sip of his drink. 'I never expected him to get back to me. But twenty minutes ago . . . he did.'

I stared at the email on Gabriel's phone. The subject line read: 'Little Boy Blue: can you help??'

Gabriel glanced around, keeping his voice low.

'So we already knew that our parents died one day apart, right? And even before we found out your mum was in the band, we knew their deaths had to be connected.'

I nodded. He pointed at his phone.

'Well, they are.'

Adam,

Researching obscure indie bands, eh?? That's a job I wouldn't mind myself. (I mean, I'm a hard rock guy at heart, but not everyone can be Black Sabbath, right?!)

But, yeah: Little Boy Blue. I remember them. Great band while they lasted, but it didn't end well. Talk about rock 'n' roll casualties.

My breath was unsteady. Even after all this time, I wasn't sure if I was ready to hear this.

I don't know the whole story, but I used to knock around with this bloke – Jogger, we called him – who roadied for a few labels back in the 90s. He worked with Little Boy Blue now and again, and he said the lead singer, Harry something, was a real messed up guy. Casual drug dealer, god knows what else. Anyway, the band are on tour in the States, and one night, halfway through the tour, he just walks offstage. Middle of a gig. Doesn't come back. Jogger says Harry owed a ton of money to his suppliers, some London drug ring, and they were threatening his family back home. He had a little kid, or something. So the band keep going without him for a few gigs, seeing out their contracts and whatnot, but it's not the same. Harry might have been a waster, but Jogger says he was one hell of a lead singer, and it kind of tanked without him. The band are strung out, the label are talking about pulling the tour and the piano player, Kit, she's missing her daughter like crazy. But she doesn't want to give up. She knows it's all over if they leave the States now. So, anyway, the pressure must have got to her, 'cos a week or so later, she's driving back from a gig and she's killed in a car accident. Runs off the road into a tree. Dead on the scene.

The air rushed out of me, and my gut, my whole body, felt hollow and raw, like I'd been suddenly scraped empty.

The image of the wrecked car bled on to my retinas: twisted metal and shattered glass, smoke rising from the engine, the bonnet concertinaed. Lights flashing all around. I pressed a hand to my mouth.

Gabriel reached across the table, closing his hand over mine, and tears collected in my eyes.

I read on.

When Harry finds out, I dunno, the guy's already screwed up, his band's falling apart and he's in debt to some nasty people . . . so he tops himself. And that's it. No more Little Boy Blue. Tragedy, really.

But, yeah, that's about all I know. Hope it helps, mate.

Good luck with the research.

SabbathRules

I discarded Gabe's phone on the table, pushing it away, and fell back into the seat. Hearing it from someone else, a stranger, somehow made it more real. Even after all these years.

I thought about my father, and the things he'd told me about how Mum had died. So it really was a car accident. He'd kept the Little Boy Blue story from me, but he'd been honest about everything else. Clearly, he'd been trying to protect me. He must have thought that knowing Mum was on tour with a band would upset me, and at first, it had.

But I had her letter now. I knew she hadn't just abandoned us. I knew she was thinking about me the whole time.

'Charlie?'

Gabe was searching my face, his eyes heavy with concern, and I suddenly felt guilty for making everything about me. I wiped my tears with the back of my hand, smearing them across my cheek.

'God, are you OK?'

He frowned.

'Don't worry about me.'

'I mean . . . at least now you know why he died. Right?'

Gabriel ran a finger down the condensation on his Coke glass. It freed up a droplet of water, which trickled on to the table.

'I thought it might make me feel better, finding out what really happened. But it hasn't.' His breathing quickened, his shoulders rising. 'He was a waste of space, Charlie.'

I reached for his hand again.

'It sounds like he came back for you, though.'

He lowered his brow.

'If he came back, it was for his money. His dealers. It wasn't for me.'

I closed my fingers around his, thinking about his many secrets, and the fact that only Barry and I knew he was an orphan. The way the press were treating him, surely they'd ease off if they knew how difficult his early life had been? And what about the rest of the band? Wouldn't it be better for Gabe if they all knew the truth?

I thought back to the restaurant, and the expression on Olly's face as we'd left. I hated keeping this a secret from him. I couldn't stand it.

'Don't you ever think you should tell Olly, and the others, about all this? They still think your parents are living in France . . . I mean, it's crazy, don't you think?'

Gabe shook his head, his teeth clenched.

'No. I can't.'

'Don't you trust them?'

His eyes went misty, his finger tracing the rim of his glass.

'I do. Honestly, I do. Olly's the most trustworthy guy on the face of the earth. You know that.' He looked at me, his face a little sad. 'But that's not the point. It's Paul Morgan I don't trust, and he can get to anyone. Believe me.'

A cold shudder trickled through my bones as I remembered the feeling of Paul's cigarette breath on the back of my neck, in the gloom of the StarBright car park. *I could make things very uncomfortable for you, Charlie.* I glanced across the bar, wishing the memory away, and when my eyes passed the main entrance, I gasped.

Olly was standing there, staring through the glass.

I pulled my hand away from Gabriel's.

29

Olly and I were sitting next to each other on the plane, not talking. Outside the windows, thirty thousand feet above sea level, pillowy clouds floated by, the sun burning orange in the distance.

I had only ever flown twice before. Those flights had been on budget airlines, and so my lasting impression of air travel was of screaming babies and weird, microwaved panini. But British Airways 'Club Europe' was another matter all together. Rows of spacious leather seats, mostly empty, enough immaculately-dressed flight attendants to staff the Titanic and an endless supply of snacks and posh sandwiches. It would have been exciting, if my stomach wasn't so tangled over Olly.

'Listen, about earlier, and cutting lunch—'

'It's fine,' interrupted Olly, turning to me, his brow furrowed. 'I'm sorry I was funny about it.'

I laughed softly, shaking my head.

'Wait. How exactly have you ended up apologising to me?'

He held air in his cheeks, then puffed it out.

'I don't know. I just . . . I don't want to be *that guy*.'

I lifted my eyebrows.

'As long as you live, Olly Samson, you will never be "that guy".'

He smiled, and we settled back into silence. After a while, he said:

'Charlie, is something . . . going on? With Gabriel, I mean?'

My muscles tensed. I had to think very carefully about how I answered this.

'We just . . . we're still friends, you know?' Olly nodded, his eyes on the floor. I took his hand. 'He's going through a rough time, and he needed someone to talk to. I don't really think he has anyone.' I stroked the back of his hand with my thumb. 'I'm sorry. This must suck for you.'

He fiddled with the latch holding up his tray table.

'I'm not a jealous person,' he said, still looking at the floor. 'Honestly. It's just . . . with Gabriel . . .'

'I know,' I said, closing my other hand around his. 'I know.'

I leaned forward and nudged his head upwards with my nose. He responded, slowly turning to face me, and our eyes met, barely millimetres apart. The air between us felt charged suddenly, and we kissed, pressing our lips together, his hand sliding upwards through my hair. I felt my skin sing, and my heart thunder, and for a moment, I felt as if the plane could disappear around us, and we wouldn't fall.

We broke apart, and I sat back in my seat. I shook my hair out.

'OK, I have to pee.'

'That's my favourite thing to hear after I've kissed someone,' said Olly. I laughed.

'Sorry. I am so gross.' I unclipped my seat belt. 'See you in a sec.' I tapped my armrest, and smiled. 'Don't let anyone steal my place.'

On my way to the loo, I attracted a few looks from the onboard staff, no doubt wondering who I was. It was their job to be discreet about popstars, but teenage girls who looked like groupies? Apparently I was fair game. They were looking at me like I'd just rolled out of one of the boys' hotel beds.

'Charlie B!'

A few minutes later, on my way back from the toilet, I passed Yuki, sitting on his own by the window. He caught my attention, and patted the seat next to him.

'Fancy joining me?' he said, his eyes pleading like a puppy's. 'I'm bored.'

I pointed across the rows of seats.

'I'm sort of sitting with Olly, actually . . . ?'

Yuki groaned.

'He gets you ALL THE TIME, bro. Pleeeeease.'

'I don't think I'm your bro, Yuks,' I said, settling down next to him. He wagged a finger at me.

'Oh, no. You are. You are fully my bro.'

He lifted up a fist, expectantly. I fist-bumped him, and he gave me a satisfied nod.

'So what's new with you?' I asked, noting the empty Jack Daniels miniatures on his tray table.

'Oh, I've just been staring out of the window, contemplating the staggering majesty of the natural world. You?'

'Same,' I said, with a one-shouldered shrug.

'Champagne?'

We both looked up to find a flight attendant standing over us, holding a tray of bubbling champagne flutes. Yuki's eyes lit up.

'Hell, yeah, sister. Bring on the fizzy goodness. Charlie?'

'You look a bit young to me,' said the attendant, with a dry smile.

'It's OK,' I said, pulling my tray table open. 'I'll just have a ginger beer.'

Yuki held his hands in the air.

'Fine . . . I'll have hers, then. Man, are you lucky I'm here.'

Yuki took two drinks from the tray, knocking back nearly half a glass in one go. After preparing my drink, the attendant moved on down the cabin, her perfect blond hair bobbing gently as she walked.

'You're smart,' said Yuki, with a nod at my ginger beer. 'Alcohol is a downward spiral. One minute you're sipping crème de menthe by the pool, the next you're waking up in a skip in Middlesbrough with a beard full of Special Brew.'

I managed a laugh, but it wasn't convincing. Yuki raised an eyebrow.

'OK, Charlie B. Let me have it. What's wrong?'

My eyes fell on his glass as he lifted it to his lips. He pulled it away.

'What . . . the booze?'

I grimaced.

'Come on, it's just a cheeky nifter to take the edge off.'

'*Yuki.*'

His shoulders dropped, and he set down the drink.

'Dude, this is like sitting next to my GP. You'll be taking my blood pressure next.'

We sat in silence for a while, listening to the furry hum of the cabin and the gentle music playing though the speakers. Yuki drummed a distracted little rhythm on his tray table.

'Something's wrong, isn't it?' I said eventually, without looking at him.

'You mean, apart from the in-flight music?'

I gave him a withering look.

'Apart from that, yeah.'

He held his breath, staring into his glass at the tiny

341

ladders of shimmering bubbles. Then he relaxed, and took another gulp.

'Nah, I'm good. Don't you worry about me, Charlie B.' He pulled his phone from his pocket, and checked the time. 'Twenty minutes until we land. Time for a snooze, maybe?'

I caught a glance of the wallpaper on his phone: a photograph of him at Christmas, wearing a jumper that read 'ALL THE JINGLE LADIES' and carrying a small child on his back, like a monkey. I looked more closely at the kid, who was waving a toy lightsaber, and a massive grin spread across my face. He looked like a mini-Yuki. He was impossibly cute.

'Is that your little brother?' I asked, pointing. Yuki's face immediately lit up.

'Yep.'

'What's his name?'

'Shinichi. But we call him Itchy, for short. He's obsessed with Star Wars, so I bought him a lightsaber for Christmas, and he carried it around *all day*. When I woke up on Boxing Day, he was lying on the bed next to me, fast asleep, still clutching it.' He smiled. 'The little tyke.'

I glanced at the champagne flutes again, then back at the photograph, thoughts churning through my mind. He was such a great guy, Yuki Harrison. I just wished I knew what was going on inside his head.

*

Snap.

My finger was poised over the camera shutter, lens darting left and right, seeking out the best angles.

Snap. Snap. Snap.

As I followed the boys through the warren of corridors that made up Northern Media Studios, I realised how soothing it was to be taking photos again. With everything that had been going on over the past few weeks, I'd almost forgotten why the band had invited me to join them in the first place. I'd hardly managed any shots at the StarBright Arena; in fact, I'd almost appeared in more pictures than I'd taken. But for the short period we were here, I was myself again. Charlie Bloom, music photographer. And it felt amazing.

Snap. Yuki walking past a life-sized stuffed bear, and making monster claws at it.

Snap. Aiden and Olly, from behind, just walking, Olly's hand on Aiden's shoulder.

Snap. Gabriel, alone, swigging from a bottle of water.

We made our way along narrow hallways, through carpeted reception areas and across spacious, high-ceilinged rooms with cables hanging down in thick, meaty tangles. Random furniture and pieces of set lay untouched in corners: a chat show sofa here, a suit of armour there. Several shows were being filmed at once, throughout the building, and every now and again, you'd spot a vaguely-recognisable TV star being led to or from the make-up room, getting briefed on the shoot ahead.

We stopped outside a dressing room, and Tara turned to me, touching her palms together.

'Give us ten minutes with the band, Charlie, and you can take some more snaps once they're made up. That cool?'

'Totally,' I said, edging away. I watched the boys file into the dressing room and, stepping backwards, looked left and right for signs of a canteen, or a vending machine. At the far end of the corridor, I spotted a water cooler, and made my way towards it.

Plucking one of the blue plastic cups from its holder, I placed it on the drip-tray and slid it under the nozzle. Just as I was about to press the button, I heard voices coming from behind a heavy black curtain on the opposite side of the corridor.

'Blake. Bloody good to see you, pal.'

'Likewise, Baz. How long's it been?'

The first voice was Barry King's – I'd recognise that gravelly tone anywhere – and the second belonged to Blake Hadaway, the country's most fashionable chat-show host. Something about the private tone of their voices made me want to listen longer.

'God, three, four years? I appreciate this, you know,' said Barry.

'Pleasure's all mine. How's Leslie?'

'She's all right. Pain in the arse, but I love her. You settling down any time soon?'

Blake laughed. Rough and throaty, like a motorcycle engine.

'You know me, squire. Too many women, not enough bottles of Merlot to go round.'

I winced. Blake Hadaway had what you might call a 'reputation', mainly for dating girls twenty years his junior. Half the general public thought he was charming and seductive, but, personally, I just thought he was a bit gross.

'Anyway, listen. Today.' Barry hushed his voice, and I took a step towards the curtain, straining my ears. 'You get where I'm coming from, right?'

'Crystal. Your boys are *persona non grata*, and you want them restored to their former, illustrious glory.'

'It's been a nightmare few weeks,' said Barry, with a sigh. 'Never work with animals or children.'

'Or popstars,' offered Blake, 'who are a bit of both.' Barry laughed drily. 'But anyway . . . time's a-tickin', I'd better get on set. And don't sweat it, my boy. You know how long I've been waiting to have your little protégés on my show. It'll be a blinder. We'll make TV history.'

'Whatever you want,' said Barry. 'Let's just fix this mess.'

A pause. I could tell they were shaking hands because I could hear Blake's jewellery rattling on his wrist.

'You can count on me, old pal. I'll see you on the other side.'

30

'Ladies and gentlefriends, let's hear it for pop's foremost Prince Charmings . . . the thinking woman's boy band . . . it's none other than . . . Fire&Lights!'

The set for *The Blake Hadaway Show* was decked out like an eighties cocktail bar, with garish neon signs, chrome furniture and a fake city skyline as a backdrop. Fire&Lights emerged from the open doorway at the back, waving, and bounded down the stairs past gold ropes and pot-plants towards the show's famous crushed-velvet sofa. Blake Hadaway was waiting for them by his leather swivel chair, wearing a suit jacket with the sleeves pulled up, a swooping V-neck T-shirt and ripped white jeans. His wrists were laddered with chunky bracelets, and his bird's nest haircut made him look like he'd just staggered backwards out of a hurricane.

Yuki arrived first, and gave him a resounding high-five.

'Steady on, lad, you'll take my arm off . . .'

Blake shook hands with Aiden, Olly and Gabriel in turn, then dropped theatrically into his chair. He spun impetuously from side to side, rubbing his hands together, while the four bandmates positioned themselves on the silver sofa.

Despite everything that had happened, I had to admit: Fire&Lights had never looked better. Their stylists had picked out crisp new suits for them in a spectrum of deep, rich colours – Olly in midnight blue, Gabriel in blood red, Aiden in royal purple, Yuki in bronze – and with their box-fresh brogues and sculpted hair, they looked almost super-real.

'So, look. Look. Lookie here.' Blake sat forward in his chair. 'It's been a naughty few weeks for you lot. Rumours flying, scandal in the papers, twitch of the curtains, etcetera. Read all about it. How are you feeling?'

'It's still amazing, to be honest,' said Olly brightly. 'We've been through a lot, but we wouldn't change it for the world.'

Blake narrowed his eyes.

'Come on, Oliver. Don't give me the party line.'

'That's not the party line!' protested Olly, turning to his bandmates for support. Yuki lifted both arms, slinging one around Aiden and the other around Gabriel.

'We're having the time of our lives,' he said, grinning. 'Look at us. Look at our little faces.'

'But what I'm *getting at*,' continued Blake, holding up an open palm, 'is this – and look, I don't want to be the one to say it – but Gabriel . . . you didn't half give that poor bloke a jimmy-licking last weekend.'

I was sitting backstage, with Barry and Tara, watching the action unfold on a wall-mounted television screen. Barry, who had been pacing back and forth since the interview started, stopped suddenly in his tracks. 'What the—?!'

'Don't believe everything you read on the internet,' said Gabriel calmly, and I shifted uncomfortably in my seat. He had said the same thing to me once.

'Don't fret, kid,' replied Blake, sorting through his cue cards, 'I'm sure he was asking for it. Now. Listen. Before the show, I thunked a thought, I did; I thought rather than sitting here gassing all night, we should play a little game . . .'

The audience whistled and cheered, and Blake clicked his fingers, prompting the studio lights to change, darkening all around, with intense, interrogation-style spotlights trained on all four band members. At the back of the set, in front of a faux-brick wall, two large light-boxes descended from the ceiling. One read TRUTH, and the other, DARE.

'Yes, that's right,' shouted Blake, above the racket from the crowd. 'We are going to play Truth Or Dare . . . with Fire&Lights!'

The booming, bassy soundtrack built to a crescendo, the audience clapping in time with the beat, strobe lights firing across the studio. A faint dread curdled inside me.

'What on *earth* is he doing?' muttered Barry, under his breath.

'Mr Harrison, we'll start with you.'

Three of the spotlights faded away, and Yuki was left exposed on the sofa, beaming at the crowd. Blake gestured to the light-boxes on the back wall.

'Make your choice.'

Yuki appealed to the audience.

'Well, it's obvious, isn't it?'

Enthusiastic shouting – 'Truth!', 'Pick dare!', 'We love you, Yuki!' – rained down on him. I knew instantly which way he would go.

'It's got to be Dare.'

Everyone started shouting and stamping their feet, and Yuki leapt off the sofa, whipping them into a frenzy. Behind him, the DARE box lit up, and an ear-piercing siren circled the studio.

'Powers That Be,' called Blake, over the noise, 'yield me a dare!'

A screen descended from above, and on it, words and phrases cycled round at lightning speed until a shrill buzzer sounded. The selected answer read: 'KISS A RANDOM AUDIENCE MEMBER'.

Jumping off the edge of the stage, Yuki hurtled towards the audience, accompanied by frantic music and the delighted roars of the crowd. He scurried up the central staircase and stopped next to a group of teenage girls, who screamed and cried, waiting for him to choose his target. At the last minute, though, he pointed at a middle-aged woman in the row behind them, squeezed past her friends, bent down and planted a big kiss on her cheek. She went instantly red, and clamped her hands to her mouth.

'What a player,' said Blake, savouring the moment. 'Are you all right, my dear?'

The camera zoomed in on the woman. She nodded, her eyes shining.

'He's lovely!' she burst out. Her friends exploded with laughter.

'Didn't even take you out for dinner first,' said Blake, shaking his head. 'Romance is dead . . .'

Yuki careered back down the stairs and on to the set, the crowd clapping in time behind him.

When he slumped on to the sofa, his hair tousled, tie askew, Blake studied him for a few moments, then said: 'Yuki, are you . . . *drunk* right now?'

Yuki's eyes flashed beneath the lights.

'I picked Dare, Hadaway. You'll have to wait your turn.'

Blake nodded, impressed.

'Well played, my friend. You have bested me.' He reached across his desk for his drink, a comically large, toilet-cleaner-blue cocktail with a massive chunk of pineapple perched on the side. 'So who's next? *Aiden Roberts?*'

Cheering erupted once more from the audience, and Aiden wrinkled his nose. Blake slurped from his cocktail through a giant curly straw.

'Truth,' he said, with the straw still in his mouth, 'or Dare?'

Aiden gave it some thought. I glanced at Barry, who was watching the screen, transfixed, his eyes flicking left and right.

'Truth, please, Blake.'

The TRUTH box lit up, and the lights in the studio shifted again, three of the spotlights disappearing, until only Aiden was visible. A long, low synth note played in the background.

'Ye Gods, spin the wheel!' exclaimed Blake, throwing his arms in the air like a toreador. Once again, phrases spun frantically on the big screen, *click-click-click*, until eventually slowing, and settling on a question.

'IS KAITLYN JONES REALLY YOUR GIRLFRIEND?'

There was a sharp intake of breath from the crowd. Backstage, Barry clasped both hands to his head. 'You have *got* to be kidding me!'

'Or,' said Blake, plucking the pineapple slice off his drink and giving it a suck, 'is it just a stunt to sell records?'

At first, Aiden said nothing. Meanwhile, the now

infamous GIF of him letting go of Kaitlyn's hand at the WorldPOP Awards played on a loop on the big screen. Blake cocked his head to one side, like a bird.

'I'm gonna have to hurry you, fella.'

Aiden stumbled for an answer.

'Well . . . Kaitlyn . . . she's just—'

'Crikey, mate,' said Blake, as the rest of the spotlights unexpectedly returned, revealing Aiden's stunned bandmates, sitting in a row. 'We were only joking.' He threw a knowing look at the audience. 'Seems I touched a nerve there.'

'I'm going to kill him,' said Barry, to no one in particular. 'I am going to tear him a new one.'

'Right, my turn,' said Gabriel, with a private glance at Aiden, who had gone tomato-red. 'Dare, Blake. Do your worst.'

Blake pulled his lips back over his teeth, and banked his head from side to side.

'I don't know . . . I'm not sure I want you boys choosing any more. I think it's more interesting if I call the shots.'

Gabriel smiled darkly.

'That's not how the game works, Blake.'

Blake returned a rakish grin.

'My game, my rules.' The audience *ooooh*-ed gleefully, and Gabriel shrugged, though I could tell, from the slight shifting of his jaw, that he knew something nasty was heading his way. 'I thought I'd read out some of your lyrics, Gabe,' continued Blake. 'Can we bring 'em up for the people at home, please?'

Words blossomed on to the screen at the back of the studio.

'This is from a track on the new EP called "Tokyo, I'm Yours", and I tell you . . . it's really quite touching. Have a look.'

The camera zoomed in on the lyrics, and the song began to play.

I pull my collar up
I've got my hair in my face so no one can see

Feel like I'm choking up
I never knew how broken my heart could be

She don't want me, no
Tokyo, I know, I know, I know the score
And if she won't be mine tonight
Then, Tokyo, I'm yours

'Sounds to me like you were pretty cut up when you wrote this, old boy,' mused Blake, slurping from his cocktail, legs crossed. He jerked a foot in Gabriel's direction. 'Who's it about?'

A hot, dry nausea spread through my body, shouts of

353

'Clara Fitzcharles!' cascading from the crowd. Gabriel interlinked his hands on the back of his head.

'This is a break-up song,' continued Blake, before Gabe could answer. 'This is about a girl who you quite clearly *adored*, and who, by the sounds of it, left you in pieces.' He set down his drink. 'Mate, I've had my fair share of women, so trust me, I understand heartbreak. And let's be honest, that Clara Fitzcharles, she might have nice hair, but Sweet Mother Mary, she's as dull as a horse's arse.'

The sickness climbed upwards through my stomach and lungs, catching in my throat. The raucous, hysterical laughter of the studio audience was like crisp wrappers being stuffed in my ears.

'If you ask me,' said Blake, stroking his chin thoughtfully, 'this song is about someone else. Someone secret.'

The crowd heckled and wolf-whistled, and I pressed a hand to my mouth. Did Blake know about me?

'You have a very wild imagination, Hadaway,' said Gabriel, his voice beginning to fray at the edges. Blake flicked his hair off his face.

'Oh, I don't know. Let's see what Oliver has to say about it.'

Olly drew in a deep breath.

'Fine. I pick Dare—'

'Nah, bored with that now,' said Blake, chucking his

cue cards over his shoulder. They fanned out in the air, scattering across the studio. 'Answer me this: have you ever dated someone that another band member had already been with?'

I closed my fingers, tight, around the edge of my chair. I could feel my blood slowing, like I was being strangled from the inside.

'What happened to the game, Blake?' said Olly, forcing a smile.

'Dooon't dodge the question!' retorted Blake, slapping him on the knee. The audience was laughing nervously, and there was a charged atmosphere in the studio. 'You see, I've had a very interesting tip-off, and I think this secret, special someone, the girl in the song . . .' He pointed back and forth between Olly and Gabriel. 'I think she connects you two together.'

I doubled over in my chair, eyes shut tight, willing it all away. The interview was going out live. This couldn't be happening.

'You're pathetic, you know that?'

I sat up, abruptly, at the sound of Gabriel's voice. He had stood up from the sofa, and was confronting Blake. The audience were booing, jeering and throwing insults, though who exactly they were aiming at was unclear.

'Manners, my boy!' said Blake, looking absolutely delighted with himself. 'Your mother might be watching.'

Gabriel sneered at him.

'We came on here to talk about music, and all you've done is peddle rumours. You're worse than the paparazzi.'

Blake grinned, his eyes gleaming.

'Are you going to hit me, Gabe?'

Gabriel squared his shoulders, locks of hair breaking loose on his forehead. The audience had been cowed into a brittle silence, and for a terrible moment, I thought Gabriel really *was* going to hit him.

Instead, he turned to face his band.

'Boys?'

They all looked up at him, and he muttered something inaudible. One by one, they stood up to join him.

Then, in their first act of unity in weeks, Gabriel, Olly, Yuki and Aiden filed past Blake without a word, and walked off the set.

'Are you having a *laugh*, mate?'

The five of us were sitting silently in the dressing room, waiting to be escorted from the building. Outside the door, we could hear Barry laying into Blake.

'Explain the absolute train-wreck I just witnessed out there.'

'Baz, even you have to admit that was fantastic television.'

'I'm not an idiot, Blake. I saw what you were doing. We've been friends for nearly ten years. Doesn't that mean anything to you?'

'Now, hang on a minute. You know as well as I do that ratings are king.' A pause. 'If you'll pardon the pun.'

I glanced up, and happened to catch Gabriel's eye. He shifted in his chair, and I tore my gaze away.

'Ratings?' spat Barry. 'You just tried to destroy my band!'

'On the contrary, I'd say they're doing a perfectly good job of destroying themselves.'

'Come off it! I know a set-up when I see one. What in the hell were you thinking?'

'I said I'd make history, didn't I?'

The door to the dressing room swung open, and Barry backed in. He clicked his fingers at us.

'We're off, guys. Come on.'

Quickly, we gathered our things and followed him from the room. Tara was waiting in the corridor, and once we were all standing together, as a group, Barry turned round and pointed a chubby finger at the presenter.

'I will end you, Hadaway, make no mistake about it. *I will end you.*'

Grinding his teeth, Barry strode off down the corridor, and the rest of us followed, browbeaten and mute, like a line of schoolchildren. Blake called after us.

'Pleasure having you, my loves. Do call again!'

As we made our way through the maze of corridors towards the studio exit, nobody spoke except Barry, who

357

was on the phone, making a series of angry demands. I figured it was his lawyer on the other end.

My phone buzzed inside my camera case, and I pulled it out.

Don't suppose Blake was talking about you there, was he? Are you the secret girl in the song??!

The message had come from an unknown number. I glared at the screen.

Who is this? I wrote back.

Sounds like you really are in the inner circle now, Charlotte. Which means you owe us a support slot. Love, Thumper & the Diamond Storm boys

31

Behind The Band, Part Nine
'Live Finals'

A group of excitable contestants buzz and chatter in the Make or Break green room. A voiceover sweeps in over the top.

'Aiden Roberts, Irish singer from boy band sensation Fire&Lights, has been openly struggling with the pressure of the live finals. Ten minutes before Fire&Lights are due onstage for Saturday's performance, he has yet to emerge from his dressing room.'

'What's happening, boys?' says Barry King, who has taken Aiden's bandmates aside for a private talk. Yuki shrugs.

'He doesn't want to sing today. He doesn't think he's good enough.'

Barry, chewing gum, presses a finger and thumb into his forehead.

'Jeez. All right.' He glances out into the hallway. 'Wait here.'

The camera cuts to Aiden, alone in a small dressing room. His eyes look a little red. Barry is standing in the doorway.

'They need you out there, Aid.'

Aiden hangs his head.

'They don't. They're better off without me.'

'Why would you think that?'

'I shouldn't be here. The other guys are way better than me. I feel like an idiot.'

Barry walks into the room, and sits down opposite Aiden.

'What are you afraid of?' he asks.

'I'm going to get it wrong again, like last week, and let them down. I'm not a popstar.'

Barry spins the silver Rolex on his wrist.

'I've seen a lot of popstars, Aiden, and trust me, you've got what it takes.' He leans in closer. 'Plus, between you and me, those boys really need you. This band needs you.'

Aiden looks up.

'They do?'

'More than you realise.' Barry lays a big hand on Aiden's shoulder. 'So what do you say? You coming back?'

Aiden's eyes drop to his lap, and the music begins to build. The shot dissolves to black.

Seconds later, the camera fades up on Gabriel, Olly and Yuki, standing in the wings beside the stage, ready to start their performance. Olly is shifting from one foot to the other. Yuki is gnawing on a fingernail.

Then, over a rousing swell in the soundtrack, Aiden

360

appears behind them, hands in his pockets. Yuki spots him, his
eyes expanding, like a child's, and he runs over to give him a
hug. Barry stands, arms crossed, in the background.

'You're an idiot, Roberts,' says Yuki, ruffling his friend's hair.

'I know,' says Aiden, the smile returning to his face.

< www.poptube.com *all the pop, all the time* **>**

'You see, look . . . they are SUCH good friends. They have
to stay together. They just *have* to.'

Melissa was sitting at her desk, chin in hands, video
player open on her computer screen. She paused the
action and swivelled round on her chair.

'They're not going to split up, are they?' she said, her
face creased with concern. I was curled up on the corner
of her bed, knees against my chest. I shook my head.

'Honestly? I have no idea.'

I looked at my phone again, scrolling listlessly through
a series of depressing headlines.

LIARS & FIGHTS: THE FALL OF THE
WORLD'S BIGGEST BOY BAND

FIRE&LIGHTS CRASH AND
BURN ON LIVE TV

GABRIEL'S GOING DOWN, AND HE'S
TAKING HIS BAND WITH HIM

Saturday's episode of *The Blake Hadaway Show* had achieved the series' highest ratings yet, and people were describing Blake's take-down of the band as 'car-crash television that we won't be forgetting for many years to come'. So, in his own way, Blake had been right. He really had made TV history.

'I feel pukey,' said Melissa, collapsing the lid of her laptop. I closed my eyes.

'I really wish this weekend would just go away.'

My phone pinged. A message from Olly.

Talked to Barry: Diamond Storm are on for Troubadour.
Can you send Tara their phone number? O xx

I drew in a deep breath, relieved. Finally, I could take Thumper and Jody off the list of things I needed to worry about. But at the same time, something was niggling at me. Was I imagining it, or was there something distant about the tone of Olly's message?

'Who's that?' asked Melissa.

'Olly. He sorted that support slot for Diamond Storm.'

Melissa sat up, her face brightening.

'Oh, wow! That's really good, right?'

I nodded, tight-lipped.

'Yeah . . . it's good. I mean, I'm relieved. But . . .' I passed my phone to her. 'Does this message seem a bit off to you?'

She examined the screen, her brow furrowing.

'Hmm. I do not have the necessary boyfriend experience to answer that question.'

She tossed my phone back on to the bed, and I picked it up, opening Twitter. I thought about the celebrations Diamond Storm would have when I passed on the message.

'Also, I kind of hate that Thumper got his way.'

Melissa gave a sympathetic nod.

'I know what you mean, but you didn't exactly have a choice. Plus, you have to admit, they're actually quite good these days. Even if they do have a Grade A douche-whistle for a drummer.'

I tugged my mouth into a smile, and Melissa slid off her chair and dropped down next to me on the bed.

'So are things . . . not OK, then, with Olly?'

I rested my head against the wall.

'I just don't know. Gabe says we have to keep everything to ourselves, because that journalist is sniffing around. And it makes sense, especially after yesterday . . . but not being able to tell Olly about it, it's killing me.' I flicked at my fingernail. 'He knows something's going on with Gabe. He knows.'

Melissa's hand brushed against mine.

'Dating a popstar is hard work, man.'

'You got that right.'

She snuggled closer to me, her feet hanging off the edge of the bed. She wiggled her toes.

'And Gabe's email, from the forum guy ... that was pretty heavy, huh?'

I thought about SabbathRules, and the story in his email. *The piano player, Kit, she's missing her daughter like crazy. But she doesn't want to give up. She knows it's all over if she leaves the States now ...*

'Yeah, it was. I mean, it made me sad at first, but at least now I know the truth. And I can understand why Dad didn't tell me about the band. If it hadn't been for Little Boy Blue, I don't know ... maybe she'd still be here.'

Melissa squeezed my hand, and we sat there for a moment in silence, birds tweeting in the trees outside.

Her phone buzzed, and she picked it up.

'No. No, no, no, NO!'

I looked up. Melissa was glaring, pale-faced, at her phone.

'What's happened?'

'The secret gig,' she said, crestfallen. 'I can't come.'

'What? Why?'

She showed me her phone.

Great Uncle Ed confirmed for Fri. Family dinner at 7.30.
Phone ban in full force!! Will be fun, though, promise.
Love you, Ma xxx ps. Back in 20 mins, am bringing ice
cream!!

My face fell.

'That really sucks. I wanted you to be there.'

'WORST. DAY. EVER.'

'Also . . . you have a Great Uncle Ed?'

'Yep,' said Melissa, pouting. 'He's older than most fossils.'

'Can't you just tell your mum you have a Diamond Storm gig?'

Melissa shook her head solemnly.

'I already did, but it makes no difference. Uncle Ed lives in Australia, and he only comes over, like, once every twelve hundred years. Plus Mum says he wants to pass some money down to me and Tom, so I have to be there to make polite conversation.' She sighed. 'He talks a LOT about The Great Depression. And Bovril.'

I winced, thinking ahead to the weekend. Friday felt like a night when I could really do with my best friend by my side.

'Worst thing is,' she continued, 'Mum's imposing one of her "family time" phone bans, so I won't even be able to get text updates from you. Man, this week is sucking harder than a hungry anteater.' She glanced at her ant farm, on the window sill. 'Sorry, ants.'

I stared at her, right into her open, innocent face, thinking about how she had genuinely meant that apology, and something about it tickled me. My shoulders began to shake and, despite all the gloom, I started to giggle.

'What?' said Melissa, glancing around the room. 'What are you laughing at?'

I caught my breath, holding one hand to my chest.

'Nothing,' I said, with a smile. 'Just never change, OK?'

Wednesday evening. I stepped out of the house into the cool spring air, breathing it in through my nose, and headed for the local shop.

Two days until the *Songs About Us* launch gig. Two days until I got to see the venue that had been so important to my mum, and to Gabriel's father, before everything went so wrong for Little Boy Blue. There were lots of knots in my stomach about Friday – would Olly be OK? Had anything happened between him and Gabriel? – but until then, at least I had that thought to comfort me. In a way, it would be like stepping into a Katherine Bloom time capsule. A window to the past.

I arrived at the shop and, as I was reaching for the door handle, I noticed a car parked by the bus stop on the opposite side of the road. It looked like the driver was watching me, but from that distance, it was impossible to be sure.

I shook it off, and stepped inside.

'Evening, Charlie,' said Benjamin, the shopkeeper, at the ringing of the bell. 'You well?'

'Not too bad,' I said, with a little smile, as I passed the till. 'We've run out of lemons.'

Benjamin leaned on the counter.

'Useful things, lemons. How's your dad?'

'Oh, he's OK,' I said, over my shoulder, as I reached the fruit basket. 'He's got himself a girlfriend.'

'Well, well! Hats off to Mr Bloom.'

I picked through the lemons, looking for the best one.

'It's kinda icky when he's your dad, though,' I said, walking up to the counter with my lemon-of-choice and a fifty-pence piece. Benjamin smiled at me.

'Dads are people too, you know,' he said, with a wink. He handed me my change. 'Say hi to him for me.'

'I will.'

'See you soon.'

I stepped out of the shop, rolling the lemon around in my hand, and froze as I noticed the car from before still sitting there, the driver watching me from behind the wheel. Feeling the faintest quiver pass over my skin, I took a sharp left and headed for my road.

The car moved with me.

I was walking pretty fast, but for a car, it was slow, and out of the corner of my eye I could see that the driver was matching my pace exactly. On a busy road. I didn't dare look up; I just kept walking, my heart pulsing behind my ribs, until I reached the turn-off for Tower Close.

I rounded the corner, lemon gripped tightly in my hand, and let out a trembling breath as the car continued on its way, along the main road, blending into the traffic. As I watched it drive off, a hand stretched out of the open window, holding a lit cigarette. It tapped ash on to the ground.

Glinting in the evening sun was a heavy gold watch, hanging from a skinny wrist.

32

Earl's Court, West London. I was standing outside the Troubadour club, in the exact spot my mother had stood fifteen years ago with her band, Little Boy Blue, and had her photograph taken with fans. I was even wearing the hat she had on in the picture, though it wasn't really cold enough for it any more.

'You OK?'

I looked sideways to find Gabriel next to me, dressed in his 'everyday' clothes, grey hoodie pulled up over his head. We were flanked on both sides by security guards, shielding us from prying eyes.

'I'm fine,' I said, with a careful smile. I nodded towards the venue. 'Just . . . thinking about the photograph.'

Gabriel looked up at the club sign, which was written in a grand, faux-medieval font: TROUBADOUR.

'Pretty spooky, eh?' he said, his face half-hidden by his hood.

He glanced back at me, and suddenly, all I could see was Harry West.

'You didn't . . . pick this venue, did you?' I said.

'Nope. I had no idea we were coming here until just now.'

I stared at him.

'Really?'

'I just go where they tell me, Charlie Brown.'

My chest went tight. He'd said it so casually, but he must have known what he was doing. *Charlie Brown*. He hadn't called me that in months.

'. . . Yes, we've been outside for several minutes already,' Tara was saying impatiently into her phone. 'I've got four high-profile popstars just hanging around on the streets up here. Uh-huh . . . thank you.' She pulled the phone away from her ear, and blew a curl out of her face. 'Seriously, this is something I don't miss about small venues . . .'

I moved closer to Gabriel.

'Don't you think it's weird that we're here, though?'

Gabe ran a hand slowly though his hair.

'Yeah. Yeah, it is.'

I peered into the road, watching the traffic stream by, and my gaze settled on a newsagents called Brompton Food & Wine. A memory stirred inside me.

'Hang on, which road are we on?'

Gabriel smirked at me.

'Charlie, I barely know what time zone we're in.'

Whipping my phone out, I opened the map and zoomed in. I tapped my finger against the screen.

'That's what I thought. Old Brompton Road.'

Gabriel shrugged.

'What's so special about the Brompton Road?'

I thought back to my conversation with Olly, the previous month, at Kingdom Records. I'd asked him why the recording studio was called Studio Six – when it was the only one – and he'd told me how superstitious Barry was. How six was his lucky number, a reference to his family, and how he'd opened his first office on the Old Brompton Road because he had some kind of 'sentimental attachment' to it.

'This venue is totally random,' I said, gesturing through the window. Inside, people were sitting at tables, reading newspapers and sipping lattes. 'It's underneath a coffee house. Barry must have picked it for a reason.'

'Like what?'

I tugged at the rim of my hat.

'Like, I don't know. Because he has some ... connection to this area, or something.'

Gabriel looked amused.

'How on earth do you know that?'

'Olly told me.'

'Olly told you what?'

We both turned to find Olly beside us, hands in his pockets. Gabriel cleared his throat. I opened my mouth, but no words came out.

'Guys . . . ?' said Olly, his brow lowered. 'What were you talking about?'

'Oh, nothing.' I stole a glance at Gabriel. 'We were just—'

'People, where the hell is Yuki?'

Tara was glancing up and down the street, looking stressed. Aiden, who was standing a few metres away, took a step towards her.

'He took a separate car. With that new guy, Dane.'

'Dane? Christ. I'll call him.'

She dialled a number, and paced side to side as it rang. My eyes were locked on the pavement, but I could feel Olly watching me.

'Dane?' snapped Tara, suddenly standing still. 'Dane, it's Tara. Where are you?'

A pause.

'Eclipse? What is th—? A cocktail club?! . . . Well, I don't care if he wanted a drink, we've got soundcheck! Who hired you, exactly? . . . Oh, really?' She pressed a hand into her temple. 'Look, enough of this. Just fetch him for me.'

Twenty seconds passed. Tara checked her watch, then massaged her forehead with her fingers. I was still avoiding Olly's eyes.

'What do you mean he's not coming?' said Tara, back on the phone. 'That's not an answer, Da—'

'Tara . . . Tara.'

Aiden had stepped in front of her.

'Aid, I'm kinda busy here.'

'Will you let me go and talk to Yuki?' He glanced at me. 'I'll take Charlie. He might listen to us.'

Tara lowered her phone, holding her breath. She looked at me, then back at Aiden.

'OK, fine. But take James.' She indicated a nearby guard. 'And don't draw any attention to yourselves.' She checked her watch again. 'And be back in ten minutes. Jesus, I can already tell tonight is going to do my head in . . .'

I gazed out of the window, anxiety gnawing at my chest, as the shops, pubs and restaurants of the Old Brompton Road drifted by. Things had already turned awkward with Olly and Gabriel, and we'd only just arrived. We all had a long evening ahead of us.

The Eclipse Bar was only a short walk away, but James had driven us there in his dark-windowed car because, I guessed, if you were Aiden Roberts from Fire&Lights, you didn't just go wandering the streets of London on a Friday night.

'OK, this is it,' said James, pulling up outside a small, chic-looking cocktail club. Bouncers stood guard on either side of the glass entrance. 'Make it quick. I'll be out here if you need me.'

We both slid out of the car and hurried across the

pavement towards the bouncers. They nodded at Aiden, clearly recognising him, and opened the door for us.

The second we stepped inside, deafening music and the smell of alcohol hit me like a slap in the face. The scene in the club was like something out of an advert: couples pressed against walls, drinks pouring everywhere, dance music pounding. Barmen were spinning cocktail shakers, people were laughing, shouting, taking selfies. And in the middle of it all, standing on the bar brandishing open bottles of liquor, were three familiar punk-rockers.

Below them, Yuki was slumped on a stool.

'Yuki.'

Aiden grabbed his arm, and tugged.

'Yuki, you need to come with us.'

Yuki stirred drowsily, and batted a hand at us.

'What? No, you don't need me. Just leave me here.'

Ratty, his pink hair glowing beneath the lights, yelled at us from above.

'Oi, leave him! He's having the time of his life.'

'We've got a show tonight,' shouted Aiden. 'How could you let this happen?'

Ratty took a swig from his expensive-looking whiskey bottle. I had a pretty solid hunch whose credit card would be behind the bar.

'Who are you, his mum?' he said, splashing liquor across the bar. Aiden steeled himself.

'I'm his friend.'

The punks laughed.

'Oooh,' taunted Ratty, 'Yuki's got a friend. What you gonna do?' He pointed his bottle at me. 'Set your girlfriend on us?'

'You three are pathetic,' I spat. 'You don't give a crap about Yuki.'

Ratty shared a surprised look with his bandmates, then jumped off the bar, steadied himself, and pressed up against me. I could smell the alcohol on his breath.

'The hottie's getting angry.'

'Don't call me that.'

'I'll call you what I want.'

I held his gaze.

'I think you should go.'

'What?' He looked me up and down. 'I'm not going just because you're on your period.'

Before I could reply, Ratty had been dragged away from me and pinned against the bar. It all happened so quickly, I'd assumed it was James, but I'd been wrong. It was Yuki.

'Don't talk to Charlie like that. *Don't you ever talk to her like that.*'

Yuki's eyes were filled with rage, and Ratty held his palms in the air. For the first time, he actually looked scared.

'Calm down, Harrison, it was a joke. It was a joke.'

'I'm serious,' snarled Yuki, leaning into Ratty's face. 'If you even look at her—'

'OK, OK,' said Ratty, trying to pull away, 'I won't. Just
. . . let me go.'

Yuki relaxed his grip and Ratty stumbled away, wiping
his hand on his mouth. Once he was at a safe distance,
he gave a theatrical bow.

'See you later, losers.'

Then, flanked by his bandmates, he spun on his heel
and walked out of the club, flicking us a backwards
finger as he went. Yuki slouched against the bar like a
puppet that had been dropped by its master.

'Charlie . . . Aid . . . I'm sorry. I messed up.'

Aiden grabbed him under the armpit, and tried to
straighten him.

'You can't go on this way, Yuk. You have to tell me
what's going on. You've been like this for months—'

'My parents are getting divorced.'

Aiden froze. Yuki's breathing was slow, laborious, his
shoulders rising and falling, his eyes blinking.

'What . . . ? Why?'

'Dad was having an affair, Mum says. She found
messages on his phone, and when we were away on
tour, she just left in the middle of the night. Took my
little brother.' Yuki pressed a palm into his eye, and
groaned. He was slurring his words. 'She flew Itchy
back to Japan. I don't . . . I don't think they're ever
coming back.'

I thought of the photograph I'd seen on the plane, of

376

the two brothers, inseparable, playing together at Christmas time.

Aiden held him by the shoulders, steadying him.

'But . . . what? Why didn't you tell me this before?'

Yuki waved a hand.

'Come on, man. I'm supposed to be the funny guy. People want *Good-time Yuki*.'

'But I'm not people, Yuks. I'm your best friend. And best friends . . .' He glanced at me, nodding slightly. 'Best friends tell each other everything.'

Yuki gazed back at him, forlorn, under the flickering lights. All around us, revellers laughed and sang, kissed, danced and drank their cares away.

'My whole life,' he said, his voice hoarse, 'everyone's looked at me like, hey, Yuki . . . *he's a fun guy*. You know? He'll bring the party. But this . . . jokes won't fix this. I don't know how to fix this.' He paused, clamping both hands to his head. 'Itchy, he sends me these messages, every night. He wants to know when he's coming home. He says, "Will it be OK, Yuk?", like he used to when we were little and he'd fallen over in the playground, and . . .' Yuki shut his eyes hard, a tremble on his jaw. 'He's waiting for an answer, as if *I have the answer*.' There were tears in his eyes. 'It's killing me, Aid. He's just a kid . . . he's terrified.'

I glanced out through the main doors, where James was waiting dutifully with his hands on the wheel.

377

'We should go, Aiden,' I said. Aiden patted Yuki on the shoulder.

'Come on, dude. We have to get back to the club.'

Yuki wiped his eyes with his sleeve.

'You don't want me, man. Look at me. I'm no good to you boys tonight . . .'

'Shut up, doofus,' said Aiden, guiding his friend towards the entrance. 'Of course we need you. Who's going to moonwalk on to the stage if you're not there?'

As we led Yuki from the club and into the waiting car, I stared back inside at the madness, at the shouting and the partying and the barmen tossing cocktail shakers in the air. My heart ached, so hard, for Yuki. Just like his best friend, he'd been carrying around a secret that he didn't think anyone wanted to hear, and it was slowly crushing him from the inside.

But when he'd told Aiden he was no good to the band tonight, the state he was in, I had to admit . . . a small part of me wondered whether he was right.

33

I was sitting downstairs in the empty club, freeing up space on my camera. The room was quiet, serene, save for the gentle clink of glasses as a member of staff stocked the bar behind me.

I looked around, taking in the exposed brick walls, the paint peeling off the woodwork and the wine-bottle candles on the tables. I could see why Mum would have liked this place. It was scruffy, charming and old fashioned. You could practically smell the history in the air. A poster on the wall listed the names of famous artists who had played here in the past – Bob Dylan, Paul Simon, Joni Mitchell – but the one I was most excited about was Katherine Bloom, and her relatively unknown indie-rock band, Little Boy Blue. Staring at the stage, with the instruments in place and ready to go, I could almost hear them, singing to me from the past. I could almost see my mum, sitting behind the piano, her fingers dancing over the keys, hair falling across her face.

Of course, to call it a 'stage' was actually a little misleading. Wedged into a corner, it was raised only a few centimetres off the ground, and there was barely enough room on it for the drum kit, keyboard and guitars that had already been set up. It would be a squeeze this evening, with all four boys on there, plus the musicians. The fans would be closer to their idols than they'd ever been before.

A black curtain was hanging down at the back of the stage, and I noticed that, where one of the guitar amps had been shoved against the wall, the curtain had snagged on its corner and been forced upwards, revealing the concrete underneath. It had caught my eye because the exposed wall, which was crumbling and uneven and probably in need of repair, looked like it was covered in handwriting.

I glanced over my shoulder. The barman was stacking glasses, and his back was turned.

Standing up, I walked silently on to the stage and snaked through the instruments. Reaching the curtain, I tugged it aside, along its metal rail, and found that the entire wall was riddled with signatures. A mess of names, tangled and twisted like spaghetti, covering the concrete from top to bottom. *Billy Franks. Playtone. Benjamin Kane. The Blackwater Jacks.* They weren't names I knew, but it didn't matter. It was thrilling. All these people had stood on this stage, singing their songs, gazing out into the watching eyes of the Troubadour crowd.

My heart began to tumble, and a voice inside me said: *She might be on here.* It was a long shot, but I couldn't let it slide. I started running my fingers up and down the rough, powdery concrete, eyes searching left and right for familiar names, but there were just so many, and lots of them had faded over time.

Kneeling, I nudged a thick cable out of my way and sat on the floor. I walked my fingers across the cool, craggy surface, reading endless names, picking up speed, until finally, hidden away near the bottom, where the wall met the floor, I found it. The last two letters were missing – a chip of concrete had fallen away, long ago, and disintegrated – but still, it was unmistakable: LITTLE BOY BL. And underneath the band name, each member had scrawled their signature: Harry West, Owen Isaac, Jermaine Jacobs. And there, on the end, beside a quirky little sketch of a piano keyboard: *Kit Bloom, June '96.* A smile warmed my face, my skin tingling. This was a genuine little piece of her, real enough to touch.

I traced the letters with my finger, imagining I was her, scrawling it across the concrete. If I believed in fate, I might have said that she'd left it there especially for me.

'Charlie?'

I jumped, tearing my gaze from the wall, and scrambled to my feet. Duffy and Campbell were looking up at me from the floor.

'What are you doing?' asked Duffy, with a frown. I reached for the curtain, and pulled it back across.

'Just . . . looking for a . . . power socket,' I said, praying that my cheeks weren't turning too red. 'Phone's dying. H-how are you guys?'

'We're OK, I guess,' said Campbell, with a glance at the backstage door. A sign had been pinned up that read: DO NOT DISTURB.

'Melissa's really sad she couldn't come tonight,' I said, hopping across the stage, narrowly avoiding the curled cables beneath my feet. I joined Campbell and Duffy, rubbing the concrete dust off my fingers. 'Seriously, she was gutted. She'll be at home right now, making small talk with a seventy-year-old.'

Neither of them spoke. I cleared my throat.

'So . . . you must be pretty excited about tonight, then? Lots of VIP fans to hang out with.'

They exchanged looks.

'We are,' said Campbell, wringing his hands. 'But we're worried too.'

I tugged my sleeves down over my wrists. I was still thinking about Mum's signature, hidden behind the curtain.

'Oh, really? What about?'

'We heard . . .' Duffy stopped herself, and lowered her voice. 'I mean, we got the impression that something's up with the band. You know, after everything that's happened.'

'They're . . . fine,' I said, shrugging it off. Campbell leaned towards me.

'Honestly, you can tell us. Are they going to be all right?'

'Look, I think we just have to concentrate on our jobs, you know? Leave the band stuff to the band.'

Campbell nodded thoughtfully. Duffy folded her arms.

'I guess you're right.'

'But you will tell us,' said Campbell, 'if you hear anything at all?'

I slid my hands into my back pockets.

'Um . . . sure. 'Course.'

They started to walk away, whispering to each other, and I called after them.

'Guys?'

They spun round to face me.

'Tonight's going to be great.'

'I know,' said Duffy, opening the door. 'See you in a bit.'

I watched the door swing closed behind them, and leaned back against the wall, sighing. We could all pretend there was nothing wrong with Fire&Lights, but we wouldn't really know for sure until they stepped out on to that stage.

'Hey, Bloom.'

The door bearing the DO NOT DISTURB sign had been opened. Barry King was standing on the other side, his hand on the knob.

'We need you.'

I pointed at my chest.

'Me?'

'Uh-huh.'

'R-right . . .' Tentatively, I pushed away from the wall. Barry pointed at the table where I'd been sitting.

'And bring your camera.'

Moments later, when I walked into the dark, cramped green room behind Barry, I found Gabriel, Olly, Yuki and Aiden dotted around the space, two sitting, two standing, none of them looking at each other. The room was starved of natural light, and barely big enough for the six of us. Old files and dusty guitar cases were piled up in the corners.

'I want a photo of these boys,' Barry said to me, 'exactly as they are.'

My camera was hanging off my neck. I closed my fingers around it.

'What, you mean . . . now?'

It seemed strange to me that Barry would want to capture this moment. Yuki looked broken, his eyes dark and sullen; Gabriel seemed distracted; Olly just looked tired. Aiden was chewing on a fingernail.

Barry nodded.

'Yep. I want them to remember this moment and understand how close they came to the edge.'

I took a deep breath. I felt like I was betraying my instincts as a photographer – there was nothing natural about how this picture was coming about – but Barry was the boss, so I didn't really have a choice. Feeling weirdly like I was taking photos at a funeral, I lifted my camera and clicked the shutter, three times. No one looked into the lens.

No one but Gabriel.

'Thanks, Charlie,' said Barry, folding his arms across his chest. He surveyed his band. 'Now . . . lads. They're opening the doors in fifteen minutes, and trust me, I'm not exaggerating when I tell you this might just be one of the most important nights of your lives.' He spoke slowly, deliberately. 'There aren't many things harder in this world than keeping a band together. I've seen it a hundred times, and most bands, they buckle under the pressure. Money, fame, sex. Power. They break you, unless you have that bond. Unless you're true brothers.'

I thought about the signatures on the other side of the wall. Harry, Kit, Owen and Jermaine. What was it that really destroyed Little Boy Blue, in the end? Money? Drugs? Being on the road? Maybe we'd never know for sure.

'And that's why you're different,' continued Barry, his voice softening, ever so slightly. 'Boys, I've known it since the day I first saw the four of you standing in a room together. You're a team. You're a *family*. But you have to fight for it. Understand?'

He pointed a thumb over his shoulder.

'You've seen what the press have been saying about you this week. They're saying you're finished. But you're not. *We're* not. You hear me?'

No one spoke.

'I said . . . do you hear me?'

'Yes,' said the boys in unison.

'Good,' continued Barry, undoing the top button of his shirt. 'Now, you've got two hours until you're on, and I want you to spend that time thinking about what you've come through together. Places you've been, things you've achieved. Tonight, you fight for all of th—'

The door burst open, and four excitable teenagers tumbled in. Jody Baxter, at the front of the group, stopped dead in his tracks as his eyes met Barry's.

'Oh, god . . . s-sorry,' he stammered, blushing an intense red. Barry considered him for a moment.

'No . . . no. Come on in, close the door.' He beckoned them inside, and Diamond Storm shuffled into the room, one by one. They'd all gone very pale, even Thumper. Sometimes I forgot how scary Barry King was on the television.

'You're the support band, right?' The boys nodded, hands in pockets. 'Lightning Storm, isn't it?'

Jody coughed.

'Diamond Storm,' he said meekly.

'Diamond Storm.' He turned to Fire&Lights. 'Right. Take a look at them, lads. Take a good, long look at their faces. What do you see?'

Silence. Barry smacked a hand on the table, and Jody twitched.

'Hunger, that's what I see. They're *hungry* for it. You understand? Just like you were, when all this started.' He pointed at each member of Fire&Lights in turn. 'Don't forget that.'

Olly caught Jody's eye, and smiled.

'Pleasure having you, guys,' he said. 'Just don't go playing us off the stage, OK?'

Jody let out a nervous laugh.

'We won't.'

Barry walked across the room and laid a chunky hand on Jody's shoulder. Jody's lips were pressed tightly together, his entire body tensed.

'You have fun tonight, fellas,' said Barry, squeezing his shoulder. 'But right now, if you don't mind buggering off, I have to finish up with my band.'

Mumbling more apologies, Jody set about herding his friends from the room, his face still burning.

'I'll see them out,' I said, moving away from the wall. Barry gave me the nod, and I followed Diamond Storm through the open door, closing it behind me.

For a few seconds, the five of us stood together in the corridor, not talking. Jody was trying to catch my eye.

'Charlie, thank you *so much* for doing this, it's just amaz—'

'That's OK,' I interrupted icily.

Thumper spun a drumstick at me. 'Don't be like that, Charlotte. We were only kidding around.'

'Of course you were.'

He pressed a hand on to my shoulder.

'Tell you what, when we're living in our mansion in Beverly Hills, we'll invite you round for a hot-tub party.'

I shook him off.

'I wouldn't get in a hot tub with you if you paid me.'

The bassist and the guitar player – the ones who never seemed to talk – sniggered at this. Thumper poked his tongue into his cheek.

'Whatever, Charlie. You know you want me.'

'Thumper, just leave it, OK?' said Jody, glaring at him. Then he turned to me. 'Look, Charlie, I mean it. Thank you, for everything. For making this happen, for taking photos later . . . this is a seriously big deal for us.'

I finally met Jody's gaze, my face stiff with anger. This whole thing had been Thumper's idea; that was obvious from the beginning. Jody wasn't a bad guy, but he could have stopped it. He could have done the decent thing and stood up to him.

'Break a leg,' I said, hanging my camera bag on my shoulder. Then I pushed past them and walked back into the club.

'Guys, we are so happy to be here. Thanks for having us! We're Diamond Storm, from Reading, and this song is called "Robot Romance" . . .'

From my post beside the stage, I zoomed in on Jody's face. He was bathed in blue light and, though I still hadn't forgiven him, I had to admit that, these days, he was looking ever more the rockstar. I tried to tweak the focus, to bring out his eyes, but I couldn't get it right. I cursed myself behind the lens. In truth, I was finding it hard to concentrate on Diamond Storm.

Turning away from the stage, I peered into the crowd, wondering whether I ought to try for some shots of the audience. I noticed a chair behind me and climbed up on to it, looking across all the heads. The club was packed. The Troubadour was tiny, at least compared to every other Fire&Lights gig I'd been to, and full to capacity. Fans were crammed into the space, filling every corner, and the air around me was heavy and hot.

I swept my camera in an arc across the room, catching the bobbing heads, the excited faces. It was a sea of people, a rippling mass, and I drew in a breath as I imagined it erupting when the headline act came onstage. Squeezing the shutter, I fired off a round of shots, then checked the screen to see if I'd got the lighting right.

It wasn't ideal. Maybe I could find a different angle.

But first: that person, squeezed against the back wall, glasses glinting beneath the lights. It couldn't be . . . could it? I zoomed in, but the picture was fuzzy, and I couldn't quite make out the face.

Cautiously, I looked up, and our eyes met. I'd been right the first time.

The man at the back was my father.

34

I was trapped, like a rat in a cage.

I couldn't have got out of that building if I'd tried, and in any case, it was too late for that. Dad had seen me, and I was holding a camera. There could be no doubt in his mind that it was me.

But then, as I stood helpless on that chair, wedged behind a two hundred-strong crowd, I noticed something curious. My father was waving at me, and smiling.

And then it hit me. This whole time, I'd been telling him that I was taking photos at Diamond Storm concerts, and tonight, that was actually true. As far as my father knew, it was business as usual.

My phone buzzed with a text message.

You look great up there, Charlie. Sorry I didn't mention I was coming – it was a bit of a last minute thing, Christine had a plus one x

I typed a hasty reply.

That's cool, hope you enjoy it! x

Moments later, I got Dad's response.

Strange to be back in this old place. What a weird
coincidence! Your mum loved it here.

I closed my eyes, a barrage of pictures, thoughts and
memories flooding my brain. Mum, standing outside the
Troubadour with Harry West and the rest of Little Boy
Blue, in Gemstar's photograph. Dad, telling Melissa about
the last time he went to a gig, in this very building back
in 1999. My mother's signature on the concrete wall. The
fact that Barry King, a man prone to superstition, had
picked this small, seemingly random venue to launch the
EP of a world-famous boy band.

In some way, all of this was connected. All we had to
do was join the dots.

Ping. Dad again.

I hear Jody's lot are supporting a famous boy band
tonight! Exciting. Maybe you'll get a chance to meet
them?

I struggled to keep my breathing steady, my throat
slowly closing, my brow beading with sweat. Inside my
head, the possible consequences of my father being here

began to trickle into my brain. What would happen when Fire&Lights came onstage? Would Dad recognise Gabriel? Something had definitely stirred in him when he'd seen Gabe's picture in the Carrie Shakes exhibition, and maybe being back here, at the Troubadour, the pieces would fall into place in his mind. Wasn't there every chance that he would connect his past with my present?

Ping.

By the way, do you want a lift home? x

I paused, staring at the message. The late train back to Reading was always a drag, but I really didn't fancy an hour in the car with Dad, Christine and Jody, trying to make small talk without giving myself away.

No, I'm fine. The main band said I could do their photos too, so might have to stay later than you guys. I can take the train. Enjoy the show x

Well done, kiddo. That's amazing. Have fun! x

Diamond Storm launched into their second song, a chirpy, bouncy number that was soon inspiring random pockets of dancing in the crowd. I forced my gaze back to the stage and, behind the drums, Thumper caught my eye. He winked smugly, and two drops of sweat slid from his hairline and down his face.

I looked away. If things had been different, I might have simply walked off and left them to it. But now, with my father here, I had to keep up appearances. I had to maintain my cover.

Lifting up my camera again, I trained the lens on the guitarist's fingers, catching him as he moved to a new chord, skin glowing with sweat, knuckles turning white. I had a feeling that Diamond Storm's triumphant Troubadour photo album would be strangely short on close-ups of the drummer.

I had never been nervous for Fire&Lights before. At their concerts, it had never occurred to me that they wouldn't deliver, because they always did. But tonight, with the pressure on, with leading music journalists in the house, with their most devoted fans waiting and watching, it felt like their entire future was hanging in the balance.

'Fire – and – Lights! Fire – and – Lights!'

A relentless chanting was willing the boys to arrive onstage, every pair of hands in the venue clapping to the same beat. *Snap. Snap.* From the vantage point of my chair, I was perfectly placed to capture the electric atmosphere in the club, and it was like nothing I'd ever experienced. *Snap.* When people talked about the unifying power of music, *this*, right here, was what they meant.

393

Finally, the four boys appeared through the back door and stepped on to the stage, and the whole building thundered.

Fire&Lights had arrived.

From the very first chord, the music was like a rocket going off. They didn't have the light shows or the pyrotechnics of their arena concerts, but that didn't matter. They had fire inside them, they were fearless, and they owned the hearts of every single person in that room. It was so loud I thought my head would explode, or the walls would cave in; the screaming of the fans melded with the roar from the guitars and the pounding of the drum kit, and I could feel my blood sing, my skin prickle and my bones shake.

They opened with 'Dance With You', and when Olly sang those opening lines, familiar shivers sparkled up my spine.

Take me home
'Cos I've been dreaming of a girl I know . . .

As the song unfolded, filling the room, a thought nagged at me. Might Dad notice Mum's lyrics, hidden in the boys' songs? Would he remember them? I didn't know how closely he'd read her notebook, or listened to Little Boy Blue, but memory was an unpredictable thing. Nervously, I searched the room for him, finding him standing in the same place by the back wall, spectacles still winking under the lights.

And he was staring, entranced, at Gabriel.

'Olly, sing your song!'

I turned my head. In the lull between songs, someone was shouting at the boys from the back of the room.

'What was that?' called Olly, craning his neck to find the source.

'Sing your song!' repeated the girl. '"She Is The Fire".'

I lowered my camera, forgetting, momentarily, about my father. Glancing across the crush of people, I spotted the girl on the far side of the room, by the DJ booth, towering above the crowd. She was nearly a head taller than the girls around her.

It was Thumper's little sister. She must have remembered the song from Olly's visit to Caversham High.

'Oh, I can't,' said Olly, with an apologetic smile. 'That's against the rules.'

He gave a nod to the drummer, presumably to cue the next number, but before the beat could start, Thumper's sister started singing Olly's song at him. Two of her friends joined in.

She is the fire in my fingertips
The warm rain that tells me where the thunder is . . .

The girls were word-perfect. We weren't allowed phones in assembly, so they must have secretly recorded it from a pocket, and learned it off-by-heart.

. . . And I know that somebody has found her heart
But that won't keep us apart

Olly's lungs expanded as he heard his lyrics sung back to him, for the first time, and he couldn't keep the smile off his face. I watched him, mirroring his smile, because he was right. His prediction had come good.

It hadn't kept us apart.

'Who wants to hear "Meet Me At Midnight"?' called Gabriel, pointing into the crowd. Whistles and cheers rained back on him, and he turned to Olly, who weighed his hands, up and down, like a set of scales.

'I dunno, Gabe. I think there are some people in here who want to hear my song . . .'

Scattered cheers erupted around the room, and the guitarist exchanged baffled looks with the other musicians. Gabriel, meanwhile, tossed Olly a discreet glance, a glance that might have remained secret on a larger stage, but in here, was obvious to everyone.

'But the band don't know it,' said Gabriel, gesturing at the drummer. The tone of his voice was light, even jokey, but his eyes told another story.

'Actually,' replied Olly, 'I taught it to them last week on the tour bus. Right, guys?'

The musicians returned a combination of nods and shrugs.

'Or ... maybe we should stick to the set-list?' suggested Gabriel, his jaw locking. 'I think the people wanna hear Kaitlyn's song.'

The crowd began to get restless, calling out songs and arguing among themselves. At the back of the stage, I noticed the drummer touching a finger to her ear, as if listening to instructions. She nodded, mouthed 'Meet Me At Midnight' at the guitarist, and they crashed instantly into the opening riff.

Olly's face dropped.

Soon, the first verse had begun, and Aiden was singing the opening lines, one hand outstretched, the girls in the front row reaching for his arm. By the chorus, every voice in the club was belting out the words at full volume, and I managed to capture a striking photograph of two hundred mouths united in song, their faces lit up, eyes shining bright.

On the other side of the stage, though, Olly was failing to disguise his irritation. His mouth was set in a flat line, his brow lowered, and when the second verse began, he missed his cue. Gritting his teeth, Gabriel took hold of his upper arm and whispered in his ear, while Yuki and Aiden carried the song. Olly took exception, shouting something angry right into Gabe's face, and soon, most of the fans in the front row were watching them instead of the singing. Gabriel shoved him away, just slightly, but it was enough to push Olly over the edge. Olly pushed him back, harder, and Gabriel crashed over into the drum kit, sending a cymbal flying across the stage. Yuki went to pick him up, but he didn't make it in time. Gabe was already launching himself at Olly, pinning him against the wall, knocking the guitarist into the back curtain and causing an ear-piercing screech of feedback. Around the room, security guards were starting to mobilise, but it was too late. In that confined space, with all the heat and the noise and the madness, the stage was like a rag soaked in petrol. All it took was one lit match.

Chaos was unleashed. The fans closest to the band surged forward, grabbing for Olly and Gabriel, shouting and crying, some of the smaller girls stumbling beneath the stampede. The whole room seemed to move as one beast, one baying monster, and before long the stage had been smothered. Frantically, the musicians disentangled themselves from their instruments, and three security guards charged the stage, gathering up the boys and herding them out of the main room, fans grabbing for them as they went.

Still standing on my chair, I could feel it being repeatedly knocked by the seething crowd, and soon, it buckled underneath me. I tumbled to the floor, camera swinging round my neck, strap burning my skin, and was instantly trampled by the forest of legs rushing towards the stage. Desperately, I heaved myself to my feet, holding my camera tight to my chest, and pushed sideways through the chaos, heading for the backstage door.

I had to see them.

I had to make sure everything was OK.

But the minute I fell through the door and slumped against the green room wall, it became absolutely clear that it wasn't.

'You've really done it this time.'

Standing in the backstage corridor, I was caught between two worlds. Behind me, the chaos of the venue: fans running, yelling and climbing across tables, security trying desperately to funnel everyone upstairs and out of the club. In front of me, the unnerving quiet of the green room: the boys, visible through the door's grubby window, sitting at the table or leaning against the walls, heads down, waiting for Barry's tirade to continue.

'Are you OK?'

James was standing guard at the door to the main room. He had let me in discreetly, when he'd heard me banging on the other side with the flat of my palm.

'I'm fine,' I said, touching my hand to my neck, where

the camera strap had left a raw burn mark. 'Kinda crazy out there, though.'

James opened the door a few centimetres, and the noise suddenly ballooned. He pursed his lips, and closed it again.

'They'll get it sorted,' he said, in that stubbornly neutral way security guards always spoke. 'You'll be out of here soon.'

'You all knew how important tonight was, but you couldn't keep it together, could you?' Barry had found his flow again. James and I both pretended not to listen. 'One damn night, that's all I asked for. The papers'll tear you apart.'

'Screw the papers,' said Gabriel, his voice hollow and flat. He was leaning back against a filing cabinet, nursing a bruised wrist.

'*Screw the p*—?' spluttered Barry. He pointed a heavily ringed finger at Gabe. 'Boy, the papers *made* you. They run things in this business, in case you hadn't noticed, and when they see photos of two hundred teenage girls rioting at a Fire&Lights show, you'll be all over the front page again. And not in a good way.'

'Maybe they'll chalk it up to rock and roll antics,' said Yuki hopefully, his eyes wide. Barry waved an exasperated palm at him, shaking his head.

'Don't even start me on you, Harrison. Rock and roll's all right if you're Led-sodding-Zeppelin, but you're not. You're a boy band. You're supposed to be the ones they

400

take home to their mums, not smashing up venues and falling asleep in a puddle of your own puke.'

Yuki, who had a pithy comeback for most situations, clammed up and stared at his hands. Aiden looked at his best friend, and I knew exactly what was on his mind. He was thinking about Itchy, and the things Yuki had told us in the cocktail bar.

He took a careful step towards Barry.

'It's not our fault, Barry. It's this venue. It's too small.'

Barry's face opened up with incredulity.

'Sorry, what? You're blaming the bloody *bricks and mortar* now, are you? Aiden, you lot screwed up, big time. Simple as that.'

'Yep, sure,' said James, into his walkie-talkie. 'I'll be out in two.'

James gave me a polite nod before slipping through the stage door into the club. It sounded a little calmer now; I could hear security guards ushering people out, and the sound of shoes crunching on broken glass. Softly, he closed the door behind him.

'So come on, then,' continued Barry. 'What have you got for me, fellas? What's your best excuse?'

Nobody spoke. Barry turned on Olly, who was sitting at the far end of the table.

'Why'd you have to wind Gabe up like that?'

Olly narrowed his eyes.

'What?'

'You push his buttons, you know you're doing it.'

Olly stood up, knocking his chair backwards with a scrape.

'This wasn't about Gabe. Those girls wanted my song. I couldn't help that.'

'Really? You couldn't help turning a perfectly decent show into a total bloody circus?'

Olly's jaw hung open.

'Hang on . . . are you blaming this on *me*?'

'All I've heard from you this year is "listen to my songs, Barry". "I wanna be a songwriter". Olly, you're a talented kid, but I make the decisions around here. You understand?' Barry locked eyes with him. 'This is my band, Olly. Not yours.'

Barry's words hung in the air. Olly spread his arms wide.

'What about your big speech, Barry, huh? The one about being a "family"?'

'Doesn't change the fact that I'm in charge, Samson. Every family needs a head.'

'I cannot believe you think this is my fault.'

Aiden moved to Olly's side, touching his forearm.

'Olly, please—'

'No, Aid, don't,' said Olly, throwing him off. 'I don't have to listen to this. It's ridiculous.'

'He's right, Olly,' said Gabe, without looking up from his wrist. 'This is Barry's band. He calls the shots.'

Olly scoffed.

'That's rich, coming from you.'

Gabriel slowly lifted his gaze.

'What's that supposed to mean?'

A nervy silence fell, and Olly walked over to his bandmate. He came so close that Gabriel was forced right up against the filing cabinet, and it toppled slightly as his back pressed into the metal.

'Didn't you tell me, last year, that you don't need me?' They were eye-to-eye now. 'On that hotel rooftop . . . ?'

I remembered that night so clearly. The lashing of the rain, the wailing of sirens, the glowing neon on the streets below. I knew Gabriel remembered it too. I knew, from his songs, that it still haunted him.

'What are you talking about?' said Gabriel, swallowing hard. Olly closed the centimetre of space between them, and lowered his voice.

'You looked me right in the eye, and you said . . . *I am the band*. Remember?' Gabriel's eyes dropped, but Olly pressed a hand to his chest, forcing them back up again. 'Well, guess what, Gabe? This is your chance to prove it.'

Olly stepped away, and fixed his gaze on Barry.

'Because I quit.'

35

Before I knew it, Olly was at the door. The handle began to turn, and I thought for a second about dashing back into the club, to give him some time on his own. But I wanted to see him. I wanted to make sure he was all right.

He stepped out into the corridor and slammed the door behind him, his cheeks red, eyes raging. At first, he didn't notice I was there.

'Olly, what's going on?'

When he lifted his head, there was a look in his eyes that I didn't recognise. A desperation. A fear.

'I quit,' he said, dazed. He was staring at the wall behind me, as if still processing it himself.

'God . . .' I suddenly felt guilty for eavesdropping. 'What happened?'

'It's Gabriel.'

'What do you mean?'

He began to search my face, but his eyes weren't meeting mine. It felt like he was gazing right through me.

'I see the way you look at him, Charlie. You don't mean to, but you do.'

I took a step towards him.

'Olly, you're not making sen—'

'Just let me finish . . . OK? Just let me finish.' He took a long, quiet breath. 'I see you talking to him, in whispers, wherever we go. I catch you looking at him like he's the only person who understands you. It's like you have all these secrets that I'm not a part of . . . that I can never be a part of.'

A nasty heat prickled my face.

'I don't know what you're talking about.'

Olly met my gaze, finally, but his eyes didn't gleam. They always used to gleam.

'You're in love with him, Charlie. Maybe you don't realise it . . . but that's the truth.' Determination blossomed in his face. 'And I won't play second string to Gabriel. It's all I've ever done. This is over. I can't do it any more.'

I grabbed his T-shirt and tried to pull him towards me. He didn't move.

'You mean . . . the band?'

My voice sounded small, paper-thin. Olly exhaled sadly, and pushed my hand away.

'No, Charlie, I mean us. It's over. I'm sorry.'

Then he opened the door and walked out, leaving me standing alone in the dark.

36

Tube platforms at night were very lonely places.

I was standing on the yellow line, just a few steps from the edge, watching mice scurry beneath the tracks. Further down the platform, a few lone strangers were scattered about, tapping idly at their phones. Occasional, robotic announcements rang out across the station.

This didn't feel real. It couldn't be real. Losing Olly, the band falling apart . . . it felt like a hideous dream.

Ping. My phone buzzed with a message.

Well, glad you're all right. I was worried.

Dad had called, to make sure I'd got safely out of the venue, but instead of answering, I'd just sent a text. I wasn't ready to talk to him yet. What if he'd recognised Gabriel during the band's set? What if all my lies were about to come crashing down around me?

I'm fine. Security looked after me.

> OK then. Expect I'll be asleep by the time you get home.
>
> See you in the morning x

I tried to read my father's tone. Was he angry? Had he made the connection? It wasn't unusual for people to be awe-struck by Gabriel while he was singing, but they were normally teenage girls, not middle-aged men. I re-read his text several times, but my brain was tangled, exhausted. I just didn't know any more.

I didn't know anything.

'Charlie.'

I felt the hairs on the back of my neck stand up. It was him.

'What are you doing?' I said, turning round. I glanced up the staircase, the way he'd come. 'People will recognise you.'

'I don't care,' said Gabriel. 'I was worried about you. Why did you wander off on your own? I can send for a driver.'

I pulled my coat tight around my body.

'Don't, honestly. I'd rather take the train.'

Gabriel took a step closer.

'What happened back there?'

I felt a sadness welling up inside me, pushing against the walls of my throat.

'Olly ended it with me.'

Gabriel sighed deeply.

'You don't have to pretend to be upset, you know,' I said.

He shook his head. 'I never wanted this to happen, Charlie. I just want you to be happy. That's all I've ever wanted.'

I glanced at the information screen. One minute until the next train.

Gabriel hugged his arms to his chest.

'So why did he do it?'

I fought the tears that were rising behind my eyes. I didn't want to cry in front of him.

'He says . . .' Before I had decided whether or not it was a good idea, the words were coming out of my mouth. 'Olly says he can't be with me . . . because I'm in love with you.'

The underground rumbled with a distant train: a deep, gentle thunder, the faint screech of brakes. Gabriel stepped towards me, and my blood stirred. I felt the evening begin to overwhelm me. My heart started to burn and tears brimmed in my eyes, spilling over to fall down my cheeks.

Gabriel locked his gaze on to mine.

'Are you?' he said.

Time slowed, the seconds grinding by, while beside us, the train rumbled in. Gabriel reached for my hand, but before our fingers could touch, I turned and walked towards the train, my face wet with tears. As the doors opened, I heard the sound of screaming girls.

408

They'd found him.

I stepped on to the train and sat down, trying to resist the urge to look back. But I couldn't. Staring out of the window, I saw Gabriel still standing on the platform, being mobbed by hysterical fans. He was just standing there, on the spot, motionless and detached, watching me, as the girls screamed and sobbed around him.

I thought about Olly. Perfect Olly. He'd been such an amazing friend to me, from the very beginning, and had never expected anything in return. He was the sweetest, kindest boy I knew. He was everything.

He was everything, everything, everything.

And I'd pushed him away.

'Excuse me, is that yours?'

A man was standing above me, holding on to a rubber ceiling handle and pointing at the floor. I looked down, and spotted my phone. I'd been so caught up in myself that it had slipped out of my hand.

'Oh, yes. Thank you. Thanks.'

Picking it up and dropping it into my bag, I looked out of the window one final time. Gabriel's eyes found mine, and the train began to pull away.

As we disappeared into the tunnel, he kept watching me until the very last second.

Fifteen minutes later, I emerged on to the concourse at Paddington station, and stepped off the escalator. I felt numb. My skin was tacky from tears I had cried on the train and hadn't wiped away. A harsh tingle, like radio static, had settled over me like a shawl, and I could feel a dull ache, deep in my bones. I didn't want to listen to music, or check my phone, or do anything. I just wanted to be asleep.

I crossed over towards the departure screens, gazing at the shimmering orange letters, trying to block out the pictures in my mind. Olly, slamming the door, white-hot rage in his eyes. His hand, pushing mine away. Gabriel, reaching out to touch me, as the train screeched into the station. It was as if the more I tried to bury the memories, the bigger they became. The brighter they burned.

A hand landed on my shoulder. I twisted round.

Campbell was standing behind me, breathing fast, his normally neat hair askew. I smeared a trembling hand across my cheek.

'Cam? Is everything . . . all right?' I asked tentatively, aware that my train would be leaving soon. He glanced over his shoulder, and I saw Duffy approaching.

'Cam, don't,' she called out.

'She filmed you,' he said urgently.

I frowned at him. 'She . . . what?'

Duffy was getting closer. Cam grabbed my sleeve.

'You and Olly, just now. At the Troubadour.'

'It's too late, Cam.' Duffy had reached his side. 'There's nothing you can do.'

I scanned the departures board above our heads. The next Reading train was leaving in four minutes.

'Would one of you please tell me what's going on?'

Duffy rolled her eyes, and flicked her bright-red hair from her face.

'Look, Charlie—'

'She filmed you and Olly breaking up,' interrupted Campbell, his cheeks pink with anger. 'On her phone. And she's made it into this horrid vlog, and she's going to tell everyone it's your fault he quit the band.'

Duffy exhaled huffily.

'You're blowing this out of proportion.'

'Am I?' he said, glaring at her. 'I don't think so.' He turned back to me. 'She said in the video that you're only taking photos for the band to get a celebrity boyfriend, and be Insta-famous. And she says you broke Olly's heart, just like you broke Gabriel's, and you're tearing the band apart. She's putting it online tomorrow morning, on the FireLighters site.'

A quiet panic hardened under my skin. Was that . . . true? Was that really what she thought of me?

My fingers began to shake, and I curled them into my palms.

'Duffy, what the hell?'

'The music business is cut-throat, Charlie. That's not my fault, and if you can't accept it, then . . .'

There was a black knot tightening inside me, deep in

my gut, and it began to pulse with fear. I tried to catch Duffy's eye, but she wouldn't look at me.

'Why would you do this?' I said, desperation creeping into my voice. She shrugged. 'You can't publish that video. *Please.*'

'It's done, it's all scheduled. If I don't publish it, he won't keep his side of the deal.'

I pressed my hands to my chest.

'What do you mean . . . "his side of the deal"?'

'N-nothing,' said Duffy, shaking her head. 'Cam, we have to g—'

'Someone's making you do this, aren't they?' I said, grabbing her arm, willing her to look at me. 'Duffy?'

She tugged herself free and looked at Campbell, her face blotchy, fists clenched. He glared at her, incensed.

'He said he'd get me an internship at his paper,' she said, braving a glance at me. 'He said he could launch my whole career. He knows people.'

I stumbled backwards, clasping a cold hand to my mouth. It was exactly like Gabriel had told me, at the airport. *It's Paul Morgan I don't trust, and he can get to anyone.*

'It's Paul, isn't it?' I said, my voice cracking. Duffy shook her head.

'It doesn't matter who it is.'

'Don't listen to him, he's a crook. He's using you.'

'What, like you used Olly?'

412

I froze, my mouth hanging open.

'You don't believe that. You *know* that's not how it was. It's Paul, he's . . . poisoned you. You have to take the video down.'

'It's too late. I made a deal.'

Memories from our time at the StarBright Arena began to play frantically inside my head, like a slideshow moving too quickly. Duffy, telling us she was leaving to meet a journalist. Me, five minutes later, giving Olly a peck on the cheek, thinking, hey, it was risky, but no one was watching. Paul, waiting for me in the car park after the ceremony, somehow knowing I was there. And then Blake Hadaway, interrogating Olly and Gabriel about me on live television, boasting about his 'interesting tip-off'.

Paul had been tapping Duffy for information, this whole time.

'Duffy, this isn't you. I know you wouldn't do this if it wasn't for him. *He's using you to get to me.*'

'You're wrong, Charlie,' she snapped angrily. She was almost snarling. 'I want this more than anything in the world, and Paul Morgan can give it to me. We're not all lucky enough to go to school with a popstar, you know.' She gritted her teeth, and stared me down. 'You've had your big break, now I deserve mine.'

A sickness rose up inside my throat, hot and bitter, as I thought back to our conversation at the Pop4Progress concert. The clues had been there, the whole time. *I'm not some fangirl . . . I want what you've got . . . I just need to meet the right people.* I should have seen this coming.

'Please, Duffy. You know what the fans'll do to me. You know what they're like.' Emotion clenched inside me, like a fist. 'They'll tear me apart.'

She was breathing hard through her nose.

'That's not my problem.'

Fresh tears gathered in my eyes as I realised I'd lost. I wasn't going to change her mind. It didn't matter what I said, or how much I begged.

'It's nothing personal,' she added, tugging her handbag up over her shoulder. 'Everyone gets screwed over eventually, right?'

Before I could reply, she had turned on her heel and walked off, heading for the station exit. I watched her leave, stunned, utterly helpless, and Campbell began to stammer at me, searching for the right words. But there was nothing left to say.

'I'm sorry, Charlie . . . I'm so sorry . . .'

He threw me a pained look, then hurried after her, trailing behind, still pleading with her as they stepped into the night and disappeared from view.

For several minutes, I just stood there, on the concourse, staring out at the London streets, feverish heart thudding beneath my skin. People were rushing past me, laughing and talking on their phones, excited to be heading home for the weekend. I was invisible to them, another anonymous traveller, but I wouldn't stay that way for long. Not once Duffy's video was out in the world.

Dark thoughts began to crawl into my brain. Maybe she was right. Maybe it *was* all my fault.

Maybe I'd just destroyed the biggest pop band in the world.

I closed the front door behind me and stood in the hallway, listening for signs of life. The house was dripping in silence. All I could hear was the sober tick of the clock in Dad's study, and the occasional click in the pipes.

Through the kitchen doorway, I noticed two spent wine glasses standing by the sink, one with a slight lipstick stain on the rim. Since Dad was already asleep, I wouldn't know until the morning whether he had managed to connect Gabriel to Little Boy Blue. Whether he was upstairs right now, lying awake in bed, wondering how his daughter had tracked down Harry West's only son, when he'd been so careful, all these years, to shield me from the truth.

I drifted up the stairs and, in a trance, got ready for bed. I plugged in my phone, which had died on the train, and waited for it to power up. A single message hit the screen.

So I heard something SUPER-INTENSE went down at the Troubadour?? Like a riot or something? Can't believe I missed it. Gotta crash now – knackered. But I want to hear EVERYTHING in the morning. Big love x

I wasn't sure how to reply to Melissa. So much had happened; things I needed to tell her face to face. It would have to wait until tomorrow.

Just got home. Tired. Call you in the morning x

I watched the message deliver, and waited for the ticks to turn blue. A minute passed, but Melissa didn't read it. She must have already been asleep. Trying to ignore the churning in the pit of my stomach, I switched the phone off and hid it in my desk drawer. When Duffy's video went live tomorrow, my notifications would be off the chart. And while I couldn't stop that happening, I could at least ignore it for a while.

Sinking my head into the pillow, I flicked off my bedside lamp and closed my eyes.

I felt like a defendant, the night before the verdict. Tomorrow, I would wake up, and the entire world would judge me.

37

I woke up feeling hollow, and dry-mouthed. *Something* was wrong. Something that happened last night . . .

A nausea climbed my throat, quick and vicious, like a swarm of spiders, and I pressed a hand to my mouth, almost gagging as I remembered. All the horrible things Duffy had said in the station flooded back to me, things that, at that very second, millions of teenagers all over the world would be sharing with their friends. I would be made responsible for destroying the band they loved more than anything in the world, and as I lay in bed, totally powerless, they would be turning to their phones, tablets and computers, and seeking me out online.

The second I turned on my phone, the hatred would pour into my life like molten lava.

'Oh, hi, Melissa.'

Dad's voice, downstairs. The front door closing. Melissa talking, and wiping her feet on the mat. Listening hard, my eyes closed, I tried to unravel the tone of my father's voice. Was he stressed, relieved . . . upset? Had he finally figured out what I'd been doing all this time?

All I knew for sure was that, very soon, I would find out.

'She's in her room,' I heard Dad say. 'Still asleep, I think.'

The familiar sound of Melissa climbing the stairs. Seconds later, she was standing in the doorway.

'Hey,' she said.

'Hey.'

She closed the door, walked over and sat down on my bed. The duvet crumpled beneath her.

I felt my heart start to shake.

'Have you seen . . . I mean, do you know about . . .'

'You and Olly?' she said, trying to stay calm. 'And Duffy's disgusting, hateful video?'

I nodded dumbly.

'Yep. I do.' Her face almost succumbed to anger, but she took a deep breath, and staved it off. 'And I have something very important to say to you.'

I looked into Melissa's eyes. I'd just about held it together since waking up, but now, with my best friend sitting in front of me, I could feel the sadness coming. Welling up in my throat, quivering in the corners of my eyes.

'What is it?' I said, the first tear tumbling down my cheek. Melissa grabbed my hand, and squeezed.

'Charlotte Katherine Bloom . . . I've basically just saved your life.'

38

I stared back at her, my toes curling.

This wasn't the time for banter.

'Mel, I don't think you understand. Every Fire&Lights fan in the country . . . in the world . . . will watch that video. It could ruin my life.'

'Oh, absolutely,' said Melissa, nodding. She pulled a packet of sweets from her pocket. 'That video *would* ruin your life. If it had ever made it on to the internet.'

I snapped my head up.

'What?'

She tugged open the packet, and peered inside.

'In order for Duffy's video to ruin your life, it would have to be on the web.' She rummaged around for a sweet. 'And it is not.'

The cogs in my brain didn't know which way to spin. I brushed my hair back from my face.

'What on earth are you talking about?'

Melissa hitched her legs on to the bed, and spun round to face me. 'Gummy bear?'

'Huh?'

She shook her bag of sweets.

'Take a bear. You're going to need it.'

Very slowly, without taking my eyes off her, I reached into the packet and pulled out a gummy bear. Then I sank back into my pillow, clutching it in my hand. My chest was pounding like a bass drum.

'So,' began Melissa, 'I woke up last night at, like, three a.m., with this nagging feeling. At first I thought it might be the four-cheese pizza I ate before bed, but then I remembered . . . four-cheese pizza is THE BOMB, so no. It had to be something else. And that's when I realised: I'd left my phone on silent, and I had a TON of messages. There was one from you, obviously, which didn't say much, but there were fifteen from Campbell, and some missed calls too.' She paused, momentarily, for breath. 'So, Campbell's messages were SERIOUSLY freaking me out. He told me everything. He told me that Duffy had filmed you and Olly splitting up' – she stopped to squeeze my hand again, her face pinched, as if to say *we'll talk about that in a minute* – 'and that she'd turned it into this horrible vlog, auto-scheduled to post this morning, at seven on the dot. And he told me how it's all because of this shady Paul Morgan creature, who by the way NEEDS TO BACK THE HELL OFF . . . but that's for another day. More gummies?'

I shook my head, blinking. I hadn't even eaten the first one.

'Campbell's messages were all confused and wonky,' continued Melissa, 'so I called him up, old-school like, and he sounded really upset. He said that Duffy was trying to force him to keep quiet about it, by threatening to get him sacked from the FireLighters. She's been in charge since the beginning, and was always the one who spoke to Tara and stuff, so she could pretty much do what she wanted. Cam wanted to tell Tara himself, but he didn't have her number, and it was the middle of the night, and anyway . . . what could she have done? Duffy runs the FireLighters website, and *she had changed all the passwords.*'

I was staring at Melissa, transfixed. I pressed the gummy bear into my mouth.

'That's right, my lovely, confused friend,' she said. '*This* is where Melissa Morris comes in. Because Campbell thought he was out of options, you see, until he remembered that I'd told him I was into computers, and coding, and he thought . . . *maybe* . . . I could hack into the site. Which is why he came to me.'

I chewed, very slowly, on the sweet.

'Of course, you might assume it was easy from here on in,' said Melissa, pointing right into my face, 'but you'd be wrong. I may be the Bill Gates of North Berkshire, but that doesn't mean I can just waltz into the back-end of password-secure websites, willy-nilly.' She raised both eyebrows. 'Charlie, it took *hours*. I started with all the

421

basic idiot passwords – *password*, *12345*, *fireandlights* and so on – but, of course, no dice. Duffy's too devious for that. So I tried punching in a bunch of words and phrases from the last month or so: *blakehadaway*, *pop4progress*, *songsaboutus*. Nothing worked.' Her face crumpled, and her cheeks went a bit red. 'By this point, time was running out. At about five a.m., I realised I only had two hours left, and I had to have a little cry. I was just so frustrated and tired, and I couldn't guess the password, and I knew that if I failed, then your whole life . . . it would be wrecked. And it would be my fault.'

I reached for her little finger with mine, and hooked them together.

'I almost gave up, but one thing kept me going.' She pressed her lips together. They were trembling. 'I thought about last year. I thought about the awful thing I did to you, on that stupid fan-blog, and I knew . . . I *knew* I had to stay awake. I knew I had to solve it. For you. Because you're my best friend, and I love you, more than you'll ever know.'

My heart quivered in my chest. I bit back tears.

'And that's when it hit me,' she continued, her face brightening. 'My FireLighters interview. D'you remember? Duffy and Campbell were sitting in her bedroom, and she had a poster on her wall for a movie called *Fear and Loathing in Las Vegas*, which is about some journalist who goes totally off the rails on drugs, or something. And I thought . . . *that could be it.*'

'Wait . . .' I touched a hand to her knee. 'You remembered the name of a film – from a poster – from a conversation we had nearly three weeks ago?'

'Actually, not the name of the film. The director.'

I stared at the wall, shaking my head in disbelief.

'No *wonder* you aced all your exams . . .'

'His name's Terry Gilliam, and by golly, *he* was the password! Bingo. And of course, once I was inside the site, all I had to do was find the video post, which was auto-scheduled for this morning, and delete it. Then I logged into the FireLighters' iCloud account (same password, the dinkus) and permanently erased the video, from all devices.' She slapped her hands together. 'Which means you, my friend, are totally in the clear.'

I pressed a cold palm against my hot, clammy forehead, trying to process Melissa's story. She seemed so confident, but what if this wasn't over?

'But, hang on . . . when Duffy works out what you've done, won't she just make a new video, or write a blog, or something?'

'That's the brilliant part,' said Melissa, a giant grin on her face.

'What do you mean?'

She pulled my laptop off the desk, and fired it up. When it had loaded, she opened the browser and spun it round to face me.

'Google "FireLighters Olly Samson",' she said,

waggling a finger at the keyboard. I typed the words, exactly as she'd said, and an official-looking article appeared as the top hit.

<><><> www.musicnews24.com <><><>

OLLY SAMSON QUITS FIRE&LIGHTS

In an announcement that has shocked the world, Barry King – manager of chart-topping boy band Fire&Lights – has revealed that Olly Samson has left the group.

The announcement came after a disastrous concert last night at the Troubadour club, a small coffee-house venue in West London. The band had chosen the club for a secret gig, open only to VIP fans and a handful of journalists, to celebrate the launch of their latest EP, Songs About Us. However, an altercation on stage, reportedly between Samson and bandmate Gabriel West, led to a stage invasion and a minor riot. The concert was curtailed immediately, and the fans sent home. Nobody was hurt in the incident.

'We're very sad to see Olly go,' said King, in his official statement. 'He's been an integral part of the group's success, and we know how popular he is with the fans. However, he's still very young, and has his whole career ahead of him. We wish Olly all the best for his future in the music industry.'

Millions of fans have united in their sadness at Olly Samson's departure, and although King is insisting that the three remaining members will stay together as a group – ahead of upcoming tour dates in the USA – the response from the online community has been sceptical. Across the world, fans are asking: is this the end for Fire&Lights?

In the same statement, it was also confirmed that bandmate Aiden Roberts has split from superstar girlfriend Kaitlyn Jones, and Yuki Harrison will be taking a short break from the media spotlight to spend time with his family.

Finally, King revealed that the 'FireLighters' fan club, recently set up to promote Fire&Lights among fans worldwide, has been dissolved on account of 'not having the band's best interests at heart'. The club's website has been taken down, and their social media accounts are suspended. It is unclear whether this move was related to Samson's departure.

~ Stream SONGS ABOUT US, the brand-new EP from
Fire&Lights ~
Wild Inside
Tokyo, I'm Yours
Tear Up The Night

<><><> www.musicnews24.com <><><>

I looked up from the article, stunned. Melissa crossed her arms.

'So, you see, it's too late now for Duffy to do anything about it. There's no way she could compete with the official statement, even if she did still have the platform for it, or the video evidence. Which she doesn't. Plus her reputation in the fan community is toast. She's been sacked, in public, so she'd basically just be another crazy groupie, yelling into the void.'

'What about Paul Morgan, though? He can write anything he wants in *The Record*.'

'Sure, but think about it: the whole point for Paul was that the story was coming from someone the fans trusted. Someone who had a video to back up her crazy claims. And now that's all gone.'

I pushed my hair off my face, the knot in my stomach beginning, finally, to unravel. I glanced at the article again. *The club's website has been taken down, and their social media accounts are suspended.*

'But, the FireLighters, and their website . . . I don't understand. How did they get found out?'

'Before I deleted the video, I took screenshots of it and sent them to the record label. I explained what Duffy had been planning to do, and they acted straightaway. Took the website down, and fired her ass.'

I fell back against the headboard.

'Oh my god. Melissa, you . . . I can't believe . . .'

I couldn't form a sentence. Melissa was beaming at me.

'This is the most incredible thing anyone's ever done for me.'

I gazed at her, breathless and bewildered, holding both hands to my heart. I felt like it might burst right out of me.

But Melissa's smile faltered.

'Charlie . . . the thing is . . .' She drew in a deep breath. 'I let you down last year, big time. I did something a real friend should never do, and I've been looking for a way to make up for it ever since.' I started to answer, but she stopped me. 'I know you've forgiven me, but I haven't forgiven myself.' Her chin wobbled. 'I don't think I ever will.'

I shook my head desperately, a well of happiness and heartache ballooning inside me.

'Thank you, Mel. You saved me. I don't know what I'd do without you.'

She chewed her lip, trying not to cry.

'I guess, sometimes, Scrappy Doo gets to save the day.'

I laughed tearfully, and she fell into me, nuzzling my neck. We hugged so tight, neither of us wanting to let go, and I could hear her sniffling in my ear. Eventually, she pulled away, her face wet from crying, and gave me a funny little smile.

'So . . . what now?' I said.

She glanced down at our hands, still interlocked.

'You could talk to me about Olly, if you want?'

My shoulders sagged. I had barely had time to process my feelings for Olly. It was too big, too sad, to even think about. And was he right about Gabriel? Was I in love with him? I couldn't be. I had spent the last four months talking myself *out* of love with him.

I pushed it all to the back of my mind.

'I don't know, Mel. I can't focus on it. It's like a storm in my head that I can't see, but I know is there. Am I crazy?'

Melissa shook her head.

'Not one bit. We'll talk about Olly tomorrow, or next week, or never. Whatever you want.'

I stared into her tear-sticky face.

'Do you know what I think I need, Mel?'

'What's that?'

'Twenty-four hours of not thinking about Olly, or Gabriel, or anything to do with the band at all. Can we do that?'

She nodded emphatically.

'Of course: your wish is my command.' She tapped a finger against her lips. 'How about a day of fun? You know, stupid, meaningless teenage fun that doesn't involve anyone snogging any popstars.'

I nodded, and smiled.

'That sounds perfect.'

'I'm thinking shopping, cinema, junk food? Things normal kids do. We can spend some of Great Uncle Ed's money. Oh, and I won't mention Fire&Lights even once. That's a promise.'

I wiggled my feet inside my duvet, warm and snug, and picked another gummy bear from the packet.

'How did it go last night, by the way? With Uncle Ed?'

Melissa shrugged.

'He's actually a really sweet old man. But he's, like, totally obsessed with Spam. You know, the canned meat?' She dropped to a whisper. '*He brought a tin with him.*'

I laughed, enjoying the sweet, sugary hit from the gummy bear. There was a grumble in my stomach.

'Speaking of which, I'm kind of hungry right now . . .' I looked around the room for more snacks. Melissa suddenly leapt up from the bed.

'What are you doing?' I said, as she headed for the door.

'I just realised I forgot the best thing!'

Before I could quiz her on it, Melissa had scampered out of the room. After a brief pause, she crept in again, hiding something behind her back.

She walked up to the bed and ceremoniously produced a large plastic bucket. Grinning, she lifted off the lid.

'I brought marshmallows for breakfast.'

39

'I feel a bit sick.'

Melissa and I had eaten nearly all of the marshmallows, and a disturbing thought was trickling back into my mind.

I had to face my father.

'Yeah ... maybe we should get some fresh air?' suggested Melissa, gesturing to the window. I concentrated for a moment, listening to the sound of the kettle boiling downstairs, and the clink of the cutlery drawer.

'When you got here, just now, did my dad seem ... OK?' I asked. Melissa stuck out her bottom lip.

'He seemed pretty normal to me.' She was rolling one of the last marshmallows between her fingers, as if debating whether or not to eat it. 'Why?'

I lowered my voice.

'He was at the gig last night.'

'NO. FREAKING. WAY.'

I pressed my finger to her lips.

'Quiet, he's in the kitchen ...' I glanced towards my bedroom door. 'He came with Christine to watch Jody perform. We saw each other, and it was fine; I just said I was there with Diamond Storm. But, I don't know, when Fire&Lights were onstage, he was staring at Gabriel in this really weird way, and I'm just scared that I'll go downstairs and everything will turn horrible again.' I picked up the nearly empty bucket. 'Hey, what if we just camped out in this room? We could stay up here forever, eating marshmallows, and then I'd never have to face him.'

Melissa glanced inside the bucket.

'But there's only one left.'

Ten minutes later, dressed and showered, I was walking down the stairs, with Melissa behind me, trying to appear calm. My father was in the kitchen.

'Hey,' he said, from the door, as we reached the hallway.

'Hey,' I said.

'You girls OK?'

We both nodded. My dad glanced at his slippered feet, then back at me.

'Charlie, can I have a word?'

I took a deep breath. This was it.

'Sure. Mel, I'll see you outside?'

Melissa gave my hand a little squeeze, then slipped out of the front door. I joined Dad in the kitchen.

'Take a seat,' he said, in a strangely formal way. I did,

431

and he sat opposite me, placing a fresh cup of tea on the table.

He cleared his throat. Then he cleared it again.

'You've obviously figured out by now that there are things I haven't told you about your mother.' My muscles tightened. 'And when I saw you up there last night, in the Troubadour, you reminded me so much of her, it . . .'

He trailed off, searching the tabletop, as if for the right words. I decided to intervene.

'Dad, I can explai—'

'I have something to say to you,' he interrupted, holding up a hand. 'Something I should have said a long time ago.'

He looked up at me.

'I'm incredibly proud of you, Charlie.'

I felt my eyes go wide.

'You . . . are?'

'What I realised yesterday, watching you working, watching you up there, following your dreams, is that you're an adult now. You're not my little girl any more. And it's time I told you the truth . . . about your mum.'

My heart was beating furiously in my chest. It felt so good to finally hear those words from him, but where was this conversation heading? Had he recognised Gabriel, or not?

'What do you mean . . . the truth?' I said.

'Look, Rosie mentioned a while back that you're interested in Katherine's life, and of *course* you are. She was your mother. I suppose I've always avoided talking about it because . . . well, it's not easy for me. In fact, it's the hardest thing in the world. But that's selfish, and I want to change. Now that I'm moving on with my life, you should be able to do the same, and part of that is understanding more about your mother, and who she really was.'

He swallowed thoughtfully, and ran a finger along the handle of his mug.

'Also . . . your grandmother called last week, after your visit. She said that seeing you, even for only a few hours, had been the highlight of her year. She wants to patch things up, with both of us. She wants to be a family again.'

I smiled, thinking back to my time with Gran. The clink of the spoon against china teacups. The biscuits piled neatly on a plate.

'That's nice,' I said, nodding. 'I'd like that.'

Dad wrapped his hands around his mug.

'So . . . what would you say to dinner sometime, all three of us? We could go to Basingstoke, eat somewhere in town. Tonight, even?'

'Tonight?'

'Only if you're not busy,' he said, with a little smile. 'But we can sit and talk, and you can ask us anything you want about Katherine. About her life, and the things she loved, and . . . whatever you like.'

I nodded, feeling relief settle inside me, warm and comforting, like a hot drink on a cold day.

'Definitely, let's do that. Tonight.'

We sat in silence for a bit, our eyes occasionally meeting. Across the hallway, Dad's clock ticked quietly in his study.

'Mel and I are going out today,' I said, nodding towards the front door. 'Just to hang around town, do some shopping and stuff.'

'Sure,' said Dad contentedly. 'You girls have fun.'

I nearly got up from my chair, but stopped myself. I had to ask.

'So . . . what did you think of Fire&Lights last night?'

Dad took a sip of tea.

'Oh, we couldn't see much from where we were. Then of course it all went a bit downhill. But they did sound very good. And that lad from round here, Olly Samson . . . he's done well, hasn't he?'

I felt a twinge in my heart, thinking about Olly. I flicked at a fingernail.

'Actually, he quit the band last night.'

'Oh. Gosh. Well. From what I heard, he's a talented young man. I'm sure he'll be fine on his own.'

Another smile crept on to my face. It was entirely by accident, maybe, but my dad was almost certainly right.

This was turning into one of the most surprising days of my life.

I clicked my gate open, and Melissa and I wandered along the path to the front door. Our arms were weighed down with shopping bags, and our brains were buzzing from all the sugar we'd consumed at the cinema.

Best of all, Melissa had kept her promise. She hadn't mentioned Fire&Lights once.

'Now *that*,' she said, dropping her bags with a thud, 'was what I call a day of fun.'

Ding. The sound of an email hitting my inbox. Gratefully, I lowered my shopping on to the doorstep and pulled out my phone, along with my keys. I was about to open the door when I spotted the name on the screen. *Carrie Shakes.*

'Oh my god. Mel . . . look at this.'

Melissa had her face buried in her handbag, searching for something.

'Look at what?'

'Carrie Shakes. She got back to me.'

She froze, then popped up, out of her handbag, her mouth hanging open.

'OH NO SHE DIDN'T.'

I unlocked the screen and began to read Carrie's message. My face opened out into a smile.

'She says . . . *no*. No way.'

'OK,' said Mel, dropping her shopping bags. 'I need to see this.'

She passed behind me and peered over my shoulder, squeezing my arms with excitement.

Charlie, I AM SO SORRY!! You must think I'm super-flaky. You emailed me weeks ago, and I guess it got filtered into junk, no clue why, but anyways, that total babe Olly Samson got in touch last week and said had I got back to you and I was all WTF??

Olly had reminded her. Of course he had. A hidden pain tugged at my heart, but I willed it away, and read on.

Point is, I checked out your photos and DAMN. My eyes popped right outta my sockets. Olly was right . . . whatever it is, you got it. I'm not back in the UK till next year, but I'll be in NYC all summer – so if you find your sweet self out this way anytime soon, you just holler, OK? Number's below. I'd kill to meet you. We can talk photos, cameras, boy bands, the whole shebang.

Big love,

Carrie xox

I gazed at my front door, speechless. Carrie Shakes liked my photographs. She wanted to meet me. I mean, sure, she was in New York, so it would never happen, but still. *Carrie Shakes wanted to meet me.*

'This is turning into an epic day,' said Melissa cheerfully. 'Funny how the universe can surprise you.'

My phone beeped again. Melissa reached for her shopping bags.

'Man, it's like Piccadilly Circus round here.'

I opened the message, and an uneasy feeling prickled in the pit of my stomach.

'Charlie?' Melissa was watching me, confused. 'Who is it?'

I lifted up my phone.

'It's . . . Gabe.'

'Oh. Ah.' She looked at the message.

I'm in the Milldown Hotel, by the train station. Room 45. Meet me there.

My face crumpled into a frown.

'Should I go?'

'Definitely,' she said, with a vigorous nod. 'Who knows, maybe he wants to get back together?'

I threw her a pointed look.

'No, Mel. *No.*' I lifted my keys to the front door, remembering the way Gabriel had stared at me the night before, as my train pulled away. What *did* he want . . . ? 'He probably just needs a friend, after last night.'

'Then go,' said Melissa, pushing my hand away from the lock. 'I'll take your clothes back to my place for now, your dad will just assume you're still in town with me, and you can be back in time for dinner. You go, girl.'

I raised my eyebrows at her.

'What did we agree about "you go, girl"?'

She pouted, and hung her head.

'That I must never ever say it.'

I nudged her on the arm.

'Nah, I'm kidding. You say whatever you want, Morris.'

She grinned at me.

'In that case' – she waved me off down the path – 'you go, girl!'

When I reached the door to Gabriel's hotel room, I paused, gathering my thoughts. I couldn't help but think of what had happened the last time I'd turned up to meet him at a hotel, on that rainy night in December. Finding him with a movie star, jumping to conclusions. Running out on to the rooftop.

Then I thought of the very last thing we had said to each other in the underground station the previous evening, just before I had stepped on to the train.

'Olly says he can't be with me, because I'm in love with you.'

'Are you?'

I stared into the rich, mahogany panelling, a small voice inside telling me to run, run away, and never look back. Was this really a good idea? Meeting up again, so soon? The answer was probably no, but if Gabriel was feeling low after last night, I wanted to be there for him. Whatever we'd been through – whatever we'd *all* been through – I still considered him a friend.

I knocked on the door, and waited.

When Gabriel opened it, he didn't look good. He looked sick, somehow. Hungry.

I walked past him into the room, and he shut the door, slumping down on the bed. I turned round to face him.

'Are you all right?' I said. He looked at me, but didn't reply. His eyes were haunted, sunken.

'What's going to happen?' I said. 'With the band, I mean? People are saying you're going to spli—'

'That doesn't matter,' he said coldly. 'None of that matters.'

I screwed my face up.

'But . . . I don't understand.'

He pulled open the small bedside drawer next to him, and took out a folded piece of paper. He held it towards me.

'What's that?'

He shook it.

'Just read it.'

I took the piece of paper from him, and unfolded it. It was a letter. And when I read the name at the bottom, my heart stuttered.

Harry.

'Where did you get this?' I asked.

'My foster home. They noticed the press were after me, said it was time for me to see it.'

I traced a finger across the paper, which was dry with age. I thought of my own letter, from Mum, and the beautiful words she'd written to me.

'Gabe, wh—'

'I need you to read it.'

The expression on Gabriel's face was like nothing I'd ever seen before. His tanned skin looked somehow pale and drained, and his eyes were struggling to focus. He stood up slowly, and walked to the window.

He turned his back while I read.

Gabriel,

I don't know if you'll ever read this, but I want you to know I'm sorry. I've been no father to you.

I'm about to do something terrible. You'll hate me, and you'll never understand it, but I need you to know – I don't feel right. I never have. I always felt like I didn't deserve to be here. They say suicide is for cowards, but then people tell me I'm a coward all the time, so hey. That's destiny for you.

One day, maybe, you'll forgive me. Or maybe you won't. There's not much I can do about it now. I just know I can't go on living any longer, not after what's happened.

She's gone, Gabriel. Katherine's gone. She was the only real friend I've ever had, and now she's never coming back.

But I need you to know — I need everyone to know — that I never meant to kill her.

I never meant for her to die.

Slowly, I lowered the note, my heart lurching.

Gabriel stared back at me, his eyes wild, while in the distance, the lights of my hometown burned.

WILD INSIDE
Fire&Lights

Turn off the TV
Shut off the phone
I know what the headlines are

You were beside me
On a road to nowhere
But I can never go
I can never go back there

When we were wild inside
I believed you and I could do anything
When we were wild inside

When we were wild inside
And you were mine, I'd have given you everything
Everything

The fire in your heartbeat
And the light of your skin
The memory of you
Is pulling me further in

Maybe I'll see you
After my show
And maybe you will smile
Or maybe you will never know

When we were wild inside
I believed you and I could do anything
When we were wild inside

When we were wild inside
And you were mine, I'd have given you everything
Everything

I never asked to be forever
I never asked for anything
I only want to see you one last time

I know that we can't be together
I know you gave your heart to him
I only want to see you one last time

Chris Russell has written and recorded several of the songs that feature in this series, including 'Wild Inside'. To find out more, visit www.songsaboutagirl.com

Don't miss the
final book in the

Songs About
a Girl

trilogy

Coming
soon ...